HAIL, <u>PROCURATOR!</u>

"Intriguingly thought out . . . This subgenre is one of the most difficult in the field—the author must have extrapolative talent *and* know his history—and an addition to it based on this much knowledge is good to find."
—*Isaac Asimov's Science Fiction Magazine*

"The best the year has produced so far . . . the action scenes are terrific! For those looking for a good read, there is not much better around."
—*Whispers*

Kirk Mitchell's saga
of alternate worlds continues . . .
The Procurator is now Caesar—
and the NEW BARBARIANS must be destroyed.

Ace Science Fiction books by Kirk Mitchell

PROCURATOR
NEW BARBARIANS

New Barbarians

KIRK MITCHELL

ACE SCIENCE FICTION BOOKS
NEW YORK

This book is an Ace Science Fiction original edition,
and has never been previously published.

NEW BARBARIANS

An Ace Science Fiction Book/published by arrangement with
the author

PRINTING HISTORY
Ace Science Fiction edition/December 1986

ISBN: 0-441-57101-8

Ace Science Fiction Books are published by
The Berkley Publishing Group,
200 Madison Avenue, New York, New York 10016.
PRINTED IN THE UNITED STATES OF AMERICA

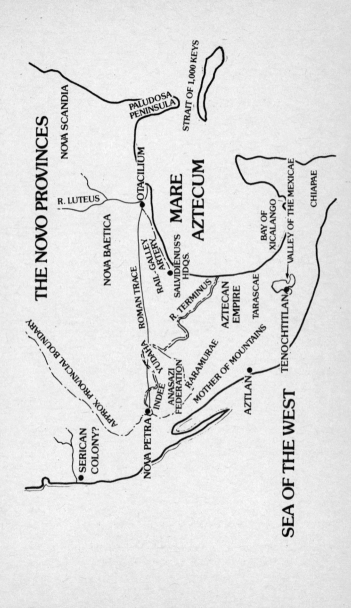

THE NOVO PROVINCES

NOVA SCANDIA

PALUDOSA PENINSULA

STRAIT OF 1,000 KEYS

OTACILIUM

R. LUTEUS

MARE AZTECUM

CHIAPAE

VALLEY OF THE MEXICAE

BAY OF XICALANGO

NOVA BAETICA

ROMAN TRACE

RAIL-GALLEY ARTERY

SALVIDIENUS'S HDQS.

R. TERMINUS

AZTECAN EMPIRE

TARASCAE

APPROX. PROVINCIAL BOUNDARY

YUDAHA

INDEE

ANASAZI FEDERATION

RARAMURAE

MOTHER OF MOUNTAINS

TENOCHTITLAN

SERICAN COLONY?

NOVA PETRA

AZTLAN

SEA OF THE WEST

VALLEY OF THE MEXICAE
MMDCCXL ANNO VRBIS CONDITAE

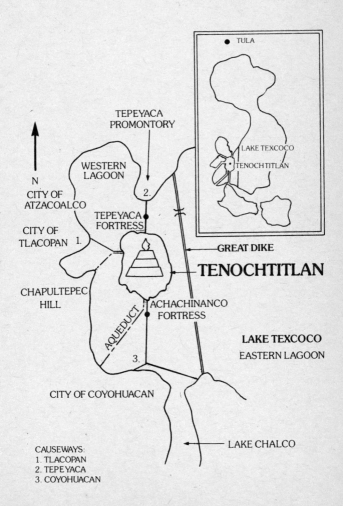

TEPEYACA
PROMONTORY

TULA

LAKE TEXCOCO

TENOCHTITLAN

WESTERN
LAGOON

N

CITY OF
ATZACOALCO

2.

TEPEYACA
FORTRESS

GREAT DIKE

CITY OF
TLACOPAN

1.

TENOCHTITLAN

CHAPULTEPEC
HILL

ACHACHINANCO
FORTRESS

AQUEDUCT

LAKE TEXCOCO
EASTERN LAGOON

3.

CITY OF COYOHUACAN

CAUSEWAYS:
1. TLACOPAN
2. TEPEYACA
3. COYOHUACAN

LAKE CHALCO

And this is how it was before the Compassionate, the Merciful, arose out of the east, having taken flight there long ago on a raft of serpents:

There was a vast chamber bright and sweet for its myriad blooms; a lake shimmered through the windows on all sides, a placidity of golden waters wherever one gazed; yet, herein an old king dwelt in darkness, prayed to darkness, and spoke from the soul of darkness. To his lord general, a nephew whom he loved as his own son, he said, "The fateful hour should come without warning."

This troubled Lord Tizoc. "Reverend one, is it not honorable to declare the Flowery Way to our brothers whose blood the Fifth Sun will taste as nectar?"

"No," the old man said, "we must never share the truth of why we make this war. Let them believe it is for flesh, fuel, or even the ground on which we stand. We alone must know: We have chosen to fight because they are vigorous and new to this country—as we were once vigorous and new to this valley that now bears our ancient name, the Mexicae. We make war because we recognize ourselves in their bold manner and are thus assured they will satisfy the thirst of Lord Tonatiuh . . ."

1

THE ROMAN ENVOY to the court of Maxtla III closeted himself in his apartments whenever the Aztecan priests were butchering human flesh to their gods. And Britannicus Musa was careful not to linger at the upper-story window that afforded a view across the shallow waters of Lake Texcoco at the Great Temple that dominated the island capital.

Shortly after his arrival in Tenochtitlan two months before, he had not been so wary. What he had witnessed made him anxious to bolt from this dusky mountain valley, and his grasp on reality—previously so concrete, so *Roman*—was more tenuous than he cared to admit. Britannicus saw no healing possible as long as he remained among a race that reveled in both flowers and gore. Prior to that day, he had never imagined that blood could gush down a flight of stone stairs like a Caledonian freshet, its progress slowed only by congealment at the lowermost steps.

But a strong sense of duty—and the comfort he took from wine—induced him to remain.

His orders had originated from the Emperor Germanicus in Rome: The colonel was to open negotiations with Maxtla in the hope of easing friction between Aztecan and Roman forces glaring at each other across the muddy flow of the River Terminus. The two hundred and forty-third heir to Caesar Augustus desired peace in the Novo Provinces with a desperation that confused the younger officers of his legions. But, so far, little of substance had been resolved, and although the octogenarian reverend speaker had absented himself from the

3

talks, Maxtla's nobles had been exquisitely polite, almost brotherly in their attempts to please the Roman ambassador—in all matters of no consequence.

In his bare feet, Britannicus padded across the airy chamber to the window that faced northeast—away from the Great Temple and its crimson fountainhead of a sacrificial stone. He stared through the haze at the Tepeyaca Fortress. This lofty, cylindrical redoubt straddled one of three causeways that joined the capital to the mainland; its twin sister, the Acachinanco, stood guard south of Tenochtitlan. They easily could be counted among the largest structures in the world, and the causeway tunnels passing through them were large enough to admit a sand-galley.

He could espy a barracks atop the Tepeyaca that, with its upturned eaves, might have been modeled on Serican architecture. This and things his most trusted agent had whispered to him were convincing Britannicus that the Aztecae enjoyed ties with that great silk-dispensing realm Rome knew only through the accounts of Baluchi traders—the Sericans allowed no one else to penetrate their western hinterlands. To Romans, this empire seemed as legendary as Troy—and there existed no Virgil capable of translating its mysteries for patrician dinner parties.

The fortress bleared out of focus, and Britannicus's mind drifted back to a day one week ago when Lord Tizoc, Maxtla's ablest general and most likely successor, had conducted him on a tour of the Tepeyaca. There were no embrasures in the structure, but this was explained when two enormous bronze doors were pulled open against a strong suction: The Tepeyaca was largely a granary—an admirably airtight one, too, and only its expansive roof was dedicated to military purposes.

Traipsing up the ramp that wound around the outer wall to the battlements on the dome, smirking at the haughtiness of his Aztecan host, Britannicus tried to estimate the volume of this store of grain. As usual, he found Roman numerals too cumbersome for quick computation. Tizoc must have been reading his thoughts, for once they had reached the summit of the fortress, the general pointed at a serpent-shaped chimney rearing up from Tenochtitlan's skyline, its fanged mouth vomiting white smoke into the already foul air: "We would starve but for the godly gift of spirulina—it is processed there, Lord Musa."

This was the second time Britannicus had been informed that this algae, harvested from the lagoons of Texcoco, was the chief source of protein for the Aztecae. In the interests of diplomacy, he had swallowed his skepticism. There was no way a body of brackish water, slightly larger than the new harbor at Ostia, could substantially help feed the ten million people crammed into this volcano-ringed bowl. But Britannicus had politely nodded at the immobile barbarian face: "I see."

Sandals now scraped the stone floor behind him.

Britannicus started, then recovered himself before meeting the smile of one of the slave girls Tizoc had provided the Roman emissaries for their comfort—and pleasure. She was the prettiest of the dozen, with full breasts and a waspish waist. Britannicus suspected that his adjutant, Lucius Balbus —who at this moment was downstairs having his body oiled— had already bedded her. His agent believed this girl to be one of the reverend speaker's most trusted spies. So, when Britannicus looked upon her, he imagined that Maxtla's ears were sewn to her head. In this way, he felt free to address the god-ruler he was never permitted to see.

"To whose glory do your priests murder captives this afternoon?" he asked in his rough Nahuatl.

She avoided his eyes as she laid out his clean tunic and cloak on a couch. "To the goddess Chalchiuhtlicue, lord."

"What place does she hold among your other gods?"

"She is mistress to Tlaloc."

"You mean the fellow to whom you sacrifice children?"

"Yes, lord," she said matter-of-factly.

"Worshipers of Ba'al-Hammon," Britannicus said in Latin, naming the fiery Punic diety to whom the Carthaginians had fed their children. He had already learned from a less circumspect slave that Chalchiuhtlicue was patroness of ventures by water. Something was coming—by water. It had not taken the Roman long to realize that Maxtla's next move could sometimes be predicted by taking note of the god his grubby priests had chosen to honor with human sacrifice.

Britannicus's expression became wistful: Her thin smock was penetrated by the sunlight slanting in through the window. The silhouette of her naked body was defined inside the glowing cloth. Absently, he ran his mind through his thinning red hair, then gave her his back and gazed off at the Tepeyaca

Fortress again, blaming his errant thoughts on a weariness
that had infiltrated all of his moods in the past few months.
He was far too tired for a man of thirty.

Before this posting in Tenochtitlan, Balbus and he had endured five years of Hibernia with the most wretched of
legions—the Third. In the last month of their tour, they had
been captured by rebels and herded blindfolded from fen to
virulent bog, never knowing when the knives would skid
across their throats. Rescued at last, they transferred to the
Tenth Legion in the Novo Provinces (as far as one could get
from Hibernia in the Roman world)—and nearly lost their
lives in the wholesale insanity of the Pamphilean Plot. A
praetorian colonel fancied that the newly arrived officers
might have had something to do with the Emperor Fabius's
murder. Only the general amnesty declared by his successor,
Germanicus Julius Agricola, had spared Britannicus and
Balbus the infamous "pink bath"—opening a vein in a tub of
warm water under the flinty eyes of praetorian guards.

"Lord Musa." A child's voice intruded on his thoughts
from the corridor.

"Come." The Roman found himself smiling at the small
boy whose chore it was to guard the portal to the dwelling.
"What is it?"

"A *pochtecatl* from Chalcatzingo begs to lay his wares at
your feet." The boy was holding something behind him.

"Show me what you have there."

Grinning, the child offered Britannicus a small stone
jaguar. "A god—he has many more."

"Tell this merchant I have no need of gods," Britannicus
said gently. "Return this to him."

"But he promises a fair price, lord."

Britannicus touched the boy's soft brown hair. "There is no
fairness where gods are concerned, my young friend." He
could feel the slave girl's eyes scrutinizing him. Britannicus
feigned a yawn, then indicated with a wave for her to dress
him. The hand he held behind him was trembling.

The stone causeway that linked the foreign quarter in
Tlacopan to Tenochtitlan was the shortest but the most heavily used. A glimpse of the crush of foot traffic on the narrow
lane convinced Britannicus to march off in a different direc-

tion—toward the quay where he could catch a barge to the island.

He hoped that his face had remained expressionless upon hearing from the boy that a merchant from Chalcatzingo wished an audience. The slave girl, who had not missed a word—who never missed a word—was certainly canny enough to sniff out a coded message. Previously, Britannicus had arranged for his agent to contact him in this way if some sudden peril arose. Then he would proceed without delay to the Great Temple, the most public place in the valley and therefore the least conspicuous for an outlander. The delivery of the message without the jaguar would have meant that his agent had been unmasked and was probably already dead. Britannicus had been enormously relieved to see the figurine in the child's hands; he was in love with his agent, something he admitted only to himself.

Britannicus thought that all the benches on the barge had been taken until the steersman good-naturedly gestured for the Roman to come aft and sit beside him. As he worked his way toward the stern, he realized that one of the muscular polers had furtively touched the pale skin of his forearm. Britannicus glowered at him.

"Forgive me, lord," the bargeman said, "but I have been curious too long now."

"About what?"

"Whether or not you have blood. You are warm, so you must have blood."

Trying not to smile, Britannicus continued to sidestep his way down a gauntlet of bare knees. Every barbarian tribe under the sway of the Aztecae was represented among the passengers. A macaw pecked at his silvered cuirass from the shoulder of a Chiapan merchant, who sought the Roman's pardon with a giggle, revealing the shyness of a people who lived in a dense privacy of tropical forest. A pair of stoical Tarascans, soldiers on leave perhaps, met Britannicus's eyes briefly, then glared off with disdain. He had heard that these northerners were as pitiless as their desert homeland.

One man, whose eyes were more almond-shaped than those of the others, appeared to belong to none of the peoples Britannicus had mentally catalogued during his stay. All at once, this barbarian drew a hood over his top-knotted hair as if the breeze were pestering him and shuffled toward the bow before Britannicus could engage him in conversation.

The steersman patted his worn plank for the Roman to sit. "Here, please—we must be off. You are quite a curiosity." Like many Aztecae, the man had a hooked nose and mahogany-colored hair. "I have seen you before. But you always took one of the other barges. You are a Person of the Sun, yes?"

"I'm a citizen of Rome."

"You are free to call yourself as you like, lord. But to us you are a Person of the Sun. You rise up out of the east, as does our god Tonatiuh. Please tell me, have you made the acquaintance of Quetzalcoatl in your land?"

"I don't think so," Britannicus said with measured civility. He had been hounded by this question again and again. Apparently, one of the local gods could not be accounted for and each responsible Azteca was taking it upon himself to discover the whereabouts of this missing deity. "Our realm covers half the world and I have not seen it all."

"What of your reverend speaker—is he a god?"

"So far, the Emperor Germanicus has declined that honor."

"How can a god choose not to be one?"

Britannicus smiled. "In our world, we hold everything to be possible."

The steersman fell silent, looking somewhat dissatisfied by the answers he had received.

The Roman was glad to have been invited to sit so near the stern post. It gave him the opportunity to corroborate something his agent had told him: "What you see is all a dream made up for Roman eyes—the barges have run on smokes for over a year now." The inference was that Maxtla, like a cunning bride on her wedding night, was pretending to be less experienced than he actually was.

Britannicus began rubbing his eyes as if the chronically smoky air of the capital had finally gotten to them. Crouching in this feint, he peered backwards at the stern post. Like all exposed portions of Lake Texcoco barges, it was brightly painted. But a square section of it was even more vivid, as if—until quite recently—a plate of some sort had protected this area from the elements. He coughed wetly into his hand, then dangled his fingers into the waters as if to wash them, but when he brought them in he swiped the outer hull. Several minutes later, he glanced at his fingertips. They were smudged with residue. It was petroleum, and he had not encountered even the most primitive engine anywhere in the Aztecan Empire.

The reverend speaker was no virgin—but why such an elaborate deception for a Roman suitor?

"Tell me," Britannicus asked the steersman, pointing at the hooded man, who was now facing forward, "what tribe is that one?"

"Xing. That is what they call themselves."

"Where does his land lie from here?"

"Far across the Sea of the West."

From this, Britannicus understood that the man was a Serican! "Why has he come to Tenochtitlan?" He was waiting for a reply when he saw that the steersman's attention had been seized by an eagle knight, who was glaring at him from the yawning beaks of his headdress. Britannicus had learned that these elite warriors were the praetorian guards of the Aztecan Empire. The humble steersman would say no more.

Britannicus ran his elbow across the hilt of his ceremonial short sword to assure himself that the weapon was still strapped to his side. His heart was hammering, although he told himself that he had been in worse spots before. This was really nothing—an uncomfortable moment, but he was longing for a draught of wine or even *pulque*, the barbarian fare fermented from cactus juice. Just the mention of *pulque* was enough to make Balbus gag.

The barge glided under a bridge built across a gap in the causeway. This wooden span, Britannicus surmised with the practiced eye of a military engineer, could be destroyed in the event the capital was invested by an invading army.

Once the barge had cleared the cool shadow of the bridge, Britannicus could see what he had only half-jokingly named "The Forum Aztecum"—for the shrines and monuments had been laid out across the glistening marble square with a symmetry and grace that made Rome's heart seem cluttered by comparison. Everything about the place appealed to his love of order—except the blood drying on one of the twin staircases of the Great Temple.

He purchased a spray of amaranth in the bazaar at the base of the massive pyramid, then relinquished his sandals before bounding up the flight of steps the priests had not used that afternoon to dispose of the bodies of their victims. Foreigners were allowed on the sacred structure as long as certain amenities, such as making offerings of grain, were observed. The higher the Roman climbed, the stiffer the breeze became. The noise of the bazaar below faded to a soft murmuring. For the first time in weeks, Britannicus could make out the white cones of the great volcanoes on the southeastern rim of the valley.

If what the slave girl had said was true, that Chalchiuhtlicue had been honored here today, he wondered why the goddess had not been accommodated at her own gleaming new temple astride a spring on Chapultepec Hill. The twin shrines atop the Great Temple were dedicated to Tlaloc and Huitzilopochtli. The significance of the latter deity now concerned Britannicus: Huitzilopochtli was their god of war.

Reaching the uppermost tier, Britannicus began strolling around Huitzilopochtli's monument, hands clasped behind him—the perfect tourist.

"Lord, may I beg a question?" the woman asked, clutching her own bouquet of amaranth.

"Speak, daughter."

"Might you be a Person of the East?"

"I am." Britannicus ached to take her in his arms. Yet, even had there been no danger, he could not have—she had rebuffed his advances once, filling him with an exquisite pain he never wanted to feel again. "What does it matter if I come from the east?"

"I wish only to know if you have made the acquaintance of Quetzalcoatl in your distant country." She said this in a voice that carried: a temple attendant was nearby, sweeping the powder of dried blood into a pile.

"No, Quetzalcoatl has not made himself obvious to me. But if you might describe him . . ." Britannicus led her to the backside of the shrine. Only when he felt safe from eavesdroppers did he ask in Latin, "What has happened, Alope?"

"There is so little time . . ." Her usually sorrowful eyes now shone with insistence. "You must leave Tenochtitlan at once. After sending my message to you, I learned this: Tizoc dispatches assassins to your quarters in Tlacopan."

"When?"

"This minute." She urged him with a tug on his cloak to follow her toward the stairs. "Do not return to your apartments."

"What about Balbus?"

"I have sent word; we can only hope it will arrive in time. Come, I will see you to the barge for Tenayuca. Your friend can join you there."

"But the roads from Tenayuca lead *inland*. To depart, we have only to send for a bireme and within two days sailing we'll be back in Nova Baetica." Although his legs were longer than hers, he found it challenging to keep up with the woman as they descended the stairs toward the attendant who guarded their footwear when not flinging copal incense into a brazier. "We're on a diplomatic mission—our murder would bring war."

"Maxtla knows that."

Britannicus halted her by grasping the shoulder tassels of her deerskin tunic. "What are you telling me?"

"The Aztecae are gathering power to make a war against you Romans." She started walking again.

Britannicus trotted to catch up. "How soon?"

"Two weeks, if not before. A great fleet has been built in secret at the Bay of Xicalango. It will carry many warriors to your province of Nova Baetica."

Britannicus then followed in silence, watching the sun glint gold and copper in her dark hair. Alope was not an Azteca. She was of the Indee, a new barbarian people who scratched for subsistence along with thirty other tribes in a huge desert wilderness south of the Roman garrison at Nova Petra. This region was called the Anasazi Federation, and it served as a buffer between the western outposts of the Romans and the Aztecae. Alope was the Anasazi ambassadress to Maxtla's court—when she was not plotting the reverend speaker's downfall.

In his diplomatic office, Britannicus did not labor under any illusion that the Anasazi tribes thought kindly of Romans. They just despised them a bit less vigorously than they did the Aztecae. And, while mindful that the commander at Nova Petra had vouched for Alope's reliability, Britannicus had also not forgotten that Indee warriors had preyed upon Roman *coloni* without respite in the three decades since the western extremity of the province had been settled. The indelible stamp of barbarity was upon her people: they could not be broken of raiding.

It was also quite possible that Alope was in Maxtla's service as well as his. This startling news of war might be nothing more than a test of the Emperor Germanicus's intentions, which Britannicus sincerely believed to be peaceable.

All at once, he knew what to do: return to his apartments, open an amphora of his best Gaulish wine, and mull over this report with Balbus. "Alope . . . ?"

She glanced back at him, her handsome face disquieted.

He smiled as he inclined his head toward the quay for the Tlacopan departure. "I'm sorry—but I'm going back to talk this over with Lucius."

"Many of us have put ourselves in peril to make sure your emperor receives this word."

"And I will see to it that Germanicus does."

"You will not live to do so, Britannicus Musa." There were now tears of anger in her eyes, which he could not bear to see.

Britannicus strode away from her, his expression dispassionate where it had been tender a moment before. How asinine to fall in love with someone you couldn't trust! Seething at himself, he took this as one more symptom of his growing malaise. He was long overdue for a comfortable tour at the Campus Martius. But, secretly, he suspected that he'd never see Rome again. A recurring nightmare had slowly convinced Britannicus that he would die here in Tenochtitlan on the bloody steps of the Great Temple.

The crowd waiting for the barge pressed against him front and back, and then from behind came her whisper, gentle but unhappy: "Whatever happens, go north. There will be help along the way."

He turned, but she had melted from sight.

2

THE BOY WAS absent from his niche in the portal. Britannicus called out for him. There was no answer from the rooms beyond. He began listening with a keener ear, then touched his fingers to the cool white plaster of the wall as if feeling for vibrations. There was a quality to the stillness in the apartments that stole the moisture out of his mouth. "Lucius?" he hailed Balbus, not too loudly.

After a moment's hesitation, he crept around the corner into an atriumlike room that opened onto the garden. The couch on which Balbus had been receiving his massage lay overturned, and Britannicus followed a smear of oil across the floor tiles out into the dusk. The sky was being bruised by first darkness; the light in the garden had grown dim.

"Ah, there you are . . . " As Britannicus approached his friend, he slapped the soles of his sandals on the walkway. This was to awaken Balbus without startling him. But the man continued to sprawl over his stone bench without moving, his arms outstretched.

"Lucius, I've got news—"

Then Britannicus glimpsed the incision that swept down across Balbus's stomach from the man's breastbone. He knew at once by the depth of the red-rimmed hole that his adjutant's heart had been ripped and twisted from his body, as from countless other sacrificial victims.

This was so closely followed by a second shock Britannicus had no time in which to recoil with horror: three eagle knights leaped over the garden wall, their feet thudding in the soft soil of the flower beds. Each bore what he believed to be the Aztecan *pilum*, which projected a lead ball by force of compressed air. Weeks before, Lord Tizoc had privileged him with an exhibition of this weapon's capabilities. It had been all the Roman could do to keep from chuckling as a warrior furiously pumped his leather billows into the breech before lofting a projectile so slow its progress could be noted by the human eye. The target, a cactus manlike in form, had suffered no injury—an adverse wind was blamed by Tizoc.

So now, Britannicus was thunderstruck when the knights hoisted these pieces to their bare shoulders—and *fired*. Three white flashes left no doubt in the Roman's mind that the Aztecan Empire was acquainted with niter powder.

He was taking his third lunging step toward the wall opposite the warriors when, suddenly, the ground hurled up to meet him and his face was thrust down into a bed of flowers. The scent of blossoms had never seemed more piercing. Then he realized through a mounting dizziness that blood was dripping through his eyebrows and down the bridge of his nose. His fingertips discovered a ragged crease along the top of his scalp.

Britannicus staggered to his feet and threw the upper part of his body astride the wall. Before swinging his legs over, he glanced back: two of the warriors were reloading their *pili*, but the third tossed aside his *pilum* with a growl and unsheathed his obsidian knife. Then he started to give chase.

After Hibernia, where no legionary was ever safe, Britannicus had made it his habit to identify avenues of escape long before he might have need of them. He did this no matter how congenial his hosts seemed—even in Rome.

Now, pressing his palm to his head to stem the flow of blood, he sprinted down a lane between flat-roofed dwellings, whose window openings throbbed yellow from freshly lit oil lamps within, and hurdled over small children who were taking advantage of the last light. He was about to cross a temple square when the gates of a *presidium* swung open and out marched a troop of warriors that wheeled and tramped off toward the foreign quarter at a brisk pace.

Britannicus backtracked through the estate of some noble, a woodland preserve of such haunting beauty he found himself wondering how aesthetic sensibility and savagery could exist in the same people—a nation of *flowers and blood*. He hid in a

copse of ferns until the gloaming was fully night, then hurried
northwest until his progress inland was halted by a perimeter
of warriors so thick each man could tap his two adjoining
comrades on the shoulders without taking a step in either
direction.

Groaning, he turned back toward Lake Texcoco.

An hour later, he was wading down a canal that separated
two farm plots the Aztecae had created in the lake by dam-
ming up silt behind pile-driven timbers. Someone could be
heard rustling through the green maize behind him. He slogged
out into Texcoco itself and paused to wash his wound, which
had benumbed his scalp but ignited a fierce headache at the
base of his skull. Perhaps there was a blessing in this: the pain
was putting an edge on his concentration.

Britannicus unhitched his cuirass and let it sink. Next, he
fought the oozy bottom for possession of his *caligae*, which
he intended to tie together and sling over his shoulder, but he
finally gave up and loosened the shin straps, leaving the
sandals where they were mired. His sword he kept, although
the scabbard went the way of the rest of his armor. Left naked
except for his linen tunic, he was thankful that it was late June
and the waters had lost the bite in their chill.

Turning his head, he saw that someone was looming up out
of the maize on the lip of the outermost artificial island,
backdropped by a slash of pale rose—all that remained of the
sunset. The silhouette clutched a knife, and Britannicus
wondered if he might be the eagle knight who had thrown
aside his *pilum* in the garden. Perhaps the Azteca had sha-
dowed him all the way through Tlacopan, never crying out
—understanding that this would only spur a more frantic
chase. Now, he appeared to be deciding whether or not to leap
into Texcoco after his quarry or summon more help.

Britannicus started backing out deeper into the waters.

At last, the warrior bawled over his shoulder, "Here! I have
him! Canoes, brothers—fast!"

Britannicus flung away his short sword and dove headlong
toward the darkest quarter of the lake. Unlike Balbus, who
had grown up beside the warm tide of the Mare Superum, he
was not a strong swimmer, but any thrashing was better than
wallowing through this clinging muck.

Within the hour, the Aztecae launched canoes and barges to
find him. Britannicus scowled at the putt-putt sounds of

engines—the first he had heard in the Aztecan Empire. The
searchers had mounted oil lanterns on the prows of their craft,
and only by these warm-looking glows was he able to keep
track of the movements of the flotilla. He zigzagged across
Texcoco's inky surface until, near exhaustion, he was forced
to seek the bottom with his toes. Surprisingly, the lake in most
places was no deeper than his shoulders, although in one spot
he exhaled all his air and plumbed the depth: it was nearly fifteen feet.

He planned to skirt the Tepeyaca Fortress through the gap
in its causeway and then sneak ashore somewhere in the swales
of reeds near Atzacoalco. From there he would slip into the
mountains and hope for the help Alope had promised if he
struck north.

Otherwise, he despaired of ever escaping the flashing black
knives of Maxtla's priests.

The flotilla was now sweeping farther south, holding to the
Tlacopan shore, its commander perhaps doubtful that the
Roman would try to cross open water—even under cover of
darkness. Britannicus had begun to pace his exertions,
floating briefly on his back between every twenty strokes.
After he had passed under the causeway bridge without
alerting the sentry posted there, he was aware of no more
obstacles in the way of his reaching the safety of the tules. He
was close to confidence again and might have grinned to
himself had he not been clenching his teeth to keep them from
chattering.

Then, an obelisk of light shot straight up off the crown of
the Tepeyaca Fortress, so powerful it was only slightly dif-
fused by the galena-colored haze.

Electricus! Britannicus couldn't believe his eyes: Only
Rome fully enjoyed *electricus motive*. Even Hibernia, which
had been sending a senator to the Curia for a thousand years,
was still warmed by peat and illuminated by tapers. Yet here
was a barbarian flaunting its use of the Emperor Fabius's
great gift to Rome.

The beam toppled over like a tree being felled and started
sifting through the mists that clung to the lake. Britannicus
ducked beneath the surface as it swept his way. The brightness
passed over him. The blobs of spirulina suspended in the water
around him suddenly became green lanterns, then faded to
darkness again. He burst up into the air but could hoard only

a few deep breaths—for the light, obstinately, returned and loitered overhead.

Ever since his arrival in the Valley of the Mexicae, Britannicus had been haunted by an odor, one that seemed distantly familiar. At night, it wafted down through the thorn forest to Tlacopan, disagreeable even when perfumed by the floral scents of the embassy garden. At last, Britannicus *knew*: The Aztecae were burning petroleum, the same sulphurous grade once used by the boilers at the Campus Martius, to generate *electricus motive*, a process that was patently Roman. And this could only mean that Maxtla and his viper Tizoc were . . .

No, not so fast—think it all through again . . . from the beginning so the significance of this is not overlooked, Britannicus reminded himself as he surfaced again, gasping.

Any cadet who had suffered through *machinalis scientia* could recite how Fabius, as a military tribune in Alexandria, had wedded Hero's ancient steam engine model to principles the young noble had derived from study of the Parthian oil stove. Fabius's next assignment was the procuratorship of Scandia, where he bullied the empire's finest metalsmiths with the demand: "I need steel that can stand up to heat!" They gave him a carbon alloy worthy of their already splendid iron ore. Two years later, Fabius launched the first steam-powered sand-galley against an outpost of Numidian rebels. The terrified barbarians bolted into the desert, taking the mechanical innocence of the world with them on the backs of their horses.

Fabius's reputation for genius was firmly established—but not his political trustworthiness. His outspokenness was mistaken for duplicity in a plot against his uncle, the emperor, and only the intervention of the empress spared him from execution. He was exiled to Magnesia, a backwater district of western Anatolia—which, like all the apparent misfortunes that came his way, Fabius turned to advantage. He observed that local shepherds, who ranged far across the often featureless Anatolian Plateau, used a sliver of black stone on a string to find the northern direction. Fabius ferreted out the principle that made this possible, refined the device and enclosed it in a brass envelope, then presented his first *index*, or pointer, to his cousin, Admiral Isadorus Otacilius, whose fleet of wooden trireme was stationed at nearby Ephesus . . .

Laboring for breath, Britannicus rolled onto his back and watched the beam of light flicker across the face of the Great

Temple. He had now been in the water several hours, and only the gods knew how many Roman miles he had put between himself and Tlacopan. His arms ached each time he lifted them above the surface. Stroking forward again, he sought refuge from this agony in *machinalis scientia* once more:

Otacilius, as every schoolchild knew, had trusted Fabius's all-weather means of navigation so completely he sailed farther beyond the Pillars of Hercules than any previous Roman expedition. He established the imperial claim to the Novo Provinces and returned to Ostia with maize, lungweed, and, most startling of all, a score of blond and redheaded peoples who spoke what was believed to be Medius Scandian. He named all the forest and tundra within a thousand miles of their coastal island Nova Scandia; the more temperate wilderness to the south he called Nova Baetica, for its similarity to that Iberian province. Fabius was exultant: he had doubled the size of the empire—with a sliver of black stone!

Britannicus stopped swimming and began bobbing off the bottom on the tips of his toes. All thoughts dribbled out of his head and a frightening melancholy took its place, announced by a loud ringing in his ears. He wondered how painful a death drowning was. Electricus, he roused himself, *the point in all this had been* electricus motive.

At the same time Otacilius had been plying the coasts of the Novo Provinces, Ptolemaeus, a Greek living on Crete, was studying the Fabian engine and the properties of Magnesian loadstones, in order to fulfill his personal vision of *dynamikos elektron mechanes*. He was accused of witchcraft when his estate suddenly shone under the blaze of noon—at midnight. A prudent man, Ptolemaeus gave credit for the invention to Fabius, who by then was recognized as heir presumptive to the throne of Augustus. The Greek was acquitted of the charge of witchcraft and in time, like Sejanus of old, became the emperor's "partner of my labors . . . "

Britannicus sank beneath the surface again. He dug his hands into the mire to anchor himself while the aquascape turned emerald green from the passing of the search beam. *Electricus motive,* he reminded himself as the air in his lungs slowly turned to burning poison. He had to survive. Somehow, he had to cross the length of the Aztecan Empire to the Roman garrison at Nova Petra. These prim barbarians possessed *electricus* and niter powder *pili*. They also had ties

with the Serican Empire, which neatly explained everything.
Baluchi traders insisted that the Silk-Makers knew about
fulminating powder and that their imperial city was lighted by
something similar to Ptolemaeus's machine. But these merchants also claimed that Serican nobles stunted the feet of
their female children, so everything they said was suspect . . .

Choking, Britannicus clawed his way up into the night air.

His eyelid flinched as it was glanced by a raindrop.

He blinked up through a wavering screen of tules at the dark
bellies of the clouds. He tried but could not rise . . . perhaps
tomorrow. His head still ached with fever, and the mud of this
slough was cool. He could not bring himself to look down at
his tattered feet. Of all things, he should have saved his sandals.

"To task, colonel. To the task at hand," he rasped as the
rain began rattling in earnest among the reeds.

He realized that this lucid spell was no more than a speck of
terra firma in a sea of delirium. It would soon be inundated by
feverish hallucinations, so Britannicus applied his concentration to the only question that mattered: How many days had
he been on the trail north?

Alope had said that the Aztecan fleet would be unleashed
against Nova Baetica in two weeks. Three, perhaps fours days
ago, he had been stumbling through the darkened lanes of
Tula, legendary home of the absent Quetzalcoatl ("If I might
ask, lord—have you made his acquaintance in your country?"), trying to lose a patrol of neophyte warriors that had
been dogging him all evening and might have caught him but
for the concealment of a jumble of huge basaltic heads with
scowling lips. He entered Tula with the hope of confusing the
best tracker among the tireless youths . . .

Even now, lying in the cool slime, he could be jarred into
horror by the vision of naked corpses stacked like the ricks of
wood at his uncle's *aqua vitae* factory, arms and legs sawn
from trunks, heads piled like boulders—each face with the
same scowl he had seen on the glowering monoliths. "House
of the Flowery Way" the torchlit glyphs over the portal to that
Hades had declared. Britannicus moaned softly and brought a
handful of wet mud to his forehead.

Two nights before Tula, he had been thrashing across Texcoco's black waters. The countryside between the lake and

Tula had puzzled him—not for what he had found but what he'd failed to find. Yes, there were fields of amaranth and maize that sustained him on his flight, but even by the most liberal reckoning there was nowhere enough cultivation in these tropical highlands to feed the Aztecan multitudes. Britannicus had been raised on a farm in Caledonia (his Pict parents had given him a name they believed would put him in good stead with their landlord in Londinium), and he had no doubt that this empire was living beyond its agricultural means—yet without famine. And that was flabbergasting to a man who had learned his Arabian reductions in terms of production and consumption.

"But help me, gods," he cried in his thin scratch of a voice, "how many days am I out from Tenochtitlan?"

Five or six perhaps, he answered himself. Nearly half the time expended—and less than a quarter of the distance to Nova Petra covered. He knew nothing about the terrain that lay before him in awful silence, except that no legionary had ever traversed it.

"I must reach deep," he muttered, fighting down his terror.

On the voyage from Nova Baetica to the Aztecan port of Zempoala, he had read *The Anatolian Revolt*, a recently published account of how Germanicus Agricola, before taking up the purple, had skillfully put down a holy war in Asia Minor. This new emperor was known to be decorous, if not self-effacing—the kind of Caesar a professional soldier could serve with pride. Of course, all new emperors were decorous, if not self-effacing. Then Britannicus gently shook his head as if reproving himself: *Think only good of Germanicus—your life may depend on it.*

He threw himself to his feet, tottered, caught his balance, then plodded northward through the cloudburst. His friends had often chided him that he was more Roman than the Romans. "You really are *peninsular*," a patrician cadet at the Campus Martius had once told him. It was still the sweetest compliment of his life.

He was shuffling across the dry lakebed, its flats so seared by alkali even the ubiquitous saltbrush could not push up through the crust, when he shuffled to a halt, rubbed his sun-burned eyelids, and gaped ahead at the horizon.

Two apparitions could be seen advancing through the heat

waves toward him. Britannicus giggled at the comic progress
of the figures: their upper bodies shifted to the sides and
elongated like rippling banners, or vanished altogether and
left only madcap legs to prance and gallop across the waterless
expanse.

Then it occurred to him that these might be the deliverers of
his death. He squatted on his heels and thought about this. A
few moments later, he suppressed another giggle, then closed
his eyes.

Feet slapped the hardened mud around him. A shadow fell
across him—merciful shade. Merciful death. Britannicus
opened an eye on a pair of wiry brown men wearing only
loincloths.

"*Kwira-ba*," one of the barbarians said in a language
Britannicus had never heard before. His partner stood behind
him, balancing a long club on his shoulder.

"You . . . Maxtla's men?" Britannicus asked in Nahuatl.

The barbarians traded glances conveying their unease that
the Roman might be in the reverend speaker's service.

"Then . . . you Indee . . . Alope's people?" Britannicus persisted.

"No," the first to speak said in a Nahuatl even cruder than
Britannicus's. "No Indee . . . we Raramurae." He tapped his
hairless chest with a forefinger. "I one Raramura!"

"Roman." Britannicus struck his own breastbone, then
laughed with an abandon that made the barbarians step
backwards. "No, no, I won't harm you . . . can't harm you
. . . anyone else. I'm finished."

They gave him water from a bottle gourd, which was
yanked away before he could completely drain it, and then a
small, chewy tuber. It instantly soured the first saliva he'd had
in days. "For vigor," they promised him.

The club was actually a deerskin litter strung between two
stout poles, which they now unfurled. With nudges and meaningless explanations, Britannicus was instructed to lie down on
it. Then, without so much as a grunt, the barbarians hoisted
him and, incredibly, began trotting back in the direction from
which they had materialized. They breathed through their
noses all the while and in no way indicated that Britannicus
was a burden to them.

He protected his face from the sun with what remained of
his tunic, then lost consciousness.

He awoke to a leering moon after extraordinarily vivid dreams and realized that his bearers were still jostling him across the desert. "Please stop."

They ignored him, and only after much caterwauling in wineshop Latin did he get them to halt. "Listen, brothers," he struggled in Nahuatl. "This is what we must do—find me parchment or vellum, a bit of charcoal . . . " Their moonstruck eyes stared back at him, uncomprehending. " . . . things so I might make glyphs for the lord at Nova Petra."

"No-wah Pay-tra," they said brightly in unison.

"Yes, friends." Encouraged, Britannicus sat up. "And then one of you must run fast to Nova Petra and tell the lord a war is coming. Four days, perhaps fewer."

"No-wah Pay-tra," they repeated, satisfied now that everyone was agreed on what to do. They lifted Britannicus off the ground with a neck-cracking jolt and started running again. He flopped back in defeat. Obviously, their orders had been to deliver him to the Roman garrison and that was precisely what they would do. He had done his best, but it had not sufficed. For the first time in an otherwise unblemished career, Britannicus Musa had failed. He was no longer *peninsular*.

Tears filled his eyes.

3

TUCKED AWAY IN a clutch of cypresses on the Palatine Hill was a small garden. It was the emperor's own, abloom with a few of his favorite flowers, such as the humble Anatolian wild iris. There was a dolomite Venus at the garden's center, but only those of long acquaintance with Germanicus Agricola realized that her features resembled those of a female colonel who had served in his eastern command—and been executed on his orders during the Pamphilean Plot.

This morning's sun was unrelieved by a breeze, but the emperor did not mop his brow as he listened to the boy who was sharing the bench with him. The child was reading from a codex entitled *The Anatolian Revolt*, and his voice was pleasingly in tune with the background of birdsong: " ' . . . the Empress Pamphile enacted her program to supplant Fabius, and this violence rippled out across the empire: Like Archimedes of old, P . . . Ptol . . .' "

"Ptolemaeus."

" ' . . . of Crete was cut down by a legionary while unraveling some problem of mathematics; the Senate was sacked; and in Anatolia, Procurator Germanicus found himself caught between barbarian zealots and the empress's confederates, who conspired to take advantage of unrest in the province.' "

The emperor's eyes had gravitated back to the face of the statue. His jaw muscles were undulating beneath the skin. Then he realized that the boy had stopped reading. Smiling sadly, he enfolded the child under his arm. "Go on, Quintus."

"How much more, uncle?"

"Five minutes for another sesterce."

"Ten minutes for two?"

Germanicus tried to frown, but the result was not adequately grave. "Oh, very well . . . just this once." He kissed his grandnephew atop the head.

" ' . . . Poppaeus, the garrison commander at Agri Dagi, colonels Marcellus and Crispa were all implicated by their own deeds . . . ' "

Once again, Germanicus was transfixed by the Venus. Only fourteen short months ago *she* had been alive—of flesh, blood, voice, and flashing aquamarine eyes. But Crispa was no more. She had crossed the Styx, as had his wife, although poor Virgilia had died in degrees over many bedridden years. And his brother Manlius was gone too, one of Pamphile's legion victims.

This boy and his father and mother were all that remained of Germanicus's family, his circle of loved ones.

And they were not his kin by blood:

The bachelor Manlius, in what proved to be the last year of his life, had adopted his assistant at the Prefecture of Antiquities, an ambitious young scholar. This man was Quintus's father. His new legal name of Manlius Julius Agricola Ahenobarbianus proved too cumbersome for all but the most formal correspondence, so he continued to use his original first two names: Gaius Nero—especially since he shared a distant common ancestor with that fop of an emperor.

Germanicus felt that he owed his adopted nephew a great debt. Gaius Nero had uncovered the evidence that sent the praetorian prefect to his execution, thereby rescuing the empire from its eternal nemesis—schism. The traitor had gone to the Mamertine Prison shouting that Gaius Nero had his own ambitions to imperial power: "Tell Caesar not to be deceived! This cataloguer of potsherds tested the waters with the Senate and me before Germanicus ever returned from Anatolia!"

In the emperor's presence, Gaius Nero calmly heard out the prefect's accusation, then said, "Yes, that is true."

Germanicus glared at him. "Explain."

"In the confusion of those bloody hours, it occurred to me that Augustus's crown might be thrust upon me. The loss of life among the Julian lineage was that severe, as Caesar well knows. Yes, I sought counsel from certain trusted senators

—and will now gladly furnish their names, if Caesar wishes. I also discussed the matter with the late praetorian prefect. Within a few hours of this intercourse, word arrived that you had not been slain in Agri Dagi, as first had been reported."

Germanicus regarded the young man with a faint smile. "Then the matter is closed. Now, more than ever, it is vital that the Roman world not be divided by—" On the verge of elaborating, Germanicus suddenly cut himself short. "At any rate, your loyalty becomes a son."

Gaius Nero looked beside himself with joy, and Germanicus immediately realized that this had been too broad a hint that he might adopt the man himself.

Offered a proconsulship—an ancient office Fabius had abolished after the Proconsular Conspiracy and Germanicus had just reinstated—Gaius Nero politely declined: "Uncle, I have no military experience to prepare me for the future. But I'd also like to remain in Rome under your tutelage. Is it too much to ask that I assume the post so recently held by this traitor?"

Command of the emperor's guard was decidedly a rung or two below proconsular rank. "You wish to be praetorian prefect?" Germanicus asked incredulously.

"I do, Caesar."

Germanicus shrugged. "So be it." Later, he took comfort in knowing that a trusted member of his family occupied the office that had often been a stepping-stone for usurpers. Of course, Gaius Nero had no idea that his eventual inheritance of Augustus's crown was doubtful. And this is what Germanicus yearned to tell him but could not: If he had his way, there would be no more Caesars after him, for it was his secret aim to restore the republic.

Of necessity, he viewed everything through a prism of empire, republic, and *Pax Romana* regardless of the governmental form it took. Above all, Rome must remain of one body. The alternative was chaos. For this reason, his heart had skipped a beat when he learned from Gaius Nero that the praetorian prefect was conspiring to carve off the Asian provinces into a realm for himself. Division into western and eastern empires had always been Rome's greatest peril. Sometimes this danger had been obvious, as in the case of Marcus Antonius's perfidy with Cleopatra to create an oriental Rome. But Ger-

manicus now believed that some of these threats had been less
than apparent—as in the matter of Joshua Bar Joseph:

Germanicus had first become aware of the legend while
bound for the mountain wilds of Agri Dagi on a rail-galley. A
tragedian related a vision he claimed to have heard from the
Sibyl at Alexandria. Only later, as emperor, was Germanicus
able to dispatch an agent to Egypt to question the old woman
and authenticate the actor's fantastic tale.

"Indeed, Caesar," the agent had reported, "the Sibyl main-
tains that, during the reign of Tiberius, the procurator of
Judea freed a Galilean holy man from crucifixion, thus saving
the empire from division and, ultimately, collapse at the hands
of the Gothic factions."

"How can that be possible?" Germanicus shook his head.
"She *must* have explained."

"I'm sorry, Caesar, she grew impatient with my questions."

"The gist of it, man—surely you have some intuition!"

The agent, a former priest of Isis, chewed the inside of his
cheek for a moment. "I believe this Cult of Joshua could have
gained impetus from the dramatic manner of his death. It
could've gained a foothold in resurrectionist cults of the oriental provinces—and rippled across racial lines, perhaps to Italia
itself."

"And she perceives that this cult would have caused our
division?"

"I believe so." All at once, the man dropped his gaze.
"Caesar, I fear the Sibyl knew who sent me."

"Did you tell her?"

"No, never! But, in parting, she said to me, 'Caesar dreams
of Arminius's deed, but only in dreams his scouts Varus does
not heed!' "

The color drained out of Germanicus's face. An amateur
historian, he had often pondered the fate of the empire had
Augustus's general, Quintilius Varus, not thrashed Arminius
and his German tribes at the battle of Teutoburg Forest. Now,
the most renowned sibyl in the world was confirming the importance he had always placed on that distant clash. Victorious, Augustus's legions had secured the borders of the empire
all the way to the River Vistula and put Germania firmly on
the path to Romanization.

So, in a nutshell, the Sibyl was suggesting that the rise of a

new cult within the empire and barbarian arms without could
have combined to smash the Roman dream of universal peace
and prosperity. "But Rome did indeed survive," Germanicus
muttered.

"Indeed," the agent had echoed with a smirk. "Indeed,
Caesar."

Now, Quintus's boyish voice welled up out of these mus-
ings: " ' . . . and on the arrival of Germanicus Julius Agricola
in Rome a public thanksgiving of twenty days was decreed to
celebrate his victory in Anatolia and the empire's good fortune
that not all the Julian nobility had been slain. This was a
greater honor than had previously been granted to anyone, in-
cluding Gaius Julius Caesar.' " He snapped shut the codex,
startling Germanicus. "Uncle, are you a greater man than
Gaius Julius?"

"I'm a different kind of man. And we leave it to history to
sort out the greatness of men."

Quintus suddenly stood on the bench and waved. "Father!"

Through the cypresses, glints of sunlight caught Gaius
Nero's balding pate. In his lean regality, which seemed a bit
practiced at times, his nephew reminded Germanicus of statuary of Julius Caesar.

"Quintus," he quickly said, "you must run along now. I
have matters to discuss with your father. Tomorrow, bring
your Zeno along."

"Hail Caesar!"

"Yes, quite." Germanicus watched the boy skip along the
path and leap up into his father's waiting arms.

After wiping his palms on the coarse linen tunic he wore in
private, the emperor took a sip of vinegar from the battered
military canteen that had served him in dozens of campaigns.
Finally, today, he would have to break hard ground with his
nephew. On its surface, the business would not smack of anything extraordinary. But a fellow as clever as Gaius Nero
would immediately grasp its significance.

Germanicus intended to return five of the most stable provinces—the four Gauls and Germania—to the authority of the
Senate. Of itself, the move would not be revolutionary. Augustus himself had set aside senatorial provinces that were
governed by proconsuls instead of military officers. But it was
the timing of the decree that would earn it close scrutiny. Ger-

manicus had really just begun his reign, and his smallest decision was held to be a harbinger of enormous import. He was terrified to think that a leak of his true intentions might spark a civil war, but he also knew that the transition from empire to republic could not be achieved with a single blow for freedom. Gradually, the Senate would have to be given greater power. *Why, then, am I dragging my feet?* he asked himself time and again. *Because I know in my heart of hearts that the republic cannot be restored without bloodshed . . . and I'm not sure I have the strength for that anymore.*

Gaius Nero marched up in his splendid praetorian uniform and saluted. "Hail Caesar!"

Germanicus patted the stone bench. "Nephew, please sit— we have things to discuss."

"None more urgent than the news I bring, Caesar."

Reflexively, Germanicus began kneading his abdomen with one hand. "What is it?"

"Nova Baetica has been invaded."

"Good Jupiter. The Aztecae?"

Gaius Nero nodded. "They came by sea with a formidable navy. Our losses are considerable."

"What word from our mission to Maxtla?"

"None—we must assume that our two envoys are dead."

Germanicus cradled his head in his hands. "Good Jupiter."

The emperor had not yet arrived at the Curia. But, minutes before, his personal bodyguard, a German with long mustaches framing his scowl, had begun sifting through the senators. He examined each patrician as if the man might be an Aztecan warrior in disguise—and nearly came to blows with an ex-consul until the dotard revealed the bulge inside his toga to be a stylus and not a dagger. Satisfied at last that none of Maxtla's cutthroats was in attendance, the centurion stationed himself behind the ornate water clock and let his gaze blear to indifference.

The German could understand less than a quarter of what was being spoken. This was the classical Latin exhorted by senators only in the sanctity of the Curia. Like most legionaries, and even officers in their day-to-day lives, Rolf spoke *nova lingua vulgata*, a plebeian tongue adulterated by the languages of the major provinces. But the centurion's eyes brightened as the noble senator from Aquitania suddenly shouted in a Latin that would have made perfect sense to any wineshop crowd: "I say we lead this king of the Aztecae down the Via Flaminia by his staff—and I don't mean that mop of feathers he's reported to wave about!"

There was raucous applause from those who were not themselves heaping insults on Maxtla III. This only proved what Rolf had known all along: The higher the class, the fouler the mouth.

Praetorian guardsmen, a hundred strong, burst through the doors and beat their shields with their short swords in a needless demand for attention. The senators came to their feet as the emperor entered their ancient hall: "*Hail Caesar!*"

Germanicus looked as if he had been taken aback by their cry, as if this were his first inkling of how hot the war passion was running in Rome. Nevertheless, he recovered himself and warmly greeted Appius Torquatus, the president of the Senate: "I thank you, *Princeps Senatus* and all the Conscript Fathers, for this opportunity to address the Senate. You are partners to my consulship in the fullest sense of the word, and I wish to share with you all the latest information I have received . . . "

Led by a colonel, two legionaries rolled in a *luxoculus*. All three were of the Tenth Legion and had been patined by the sun of Novo Provinces to resemble Nabataean nomads. "Caesar," the officer said, "with your permission—"

"Speak, colonel, and speak frankly as you would to your own staff."

The man saluted.

The *luxoculus*, after a fit of smoking that sent one senator gagging from the chamber, projected a somewhat blurred map of the Nova Baetica on the wall. "So that Caesar and the Conscript Fathers," the colonel began, "may appreciate the distances over which military enterprises must be conducted in the Nova Provinces, this peninsula here"—he pointed with his short sword—"the Paludosa, dear to tanners for its specie of crocodilus, is about the same size as Italia—less Cisalpine Gaul, of course. From its tip to the provincial capital of Otacilium is the equivalent of a march from Rome to the German border—if there were no roads and only malarial bogs along the way. Between Otacilius and our westernmost garrison at Nova Petra lies a parched wilderness of prairie, desert, and mountains that would extend from the Rome to Londinium—"

"The only distance, colonel, we beg to know is this . . . " a nasal patrician voice cried from the gallery. "How far is it from Otacilium to that unpronounceable *capital* of theirs?"

There was a chorus of approval punctuated by the drumming of sandals on the floor that died away only when, one by one, the senators glanced up and found Caesar brooding on his curule chair. "Yes, colonel," he said gravely, "please acquaint us with that distance in Roman miles."

"Well, Caesar, if terrain is taken into account—"

"Take everything into account, colonel—as an invading army must."

"Then, I would estimate two thousand miles from Otacilium to the lake that surrounds Tenochtitlan."

"From Rome to the Parthian frontier—that is the march that would lie ahead of our legions." Germanicus paused as he ran his gaze across the somber faces. "Now, colonel, kindly limit your discourse to the vicinity of the invasion itself . . . "

When the briefing was concluded, Germanicus turned to Appius Torquatus again. Obviously, he was taking pains to venerate the titular head of the Senate. "Tell me, noble *Princeps Senatus*, what are your thoughts on this matter?"

"Well, Caesar . . . "

Everyone leaned forward from their benches as if Cicero were about to address them.

" . . . my poor tongue can do little justice to what must be said. Prefect Gaius Nero can best express what has melded all our hearts into one." Then Appius sat down to loud applause.

Germanicus glowered at him. The president of the Senate was toadying to the man everyone assumed would be their next emperor—precisely the kind of timidity that had kept the Julians in power for the two thousand and thirty-six years since Gaius Julius had crossed the Rubicon. The die was certainly cast—seemingly forever.

Gaius Nero bounded to the forefront of the assembly with a relish he could scarcely hide. He waited for all coughing to rumble to silence, then, with his fist clenched across his cuirass, said:

"In this land among strangers
He died where he chose to die.

He has his eternal bed well shaded,
And in his death is not unmourned.
My eyes are blind with tears
For weeping for you, Britannicus Musa.
The terror and the loss
Cannot be quieted.
I know you wished to die in a strange country,
Yet your death was so lonely!
Why could I not be with you?"

Dabbing their eyes with the folds of their togas, the senators took their ovation to their feet.

"Borrowed from Sophocles," Germanicus whispered to Rolf, who unobtrusively had taken his usual place a few steps behind Caesar.

The centurion shrugged as if not sure who Sophocles was.

"Friends," Gaius Nero went on, "whatever happens in the coming days or weeks of war—"

"Or *years*," Germanicus interrupted.

"Quite, Caesar." The prefect flashed a grin, then turned back to his larger audience. "Whatever happens, let us never forget that the indignities rained upon our heads by the Punic council were ended only when we struck a blow at the heart of the monster—Carthage itself. So be it with Tenochtitlan!" He held up a hand to quiet the roar of approval. "I propose a campaign of this design: We land five legions on the Aztecan coast, march inland, and invest their capital."

"What fortunate legion will form your vanguard, prefect?" a senator asked. The question sounded as if it had been rehearsed.

"Why, the Third, of course, now garrisoned in Hibernia. They have a great store of frustration to unleash on the Aztecae." The laughter attending this remark admitted the Roman despair of ever civilizing the Hibernians. "I believe we can safely say that Maxtla will capitulate no later than the first day of spring."

Germanicus leaned forward as if to say something, but then eased back again.

Gaius Nero planted his fists on his hips. "If there remains the slightest misgiving in any Roman heart, I would like to share something that Caesar's praetorians found on the field of battle in Nova Baetica." A guardsman with comical-

looking jowls hurried to the prefect's side, bearing an Aztecan
pilum at port arms. "This, citizens, is the standard issue to
Maxtla's forces. And it cannot be discharged until the following mechanical operation is completed . . . " A second
praetorian, as insipid-looking as the first, quickmarched up
to Gaius Nero. He carried bellows on a sling around his
shoulder. The first guardsman unscrewed the stop in the
breech of his weapon and his partner commenced pumping air
into the *pilum*. A few sniggers braved the attentive silence.
"The Aztecan warrior," Gaius Nero said, "must keep doing
this for two minutes before his weapon can be discharged.
Conscript Fathers, if I might direct your attention to the main
doors . . . " A third praetorian stood in the portal, holding an
aluminum shield before him, grimacing slightly as he waited.
The senators, seeing that the military men in the gallery had
plugged their ears with their fingers, now did the same.

"Fire!" Gaius Nero barked, and the guardsman beside him
hoisted the *pilum*. There was a disappointing pop of a report
and then uproarious laughter when everyone realized that the
lead ball skittering along the marble floor had done nothing
more than dent the shield, which the praetorian let clatter to
his feet to let all see that he had not been harmed in the least.
"Conscript Fathers, these are the toys with which Maxtla chal-
lenges the might of Rome!"

When the howling and whistling had died away, Germanicus said, "Tell me, prefect, were not niter pieces also found
among the enemy dead?"

"Yes, Caesar." Gaius Nero was still smirking. "A small
number."

"And might they be of Serican manufacture?"

"No one knows for sure."

Germanicus noticed that Appius Torquatus had stood to
speak. "Yes, *Princeps Senatus*, please tell us what you think
—I earnestly seek the counsel of the Senate in a matter as
weighty as this."

"Caesar, I have been told by many that, when I say this, I
give voice to the will of the entire Senate: The hour has arrived for us to march on Maxtla's palace! Let us make short
work of this tyrant!"

Germanicus's glare stifled the inklings of another noisy ovation. "Are there any present who do not share this sentiment?"

Silence.

The emperor's face reddened: once again, the consensus of the Senate would have to be overruled by a Julian—and the very man who wanted to restore the republic. "Let me point out, Conscript Fathers," he said, trying to strain the vehemence out of his voice with a smile, "that there are no short wars—any more than there are congenial divorces."

The laughter was polite but brittle.

"Noble Appius, kindly tell us what you believe to be Maxtla's greatest difficulty in making war on us."

"Roman resolve, Caesar!"

"Gaius Nero," Germanicus tried again, "what would your answer be?"

The praetorian prefect beamed like a star pupil. "The superiority of Roman arms, Caesar—as I have demonstrated."

Germanicus exhaled, then peered around the Curia until his eyes lit upon his bodyguard. "Centurion . . . "

Rolf snapped to. "Hail Kaiser!"

"If you were Maxtla, what would keep you awake at night?"

The German was discomfited for only an instant; he had been ordered to do something. "Lines of supply, Kaiser—they be too long."

"Yes!" Germanicus smacked his palm with his right fist. "Maxtla has landed a huge army hundreds of miles from his nearest stores. Now he must maintain sea lanes to supply that force!" He grinned, somewhat exasperated that he had to explain this in the first place. "Conscript Fathers, should we then duplicate the same folly—with the added disadvantage of having a powerful enemy army to our back?"

No one met Germanicus's eyes. Unintentionally, he had cowed every last one of them. He paused, remembering to smile again. "Friends, I beg the counsel of the Senate in doing this—dislodging Maxtla's warriors from the beaches of Nova Baetica and sending them home in dishonor. I hereby convene a *comita bellica* and ask the Senate to be so generous as to lend me five of its number for this committee."

"Of course, Caesar," Appius Torquatus muttered.

"We sail for the Novo Provinces the first week of August."

The "Hail Caesar!" that marked Germanicus's exit from the Curia was but a tenth as forceful as the one that had greeted him. As he was led through the doors by Rolf, he was joined by the praetorian prefect, who was tight-lipped and stared straight ahead. "Politics, my boy," Germanicus whispered, patting Gaius Nero on the shoulder.

"Yes, uncle . . . politics."

4

THE CROWD IN the Circus Fabius roared for Germanicus's attention. Frowning, he glanced up from the huge scrolls that had been unfurled across the white marble floor of his gallery. "What is it?"

Gaius Nero pointed down at the bloodied sands, where a heavily armed Thracian was poised with uplifted sword to dispatch a *retiarius* who had become entangled in his own net. "These gladiators await your decision, Caesar."

"Damn, but I have no time for this. Tomorrow we sail for the Novo Provinces—"

"Which the Senate implores you not to do, Caesar," Appius Torquatus said none too forcefully—Germanicus's unwillingness to march on Tenochtitlan had cost him much popularity with the Conscript Fathers. "Surely, as a historian, you recall the two consuls who ventured too near the Punic lines and were slain by Hannibal."

Germanicus waved off Appius's remark and instead looked to his German bodyguard. "What do you say, Rolf? Did this *retiarius* put up a decent fight?"

The centurion shrugged. "Not brilliant—but aye."

Germanicus got up from his knees and stood at the balustrade so all in the arena could see him. Then he thrust his thumb upward. "I shouldn't have come—there remains so much to do."

"It is important that the people see you before you embark for the war," Gaius Nero said, holding out his wine cup for it to be filled by a Nubian slave girl, whose hands trembled as she poured.

Clambering down to his hands and knees once more, Germanicus motioned for the marine architects to huddle around him again. "Continue . . . continue."

"Well, as I was saying, Caesar," the *architectus maximus* prattled, "the improvement of the quinquereme over the trireme can be found here, amidship. While the trireme is driven through the water by only three screw propellers, the forward movement of the quinquereme is further assisted by these two outboard floatwheels—five exerters of thrust instead of three, if you will."

Germanicus noticed that one of the architects did not appear to concur. "What's your name?"

The man paled at being singled out. "Lepidus, Caesar."

"You don't look like you agree with the *architectus maximus.*"

Lepidus hesitated only briefly before finding his courage. "Outboard assistance has proved no more fruitful an experiment than the mechanical oars of three decades ago."

"Were these floatwheels the cause of the Syracusae Disaster?"

"No . . . "

"That tragedy is still under investigation, Caesar." The *architectus maximus* wrapped his left hand in his toga, a patrician affectation that irked Germanicus. "So, it is only fitting that we wait until—"

"Let Lepidus go on. He speaks frankly."

Lepidus's eyes flickered toward his immediate superior, then back to Germanicus's stern face. "The Syracusae Disaster had nothing to do with floatwheels. It is a maxim that the length of a galley should not exceed ten times its beam. Otherwise, the ship is too slender. The ratio on these two new quinqueremes was more like twelve to one."

"Why was this done?"

"To make room for a longer *corvus.*" Lepidus spoke of the boarding ramp affixed to the prows of Roman war galleys. The younger admirals considered it to be a superfluous antique. "On the basis of Sicilian eyewitness accounts, I believe that, when these narrow ships fired practice salvos, their own *ballistae* capsized them . . . sent them to the bottom of the Bay of Thapsus."

"Good Jupiter." Germanicus began massaging his eyelids. "What has happened to us? The leading edge of the Latin League has become a race of incompetents, procrastinators. The fleet I order readied by the first of August does not assemble at Ostia until the ides." He opened his weary gaze on the architects. "This is intended to disgrace none of you—but I'm about to wage a naval war and suddenly discover that our newest ships are not seaworthy." He sighed. "Lepidus—"

"Caesar?"

"You are now *architectus maximus*. I believe you would not try to hide your own mistakes. The new quinqueremes must sail for the Mare Aztecum by the ides of December. That is all." Stiffly, Germanicus got up and was turning to call for a cup of vinegar when he smiled for the first time that day. "Epizelus!"

The imperial physician, his face burnished by the Egyptian sun, had just arrived from Alexandria. "Hail Caesar!"

"Yes, yes, how are you?"

"Exceedingly well, thank you."

Germanicus sidled up to him and whispered, "Did you learn anything?"

"I did indeed."

"Then come with me to my villa at Ostia."

"When, Caesar?"

"Right now—the older I get, the more disagreeable the Games seem."

Despite its team of twelve Iberian horses, the emperor's luxurious traveling van was actually a lorry powered by a Fabian engine. The white geldings served only the tradition that Caesar must be conveyed around Rome by gorgeous horseflesh, and an inexperienced operator could quickly run them ragged. Germanicus reminded the young praetorian of this before leaning back inside the coach window and drawing the curtains. "Very well, Epizelus," he said in a low voice, "tell me the answer to this riddle."

The Greek simpered. "I said I learned something, Germanicus, but it might only deepen the mystery."

"Go on."

Germanicus had dispatched his trusted friend to the eastern provinces out of a deep sense of his own inadequacy. Fabius would eclipse all emperors who followed him for a long time.

The gods had given him not only a mechanical genius, but the
ability to actualize what other marvelous eccentrics had only
dreamed. In his willingness to beg, borrow, and steal from all
quarters to get the job done, he had been the quintessential
Roman. But, in other equally important regards, Fabius had
transcended Latin thinking. How had this happened? What
forces had shaped Germanicus's extraordinary cousin?

And what had once been a curiosity for Germanicus was
now a grave urgency. He had inherited a complicated imperial
machinery he did not know how to use. While the reign of
Fabius was exalted for its burgeoning of knowledge, the reign
of Germanicus was already being disdained for its lethargic
bureaucracy.

"I first sailed to Crete as instructed," Epizelus's voice
welled up out of this pensive silence. "I went through
Ptolemaeus's effects. Extraordinary . . . did you realize that
his 'fire bolts' idea had less to do with combustion than the
concentration of light?"

"Yes, the emperor—" Germanicus smiled self-consciously.
"Fabius once told me about the new weapon, but it was all
beyond me. And now the legions will never have 'fire bolts' in
their arsenal."

"It was there in Ptolemaeus's library that I read of the mentor Fabius and he had shared in Alexandria."

"Yes, I got the message you were going on to Egypt. Was
this teacher of theirs Hellenic, then?"

"No, Nabataean."

"*What?*" Germanicus looked on the verge of being demor-
alized by confusion. He began rubbing red circles onto his
temples.

"One of those nomadic clans that scuttles from waterhole
to waterhole across Arabia Petraea."

"Are you sure this is the fellow we're looking for?"

"Quite."

"He is still alive?"

"Unknown, Caesar. Years ago, while in his seventies, he
traveled east. He is presumed to have died somewhere beyond
Baluchistan—but no one can say for certain."

"Bloody Hades," Germanicus whispered.

The operator had stopped pushing the horses forward, and
a glimpse out the curtain told Germanicus that they had arrived at the Subura quay. The remainder of the trip to Ostia

would be by imperial barge. "Come, hurry . . . I don't want to dine too late."

"Sometimes you sound more Greek than Roman, Caesar."

"Don't flatter yourself."

They stepped out of the van into purplish light that had been muddled by the evening mists off the Tiber. Germanicus waved off Rolf's offer to help in crossing the gap over the chuckling waters between the quay and the gilt barge. Epizelus was less bold, but still dusted his hands after being touched by the German.

As soon as they were underway, Germanicus asked his physician, "What was this Nabataean's name?"

"Al-Hamar."

"What did he teach?"

"He was something of an eclectic. But if I were to sum up the essence of his dialectic—"

"Please."

"Al-Hamar contested the Aristotelian foundations of science. He maintained that the depths of the seas cannot be deduced from the heights of their islands."

"Enough for now," Germanicus sighed. "It's been a long day." Then, with a sweep of his arm, he encompassed the Tiber-side factories that were belching phosphorescent smoke into the twilight: "This was all so much more pleasant when I was a boy."

At dawn, he hiked down to the sea from his ancestral estate, trying to forget with each step that the wooded ravines on both sides of him were teeming with praetorian guards. Fabius had once remarked to him, "I'm never alone anymore, cousin— and how lonely that makes me feel!"

But Germanicus put all of this out of mind as he approached the olive tree whose seaward leaves, in time of storm, were scorched by salt spray. Here, on a March afternoon ten years before, he had buried the urn that contained his son's ashes. In the only lie of his marriage, he had told Virgilia that he'd sent the young tribune's last vestiges out to sea on the Tiber. He had believed, perhaps wrongly, that her grief would never have abated had she been aware of this place.

He reclined against the trunk of the tree. "Ah, my Cassius . . . " As always, his eyes clouded, releasing the store of grief he had built up since last visiting here. "At noon I sail for the Novo Provinces. I won't be back for some long time. Now, for my supplications . . . all in your memory . . ."

Carefully, he prayed to each of the deities who might influence the outcome of this undertaking. Something of a reactionary in religious matters, he had never been attracted to the Cult of Isis, although he denounced persecution of its priesthood by Jovian patricians, believing that this only served to increase the sway of the cult among the plebeians. He admitted to himself that he worshiped the House of Jupiter only because these had been the gods of his heroes—and his class. Perhaps, truly, he believed only in the peace that attended this tree. The ecclesiastical convictions of a lifetime had attenuated into a simple longing: to share this quiet concord with his son.

"And Charon, my old friend," he concluded his prayers, "when the hour of my death comes, I'll pay my fare without bitterness, in eager anticipation of embracing those who await me on the far shore."

Then Germanicus rose and snapped a sprig off the lower-most bough of the olive tree. This he would carry with him on the campaign. He would offer it to Maxtla at the earliest possible opportunity. It was more than a token of peace. The sprig reminded him of something he felt his Roman blood often made him forget: In the end, ashes of men feed only the glory of trees.

Moments before Germanicus was set to depart by barge for the naval harbor, Gaius Nero informed him that a great crowd had lined the Via Claudia to watch Caesar's passing. The prefect had readied a sand-galley to transport him.

Privately, Germanicus thought this an unseemly way to leave for war. It smacked prematurely of a triumph and could even result in unfavorable auspices. But he had no desire to add any insult to the injury he had been forced to inflict on Gaius Nero, who was still smarting from the decision not to invade the Aztecan Empire. Despite being overruled, the prefect had ably served Caesar as adjutant in preparations for the campaign, and Germanicus admired the young man's sense of *authoritas*. "Of course I will go by sand-galley," he said warmly. "Lead the way. But first, where is my Quintus?"

"Ill, I'm afraid, Caesar."

"What?" Germanicus's face blanched. "Let me send Epizelus to—"

"There's no need, uncle. It's only a cold brought on by a change of humors in the air."

"Are you sure?"

"Positive."

Germanicus swatted away the assisting hands of a half-dozen praetorians and, on his own power, clambered up onto the prow deck of the gold-sheathed sand-galley that conveyed the prefect on his errands up and down the length of Italia. Trumpets blared, and the ponderous vehicle clattered forward on its cleated tracks.

Twenty minutes later, the imperial convoy emerged from a grove of umbrella pines and onto a headland that overlooked the naval harbor that had been reclaimed in the past year from ancient siltation. Germanicus ordered the operator to halt so he might gaze upon the Roman fleet and, perhaps, melt his doubts in the majesty of the sight.

Thirty enormous triremes, their drafts too great for slips constructed during the reign of Claudius, were anchored together mid-harbor, leaking smoke into the washed-out blue of the sky, their small advice boats skimming around them like water beetles. Their massed exhaust chimneys, fluted like Doric columns, resembled a roofless Parthenon floating out in the yellowly turbid flow of the Tiber. More than a hundred biremes were hugging the quays, building steam and taking aboard the last contingents of naval infantry. A flotilla of slower cargo galleys had departed two weeks before and would be overtaken at sea. "May this prove sufficient," Germanicus muttered.

"Caesar!" Gaius Nero called down to him from the after-deck. "The rabble presses against our rear guard. May we push on?"

"Proceed."

At quayside, Germanicus alighted from the sand-galley into a swirl of purple-hemmed togas: the Conscript Fathers were clotting around him for want of some encouraging word, but he felt less than ebullient as he embarked for a war he did not want. "Good morning," he finally said, sobering them with his somewhat distant manner.

Germanicus mounted the portable rostrum and, in grave-faced silence, awaited the determination of the auspices by a joint delegation of Jovian and Isiac priests.

Cages were brought forth, and from them grouse and rabbits were seized by the holy men. The animals had been recently captured in the wilds of the Novo Provinces, and every possible care had been exercised to preserve their health until this moment. The high spirits of the throng gave way to apprehension as they watched the flashing knives of the priests. One by one, the livers of the beasts were declared to be clean: all boded well for the expedition. The dignitaries around the emperor had begun to congratulate him when a sleek-eyed priest of Isis announced that this was all well and good for Roman endeavors by land—but the auspices for success on the waves of the Mare Aztecum could only be read from the liver of a sea creature. "May I proceed, Caesar?"

Germanicus gave him a slight nod.

As soon as he had made the incision in the belly of a small porpoise, the priest narrowed his eyes and gasped, leaving no question in anyone's mind that the liver was diseased. Germanicus expected him to now hedge a bit and admit that, well yes, the organ was mottled, although it probably meant nothing more than a touch of adversity along the way to eventual triumph over the Aztecae. So Germanicus was jarred when the priest cried: "The auspices are not good for battle on Neptune's fields of blue!"

Quickly, Germanicus tried to think of something reassuring to say, but his own premonition of doom had been slowly festering inside him for weeks. Now it seemed that even the gods were declaring against his plan for a cautious naval war against Maxtla. "Citizens," he shouted above the growing din of voices, "I will not disclaim what the gods themselves reveal to us. Few victories are swift and easy. But let us be confident—"

Germanicus was cut short by a sound that confused him as much as the crowd: the clopping of hooves on paving stones. The only horses in the vicinity of Rome were those of the emperor's traveling van, which he had left behind yesterday at the Subura quay.

Then, a troop of barbarian cavalry could be seen galloping up to the praetorian cordon. The lead mount, an Anatolian pony by the look of its uncropped mane, suddenly reared, spooked by a centurion who had drawn his short sword to halt the advance of the impudent riders. A reinforcement of guardsmen tramped past Germanicus, unslinging their *pili* as their ranks dissolved into the growing melee.

"Caesar!" a youthful voice was shouting desperately. "Caesar Germanicus!"

"It be wise to board this bireme." Rolf seized Germanicus by the arm and began tugging him toward the safety of the nearest galley.

"Your centurion is right," Gaius Nero said with a quaver in his voice, clearing a path to the gangway.

"*Pasa!*" the distant voice begged.

"Wait." Germanicus then recognized the headgear worn by the horsemen as the *jamadani* of the Agri Dagi tribesmen, a fierce and devout mountain people of eastern Anatolia.

The youth who had been bellowing for Caesar's attention now kicked a praetorian who was trying to confiscate the reins with one hand and ward off blows with the other.

"*All desist!*" Germanicus cried in the arresting tone of voice he had acquired from governing Hibernians.

Surprisingly, all quieted themselves, except for a few of the ponies, which continued to snort and skitter. Everyone awaited the emperor's next words. But when he spoke, the Romans were left perplexed.

Smiling, Germanicus addressed the youth in the dialect of these tribesmen: "It is a far way from your Purple Village, Prince Khalid."

"When we met our first infidel, we were already too far from home, *pasa*." Khalid doffed his *jamadani*—something he'd have never done while Germanicus's hostage fourteen months before. His matted hair was as shiny black as his eyes, but as of yet he had only a light sheen of a beard. He said in a Latin that was quite serviceable: "My father, the Great *Zaim*, the holiest of men, has seen to it I speak to Germanicus as Germanicus speaks to his own heart. This is so nothing remains hidden and all we say is touched by light."

"*Inshallah*," Germanicus said respectfully.

"As God wills," the tribesmen echoed, looking pleased that the Roman had not forgotten the piety of their ways.

"But tell me, Khalid, son of my noble enemy—why do you venture into the country of those whom you despise?" Germanicus shot a glance of censure at Gaius Nero that demanded to know how these primitive warriors had crossed the provinces of Anatolia, Thrace, Illyricum, Cisalpine Gaul, finally arriving in Rome's busiest port with the praetorian prefect none the wiser! "You once told me, prince," Germanicus went on, "that you did not want your time profaned by the stink of Roman company—is that not so?"

"True, but it has not been fully revealed to me why my father has sent me and the bravest of the brave to this region of filth and smoke. Still, we have been careful to keep only our own company and travel at night when all Romans lock themselves inside with their many vices. This much I know—my father has seen in a vision how you Romans will make a war across the seas . . . " He could not suppress a boyish grin. "I had never seen a sea until we crossed the Hellespontus." Then he remembered himself and resumed his officious bearing. "My father demands this question of Caesar Germanicus: Do you go to fight infidels?"

Germanicus shrugged. "Well, yes, I suppose the Aztecae are infidels."

"Then, truly, this shall be a *jhad*, a war of holy purpose." Satisfied, Khalid flicked his chin in the direction of the fleet. "Which of those is our boat?" All at once, he did not seem so sure of himself, for he lowered his voice to inquire: " . . . And how is it ridden?"

5

GAIUS NERO WAS smiling to himself as he clambered up a ladder toward a round of blue sky. Being appointed *legatus* to Caesar's personal command of the expedition had done much to bolster his spirits. He emerged on the afterdeck of the trireme *Aeneas*, unfurled his cloak, which he had been clutching, and let it flow behind him in the sea breeze.

Of course, Germanicus, true to the banalities that constipated him, had announced Gaius Nero's promotion not before the Conscript Fathers on the quay at Ostia, but at a scantily attended staff conference aboard this aged flagship. In the prefect's estimation, the greatest Caesars had been splendid actors, figures larger than life who'd made the empire their proscenium. Each had been so thoroughly convincing he'd validated a preposterous convention: that one man can control the world. This was not tyranny—it was high art! In reality, a man couldn't even hope to control his wife, and Gaius Nero knew this firsthand from his marriage to Claudia, a driven woman with plebeian origins she was methodically culling from society's memory.

But back to thoughts of Germanicus: Something was amiss with this emperor. And Gaius Nero was certain that he alone knew what.

It had dropped into his lap one rainy afternoon years before at the Prefecture of Antiquities. Manlius, Germanicus's older brother, was poring over a proposal to repair the Flavian Amphitheater. All at once, he threw down his stylus. "Damn, if I were emperor I'd abandon these stopgap measures and do the restoration properly!"

"Can you see that happening?" Gaius Nero quietly asked. "You becoming emperor?"

"Oh, Hades, no." Then Manlius chuckled in embarrassment. "And if by some miracle it was offered to me I'd probably turn it down."

"And let the throne of Augustus pass to your younger brother?"

Manlius's ordinarily weak eyes became even more glassy as they focused on the distant possibility. "Under that circumstance . . . it might be difficult for me to decline."

"I don't understand, sir."

"I'd only say this to you, my dear boy—but Germanicus would bring us to civil war. There's no finer man in the empire, but he believes in the republic with all his heart, as did our poor father . . . "

So, not only did Germanicus not want to be Caesar, he wanted no one to be Caesar. *Interesting material for a Plautine comedy: "The Reluctant Emperor,"* Gaius Nero thought to himself as he passed into the chilly shadow of a smoke chimney.

"Lord prefect?" a female voice called from the recess between two *ballistae* mounts.

He squinted into the darkened space. "Alope?"

"Yes—a word please."

He sauntered up to her. "Only a brief word. Our war council convenes in a few minutes."

She stared at him, her lips moving slightly as if she didn't know where to begin.

"What is it, woman? Don't waste my time."

"*Your* time, lord prefect? Seven days it took me to escape from Maxtla's realm. Another twenty to cross the Sea of the East in a Roman ship. And again that many days in Rome trying to be heard. I would like to finally know if I might speak to this council."

"Ah, didn't I tell you?"

"You have told me nothing since . . . " Her voice trailed off, and her gaze dropped to the deck. Her handsome face was briefly pained.

"This is a military council, Alope. I'm afraid that political matters won't be discussed this afternoon."

"But this *is* a military matter." She grinned, somewhat confusing the Roman, who did not know that this was how her people often revealed resentment. "I carry an offer from the Anasazi Federation—half a million warriors to fight alongside your Purple Cloaks!"

"Don't become argumentative with me." Gaius Nero stroked her forearm with his hand. "Are we not the best of friends? Didn't I listen to you after all other doors in Rome had been slammed in your face?"

"Yes," she whispered.

"Caesar will hear you out. I'll make sure of it. But the timing is important."

"When, lord prefect?"

"Soon."

The emperor and his staff were finishing a light meal on the main deck. Gaius Nero took the couch beside Germanicus's and ignored a servant's offer of dormice stuffed with pine nuts.

"Caesar, may I broach a few matters before the council comes to order?"

"Certainly." Germanicus was peering across the choppy sea at the rest of the fleet, which was steaming in column.

"A praetorian colonel aboard the *Romulus* reports that the Anatolians insist on lighting cooking fires below decks."

"Let them continue to use their braziers—but above decks. They have strict dietary laws."

"Is Caesar confident that these barbarians can be trusted?"

"I am. The *shaykh*, spiritual mentor to their Great *Zaim*, once had a vision that I, even in my ignorance as a Roman, would somehow serve their god. Whatever their reasons for helping us, this will be an important first step toward Romanization for the Agri Dagi tribesmen."

Gaius Nero did not look convinced but decided to move on to other matters. "I have a return on the inquiry about Britannicus Musa. The commander at Nova Petra wirelessed that the colonel still cannot be roused from his melancholy."

Germanicus shook his head. "What a terrible irony—the only Roman to have seen Tenochtitlan survives Maxtla's treachery but is too addled to give us a decent report."

"The physician there believes Musa will be unfit for service from now on."

Sighing, Germanicus began rising from his couch. "Well, does that conclude your agenda?"

"Not quite, Caesar." Gaius Nero waited until Germanicus had reclined again, as if insisting on the emperor's complete attention. "I took the liberty of bringing a new barbarian agent aboard."

"Ours or Maxtla's?"

"In my enterprises, uncle, that's often impossible to tell. But my people at Nova Petra vouched for her hatred of the Aztecae. Whether or not she and her Indee compatriots are truly friendly to Rome remains to be seen. They have raided our *coloni* in the past." Gaius Nero paused. "On one hand, she slipped away from Tenochtitlan without suffering so much as a scratch—at the same time our adjutant envoy was murdered. Still, the woman might have helped Colonel Musa make his escape. After all, he did reach Nova Petra in one piece."

"Less his wits," Germanicus said. His staff officers were already on their feet, waiting for him. "I'd like to question this woman later."

"As you wish, Caesar." Then the prefect strode through the hatch at the emperor's heels. He was quite pleased with himself: he had demonstrated to everyone that he had the force of personality to delay the most powerful man in the world.

Terrentius Glabrio had not arrived in Ostia expecting to be named admiral of the entire expeditionary fleet. By his own admission, he was a lesser light in naval circles. But his Lusitanian squadron was the only to present in good order a week ahead of schedule, and a restless Caesar had made inquiries about its commander. It appeared that, in addition to being punctual, Glabrio had initiative: on his way to Italia, he had been apprised of piratical attacks on merchant galleys plying the Mauretanian coast south of Tingis. He located, engaged, and boarded the pirate bireme—and still steamed into Ostia two weeks before the next squadron to drop anchor.

Summarily promoted by the emperor himself, Glabrio, a robust man with the transparent emotions of a Lusitanian, had been unable to keep his eyes from misting. "This is more honor than I can bear, Caesar."

Yet now, bearing the honor quite comfortably as he welcomed the imperial staff into his *praetoria navis,* Glabrio stood at the forefront of his former superiors without revealing the least bit of diffidence. He opened the discussion with a firm voice: "Caesar, the Aztecae offloaded their invasion cohorts at night. So no one saw the demons' manner of galley. Their army, stalemated against the Tenth Legion along an entrenched front here"—he tapped a map of Nova Baetica with his blunt fingers—"is resupplied by small boats, always under cover of darkness."

"My dear admiral," Hadrianus, the rawboned Iberian commander of Naval Infantry, asked, "have we attempted to interdict their resupply?"

"We have." Glabrio frowned. "Last night, two triremes sortied from Otacilium against the Maxtla's fleet. From ashore, our legionaries saw the flashes of our *ballistae*—and then Aztecan flashes in answer." He paused to let this news sink in. "That's right—the Aztecae have progressed beyond mechanical *ballistaery*. This morning, General Salvidienus reported the first bombardment of his positions."

"What of our galleys?" Germanicus asked.

"They never returned to Otacilium."

"Certainly some survivors must have made it to shore."

"Perhaps, Caesar. But if any were fortunate enough to be spared by the Mare Aztecum, they were taken by the enemy—a worse fate than the sea, I'm told." Glabrio took a deep breath before continuing, "What I have to say next won't be well received by everyone here. But it must be discussed before we close with the enemy." Then he looked directly at Germanicus: "We're floating the wrong kind of navy for the perils we may face."

A dry chuckle escaped the elderly admiral Glabrio had supplanted. "Then please acquaint us with the error of our ways, noble Terrentius."

"I shall. From the First Punic War to the present, our galleys have been built and appointed for a boarder's fight. We have depended on naval infantry to vanquish our foes." Glabrio nodded at Hadrianus. "And there will always be some need for our gallant marines. But we must not be the last naval power to adopt new—"

"Unless I'm mistaken," Hadrianus angrily interrupted, "I distinctly recall my marines garnering you a senatorial ovation for action against Mauretanian pirates earlier this summer!''

"Yes, which only substantiates my point in a roundabout way, Lucillus—"

"Before we haul up the *corvus* for the last time and forever forsake boarding enemy vessels by ramp," Hadrianus declared, "let us recount what successes this time-tested method has wrought us in the Mare Nostrum!"

"But the coming fight won't be in our own sea," Germanicus said quietly.

"Of course, Caesar," Hadrianus sputtered. "I meant only to suggest the predominant point of view."

"Fear not—that point of view is always with us. Please continue, Admiral Glabrio."

The Lusitanian took a moment to cool his ardor with a sip of wine. "The last time—within the waters of our empire, at least—one great fleet confronted another was at Actium. Two thousand years ago. Since then, we have applied our navy to two purposes: apprehending pirates, whose galleys had to be boarded in order to recover captives and contraband, and supporting the seiges of rebellious port cities. *That* is all we know how to do."

"Or need to know!"

"Wrong, Lucillus Hadrianus!" Glabrio shouted. "We must be prepared to outmaneuver and destroy other war galleys on the high seas!"

"Dear Terrentius," the old admiral cooed, the back of his neck a brocade of wrinkles from years of sun and wind, "if we, the mightiest empire on earth, are not so prepared, who then is?" He sat back and popped a grape into his mouth, having loosed his words in the predacious way a falconer launches his birds.

Suddenly, Glabrio seemed reluctant to press his point.

"The question's a fair one, Admiral Glabrio," Germanicus said, noting at the same time that Gaius Nero seemed to be taking pleasure from the dissension.

The Lusitanian blew a gust of air out of his cheeks. "The *Sericans*, by Jupiter!"

"Oh come now, Terrentius!" Hadrianus cried.

"Not that fable," the old admiral said through a rumbling cough. "We're in high council, lad, not couching in our cups! No reliable eyewitnesses exist to this supposed Battle of the Nihonian Sea!"

"I've never heard of this affair." Germanicus realized how little he knew of the world—except the provinces where he'd been posted. "Explain, Terrentius."

"Decades ago, the Serican Empire invaded the chain of islands to its east known as Nihonia. Preparatory to landing their army, they engaged the Nihonian coastal fleet. What ensued was perhaps the greatest naval battle in history."

"If there was a battle at all," Hadrianus said. "We have only the word of wraphead traders for that."

"Its significance was this, Caesar: The battle was fought without a single boarding. Ships sought solely to destroy other ships. The victors let the sea deal with the crews they'd defeated."

Germanicus felt the *Aeneas* rock gently beneath him. He realized that, even here, only a few miles off both the Mauretanian and Iberian coasts, he would drown unless this iron island remained afloat. "Still, it occurs to me," he finally said, "that we should be discussing the Aztecan fleet—not the Serican. What do we know for certain about their ships?"

"Proconsul Marcus Gracchus reports having seen only one at Otacilium. It was a courier boat, an old packet so unseaworthy he felt sure it had been hauled out of dereliction to mislead us about their true naval capability." Then Glabrio lowered his voice. "But the packet's anchor was *round*."

"Forgive my ignorance, but in my years of service I've tasted more dust than salt water." Germanicus waved off the cursory laughter. "Why should the shape of an anchor matter so?"

"Serican anchors are said to be round, Caesar," the Lusitanian said.

The only sound in the *praetoria navis* came from the *Aeneas* itself.

6

As HIS FLEET steamed through the Pillars of Hercules, Germanicus paced the prow deck of the *Aeneas*. To the north he could see the Mons Calpe jutting up from the Iberian shore, and to the south the dun-colored headlands of Maurentania, wreathed in dust. Ahead, the sun was lowering into rougher waters than he had experienced in the past four days: these marked the currents of the Mare Atlanticum, and across them a ray of gilt spangles raced at the same speed as the trireme.

Twenty minutes before, he had snapped at Rolf, "Will you grant me some space—or must I draw to have it?" The centurion had retreated, scowling. But each time Germanicus turned aftward, he glimpsed the mustachioed German peeking out from behind a coil of hawsers or the bronze effigy of Neptune.

I have gained nothing but an utter lack of privacy! he fumed to himself. *And here I am sailing full steam—away from the restoration of the republic!*

By this week of August he had hoped to have completed transfer of Gaul and Germania to senatorial control. He damned Maxtla, knowing that this campaign—which most Romans anticipated with high spirits—might easily become a Sisyphean labor, delaying the restoration forever. And for what? To hang on to a remote province that was already grumbling with discontent?

"Caesar Germanicus?" a female voice called to him from behind.

Germanicus slowly turned: he had a brief vision of a lovely, dark-haired woman before his eyes were drawn to his centurion, who was vaulting over a series of railings down toward the prow deck. "Rolf—stand off!"

The German glared at him, but remained perched on an upper deck.

Smiling, Germanicus turned and filled his sight with the intruder again. His fleeting impression had been correct: The barbarian woman was fascinating to look upon. Her beauty was of the distinctive kind that is measured only against the power of its own effect. Her hair, as black as raven feathers, flowed over her shoulders and midway down her back. Her face, more round than oval, was so arresting for its intelligence and nobility that several moments elapsed in silence before Germanicus could divert his eyes to examine her unusual dress. Her costume was more regal than anything the Empress Pamphile had ever flaunted, yet it consisted only of a choker of glass beads, a buckskin tunic, and overlapping triangles of kilt that dangled down to her slippers of tanned hide. "I am Germanicus Agricola," he said simply, not wanting to sound pompous in the presence of someone with so much natural dignity.

She took a quick breath as if forcing a patient manner upon herself. "I am called Alope. I come on behalf of the Indee people and our Anasazi allies."

"You speak an excellent Latin."

"I write it, too. I went to the lyceum at Nova Petra. I also know five barbarian tongues."

"Do you speak the Aztecan language, Alope?"

"Nahuatl? All too well, Caesar. I was ambassadress to the court of Maxtla—until he ordered the deaths of your envoys."

Briefly, Germanicus broke off his stare by glancing seaward. "Having never visited the Novo Provinces until now, I'm not familiar with your tribe. Are you the people of the Great Red Chasm?"

"Caesar speaks of the Saikine." Her eyes dimmed. "They are our enemies—and subjects of Rome."

"Then are the Indee enemies to Rome?"

"I did not say so. We are enemies to three tribes other than the Aztecae. Our warriors have raided you Romans in the past. But that was commerce, not war."

Germanicus wondered if the distinction had been clear to the ravaged *coloni* of western Nova Baetica. But he said nothing.

"Now," Alope went on, "we wish to join you Romans in a war against Tenochtitlan."

"I'm sure General Salvidienus would welcome the help of your warriors in defending the approaches to Otacilium."

"No." Her face hardened. "We will join only a drive on Tenochtitlan."

"I've brought no force capable of doing that."

She glanced meaningfully at the scores of ships on all sides of them. "I can speak for Skinyea, war chief of the Indee. The other chiefs may wish to speak for themselves when the time comes. But still, it is within my place to say this—all the peoples of the Anasazi Federation will follow Caesar if he strikes at the heart of Maxtla's country."

Germanicus smiled, hoping to uncover a chink in her resolve. "Isn't it enough to send the Aztecae back into their own homeland?"

"No, it is not. They are like the seasons. They will always return—unless we cut them off from their sun."

"Is your hatred for them that strong?"

"It is." She refused to lower her eyes from his. The breeze whipped the tassels of her tunic.

In the past months, he had been besieged by a cohort of patrician maidens, each powdered and perfumed, hair sprinkled with gold dust in the hope of catching Caesar's fancy. Not one of those vapid beauties had done so. Yet here stood a primitive of the Novo wilds who had him struggling to maintain his composure. "Will you share with us what you know firsthand of the Aztecan Empire?"

Black eyes darting in search of advantage, she paused. Obviously, she would grant nothing without receiving something better in return. "Yes . . . if Caesar will not refuse to drive on Tenochtitlan—until he has spoken to the Anasazi chiefs and looked inside their hearts."

Germanicus wanted to make no promises, but he reassured himself by hoping that the barbarian horde she represented might yet be won over to the Roman purpose of ejecting the Aztecae from Nova Baetica. Also, there was another reason for what he next said. He desired to please her. "I shall withhold judgment on this matter until such time as I meet with your leaders.''

For the first time, she smiled fully, without restraint. It was thrilling, and he felt foolish for thinking so.

"What does Caesar wish to know about the Aztecae?"

Germanicus led her aftward; the spray breaking over the prow was suddenly needle-sharp. "Tell me about this reverend speaker of theirs."

"I have never seen Maxtla."

"You just said you were an ambassadress to his court."

"I was. But it is forbidden for commoners to look upon his person. He is believed to be a god. And those caught peeking up at him from the floor are slain."

"Well, then, have you heard him speak?"

"Yes, many times."

"What things could you tell from his voice?" Germanicus asked.

"Maxtla sounds very old. They say his blood flows through his veins like pitch and he must be set out in the warm sunlight for an hour each day to improve his circulation." Her hand floated up to the beaded choker at her throat. "He speaks with great tenderness. He refers to others always as brother or sister. He is fond of flowers, as are all Aztecae, and poetry." Self-consciously, she looked at Germanicus. "Are these the things Caesar wishes to learn?"

"Yes, in time, but first a question: If Maxtla is so infirm, who then manages his empire?"

"Lord Tizoc, the greatest of his warriors."

"Is he old as well?"

"No, he is younger . . . with a young man's body." Almost visibly, she seemed to withdraw into herself, and Germanicus felt in no mood at the moment to press her about this formidable-sounding Aztecan.

He instead asked, "Do you know of a people called the Sericans?"

"Yes, those with pulled-up eyes. They are known as the Xing among the Aztecae."

Germanicus hid his excitement by feigning absorption with the last crescent of sun that was sliding under the waves. "Will you dine with Admiral Glabrio and myself?"

●　　　●　　　●

Only when the long meal was concluded did Germanicus say matter-of-factly, "Alope has seen Sericans in Tenochtitlan."

"Many times," she added, relishing the last of her lemon ice.

"*What?*" Glabrio roared, upsetting his wine cup. "Were they military men? Any mariners?"

The admiral's agitation made her cautious. Slightly bemused, she looked to Germanicus, who saw in her behavior all the scars of someone who has survived extraordinary danger. He smiled at her: "Please tell noble Terrentius what you mentioned to me."

"The first Xing arrived three years ago. But I should not say the first. Their ships have sailed up and down the coast of the Sea of the West for longer than anyone can remember."

"Doing what—trading?" Glabrio demanded.

"Yes."

The Lusitanian slowly shook his head. "But why haven't we found evidence of this commerce?"

"You have not looked closely enough." Alope unfastened her choker and laid it backside up on one of the admiral's couch cushions. "This was my grandmother's."

Glabrio ran his thumbs over the satiny lining. "Bloody silk," he whispered, rousing himself from a deep distraction to hand it to Germanicus. "What did the Sericans want from the Aztecae?"

"Gold, buyers for the things they make, refuge for their shipwrecked sailors."

"And what did they offer Maxtla?" Germanicus asked, careful not to touch her hand as he returned the choker.

"I do not know. These things were discussed in secret and"—she lowered her eyes—"Tizoc would not tell me of them. But one of his servants had a brother who was an ironsmith. She said he had gone to Xicalango to learn from the Xing—Sericans, as you call them—how to make war galleys. A great fleet was being built there. Later I learned that these ships would be sent to fight you Romans. I do not think Britannicus Musa believed me."

Glabrio's tense grin betrayed a curious mixture of alarm and satisfaction that his hunch had proved correct. "Have you seen any of the Aztecan galleys with your own eyes?"

"No outlanders were permitted to travel to Xicalango."

"Drawings, then—did you get a look at any plans?"

"I did not."

Glabrio groaned and then motioned for a servant to bring him more wine. "I can see them as if they were steaming on the other side of this porthole—sleek, low to the water, and with nothing as antiquated as *corvi* on their bows!"

Germanicus leaned toward the admiral and whispered, "Can we defeat this kind of galley you describe?"

"If our crews become more proficient at firing their *ballistae* at full speed. If . . . " The Lusitanian suddenly sighed and threw up his hands. "I don't know, Caesar. This is a slothful answer, I admit, but we shall find out soon enough."

Germanicus turned back to Alope. "Perhaps more than anything else, it's important for me to understand *why* the Aztecae have invaded our province. Do you have any idea?"

Carefully, she returned her bowl of ice to the table she shared with the emperor. "Tizoc once said that the Sericans like to create mischief with their gifts. Only after they gave Maxtla machines that drink oil did they reveal to him that you Romans had all the oil."

"Then it was for our petroleum enterprises on the coast of Nova Baetica?"

"Perhaps . . . but I think not."

"What, then?"

"Fire came to Tizoc's face whenever he counted the lands Caesar Fabius had stolen from the Aztecae."

"What lands?" Germanicus asked, confused. "Our legions encountered no Aztecan garrisons as they advanced westward. Nothing but empty wilderness and new barbarian tribes such as yours. Nor were we fully aware of the existence of another civilization in this part of the world until Otacilium had streets of stone instead of mud."

"The wilderness is empty only to Roman eyes." Then she became quiet; an unhappy smile visited her lips. It seemed to Germanicus that she was working around the edges of a torment that she would have sooner left alone. Yet, for whatever reasons, she persisted. "Caesar Fabius took for his subjects the choicest . . . " Her voice thickened and trailed off.

"I don't understand," Germanicus said, avoiding her eyes because they had clouded with tears.

"Has Caesar heard of a War of the Flowery Way?"

"No, I haven't." Germanicus looked to Glabrio to see if the Lusitanian had, but the admiral was mired in his own worries.

"Neither had we," she went on, "until sixty years ago. Oh, we knew of the Aztecae through their wily *pochteca*, who are both merchants and spies. We had even raided Maxtla's villages deep in the south with the help of our friends, the Raramurae. But it was not until the Aztecae killed one of our warriors and we were obligated to make a war on them did we learn of the Flowery Way." She waited until the emperor looked directly at her. "The Aztecae devour their enemies."

Germanicus kept the smirk off his face, but he felt certain that Alope, in her barbarian grasp of Latin, had really meant to use a word more figurative than *devorant*. "You mean . . . in the sense that they are consummate warriors?"

"No. In the sense that they murder us atop their temples and feed our bodies to their masses." Her light brown fingers clawed at the sides of the couch for a few moments before she could still them.

Here it was, right on schedule: that barbarian propensity to fantasticate when reason and proportion were the surest route to a Roman's sympathies. "We'd heard that there is token sacrifice in Tenochtitlan from time to time."

"Ten thousand deaths on the Great Temple in one day is not token, Caesar," she snapped. "And the Flowery Way is practiced in every city of their realm, not just Tenochtitlan."

"I'm sure it is." Germanicus rose, stretching as a signal that the dinner was concluded. An air of disappointment pressed down on his shoulders, and on Glabrio's as well. With one slip, Alope had reduced her priceless intelligence to folklore. Or had she? Germanicus wondered if Maxtla was using the fetching Indee woman to outwit him. It was a thought he would sleep on. "I thank you, Alope, for your help. I wish to retire now." Rolf materialized out of a darkened corner of the cabin and tramped unsteadily across the rolling deck to Germanicus's side.

"Goodnight, Caesar," Glabrio muttered.

Alope glared at Germanicus as he withdrew.

7

HIS SLEEP WAS wretched, but Germanicus was helpless to rouse himself from it.

At least twice, he had imagined that the silk pillow cover had wrapped itself around his face, forming a sweaty gag over his nose and mouth, and he had sat upright to pummel the Serican material with his fists before sighing in exasperation and flopping down again.

These phantasms were followed by dreams of ever-deepening sadness. Once again, he was a young tribune, shuffling through the sun-baked lanes of that *castrum* in Numidia at the side of a praetorian assigned to guard him, feeling nothing but the heat as the tents of the bivouac drifted past in a tunnel of canvas, telling himself for the dozenth time what he had just learned beside the colonel's enormous, hissing wireless: *"Antoninus Julius Agricola has been assassinated for a cause not yet clarified. Guard the person of his son, Germanicus, by order of the emperor."* And later, as he lay roasting on his pallet, Germanicus heard but ignored a curious rumbling noise that was approaching the camp. Soon, his cousin Fabius burst through the flaps, chattering about the wondrous seige machine he had conveyed by its own internal motive from Hippo Regius to batter a rebel stronghold. Apparently, Fabius had already forgotten that he had let Germanicus preview this craft at the imperial palace, where the young god Vulcan had been laboring under the protection of his aunt, the empress. "Think of it, Germanicus Julius—my sand-galley can take the place of a thousand men!"

"Some men cannot be replaced."

"Nonsense, cousin. Within our lifetime, war will be an intercourse strictly between machines."

"What honor would there be in that?"

Fabius chuckled. "I don't understand how Agricolan sentimentality can be strained through the loins of fifty generations and still be so potent!" Of course, Fabius had not yet learned of Antoninus Agricola's murder before saying these things; but, so informed by the praetorian attending Germanicus, he became only slightly less blunt. It was both Fabius's strength and weakness that his emotions were forever eclipsed by his ideas. "Well, I'm sure the culprits will be caught." They never had been. And Germanicus had vowed to unravel the mystery before he himself set foot in Charon's boat.

Groaning now, Germanicus rolled onto his back in the darkness of his cabin. He threw his forearm over his feverish eyes.

"*Germanicussssss*," a murderous voice seemed to hiss at him out of the past, the stifling blackness, the bowels of the ship.

He opened his eyes. "Jupiter!" The cabin was as torrid as the steam room in a public bath. He lowered his bare feet to the deck and recoiled with a sharp gasp. Standing on the iron plates was impossible without wearing slippers: even then, the soft leather soles provided poor insulation against such fierce heat.

"Rolf?" he shouted crossly, fumbling for the light lever and, after no success in his search for that, the porthole latch, which would not budge even under the most frantic pressure. "Damn—this cabin's an oven! Centurion!" There was a peculiar density to the sound of his own voice, as if he were far underground. "Rolf?" he cried again, perplexed that the German was not answering when they were separated only by a small vestibule.

Hopping now rather than walking—contact with the deck had become torture—Germanicus crossed the compartment and groped for the brass wheel that would open the hatch. "Ah!" he roared, having burned his fingers.

The only thing he could now imagine was that the *Aeneas* was aflame. He had to reach the upper decks, even if it meant braving smoke in the passageways.

Germanicus draped his bed covers over his head, then used

a corner of the thickest blanket to grasp the hatch wheel. Slowly, it began to give . . .

Rolf snapped out of his catnap. Over the muffled clatter and groaning of steam propulsion, footfalls could be heard approaching—that would be the relief for the praetorian posted in the main passageway. Grunting wearily, the German heaved himself off the couch in Caesar's outer cabin and, although another compartment lay between him and where Germanicus slept, leaned against the bulkhead to listen.

He sprang back, amazed, rubbing his ear madly with his palm.

The centurion considered this for an instant, his eyes frantic. Then, gingerly, he ran his hand down the iron partition until reaching a level that was too hot to brush for even a few seconds. He had already practiced activating the light lever in total darkness, so it bewildered him when he flipped it up and nothing happened. Next, he tried to start the self-igniting oil lamp, but its wick refused to accept the phosphorus flame. Finally, he got adequate illumination only by throwing open the hatch to the main passageway.

Outside, the praetorians were murmuring sleepily to each other. Obviously, no fire alarm had been given.

Turning again, Rolf noticed something at the base of the hatch that led to Caesar's inner cabin: Water was trickling out of the seal, skittering back and forth across the deck in keeping with the ponderous roll of the trireme. Steam was roiling up out of this leakage.

He tested the bulkhead again with his now throbbing fingers: the iron plate was searing as high as his shoulders—and rising.

Bursting out into the passageway with sword drawn, Rolf bawled at the startled praetorians, "The way to Kaiser's cabin be flooded. You—!" He pointed his blade at the fleeter-looking of the two. "Run for the *machinator*!" The second praetorian he spun around by the cloak. "And you stand fast —be ready for the worst!"

Rolf ducked back inside the compartment, feeling the full brunt of the heat after the coolness of the passageway, his fair skin erupting into red blotches. "Kaiser!" he shouted at the top of his lungs. "Germanicus!" There was no reply. He nearly retched on the thought that his emperor's cabin had already filled to its top while he himself had been slumbering on a couch two compartments away, dreaming of pork sausages and beer.

Then his eyes lit on the hatch wheel.

Rolf's price for saving Caesar's life this way would be his own death. The centurion had conditioned himself for such an eventuality. He had dwelt liturgically upon it each day so time would not have eroded his resolve when the moment presented itself. But, as his outstretched hand trembled a few inches short of the wheel, it came to him that the act would be meaningless as long as any other option remained open.

Growling, he raced out into the passageway, up a maze of ladders and finally onto the blustery afterdeck. Leaning precariously over the railing, he began counting portholes. The tenth from the stern, he had previously determined in his inspection of the *Aeneas*, was Caesar's.

Sheathing his sword, he tied the end of a hawser to a stanchion and flung the coil over the side. He straddled the railing and hesitated. Fifty feet below, the sea gushed past in tumults of foam.

Then he looped the rope over one shoulder and between his thighs—as he had seen Helvetian legionaries do—and lowered himself away. Once, he began twirling wildly and had to close his eyes until the tension in the line played itself out.

The centurion could not swim.

Pausing to regain his nerve, he gazed down between his sandals at the starshine on the silver garland that girded the hull of the great galley. But this only made him dizzy, and he was forced to fix his eyes on the horizon. The other vessels of the fleet looked like darkened temples gliding across the deep. His fingers on the verge of cramping, he continued his descent.

The porthole glazing was tinted emerald, and Rolf could not discern Caesar's whereabouts within the blacked-out cabin. Only after wrapping the hawser twice around his ankle did he feel secure enough to let go with his right fist and pound the thick glass. "Germanicus!"

A greenish face rippled into view. Its distorted lips were moving, but Rolf could catch no words over the wind and the churning of the screw propellers. "Kaiser, I cannot hear!"

Germanicus flattened his palms against the glazing, and Rolf realized what was preventing Caesar from breathing the cool night air. "Stand aside!" The centurion pushed off the hull and came crashing back against the porthole with his *caligae*. The round of glass opened cleanly out of its frame and shattered on the deck within. Rolf found himself protruding halfway into the *Aeneas*, steam surging around him and stinging his nostrils like acid.

Germanicus's breath rattled in his throat as he tried to cool his lungs. He clutched the centurion's knees to keep himself upright.

"Kaiser," Rolf gasped, "what be that dripping noise?"

"I was cracking the hatch just as you knocked for me."

"Come!" But the centurion had no sooner screamed this and seized Germanicus by the nape of his sweaty nightclothes than the hatch collar could be heard spitting its rivets onto the deck. Next, the hinges began groaning under great pressure. "Come, Germanicus!"

An instant later, both men were dangling on the hawser outside the trireme, their heads thudding against the hull as they struggled to keep their purchase on the line. A deluge of boiling water gushed into the cabin Germanicus had just abandoned, and more steam shot out the porthole, forcing them to bury their faces against their shoulders. Rolf had not released Germanicus's undergarment, making a noose of its neckline. Germanicus was choking fitfully. Those marines not occupied in hoisting up the twosome were shouting for the exhausted centurion to quit strangling the emperor. At last, Rolf understood and gently released his charge.

Both sea and dawn sky were equally cheerless. "It isn't the peril . . . I suppose," Germanicus said quietly to Terrentius Glabrio. "It's this awful sense of loneliness that comes afterward."

"Caesar, I don't know how to apologize," the Lusitanian said miserably. "On the flagship yet . . . "

"We suffered little more than a few blisters. I only ordered my centurion below to the *valetudinarium* so he'd finally rest."

"There's a bold one, that German of yours."

"Yes . . . " Germanicus started to say more but tears threatened his eyes, so he looked out at the pale gray morning again.

The wait was making both men uncomfortable.

When Epizelus had finished ministering to Germanicus, he, the praetorian prefect and the *machinator*, or engineering officer, of the *Aeneas*, had been sent below to the flooded cabin to investigate what had gone awry. No one had to say that they were looking for evidence of an assassination attempt.

"Your *machinator*'s an Abyssinian, isn't he?" Germanicus asked, mostly to stir the silence.

"Yes, Caesar," Glabrio said. "Fiducio's been with me since my days on the *Cincinnatus*. He's a freedman, you know."

"Really."

"And quite outspoken about the injuries he believes he suffered. So I may have to beg your indulgence."

"What quarrel does he have with slavery now that he himself is a man of property and license?"

"Fiducio claims—" Glabrio looked relieved to have been interrupted by tramping footfalls. "Ah, here's our commission now."

The three men formed a line before Caesar but did not speak. Their faces revealed their findings for them.

"I see," Germanicus said at last.

Gaius Nero exhaled loudly. "All I want to know is *why* were those bloody hatches closed in the first place?"

Fiducio stared down his thin nose at the prefect. "It is regulation during a war sailing; you may check the codex if you wish. In this way, there is a watertight envelope completely around the inside of the hull. Now, a live steam conduit winds through that compartment to power the largest *ballista* mount and—"

"The valve had been rigged to engage!" Epizelus said.

"Pardon me, physician, I was not finished." Fiducio gave him a barren smile, then turned to Germanicus. "Two containers had been clamped to the conduit in such a way that one dripped quicksilver into the other. As the lower one filled, it put pressure on the lever. After several hours, the valve opened, and the steam condensed into water that was heated by more escaping steam."

"Caesar," Gaius Nero said, showing a half-dozen metal buttons in his palm, "these hatch collar rivets had been fouled." He looked to the *machinator*. "I trust that's the proper term."

The Abyssinian nodded serenely.

Gaius Nero continued, "I'll preserve them for a proper examination once we return to Rome. And I've commenced the interrogations, deck by deck.''

"Yes, yes, nephew . . . '' Germanicus grinned, although his heart felt as if it were sagging against the breastbone. He wanted to convey to his subordinates that he hadn't been unduly rattled by the attempt on his life. As if he'd heard enough of this irksome assassination business, he fixed an amused eye on Fiducio. "The admiral tells me you have some rather contentious opinions about slavery.''

Fiducio was caught off guard but quickly recovered himself. "I don't know if my opinions are contentious, Caesar. But they're honestly held.''

"Do you have slaves of your own now?''

"No, Caesar.''

"Why not? You appear to be an ambitious, worldly man—I hope no offense is taken.''

"None is . . . from the last surviving relative of the noble Fabius,'' Fiducio said curtly, smiling only as an afterthought. "I am an ambitious man, and for that reason I refuse to burden myself with slaves.''

"*Burden* yourself?'' Gaius Nero asked with a smirk.

"Yes. Oh, I know how most good Romans feel about this. Cicero captured the sentiment most succinctly: ' . . . for the very wages the laborer receives are a badge of slavery. The work of the mechanic is also degrading; there is nothing noble about a workshop.' '' The Abyssinian chuckled, then sobered in a manner that revealed a great store of bitterness beneath his civility. "Be forewarned, Caesar—he who relinquishes his labor to another, no matter how distasteful that enterprise may seem, also relinquishes his future.''

"The future of Rome, then,'' Germanicus asked with a thin smile, "what will it be?''

"It will be in the hands of those whom she has heretofore oppressed.''

8

"HOW DO YOU expect to find the Aztecae?" Germanicus asked Terrentius Glabrio.

Squinting into the wind, the admiral said nothing for a moment. During the night, the fleet had caught up with and then taken formation to protect the cargo galleys that had departed earlier from Ostia. And now, within the Strait of a Thousand Keys, the armada had further reduced its speed in the expectation of rendezvousing with a squadron of biremes from Britannia. So far there had been no trace of these war galleys, the swiftest and most capably handled in the Roman navy, which should have already reached the coral islets off the Paludosa Peninsula and started screening for the slower vessels. Glabrio was scanning the northeastern horizon for these, his "lost sheep," as he called them with mounting alarm. "The Aztecae will find us first, Caesar," he said at last. "I only hope it's in the waters west of the River Luteus's delta, after our merchant galleys are safely moored at Otacilium."

"The battle won't be fought off the beaches where both armies are entrenched?"

"I doubt it. If I were Maxtla's admiral, I'd strike against the Roman fleet far east of there. He knows the Aztecan legions will wither like grapes on a broken vine if their channels of supply are cut."

"Then we can expect to be intercepted at any time?"

"Aye." Glabrio peered northeast again. After a moment of fruitless searching, he sighed. "Caesar, I'm loath to ask this . . . " Then, with a pained expression, Glabrio gave argu-

66

ments against his own counsel: This strait, with its strong
west-to-east current, was no place to tarry, especially for ships
low on fuel; that the *procella* season had already begun could
be seen by any fool—the sky astern was flocked with towering
masses of clouds; and he feared that his fleet might be dashed
against the keys by sudden gales. Nevertheless, the admiral
begged to delay here until sundown for the tardy squadron. "I
know its commander. A reliable man, I assure you. This is
quite unlike him."

"As you think," Germanicus said absently. He glanced
over his shoulder to remind himself that Rolf was close at
hand. It shamed him, slightly, that he needed this reassurance.

"It is not proper for a woman to be in the presence of a man
at his bath." Alope kept her eyes on the deck as she spoke.
"To the Indee, the bath is a spiritual cleansing."

"To a Roman, it isn't proper to share one's bath with an
assassin."

Her startled gaze flashed from the prefect's face to the
glistening hands of the slave who was kneading perfumed oil
into Gaius Nero's white flesh. "I must go," she whispered.

"You'll go when I dismiss you." He winked conspiratori-
ally. "And don't fret about old Bernardus here. Thirty years
ago it was fashionable to deafen masseurs."

A mask had dropped over Alope's features; not even the
most trivial expression escaped it. Galatea had reverted to fine
ivory with a soft tawny patina.

"Let me share something with you," Gaius Nero went on,
his voice quavering from the gentle blows being delivered to
his back by the slave. "Germanicus Julius Agricola was looking forward to an early retirement when the imperial crown
was thrust upon him by certain dotards in the Senate and
army. In all fairness to my uncle—soon to be my father, he
had spent thirty years sleeping in mildewy blankets, eating
food fit only for maggots, touring locales like Hibernia, where
the sun will not shine, or Anatolia, where it penetrates a man's
skull and simmers the juices of his brain until he is quite addled . . . until he has no idea what he really wants anymore . . .
until he confuses the past with the present. How does one say
debilitated in your tongue?"

"I do not . . . ?"

"*Exhausted*, Alope!"

"*Ninldag.*"

"So, the present emperor of Rome is quite *ninldag.*" Gaius Nero groaned with pleasure as Bernardus began working on the small of his back. "Approach me, Alope." When she hesitated, he barked, "Quickly, dammit!" Then, with eyes closed, he soughed, "Touch me . . . "

She brushed his shoulder with her fingers, then withdrew a step.

"No, not that way. Take hold of my flesh. Feel the texture of it." After she had done so, he said, "I am smooth. I am thirty-two years of age. Bear that in mind during the coming days. Now go. You were correct: A man's bath is for purification. And soon everything will be scoured away—except the bedrock of my dreams."

Over two thousand pairs of eyes strained toward the northeast for a squiggle of smoke, a signal lamp, even a flare. But nothing showed, and night finally closed on that quarter of the ocean. Germanicus had joined the fleet-wide call for all hands not otherwise occupied to go topside in one last effort to locate the missing squadron. Now, accompanied by Rolf, he began strolling along the main deck.

Nearly ruined by boiling, his own regal clothes had been given over to his fuller for repair, and Caesar had been loaned a plain white toga by a humble *quaestor* bound for Otacilium. For this reason, a middle-aged cook, who was taking a breather at the railing, took no special notice of the treasury functionary and the centurion sauntering toward him.

"What does that sunset say to you, friend?" Germanicus asked him.

"Now this could be a sneaky one, guvnor. It's not righteous red like a tame dusk. Neither's it socked in like an honest bad one. This is one what could pitch you a bloody *procella* right out of Jove's blue." The cook's arthritic fingers brought some lungweed to his lips, and he spat a flake off the tip of his tongue. "Weren't that a shame about those two lads kilt on the *Seneca?*"

"Yes," Germanicus said quietly. That afternoon, a *ballista* mishap had occurred in which a trireme and not the target she had been towing was struck, sending Admiral Glabrio into a bottomless funk.

"It never be known to a man when he must cross over,"

Rolf muttered in a way that made Germanicus carefully study the centurion's weary eyes. "How much service be left for you?" the German asked the cook.

"Tomorrow it'll be only six months more." The old man flashed a snaggletooth. "My maiden voyage was with Otacilius hisself. That's right, I was among the first to look upon these shores of the Novo Provinces."

"Now *that* must have been a voyage," Germanicus said, brightening with interest.

"Oh, it was, sir. And a bit of a fright at times. We wasn't sure how true old Fabius's *index* was. So when we'd tacked to the end of this very strait and could see nothing but nothing beyond, we come about and rode the current up the east shore of the Paludosa Peninsula. We dearly loved the sight of land in those days." He wiped his nose with his apron, and his eyes grew glassy as he watched the swells begin to slip past more quickly as the *Aeneas* built speed. "Two days north of here, we was swallowed up by an unholy fog. The bireme *Coriolanus* and us. I've always said that was an unlucky name for a Roman galley. Our sails was slack, heavy with dew, and engines wasn't much then, just enough to back a shallow drafter off a shoal." He chuckled bitterly. "So that madman Otacilius had us break out the ash twelve-footers and lock them in tholes what was half-froze with rust. And we rowed. The gods, how we rowed. All day, through the night, and unto the next day, burning lamps fore and aft, hailing the *Coriolanus* so we wouldn't lose her whenever that demon mist thickened and hid her from our sight." The old man cupped his knobby hand around his mouth and cried as if to a distant ship, " '*Coriolanus*—from flagship *Cato*!' And a voice would drift back to us across the flattened sea: '*Cato* from *Coriolanus*! All's well!' Otacilius didn't tell us then"—the cook could not resist more grim laughter—"but in them bedeviled waters Fabius's *index* was deeming points north what'd never even visited the place! The guvnor was staking our lives on a blind guess—and all the while he looked as bored as the captain of the ferry from Puteoli to Capri!''

Germanicus crossed his arms over his chest. "I'd always heard that the *Coriolanus* was lost in a storm."

"Aye, she *was*, but no storm of this world, guvnor. At eight bells of the second day, we still was not back under the fair blue skirts of Juno. I was slumped over the port gunwale, waiting my spell at the oar again, when I saw not just two lights from the *Coriolanus*, but four and then eight and finally swarms of the things. They wasn't a golden blur like lamp-shine in fog, but blue and red and white, bright like little suns. Oh, these did a merry dance about us for a time. But then they vanished—I mean every last blaze. Once more, there was nothing but wool before our eyes. And the stench of lightning in our nostrils—you'd know what I mean if you've ever been near-struck. '*Coriolanus*—from flagship *Cato*!' Otacilius cried. But there came back no answer. Again and again, he hailed that galley. When his voice gave out, others kept up the call. The next dawn was clear and lovely bright. But we had no sign of the *Coriolanus* . . . nor after circling in those waters three days.''

''What be her fate?'' Rolf asked.

The cook shrugged. ''I was born in Genua. So I can only see things through Genuan eyes.''

''Do you believe that this is what has befallen the squadron from Britannia?''

He frowned at Germanicus. ''Please, sir—let's not spoil what little luck those lads might have left to them.''

''Of course. You must pardon my curiosity.'' Germanicus quickly changed the subject: ''You must have seen great changes during your years of service.''

''That I have, guvnor. The whole bloody empire has—and it's high time for slack latitudes.''

''What do you mean?''

''Well, take this emperor we got now. He may not be the swiftest chap for the job. But old Germanicus could be just what we need for a year or two—he'll keel over soon enough.''

Germanicus hid his mouth behind his hand. ''How does he suit our needs? Just between us, of course.''

''Well, look upon it this way: People was playing the same game at the same slow clip for thousands of years. Then along come beggars swifter than the lot of us—Fabius, the swiftest of the crop—and in a blink shy of fifty years the world's sud-denly galloping past the likes of you and me. Why, it's more than what a normal nervous system can bear just to under-stand the cookstoves they're putting aboard the new quinque-remes. If stoves can baffle a lad, what of the things witched up by that fellow on Crete?''

''Ptolemaeus?''

"That's him. When first there was talk of him working on 'fire bolts,' I said good enough—they're figuring ways to get a Greek firer to squirt a pace or two further. But I hear it has nothing to do with that. This Ptolemaeus was scheming to make a weapon out of light. *Light*, mind you! Finally, they're playing with what Jupiter wishes kept to hisself." The cook raised his finger in a gesture worthy of Demosthenes. "It's one empire, the swift and the slow together. There's those on this very trireme what look down on me because I don't understand their business. But those same beggars would be screaming to wake Gaius Julius Caesar if I was off musing instead of staying elbow-deep in my pots and pans to make their supper!"

Germanicus shrugged. "But what can this new emperor do to benefit all Romans?"

"First off the top of my head, Germanicus is one of us—"

"But he's as patrician as they come, isn't he?"

"There are many ways to halve an apple, good sir."

"Ah, you mean this Caesar's *slow*—as opposed to swift."

"There you have it, as neatly cut as quince cakes. Mark my words: he'll give a healthy yank on the reins before you know what."

"I'm sorry, I'm afraid I don't."

"Before only two or three chaps know what the bloody empire's up to! We got to know where we're headed before we push on again. I mean *all of us.*"

"You are quite right, citizen," Germanicus said.

The cook looked pleased with himself over the obvious impression he had made on this serious-minded stranger. His conversation took a more relaxed turn. "Is this your last stint in the provinces, sir?"

"I hope so."

"And how soon are you two for retirement?"

"Later than you might expect, my friend, but much sooner than most believe."

"How's that?"

Germanicus motioned to Rolf that it was a good moment in which to continue their stroll.

9

At DAWN, A GALE began blowing out of the northeast. It whipped against the prevailing current in the strait, churning up a riot of waters that spalled sheets of foam over one another in no semblance of order. Huge sprays erupted over the prow of the *Aeneas* and threatened to wash the forwardmost decks clean of lookouts. But no Roman sailor or marine complained of this tumultuous peril, for first light had also delivered a glimpse of small craft on the western horizon. These, Glabrio suspected, were the advice boats of the Aztecan fleet. He so informed Caesar through the praetorian prefect, who in the last day had made himself a permanent fixture on the *pontis* deck.

With seas still rising, the admiral directed the armada to head into the wind, which amounted to ordering a full stop, and then to launch its own reconnaissance craft. This effort was soon aborted: a boat from the *Vespasianus* was dashed against the hull of the mother ship even before its lines could be cast off.

"Damn you!" Glabrio railed against the absent commander of the Britannican squadron. "Where are my screening bireme?"

Below, Gaius Nero staggered down the last pitching corridor to Caesar's new quarters, on the deck where the praetorian force was billeted. He whisked past Germanicus's centurion, who was bracing himself against another ungodly lurch of the *Aeneas* by wedging his long arms between two bulkheads.

"Caesar?" Gaius Nero rapped softly.

"Enter." Germanicus was being fitted into his military uniform by a servant. "Good morning, nephew."

"I bring word that the enemy may have been sighted—but I see that Caesar is already so apprised."

Germanicus smiled. "Rumors run faster than feet." He tugged at the hem of his tunic. "It shrank an inch everywhere after that steam business . . . ruined. Well, so what, yes? Tell the good admiral I'll be on the *pontis* deck in a few minutes."

"Caesar, I beg a word in private first."

"Very well." Germanicus dismissed the servant and sank onto a couch: invariably, this was how his nephew broached unpleasant news. "Go ahead."

"Safeguarding your life is not a simple task."

"I appreciate that."

"And I must bait many traps in a day. So please, uncle, if ever you hear some rumor that casts my loyalty into doubt, you must recall the intricacies of my duties and—"

"Hold, nephew," Germanicus said warmly. "If I hear such things, I'll receive you in private and ask you to explain. You see, jealousy and intrigue have cost me my entire family. You, your lovely Claudia, and Quintus are all I have left. So you may trust that I'll never act in haste."

"Thank you, Caesar. You cannot imagine how that puts my mind at rest."

"Now, what trap have you baited on my behalf?"

"Believe me, my guardsmen and I have not stopped hounding those who mean you harm since that night—"

"Yes, yes. What have you learned?"

"We have opened some promising avenues of investigation. One concerns the *machinator* of this galley."

"The Abyssinian, Fiducio? What of him?"

"His father was a skilled slave at the Alexandrian glazing works. At the onset of our troubles in Abyssinia some years ago, he conspired with others of his race to make optical aimers for our sand-galleys that distorted *ballista* range. The Emperor Fabius learned of the plot and personally saw to it that the culprits were crucified."

"Is there any evidence the son has followed after the father in this regard?" Germanicus asked.

"We are on the verge of developing such evidence, uncle."

"Be certain that when you say *develop* you do not mean

invent. I will not have that praetorian tradition continued during my reign.''

"Of course, Caesar.'' Gaius Nero's eyes widened as he waited for the *Aeneas* to right herself after an especially acute roll. The trireme finally did, and he released the breath he had pent up. "And then there is the Indee woman . . .''

"Alope?''

"Yes, it's a simple matter of course that we should suspect her.''

"Explain.''

"Why, she's the daughter of an aberrant people. The praetorian commander at Nova Petra informs me that they are liars, thieves, and cutthroats of the first order. What is worse, these new barbarians are actually proud of their lowly moral condition.''

"But the woman seems so *noble*.''

"As seemed Messalina of old and Pamphile of late.''

"How would Alope know how to rig a steam valve on a trireme?''

"She wouldn't,'' Gaius Nero said evenly. "Not without the help of a certain *machinator* who has his own *vindicta* to carry out against the imperial family.''

Germanicus grew pensive. "How can we be positively sure?''

"If we are to remain nimble enough to survive, Caesar, we must settle for being *relatively* sure.'' The prefect reached for the hatch wheel as a shudder groaned down the length of the galley. "Alope came to Rome to petition you to invade the Aztecan Empire. If you refuse, she'll plot your removal and hope for a more amenable successor.'' He eased down beside Germanicus on the couch and looked squarely into his eyes. "I have indicated to her that *I* would be such a successor.''

"What did the woman say?'' Germanicus asked guardedly.

"Nothing. She simply withdrew. Oh, she's wily, this one. No doubt she'll test my sincerity before making her next move. And what will she hear from everyone?'' Gaius Nero smirked. "That I counseled Caesar to march directly on Tenochtitlan!'' He threw back his head and laughed. "It's perfect, uncle, because she'll never fathom a Roman's concept of obedient duty. Yes, I once believed that an invasion was the solution to our difficulties. But Caesar ordered otherwise, and

I obey—willingly, with all my energies."

Germanicus could not pinpoint why his nephew's words failed to lift his spirits, but he would not let such a declaration of loyalty pass unrewarded. "More and more, I see why my brother had such high regard for you."

The prefect's eyes dampened. "Thank you, Caesar."

"But all this might prove superfluous if our enemies send both Caesar and those who conspire against him to the bottom of the Mare Aztecum today."

"I see nothing so far," Germanicus said. The wind continued to pile water against the windows of the *pontis* deck. "Where are they?"

"You'll catch a glimpse momentarily, Caesar." Glabrio's gaze was fixed on the shimmering screen. "Actually, we've cleared the strait and the sea's calmer than it was."

"Are you preparing to launch your advice boats?"

"There's no need—"

All at once, the bow of the *Aeneas* reared up out of the waves and the spray fell away from the glazing. "Neptune preserve us," Germanicus whispered.

The Aztecan warships were steaming directly for the Roman armada. They were arrayed in a formation of eight columns abreast, and each column was a double one; otherwise, their fleet would have lapped over the edges of the horizon. As if entranced, Glabrio had drifted up to the window and rested his palms against the glazing. "See how low they're built to the water!"

"Yes," the old admiral said from the gaggle of officers who, heretofore, had been standing aside in wounded silence. "All the better for our marines to rake their decks clean."

"And I'd rather fight down a *corvus* than up one any day," Lucillus Hadrianus, the commander of naval infantry, added.

Glabrio spun on them. "What they've done is make it easier for our *ballistae* to miss their galleys!" Then he ordered his adjutant: "Signal fleet to sound trumpets."

A blast of spray sizzled against the glazing, and the Aztecan fleet was lost from view again. Germanicus put his hand on Glabrio's shoulder. "What is your plan?"

"I'll not give the Aztecae any more sea in which to maneuver than I must. I'll strengthen our port flank against envelopment, protect the cargo galleys inshore of our triremes, and steam up the western coast of the Paludosa Peninsula, hoping that my noble counterpart has surmised what I have."

"Which is?" Hadrianus half-sneered.

"This northeaster is the van of a full-fledged *procella* that can sink both navies without a shot being fired."

The old admiral winked at Hadrianus. "And if we are caught at sea by one of these tempests, Admiral Glabrio—what do you propose to do?"

"There are a number of anchorages farther up this shore. But first we must outrun the Aztecae."

"Already we are talking of retreat." At last, the old admiral's lips stretched into a scowl. "I beg you, Caesar, stop this dangerous tactical experiment before it begins! First, we should steam through Maxtla's line and then turn around his flank—"

"These are the *diekplous* and *periplous* maneuvers, Caesar—as ancient as Troy! And they require superiority in numbers, which we obviously do not have!"

The old admiral gave his back to Glabrio. "Next, Caesar, we should turn smartly about and make haste to board the Aztecan galleys. *That*, Caesar, is how a Roman makes war at sea!"

A silence fell over the deck. All eyes gravitated toward Germanicus, who was staring out the window again. Watery sunshine rippled over his features. "Admiral Glabrio," he said, "signal the fleet as you see fit. I'll be on the afterdeck until the battle is concluded." Then he marched through the hatch and out into the growing storm.

"This be no time for a staff quarrel," Rolf cried over the wind as they clutched the rail and slogged through an ankle-deep swirl of foam.

"Pride runs on its own schedule. I had to get out of there. Otherwise, no one would listen to poor Terrentius."

Glancing behind, Germanicus saw that he was being followed by Gaius Nero and his praetorians. A wave snatched at the last guardsman in the file and, but for the handiness of a stanchion, would have carried him away.

The leeward side of the afterdeck provided some protection from the gale as well as a limited vantage of the Aztecan fleet. A squad of marines huddled there, trying to keep their *pili* dry and grappling lines untangled. Germanicus motioned for the men to be at their ease. "This is no inspection, lads. We save that for the Campus Martius, which does not pitch and roll even when the winds howl down from the Senate." He was smiling back at their polite chuckles when he glimpsed something across the seething waters that made him ask, "What are those bloody things?"

"Trailing behind the Aztecan galleys in the sky, Caesar?" their suboptio, a Syrian, asked.

"Yes!"

"We were asking ourselves when you came up, sir. Our scholar, Lucterius here, says—"

"They're kites, Caesar," the boyish-looking Gaul explained for himself. "I read it in a codex by a Baluchi trader who'd been to the Serican Empire. In a good bit of breeze, their fishermen hoist aloft a man strapped to a kite. He gives the word if he spots a school of fishes or whales."

"So these Icarians will have a godly view of everything we undertake today?"

The marines nodded glumly, but then their suboptio piped up: "At least until the *procella* strikes. Then our winged friends will have the sun's fire to worry about."

They were laughing boisterously when the Gaul bemoaned, "Oh, look to it, lads—here comes the missy with the powder. She did Flaccus's crew earlier."

Alope was wending her way through clusters of marines, dipping her fingers inside a hide pouch and then dusting the astonished Romans with a golden substance that was quickly wafted away by the wind. She was singing a chant with such absorption she was startled to suddenly discover the emperor standing directly in her path.

"What are you doing?" he demanded.

"I am strengthening these warriors against the Aztecae."

"What is that stuff?"

"Pollen of the cattail. It has great power."

"Whatever its properties, you will stop flinging it about at once. Some of these men are provincials and quite superstitious. I won't have them going into battle thinking they've been hexed."

She flicked her chin in the direction of the marines, then smiled. "Do you think these—and all the others on your war galleys—will be enough?"

"They will have to do."

"Caesar, we can unleash half a million—!"

"Mars, how I abhor barbarian carelessness with numbers!" Germanicus glanced over his shoulder at the eavesdropping marines, then lowered his voice. "I've made certain inquiries. There cannot be more than fifty thousand warriors in the Anasazi Federation. You know that better than I."

"I do," she said obstinately.

"Then why this pretense of five hundred thousand warriors when you have but a tenth of that at your disposal?"

"When I speak, I include men from tribes to the south of the Indee. They hate the Aztecae as much as we. No one suffers paying tribute forever, and their chiefs have sworn vengeance many times—"

Trumpets blared. Germanicus tracked the gazes of the marines to a purple banner, which was being replaced on its staff by a carmine one. "What does this herald?" he asked the suboptio.

"We're forming a battle line, Caesar."

Recalling Glabrio's desire to run north and avoid engagement, Germanicus was perplexed. "But why?"

The marine swept his hand across the Aztecan vessels speckling the western horizon. "The bastards are doing a good job of enveloping us. Their galleys are faster than ours."

As the *Aeneas* began turning to port in the heavy seas, Germanicus skidded across the deck on the soles of his sandals, crashing into Gaius Nero and his praetorians. A dozen pairs of hands brought him to his feet again, and he had to bellow for the guardsmen to release him. Massaging the nape of his neck, he glanced at the railing where Alope had been last standing. He saw nothing but a retreating surge of wave, then scanned the decks both fore and aft for a glimpse of buckskin. "Nephew!" he cried, "where is she?"

"Behind you, Caesar."

Germanicus looked sheepish, but only briefly. She was soaked, and her skirt clung to her hips. Her light brown skin was glistening with salt water. Tilting her head to first one side and then the other, she stripped the droplets out of her braids with her fingers.

"Caesar—" Gaius Nero flinched; his forearm shot up to shield his eyes from a frenzy of spray as sharp as glass chips. "I urge your return to the *pontis* deck!"

Germanicus nodded, then followed the prefect. He could now see for himself why Glabrio had been forced to countermand his own intentions in the last ten minutes: the gleaming

Aztecan ships had raced along the flank of the Roman fleet, cutting off its van and rear guards. The merchant galleys, whose cargoes were invaluable to the legionaries fighting in Nova Baetica, were scampering back and forth across the tropical green of the shoreline like sheep whose shepherds are beset by too many wolves.

His growing alarm was justified a few moments later when Glabrio's adjutant intercepted him beneath one of the towering smoke chimneys. The man drew Germanicus aside. "Caesar, the admiral has readied an advice boat for you and a dozen of your personal staff. I will captain it."

"I don't understand."

The adjutant was nearly gagging on his shame. "We will not permit Caesar to be taken captive."

"Is it thus *so soon*?"

"This is simply a precaution," the man lied, for his stricken features said otherwise. "The *Aeneas*, as flagship bearing your person, will fall back into the second echelon any second. It's unlikely our galley will be engaged at all."

"Please inform the admiral I won't have the *Aeneas* pulled from the line on my account."

"It's in the codex, Caesar."

Trumpets brayed against the wind once again, and the flagship began to slow as the triremes on both sides of it continued at attack speed. Germanicus could see the *hortator* on the main deck of the *Vespasianus* pounding out a tempo on his sounding board, serving a useless tradition now that rowers no longer propelled galleys. And, in the image of that heavily muscled man wielding his oaken gavels hand over hand, Germanicus sensed why the battle had been decided even before the first exchange of fire: Rome had prepared to fight in the past.

Now it was like choosing what valuables to take from a house on fire. "Prefect," he turned to Gaius Nero, "send your praetorians at once to find Epizelus."

"Aye, Caesar."

Although taking her aboard the boat would deny space to a Roman, Germanicus nevertheless kept a tight grip on Alope's arm. He justified this by thinking of her intelligence value. "Do not stray from my side," he commanded.

But, suddenly, she squirmed free of his clutch. "I will not flee until I have spilled the blood of at least one Azteca. My honor obligates me to do this."

Germanicus returned her glare but did not attempt to recapture her wrist. He had cautioned himself to remain austere in her presence; but now, almost tenderly, he violated this mien with a slight smile that vanished when Alope gaped upward —it sounded as if the fabric of the sky were being torn. An orange sun exploded amidship, and Germanicus was buffeted off his feet, hurled aside. He was anticipating a long fall and then a tumble into water when he slammed painfully against an iron surface and crumpled down onto a deck choked with smoke. Dazed, unable to regain his breath, he struggled to rise as salt water spiked with petroleum flowed into his mouth and nostrils.

"Caesar!" a dozen voices seemed to be crying. "The emperor—help me find him!"

The gale swiftly cleared the smoke, and Alope could be seen peering forward from the railing, her plaits of hair trailing behind her. When Germanicus tried to crawl toward her, he realized that Rolf had seized him by the cloak with no intention of letting go until the situation improved. "What happened?" Germanicus asked.

"It be Aztecan *ballista*. Our *pontis* deck be gone."

"But we were in the *second* echelon."

"Aye," Rolf said gravely.

Then Germanicus saw that Glabrio's adjutant was flat on his back beside them with a gashed chest and the meaningless grin of a man in deep shock. "Admiral Glabrio . . . ?" he asked sleepily.

"Dead." Rolf was trying to stem the flow from the man's wounds.

"Are we at full stop in water?"

"Aye, that too, lad. Be still."

The adjutant tried to sit up. The bloody froth on his lips was bright crimson. "Get Caesar off . . . they'll try to board . . . to take him."

But then Germanicus's attention was drawn seaward by Alope's cries to the fangs of an enormous cat that were biting into the waves as the Aztecan war galley rubbed alongside the *Aeneas*.

10

GERMANICUS WAS GAPING at the Aztecan war galley when Rolf seized his cloak and pulled him down behind the bulwark. Scowling, the centurion cried, "It just be a big ship—stay here!"

"Like none I've ever seen!" During his brief examination of the vessel, Germanicus had managed to glimpse two warriors on the stern, hacking at the tether to the observation kite with axes. From aloft, the spotter had watched them, a grin parting his wind-tussled lips.

Germanicus peeked over the bulwark once again: the line was unraveling in a blur of saltwater mist when suddenly the kite snapped free of its mooring, and the man swooped down to the waves, which swallowed him without leaving a trace of his parrot-blue wings.

"Why didn't they reel the poor beggar in?" Germanicus asked Alope.

"That would rob him of a Flowery Death. It is an honor for an Azteca to die thusly."

Germanicus bent over so he could peer through one of the scuppers at the enemy galley. Its prow was a great jaguar head, sheathed in hammered silver, with golden fangs and enraged eyes of some translucent red stone. Twin serpents were braided around the feline's neck and then undulated down the length of both gunwales, providing crenellations for their naval infantry to hide behind. The *ballista* mounts were in the shape of small pyramids, and atop each was a holy man of some sort, exhorting his charges to fight bravely. The otherwise slender chimneys flared out at their crowns into copper braziers, from which scarlet smoke now issued. In comparison, the *Aeneas* seemed drab despite its adornments that Germanicus had thought garish until this moment.

With a horrendous screaking, the two war galleys glanced off each other in the rough seas. When borne upward by one of the mountainous swells, the Aztecan vessel nearly equaled the height of the Roman trireme, and its warriors popped up from behind the armored serpent. Their feathered headdresses flattened by the gale, they raked the *Aeneas*'s decks with impunity. The Roman response was less than withering, and Germanicus surmised that the direct hit had cut down most of his topside marines.

The praetorian prefect came sprinting between two riddled chimneys from the protected side of the galley and leaped over the body of Glabrio's adjutant to Germanicus. His cloak was smoldering at its fringes. "I was checking advice boats. One full of holes. The other burning."

"Then we fight," Germanicus said almost in relief as he glanced at waves being flayed of their whitecaps by the wind. "What is the condition of this ship?"

"I came upon the *machinator*. He's battling the fires. He'll report to you shortly."

"All right." Germanicus gave his nephew's shoulder a reassuring squeeze. This was Gaius Nero's first battle; he was breathless and wild-eyed. "How fares our fleet?"

"Most of the Aztecan ships disengaged after their first salvo. They're steaming westward—away from us."

"But why?" Germanicus asked, taken aback.

Rolf shouted in Germanicus's ear, "This Aztecan be closing for one reason: to take you! Otherwise, they use *ballistae* to finish us!"

"Then I suppose we will have to *take* them," Germanicus said with a smile.

Rolf hesitated only briefly, then beamed back at him: There was freedom in desperation. "Aye!"

"Let's find out who's still standing."

Germanicus located a marine centurion on the shattered foredeck. But the officer, wounded in the belly, was gasping all his commands from the horizontal. When Germanicus ordered him to be carried below, the man protested, "Please, Caesar—are we going to board them?"

"I see no choice at the moment."

"Then we both know this will be the last time the *corvus* ever falls. I want to see it."

Germanicus realized that the gray waxiness working its way to the surface of the marine's skin was death. "And so you shall, centurion." He turned toward the towering contraption on the prow.

The *corvus* was not a complete mystery to him. As part of their training, all legionaries were required to jog down the "raven-ramp" at least once. Essentially, it was a long plank that was secured upright against a derrick until released to plant the metal spike or "beak" at its far end into the decking of the enemy vessel, pinning the two galleys together. But Germanicus had no clear idea how to lower away the apparatus from its derrick, so he was relieved to spot the suboptio he had met earlier on the afterdeck. The Syrian was dodging spirited fire in order to cast off Aztecan grappling hooks that had connected with the *Aeneas*'s gunwale. "Suboptio!" Germanicus cried. "Stop that!"

"Are we to board then, Caesar?"

"Yes!"

"Excellent!" Racing across the exposed deck, the Syrian joined Germanicus behind a jagged curl of scorched iron. "Why aren't you away, Caesar?"

"Too nasty for boating today. Are you ready to drop the *corvus*?"

"Aye, but I'm short of lads. Will your praetorians help out?"

Germanicus turned to Gaius Nero, who was trembling despite his best efforts to quiet his hands and pointed chin. "Of course . . . " The prefect gave the order, then looked away, humiliated by the agitation of his nervous system.

"Don't be ashamed, my boy," Germanicus said so only his nephew could hear. "It's always this way the first time."

Drawing his short sword, the suboptio bellowed for a flourish of trumpets, then dashed across the volcanic-looking wasteland of a foredeck to the *corvus* and, with the veins bulging in his neck, muscled the derrick around so the line of fall was squarely across the afterdeck of the Aztecan galley. He sliced the two ropes that were rigged to the top of the framework. The ramp groaned on its stout hinges and then toppled over, planting its tungsten spike into the softer steel of the enemy's deck.

"So that's how it's done," Germanicus murmured.

Marines, reinforced by praetorians, began funneling onto the plank, discharging their *pili* wherever sprays of bright feathers attracted their attention.

Germanicus peered down into the chasm between the heaving galleys. The shadowy waters there were slowly filling with corpses, for the outer passageways of both ships had been transformed into opposing trenches: the Romans in their wine-colored cloaks facing the Aztecae in their jaguar skins or feather capes; and, out of the necessity to make space for fresh combatants, the dead were being pitched over the sides.

Germanicus was looking amidships at the Aztecan galley when he exclaimed, "Good Jupiter—what is that?"

"Their version of the *corvus*, I'd imagine." The *machinator* Fiducio had appeared at Germanicus's side. He ran his palm over one side of his hair, which was badly scorched and disintegrated into fine gray ash under his touch.

"Are you well?"

The Abyssinian nodded yes.

Germanicus stared again at the pole that had been hoisted into a slot on the enemy's main deck. The timber began to rotate, and four ropes attached to a square crib at its apex slowly splayed outward. Four warriors, *pili* slung across their backs, trotted in circles until able to leap up and seize these lines. Then, as the device gathered speed, the men played themselves farther and farther out on their ropes, biding their time as the radius of their revolutions increased, waiting for the precise moment in which they might drop onto the tottering decks of the *Aeneas*. Some of these boarders were picked off by Roman marksmen, but others flew into the midst of the marines and began exacting a dear price for their own lives. Hunkered down in a long queue, more warriors awaited their turn to be flung onto the Roman galley.

"I see no necessity in continuing this fight," Fiducio said. "Our fires cannot be suppressed. The *Aeneas* is sinking."

Germanicus's face darkened. All at once, it might be incumbent upon him to take his own life rather than fall into Maxtla's hands. Making a hostage of the Roman emperor would successfully conclude the war for the Aztecae. "Do you suggest we surrender?"

"No, Caesar." Fiducio pointed across a foam-dappled expanse of waters to the *Romulus*. "I suggest that we be taken off."

Although her forward chimney was crumpled over like an

old boot and her decks were sprinkled with small fires, the
bireme was nevertheless steaming to the aid of her flagship.
She was several miles southeast and plowing over green ridges
twice her height. It would be some time before she could come
alongside the stricken *Aeneas*.

Then he noticed something looming above the *Romulus* that
took his breath away. "Damn . . . "

"Yes, Caesar," Fiducio said, almost taking pleasure in Germanicus's distress. "*That* is why the Aztecae have not remained to claim their victory."

The *procella* reminded Germanicus of a Numidian dust
storm, although its monstrous cloud was dark gray rather than
buff-colored. From this central mass of moisture, a dark hood
projected westward over the strait, sheeting rain across the
waves. "How long before it overtakes us?" Germanicus
asked.

"That would depend on the path—"

"Very soon," Alope interrupted.

Germanicus spun around, then snapped at her: "Where
have you been?"

"Invoking the power of the sun to help your warriors."

"Not dusting them with pollen again, I hope."

She refused to answer.

"You were commanded not to—"

Germanicus's words were cut short by a flurry of *pili* fire
that rose and crackled above the din. Two marines bounded
back across the *corvus* from the Aztecan galley, dragging between them a slight man who appeared to be unconscious.
Moments later, they dropped the prisoner at Germanicus's
feet. "Our suboptio sends Caesar his compliments," one of
them said, "and a Serican."

The captive, perhaps in his late twenties, had an elongated
face of light complexion and wore his coarse, black hair in a
topknot. Germanicus felt the skin of the man's right palm. It
had not been toughened by handling hawsers: the Serican was
not a common mariner.

"Little fellow addressed me proper like, Caesar," the second marine said, smirking as he held a curved sword up to
view. "Even gave me a bit of a bow before he commenced to
flash this in my face. Nothing serious, just a hello there, you
know. Might've done my shave for me, too—what if my mate
hadn't snuck up behind and clouted him. Little fellow went
out, but not before he twisted around and gave Milo here a

dose of eye-fire for not sporting fair."

"Good work, lads." Hurriedly, Germanicus checked on the progress of the bireme. "Now, take word to your suboptio to withdraw."

"Caesar?" they asked in unison, faces disappointed.

"The *Aeneas* is finished. We'll be taken off her by the *Romulus*."

"Aye. Hail Caesar!"

Groggily, the Serican opened an eye and fixed it on Germanicus. He winced as he recalled what had just befallen him, then bowed as best he could, being flat on his back. He uttered something Germanicus only intuitively thought to be Latin.

"He must know Nahuatl," Germanicus said to Alope. "Ask him if he's trying to speak classical Latin."

She prefaced the question with an obvious warning that she would tolerate no nonsense from the man. "He says he studied Latin from a codex. He apologizes for the way he speaks it. He has never heard it from a Roman's lips before."

"Ask him what business a Serican has on an Aztecan war galley."

His eyes narrowed to slits, and he answered in a cautious tone of voice. Alope spat at him. He recoiled as if he'd been slapped. "He lies that he is not a Serican," she said to Germanicus. "I have seen many of these people in Tenochtitlan —perhaps even this one. Surely, he is of Serican blood. Let me—"

The trumpets blared to life, announcing the retreat. Through strands of smoke, Germanicus saw that the vicious fight on the afterdeck of the enemy galley was drawing more and more Aztecan warriors. The Romans, who had been scrabbling back toward the *Aeneas*, were in peril of being overwhelmed by a force of fresh warriors. Armed with clubs edged with flakes of black stone, caparisoned in aquiline helmets, these fighters had come swarming out of a hatch, cutting off the Roman boarders, who were being compelled to resort to their own blades on the crowded deck.

"Eagle knights!" Alope hissed. "They appear at the last minute to take captives for the Fifth Sun!"

Germanicus had no time to ask about the Fifth Sun or any other matter, for only a handful of red cloaks could be seen in the swarm of Aztecan knights.

The suboptio must have sensed the disaster in the making. Before he himself could be felled, he broke free of the frenzied mob, flailing his sword in front of him as he groped backwards over corpses, and staggered onto the *corvus* that was now an invitation for the Aztecae to board the *Aeneas*. Fending off two warriors who had pursued him midway across the ramp, he reached down for a brass ring that opened a small hatch in the plating. Still holding the Aztecae at bay, he fumbled for the lanyard inside the cubbyhole and then pulled with all his might. Grinning, the suboptio affected the ferocious deportment of a Thracian gladiator and drove his opponents back several yards by the sheer bravado of his swordplay. When he had gained some space, he did an about-face, saluted Caesar, and vanished in the explosion that collapsed the *corvus* into the sea.

Motionlessly, Germanicus watched as the burst of smoke was shredded apart by the wind. After a few moments, he became aware of soft snuffling noises at his back.

Alope was weeping. She must have sensed his bewilderment, for she wiped her cheeks with the heels of her hands and gave him a smile that was damaged by sorrow. "I gnash my teeth for such courage," she said.

Germanicus touched her chin with his fingertips, lifted it slightly. "You're not an aberrant people, are you . . . ?"

"Caesar?"

"If you revere courage above all else, as did my people long ago?"

Suddenly, Alope shrieked and rolled away from him. Germanicus looked at her in astonishment—until a human shadow flashed across the decking in front of him. Instinctively shielding his face with his forearm, he glanced up in time to see the Aztecan war club caught and held by the edge of Rolf's short sword. The warrior and the centurion each pressed his full weight into his weapon. Neither appeared to be moving but for the quivering of their biceps. A tawny blur passed between Germanicus and the combatants, and all at once the Azteca gave out with a gasp as if someone had touched ice to his skin. His slapped his left hand to his throat, then slowly turned to glower at Alope: a knife was dripping blood from the vise of her small fist.

The scorn in the Azteca's eyes was bottomless. He began trembling wildly in the effort to hold his own against Rolf. But finally the centurion pulled back his sword, taking the club away with it. The warrior sank to his knees, bloody hand yet fastened to his throat. He tried to speak to Alope, but the words were lost in a gurgling sound. His eyelids began flutter-ing, and then his pupils rolled up into his skull. He pitched forward, dead.

Rolf widened his stance at the approach of running foot-falls, but it was only Gaius Nero at the head of a brace of prae-torians. That the prefect had been absent during the attack on Caesar was duly noted by the way in which the German said to Alope: "I be thankful to you, daughter."

She nodded once, almost defiantly in the face of Germani-cus's expectation that she might now betray some remorse.

"Caesar," Gaius Nero said, "I beg you to hurry—the *Rom-ulus* approaches."

Before he could open his mouth, Germanicus found himself being jostled away by the pair of praetorians who had clasped him under the arms and were lifting him over wreckage and bodies as if he were a dotard. He didn't resist them. What had been lurking on the edge of his thoughts now overwhelmed him: He had lost. Terrentius Glabrio, priceless for his keen mind and the boldness to speak that mind, was lost. Curi-ously, Germanicus wondered if the old cook who'd sailed with Otacilius had survived, but somehow doubted it. All was lost, and Aztecae could be espied trotting over the afterdeck of the *Aeneas* at will.

The crew of the *Romulus* was tossing lines across a heaving gulf of water in the attempt to tie up alongside. It didn't seem possible, but the Mare Aztecum had grown even more violent in the last several minutes, and the hawsers kept falling short or glancing off the hull of the *Aeneas*. His shoulders slumped, Germanicus gave his back to this difficult task—as if afraid his attention was vexing it—and stared instead at the gap in the trireme's profile where the *pontis* deck had once stood.

Then he cried, "No!," straining against the firm grasp the praetorians had on him.

The Aztecae had somehow bridged their vessel to the *Aeneas* with a rope gangway, and a squad of eagle knights was now herding a dozen Romans into captivity. Among them was Germanicus's physician.

"Epizelus!" Germanicus cried.

The Greek could not hear him above the roar of wind and battle. Prodded by a stone-barbed club, he pinched the main rope between his toes and continued the precarious traverse to the Aztecan galley.

"Follow me!" Germanicus ordered the praetorians. "That man must not be taken!"

But it was Rolf who settled the matter. "Nay—stand fast."

The guardsmen looked to their prefect, who echoed the centurion's order.

Eventually, the captain of the *Romulus* saw no alternative but to plant his own *corvus* into the deck of the flagship. Those awaiting rescue on the *Aeneas*'s foredeck cleared a space, and the beak of the ramp ripped into the iron plate with a brutal clang.

Germanicus and the praetorians were first across, with Alope and Gaius Nero directly behind them, followed by Rolf, who had taken charge of the Serican. One instant, the *corvus* was tilting upward into the gathering clouds; the next, sea was boiling where sky had just been. Germanicus boarded the bireme into the midst of the Anatolian tribesmen, who were watching the burning of the *Aeneas* and the skirmishing of the Roman rear guard with philosophical interest. "*Inshallah, pasa*," Khalid said to him.

Germanicus roused himself long enough to mutter, "Yes . . . *Inshallah*." Then his eyes became glazed again.

A niter store exploded on the flagship, hurling a *ballista* mount out into the waves. To the last man, the Anatolians said, "Ah . . . " This was expressed with an air of disappointment, as if they would have preferred seeing the *Aeneas* herself flying into pieces across the ever-darkening heavens. "This was foretold, *pasa*," Khalid commiserated. "Now we have fulfilled that which was written and would like to set foot on land again. These ships are very bad for digestion."

Germanicus gave no sign of having heard the young prince, but Rolf asked, "What be written of this day?"

" 'Caesar shall drink boiling water at the first well of his enemies.' "

The Aztecan galley cast off from the now listing *Aeneas*, and moments later a marine—delayed only as long as it took for Fiducio to stagger across the ramp—destroyed the *corvus* that linked the *Romulus* to the sinking trireme. Both captains rushed to clear the derelict and be first to open fire upon the other. But no salvos barked over the howl of the wind. The storm had fully arrived: the world had been reduced to darkness and seething waters.

And there was doom in the old king's heart even in the midst of Tenochtitlan's celebration, for he said to Lord Tizoc: "We should not taste the sweet fruits of victory because the wind god, Ehecatl, has decided against us."

"But our enemies suffered in this storm as greatly as we did, reverend speaker."

The old man took no comfort from the words of his lord general. "Long ago, when we were known as the Mexicae, before we instructed our cousins in this valley that we are all descendants of the hardy Aztecae, were we not told by the gods that our world will one day end? We do not know when this will happen, but every two and fifty years it falls upon the gods to renew this, the Fifth Sun, the last realm of our people, at the Ceremony of New Fire. That day is but a few months distant."

"I have no doubt, reverend one, that we shall be granted another two and fifty years. Do we not honor the sun with more blood and hearts than ever?"

"Yes, my lord general, but even numberless sacrifices cannot postpone the darkness and void that must close our days. Now we must see how our brother-foe does on land—and whether the gods help or hinder him as he ushers in the eternal night . . ."

11

THE ROMULUS CREPT up the River Luteus, the brown waters flattened and dimpled by a light rain. The heavily damaged galley was steaming forward so slowly it seemed constantly on the verge of being overtaken by the skein of ripples broadcast by its wake. The bireme had been joined by no other Roman vessels in the three days since her *corvus* had been blasted free of the *Aeneas*.

Of course, there had been scant visibility in that time. The horizons had damped down on the *Romulus*. What little illumination there was came suddenly in the form of lightning that twitched across the liquid membranes of the sky, then crackled to darkness again. The decks pitched and lurched at unbelievable angles, hurling gear and men from bulkhead to bulkhead. This jostling was relieved for one half-hour by a strange calm that invited Germanicus and Alope topside to gape in wonder at a circumvallation of clouds that reared up from the slack surface of the ocean. But then the storm crashed down on the lone galley again, and the couple rushed below to clutch at ladders, pipes, stanchions . . . each other . . . with fingers that had grown stiff and cramped from this endless necessity.

Word came to Germanicus that most of the Anatolian ponies were already dead and the remainder continued to thrash against their restraints. Gently, he explained the matter to Khalid, who, in grim silence, went down into the hold and dispatched them. The Anatolian refused to speak after this, which only served to deepen Germanicus's own melancholy.

Alope began to chide the emperor with her eyes.

"Why do you look at me so, woman?" he finally demanded.

"You must not let your people borrow all your power."

"What do you mean?"

"You must take some power from your people. You must *become* your people, as I am mine. Then you will know what to do—and not get twisted around yourself."

He had smiled at her, and in that instant his shame and anger began to dissipate.

Now, as the *Romulus* glided around a wooded bend in the river, Germanicus covered her hand where it rested on the railing.

They passed a Nova Baetican villa, in actuality a wooden mansion with a self-conscious dolomite facing and a pair of Corinthian columns to dignify its portal. But the surrounding fields of maize looked neatly tended, and beyond the hedgerow was a huge pasture across which a flood of horseflesh was rippling in shades of gray and umber, driven along the riverbank by mounted colonials. These Novos wore huge floppy-brimmed hats and had dispensed with togas in favor of kidskin tunics with bullhide greaves to protect their forelegs; they whooped raucously as they rode but, almost intransigently, took no notice of the *Romulus*. Germanicus had been forewarned that Novos were different.

"Magnificent country," he said.

"It is nothing compared to the lands of the Indee."

Unobtrusively, Germanicus withdrew his hand from hers. He could feel her eyes flash at him.

The bireme rounded an oxbow that cut through diked sloughs that were bright green with rice shoots, then steamed onto a broad lake, across which Germanicus viewed something that heartened him: Riding at anchor mid-channel were at least forty war galleys and an equal number of merchant vessels, all storm-worn but still afloat. The *procella*'s victory had not been complete.

This obviously was its harbor, but he could catch no glimpse of the provincial capital. "Where is Otacilium?" he asked Rolf.

The centurion pointed toward a bluff to the west. "It be built up off the floodplain."

Gaunt-looking from three days of seasickness, Gaius Nero shuffled up and saluted without his usual briskness. "Proconsul Gracchus has been advised of your arrival, Caesar. He will greet you at the landing."

"Good Jupiter," Germanicus whispered as the *Romulus*'s advice boat bumped against the quay, "they're swaddled in animal-pelt togas!"

"Aye," Rolf said, "that be the high fashion when I served here long ago."

"But they look like mounds of hair!"

"Novos *be* mounds of hair," the centurion grunted.

Alope's eyes were laughing. "Does Caesar think these Romans have mingled too much with the likes of the Indee?"

Germanicus didn't answer, although his nose was itching for want of asking if these citizens, in their thirty-year haste to replicate Rome in the wilderness, had bothered to construct a public bath.

At the urging of a Tenth Legion colonel, a band of Novos hoisted their arms and fired a volley skyward. There was an awkward lack of cheering, which the proconsul and other more recently transplanted Latins remedied by crying, "Hail Caesar!" An unintelligible rumble followed from the colonials; it might have been a salute to Germanicus's *imperium*— or simply a hundred throats being cleared at once.

Even Marcus Gracchus had relented to local custom and wore a fringe of purple-dyed fur on his toga. "Praise to the gods you're safe, Caesar," he said with a bow that set his chins to jiggling. "It is seven miles to Otacilium and we have arranged a banquet in your honor. May we proceed?"

"Proceed," Germanicus said quietly.

The sand-galleys that conveyed the imperial staff toward the city were manned by convalescing legionaries. As soon as he could shake off a swarm of fawning functionaries, Germanicus drifted across the prow deck of the proconsul's craft and asked a young soldier with a bandaged arm, "How goes the fighting?"

"Slow, Caesar," he answered almost listlessly.

"How'd you receive your wound?"

"At night, those eagle knight bastards slip into our trenches to carry us off." A little anger seeped into his voice. "I would not be carried off."

"Good lad." Smiling, Germanicus took his leave of the legionary, but in truth he'd been troubled by the disheartened look in the man's eyes. This, he knew, was the consequence of a stalemated war.

The muddy road passed through an immense bivouac of new barbarians on a marshy plain. The stagnant ponds were ringed with lodges of two basic designs: one conical with a spray of poles jutting out of the bison-hide covering, the other nothing more than a thatch of reeds lashed over a few bowed sticks. On the most pestilent piece of ground stood a small village seemingly populated only by women, who hailed the imperial procession with shrill catcalls, and their children, who were lighter-skinned than the other youngsters scampering through the piles of refuse that lay everywhere.

"These are brides for the night," Alope explained. "Your legionaries have rubbed away the grass around their *gowas*."

Germanicus frowned, then encompassed all the diverse bands of tribesmen with a sweep of his arm. "Which community is the Indee's?"

"We never camp near Otacilium."

The loud grumbling of the sand-galley's engine echoed off the fortified wall of the city, and the operator geared down as he eased the craft into the vaulted opening of the Porta Germanica. Germanicus noticed that the profile in bas-relief above the gate was his own; self-consciously, he stroked his thick lower jaw.

The convoy emerged onto a rain-flooded, cobbled street of shops that was colonnaded on both sides in logs that, Gracchus explained, had been sanded smooth with pumice to resemble stone. There was statuary—all wooden and of a rusticity that would have made it unfit for even the poorest houses in Italia. Otacilium seemed a hodgepodge city thrown together by children who knew of Rome only from the stories of their grandparents, although the Novos sheltered under the arcades here seemed friendlier than those who had welcomed him on the quay. Then Germanicus realized that this was a street consisting entirely of wine shops.

"Tomorrow, Caesar," Gracchus prattled, "we have scheduled games in your honor. Our gladiators will fight two hundred wildcats and a specie of gigantic humpbacked bear that slays more often than it is slain."

"You must pardon my absence from your games, Marcus

—and tonight's banquet as well."

The fêtes of the Gracchi family were of fabled opulence; no one had ever declined an invitation, not even an emperor. "But . . . but Caesar!" the proconsul sputtered.

"I'm sorry," Germanicus said brusquely, "but I must go where I'm most needed: to the front, immediately."

"But you haven't seen our new forum!"

"Another time. How near Salvidienus's headquarters has the artery been completed?"

"Why, within twenty miles or so."

"Is the proconsular rail-galley here?"

If his abrupt decision to visit the front plunged the imperial and provincial staffs into pandemonium, it improved Germanicus's spirits greatly.

He boarded the rail-galley at Otacilium's dank, cedarwood station—which smelled for all the world like the Jewish holy houses that were lined with panels hewn from the Phoenician variety of this tree—and reclined on a window couch in the proconsul's private car. Served a cup of chilled vinegar, he came close to smiling as he watched the young military tribunes outside, clawing over one another across the platform to complete their errands before the hour was spent and an outraged Caesar ordered something dreadful like *decimatus* —and each of them privately knowing in his sweat of sweats that he would be the tenth man to be counted in that long, tremulous line.

"What kind of emperor have they been taking me to be?" he asked, hushed, although only Rolf shared the compartment with him.

The German did not respond.

A few minutes before, Germanicus had absently muttered some idle thought to himself, bringing Rolf up off his couch to full attention. Weary of his lack of privacy, Caesar had carped at the man for crowding him: "Can't you keep someone company without listening to what is said?!"

And Rolf had growled in reply: "Aye, I be married once! And I be much reminded of those times lately!"

Germanicus had nearly chuckled; but now had he had to snap his fingers to get the German's attention. Twice.

"Kaiser?" he asked—altogether too innocently.

"I asked you a question: what kind of emperor have my

people been imagining me to be? Some cantankerous but harmless old uncle they can outwit at every turn?"

The centurion shrugged. "Maybe."

"Is that what *you* think?"

Rolf fought a rising smile—and lost. "No . . . I been on campaign with you. You be cantankerous, aye, but not harmless." Quickly, he sobered himself. "Now I stop listening again."

"Before you do, have Alope join me for dinner." Then, as an afterthought: "Bring the Serican prisoner as well."

"Aye, Kaiser."

With a neck-wrenching jolt, the rail-galley departed for the coast of Nova Baetica. Retired decades before from the Bosporus-Parthia run and shipped to the Novo Provinces where even noble passengers were less demanding of comfort, it was one of the oldest in existence. In terms of excruciation, this meant that the wheels and undercarriages of the cars were not outfitted with buffers: the science of pneumatics had been in its infancy back then.

But the jolting and clattering served to remind Germanicus of better days. His manservant Charicles and he had taken countless trips to the accompaniment of these very sensations and sounds. And the countryside flashing between random spates of woodland shadow was green, moist, bucolic—like the Cisalpine Gaul of his youth. Except that this province was less densely settled, and it was teeming with horses destined to be traded to the new barbarians farther west.

Germanicus's eyes became reflective: Charicles had been dead six months now. No one could ever wrap a toga as expertly as the old man; but Germanicus knew that there was much more to the loss than that—things his grief wouldn't let him fully recount yet. Although it was also true that Charicles, quite obnoxiously at times, had turned his deathbed into a rostrum: "You must marry as soon as possible, Germanicus. You need someone more cheerful than yourself. Marry for love—two or three times if you must. But keep trying until you find an agreeable woman!"

Softly, Germanicus chuckled to himself.

The rain had stopped, and the spent storm was being scattered into swatches of powdery cloud. Sunlight glanced down through the glazing, which had to be wiped clear of steam by servants every few minutes, and warmed Germanicus's back as he dined on his couch.

Alope reclined across from him, eating vigorously. Between Rolf and her sat the Serican cross-legged on his couch, sipping a bowl of sauce instead of dipping his fish into it. He had attempted to eat lying down, propping himself up on his left elbow as the others did, but kept choking from swallowing food down a horizontal gullet. Whispering apologies in a slightly improved Latin, he eventually eased upright, eyeing Rolf's sheathed short sword all the while.

Germanicus asked him, "In what capacity did you serve the Aztecae?" The prisoner clearly understood the question, but his accent bruised the ancient words beyond recognition. Germanicus turned to Alope: "Tell him I will assign my scribe to practice conversational Latin with him. He's the best grammarian in Rome. But for now, the prisoner must answer my questions in Nahuatl through you."

After shuttling some pleasant-sounding syllables back and forth with the Serican, Alope said, "His duties, Caesar, were like those of a *machinator* on a Roman galley. Maxtla's sailors are as children to machines and need much help. But this was only his most recent task. Before, he was a teacher in Tenochtitlan. This too was difficult. The Aztecae learn everything by rote and believe questions to be discourteous."

"What did he try to teach them?" Germanicus asked.

"He calls it *Yinshaya*."

"What does this mean?"

Further explanation by the Serican did not appear to clear up Alope's confusion. "The word is neither Serican nor Nahuatl. He says this thing was the gift from Star-Sorter."

"*Who?*"

"I do not know of this person, Caesar. But those are his words as he gave them to me in the tongue of Aztecae."

"Ask him to tell us more about this personage."

Alope barked a command at the prisoner, then waited impatiently as he replied. "He says Star-Sorter was the provider of *Yinshaya* to mankind. He walked out of the western sun into the Serican Empire many years ago. He lectured at an academy he created in the imperial capital. Finally, a very old man, overripe with wisdom, he fell off the branch of life during his sleep. In obedience to his wishes, Star-Sorter's body was carried by caravan back to his homeland, so he might lie in repose among other *sensei* in a secret underground tomb."

"Who are these *sensei*?"

"The Light-Givers. Great teachers, I think. He admits the word is from his own language—not Serican. Again, he lies that he is not a Serican."

Germanicus ran his forefinger along his lower lip: mention of such a tomb pricked his memory, but the bucket he drew up out of the past was empty. He sighed. "Why does our friend cling to this denial of being Serican? He's obviously the racial type."

The prisoner spoke so fervently he slopped wine onto his couch cushions. Alope glared at him, then said to Germanicus, "He says Roman eyes are not keen enough to tell the difference between Sericans and Nihonians."

"Ah ha!" Germanicus clapped his hands together, then met the Nihonian's stare. "I apologize. It is an honor to finally meet someone from your island country."

The man bowed, mollified.

"So there is no confusion," Germanicus went on, "tell him that I am curious about Aztecan ships—how and where they are built."

This lit a quarrel between Alope and the Nihonian. At last, she broke off the exchange with what Germanicus surmised to be an Indee oath. "He says he cannot tell Caesar such things while he is still in service to the Sericans."

"Is this a bid for a commission with me?" Germanicus asked.

"I think so. But do not trust this one. Look how he always drops his eyes."

"Does he mention terms?"

"Yes— He must be attached to your household. And his sword must be returned to him."

"Why does he so eagerly switch his allegiance?"

The Nihonian explained through Alope that he saw nothing wrong or unusual in this. He had been born to the warrior caste and his ancestors had hired themselves out as mercenaries for generations; the only dishonor was to abandon one lord before landing employment with another. Personally, he had no use for the Sericans. They had conquered his country after a great sea battle and executed his emperor-god. But business was business.

Germanicus was silent for a long moment. "What is our Nihonian's name?"

"He has already told me—Tora. It is the word for tiger in his language."

"Very well, Tora, I will take your proposal under advisement." Germanicus then motioned for Rolf to remove the prisoner.

Alone with Alope, he did not speak again. Nor did she. They scarcely exchanged glances, but when they did he was powerless to keep the delight out of his eyes. He did not rush the conclusion of their meal, and Nova Baetica gradually faded to darkness outside the glazing.

12

GERMANICUS SENSED THE closeness of the battlefield long before the rail-galley squealed to a halt and Gaius Nero crept into his darkened cabin to touch him gently on the shoulder. "Uncle . . . ?"

"I'm awake." Beneath his coverlet, Germanicus released the hilt of the short sword he'd slept with since the attempt on his life. "Is there fog?"

"Why, yes—how did you know?"

"It sits on my lungs like an old tomcat."

"We transfer here to a column of sand-galleys."

"I'll be along in a moment," Germanicus said. Rolf could be seen in the passageway, yawning and cracking his vertebrae with his knuckles.

Gaius Nero fumbled with the self-igniting oil lamp until he got a dim flame, then hesitated at the cramped entry. "Uncle, I beg forgiveness. In all honesty, I seem no closer to discovering—"

"Hold, my boy." Germanicus had been waiting for this. "You may never learn who tried to kill me. I suspect that the man responsible may have vanished forever with the *Aeneas*. But I want you to strike Alope's name from your list."

"I already have. I did it the instant she joined her knife to ours against the Aztecan warrior . . . and saved your life at the damnable moment my cloak was snagged by a piece of iron."

Germanicus studied his nephew's slender face, then smiled. "There's no shame in that. I was once captured for twenty full minutes by a claw of Hibernian willow." He accepted a cup of warmed vinegar from a servant, then winked at Gaius Nero over its lip. "I wrote young Quintus a long letter before retiring last night."

"How thoughtful of you."

"I've promised him a denarius if he can find this among my codices: 'Whatever may happen to you was prepared for you in advance from the beginning of time. In the woven tapestry of causation . . . ' " Germanicus paused, his eyes stung by some thought he quicky put aside. " ' . . . the thread of your being had been intertwined from all time with that particular incident.' "

"From Marcus Aurelius's *Sibi*, Codex Ten."

Germanicus rose and reached for his military tunic. "I knew I wouldn't be able to put anything over on a Prefecture of Antiquities man."

"Indeed, uncle, but Quintus will rip your library apart in search of it."

"Better a tyrant's library than his empire."

Gaius Nero's smile was so faint it might have been nothing more than his upper lip catching on his eyetooth. "Does Caesar consider himself to be a tyrant?"

Germanicus slapped him on the back, but did not answer.

"Help me with my cuirass, nephew."

Germanicus slipped through the shrouded air with the suspicion that he was yet asleep, gliding through a dream on winged feet, or stealing down a past that repeated itself endlessly. Eddies of legionaries and praetorians scuttled around him, but he himself was at the becalmed eye of this storm called war. Both saddened and excited, he appreciated that black and hectic mornings such as these were the engines that powered empires and kept emperors humming on their thrones. But he felt detached from it all, perhaps because he had nothing tangible to do, such as inspect a century of pimpled boys or perform last-minute repairs on a sand-galley tread. And what could all this activity ever resolve? Could it free even a single man to sit on a warm stone and be at peace with himself? *I am growing old*, he thought.

Someone brushed his arm with their cold fingers. He started: it was Alope.

"This morning, Caesar shall *see*."

She said this in such a way his heart began trip-hammering. "What will I see, woman?"

She simply repeated the utterance, her features dimmed by the fog despite the torch a guardsman carried before them.

"This one be bannered purple, Caesar," Rolf said, pounding the iron hull of a sand-galley with his fist.

And Germanicus noted no transition of time between the thump of the centurion's hand on the craft and the first throaty crackle of *ballista* fire. A flare erupted overhead, and he imagined he could feel the white heat on his face. By this muted light, he could see that the ground was a mat of reeds blown flat by the storm. There were dugouts in the higher ground, and from their crawlways lanterns shone. Streaked with woodsmoke, these amber beams were crisscrossed by the silhouettes of legionaries who were tending the spits on which they baked their gritty rolls of bread. "I can close my eyes and see this all the clearer," Germanicus whispered.

"Yes; today you shall *see*."

He gently grasped her face and turned it toward him. Only her shining black eyes penetrated the duskiness of the hour. "What are you saying?"

"There is no saying until you have *seen*."

And again, after no sense that minutes had piled on minutes, or surprise that a thin glow was suddenly irradiating the fog to the east, Germanicus found himself following Gaius Nero down a muddy trench, and Gaius Nero was slogging behind the first centurion of the Tenth Legion, who in his filthy condition seemed to have wriggled up out of this ooze. "The storm did us less harm than we ourselves expected," he said. "We were already burrowed in when it struck." The earth quaked beneath the imperial party as an Aztecan projectile blew a rent in a rampart far forward of them. The first centurion glanced over his shoulder at Gaius Nero, who was cringing under the brief downpour of slime. "No cause for alarm, prefect. We shoved them back on this flank a month ago. We're out of range."

"I was not alarmed," Gaius Nero snapped.

For the first time, Germanicus realized that his nephew was in his silvered helmet, which was properly worn only on the highest ceremonial occasions.

A file of praetorians marched above Caesar on each parapet lining the trench. The prefect had passed on word ahead that no voice was to announce the emperor's presence and perhaps alert the enemy, who might put into motion some desperate plan of capture. But this didn't stop some of the younger legionaries from gasping, "Hail Caesar!" at the vision that must have seemed apparitional to them.

Gaius Nero singled out one of those violators, a Balearic sniper, and cuffed him. "Fool!" he hissed. "Do you want to see your emperor dead?"

The youth was too terrified to speak.

"He meant no harm, prefect," the first centurion answered for him. "We're a good mile from the Aztecan lines here. And you can't imagine how it cheers these lads to see Caesar in their midst."

Germanicus drew his nephew aside before he could launch into the first centurion. "My boy, the worst thing about this degrading kind of warfare is that one imagines himself forsaken by his leaders, forgotten by his countrymen. These legionaries have had an impossible time. They've built up a heavy store of emotion these past months. Some of it must be released or they'll lose heart."

The prefect's eyes were glistening in the first light of day. "If Caesar might recall, I never suggested that we conduct this *degrading* kind of warfare. But regardless, my only concern has been Caesar's safety."

"I thank you for that," Germanicus said. "But let's defer to the advice of the first centurion in this matter."

"Good Mars, uncle, he's only a centurion."

Germanicus's kindly smile vanished. "This soldier is the chief centurion of this entire legion. By some reckonings, he is second only to its commander."

"If I'm not permitted to act as your *legatus* on this expedition, I still believe myself to be the praetorian prefect. And in that office my duties are explicit: To preserve the person of the emperor at all costs."

"You are very much my *legatus*."

"Caesar proclaims so but acts contrary at every turn."

"What would you have me do?"

"Execute the legionary—as an example."

"As an example," Germanicus echoed tonelessly.

"It may be a long campaign, as you told the Senate. It is only fair that Caesar forewarns those who would threaten him."

Germanicus fought down the words, imprisoned them behind clenched teeth: *Whenever have you bloodied those soft hands of yours*? *Or lost a son*? But he held his tongue, and—while tightening the grip on his anger—sensed that Alope was keenly awaiting his next move. He no more had to trade glances with her to realize this. He faced Gaius Nero again: "You may warn this legionary to be more careful."

"Is that *all*?"

"Yes."

"By this, am I to understand that I am no longer Caesar's *legatus*?"

"You are to understand no such thing!" Germanicus exploded. "But you shall understand that Caesar's adjutant follows Caesar's orders—as does the least legionary on this field!" Askance, he glimpsed Alope's fleeting triumphant glance.

Panic replaced the impertinence in Gaius Nero's features. He started to answer Germanicus, then thought better of it and spun around to dress down the offending Balearic: "You are reminded not to betray Caesar's presence to our enemies."

"I would never do so, sir!"

Stiffly, the prefect gestured for the first centurion to lead them onward again. His face was a deeper rose than the dawn sky's.

And Germanicus's sense of detachment, moments before so delicate and plaintive, now dissolved in the craw of this ill humor. Every perception traveled to his brain on peeled nerves, as if each breath he drew had to cross broken teeth.

Suddenly, the air had the sulfurous bite of niter powder, and the nearby explosions were intensely jangling, like thunder from a cloudless sky. The first centurion herded the imperial party into a lamplit tunnel, and Germanicus's spirits sank: he was visiting one more mean little headquarters with its crowded hospital. The misery, the loneliness his eyes so dutifully recorded might prove meaningless; everything spent and spilled here might prove meaningless.

Bunks began lining the earthen walls a few paces inside the portal, stacked three high, teeming with men too exhausted or pained by wounds to sleep well. They whimpered, gasped, mumbled in Etruscan for all anyone knew—but fell silent when the Aztecan *ballistae* walked overhead in Titan's boots. *How they suffer so, even in their rest*, Germanicus thought as he passed ever deeper into the fetid air. *Have I the strength to conclude a civil war my own convictions might ignite? Are convictions worth such human desolation as this?*

"This way, Caesar," the first centurion said, "to the general's pretorium."

Germanicus brightened at the thought of seeing Gnaeus Salvidienus again. He fondly remembered the man from their days together at the Campus Martius. Although Gnaeus's grandfather had been Prefect of Rome, it had been the youth's horsemanship—which could make or break careers prior to the sand-galley—and his stalwart character that, in actuality, had offset his difficulties with most of the academy curricula, especially *machinalis scientia*. And just when poor Gnaeus thought he'd forever escaped the clutches of Euclid and Archimedes, the Emperor Fabius had decreed that all officers above the rank of tribune were to return to the sprawling facility on the Tiber to learn Arabian reductions, a discipline which confounded the phlegmatic soldier to no end because of its admittedly valueless cipher called *zero*. "If it isn't worth anything, why fool with it?" he ranted to no avail. "What will become of us if we insist on working with that which does not exist?"

Yet Germanicus trusted that, of all the illustrious soldiers to come out of that distant class of cadets, none was better suited than Gnaeus Salvidienus to keep the Aztecae from surging up to the walls of Otacilium.

While still a tribune, Gnaeus had commanded a small garrison on the Illyrian coast where local pirates took advantage of Rome's more urgent problems in Numidia at the time. Salvidienus's out-of-the-way post was not reinforced for six weeks; in truth, it had been written off by the proconsul, who had withdrawn to Italia with his staff. So the eventual relief force of marines from Ravenna was surprised to find the tribune and a handful of survivors still manning the breastworks. Mounted on a triple cross with two of his confederates, the pirate chieftain had groused, "Can I be blamed if this Roman was too stupid to know he was beaten?"

And now, as Germanicus and his party were ushered into a bunker that reeked of mold, sweat, and lungweed, Caesar's teeth showed in a slight grin as he glimpsed this often-maligned Leonidas of Illyricum. Salvidienus raised his gleaming bald head from where it had hung over a map and exclaimed, "Why, Germanicus Julius—you still have most your hair!"

There was an embarrassed silence among the general's staff, who stood at attention behind Salvidienus, holding in their bellies.

Germanicus chuckled and offered his hand. "And you,

Aufidius Gnaeus, still ambush idle talk before it can be deployed."

Relieved cries of "Hail Caesar!" punctuated the laughter.

Assiduously, Germanicus introduced Gaius Nero as his *legatus*.

Subdued yet after his chastisement, the praetorian prefect nevertheless saluted the general—a courtesy, considering an equivalence of rank that dipped slightly in his own favor. "An honor, noble Gnaeus. I've heard so much about your exploits."

The general peered at the young prefect for a long moment, then said with a most earnest mystification, "Which exploits?"

Gaius Nero struggled to keep control of his thin lips. Quickly, he began inspecting a large copper urn. A peculiar-smelling vapor was puffing from its top. "What brews here?"

Brightness came to Salvidienus's eyes for the first time. "The last of our *cacahuhel*. I wanted Caesar to sample some before we're completely out. With the war, we can get no more from the Aztecan *pochteca* who once traded on our side of the River Terminus."

"And spied on your side of the river," Alope whispered so only Germanicus could hear.

An orderly carefully filled two lead cups and presented one to Germanicus and the second to Salvidienus.

Germanicus sniffed the head of tan froth, then took a sip. Despite its bitterness, the stuff was utterly satisfying. But he lowered the cup after a second swallow. "My dear Gnaeus, are you sure this is not addictive?"

The general hoarded the liquid in the pockets of his cheeks, then gulped loudly. "I don't know."

"What is it made from?"

"A small bean they call *cacao*."

Germanicus turned to Alope: "Do the Aztecae drink it themselves?"

"Only the nobility, Caesar. We Indee believe *cacahuhel* fills the warrior with lassitude."

"I suspect that's quite possible." Germanicus wiped his mouth with the back of his hand. "My physician was captured off the *Aeneas*. Otherwise, I'd have him look into this drink."

Sighing, Salvidienus waved for his orderly to remove the urn. Then he squeezed shut one eye and enlarged the other at

Germanicus. "You say your surgeon is in the hands of the Aztecae?"

"Yes. But now that we hold some of their people, I trust he'll be treated decently. Even these barbarians must recognize that Epizelus is an extraordinary man."

"All the worse for him . . . all the worse." The general's eyes shifted to Alope. "Have you told Caesar how things are here, daughter?"

"I have. But he must see for himself."

"Yes, isn't that the way? How sad. But I too have kept silent for the very same reason—until now. How terribly sad."

"Of what is Caesar so abysmally ignorant?" Germanicus demanded.

Salvidienus lingered over his last drop of *cacahuehl*. "Soon it will be fully light," he said in a low voice. "The fog will soon lift."

Impatiently, Germanicus approached a map of the front. "Please, Aufidius Gnaeus, tell me of the situation here."

"Ah, forgive me, Caesar . . ." And, over the next twenty minutes, Salvidienus neither embellished his successes nor glossed over his errors. He civilly answered even the praetorian prefect's questions, many of which would have been cause for a quarrel but for the lack of an arrogant bone in this general. It was not lost on Germanicus that Gaius Nero was sharing a wink now and again with a few of Salvidienus's subordinates, who no doubt felt themselves hindered by what Germanicus had always admired in Aufidius Gnaeus: his unflappable honesty.

"In those bad days right after the invasion," Salvidienus continued, "it was all we could do to repel the Aztecae short of the petroleum fields. And Caesar, that is not thanks to me but this man here—Claudius Pollio." He pointed to an officer who had been exchanging sniggering glances with Gaius Nero but who now, to his credit, looked ashamed. "Yes, noble Claudius bruised their noses for them. But we met even more stubborn resistance when the enemy found himself pressed between these two estuaries here with the sea to his back. That is when both armies took to the spade."

"Is it within your power to drive them into the waves?" Germanicus asked.

"No," Salvidienus said softly.

"Can *they* drive you back to Otacilium?"

"No," the general said in precisely the same tone of voice.

"Then what will happen?"

Salvidienus's fingers scratched at his thick neck. "Nothing for a long time, unless we can put new pressure on them someplace else, Caesar. Give me two fresh legions and land three more down the coast; why, you'll see the Aztecae hang out their gold mesh banner of truce—"

"I can't do that. The Hibernian rebels and the Gothic Revivalists are waiting like vultures for us to spirit a few of our legions half a world away."

A tribune came drumming down some wooden stairs from a higher level in the underground complex. He sought, then held Salvidienus's eyes. "It begins, sir."

"Yes, yes . . . how sad." Slowly, the general turned to Germanicus. "This is nothing for idle viewing, Caesar. And the vantage platform is quite small. I recommend yourself and your *legatus*."

"I see no need for me to gawk at this." There was a heightened timbre to Gaius Nero's voice. "A dozen reports have acquainted me with their bloody customs."

Germanicus nodded, then looked to Alope. She avoided his gaze. "Rolf will go with me." He approached the steps with a childish sense of trepidation: he had last felt anything like it more than forty years before when, as a boy, he had cowered behind the lime tree in his grandfather's Ostian garden, rubbing with his tiny thumbs the leaves that felt as waxy as the old man's face looked, expecting his mother at any instant to seize him roughly by the hand and pull him back out of hiding to view the orange and blue licks of flame snaking up around the legs of the funeral couch . . .

Salvidienus snuffled a few times, then trumpeted into a handkerchief before motioning for his orderly to bring him a third cup of steaming *cacahuhel*.

Out of his embarrassment for not accompanying Caesar above, Gaius Nero prattled, "You really should not drink from lead vessels, general."

"But these old ones have such a nice heft in the hand."

"And leave a nice toxicity in the blood."

Salvidienus looked profoundly surprised. "What?"

"Yes, I learned this from Epizelus, the emperor's physician. Lead is a splendid poison, and the average patrician already has an inordinate amount of it in his blood from using antique utensils as you do. The Empress Pamphile knew this. She killed dozens simply by giving them small doses of the metal. They were so tiny no one suspected intentional poisoning.''

"Damn her black heart," Salvidienus muttered.

"Whatever—but I'd make it your habit if I were you to drink from glass, gold, or silver.''

"Is nothing safe anymore?''

"Nothing was ever safe, noble general." Gaius Nero tried to say this in a casual manner, but the effect was not enhanced by the trembling of his hands.

Salvidienus was smiling at Alope: "You, daughter, are one of the Anasazi folk, yes?''

"The Indee.''

"I thought so. Remarkable fighters, you Indee.''

"If given the chance to fight.'' Her eyes gravitated toward the planked ceiling of the bunker. "Have the Aztecae raised a temple?''

"Yes. On a spit. They pyramid the sand up during the night, and we blast it down during the day. But that does not stop them.''

"No, it will not. They will quit only when they truly believe that the Fifth Sun is about to be destroyed.''

Salvidienus looked bemused, but did not ask her what she meant. "Perhaps you can answer this, daughter: Why no officers? The unfortunates so far have all been legionaries or Novo militiamen.''

"Your officers have been sent to Tenochtitlan . . . for a more honored death on the Great Temple.''

"Dear Mars.'' The general turned toward footfalls that were descending the stairs. They were plodding, lifeless.

Finally, Rolf drifted down across the landing. There were twin circles of red around his eyes where he had leaned into the rubber grommets of an optical aimer. He halted, appeared to recall something out of a paralyzing distraction, then stared back over his shoulder.

Germanicus had the hesitant gait and pale countenance of a man who has just risen from his sickbed for the first time in months. When he eventually spoke, his voice was husky: "Prefect?''

"Caesar?''

"Return to Rome in my stead.''

Gaius Nero was clearly shaken by the order and could not hide his astonishment. "Aye . . . of course, Caesar.''

"Take the *machinator* from the *Aeneas* with you—what was his name?"

"Fiducio."

"Have him help the *architectus maximus* modify our new quinqueremes until they're equal to the Serican design. Advise the Senate. I want the Third Legion readied to sail here. A force of detached cohorts must cover Hibernia until the Third returns." Germanicus glanced back up the stairs. "Finally, prepare the Roman people in mind and spirit for a broader war than what I first envisaged."

Gaius Nero no longer bothered to suppress his grin.

Salvidienus cleared his throat. "Caesar, will you order only the Third Legion to Nova Baetica?"

"Yes."

"But, by any manner of reckoning you please, we need at least four legions to break this stalemate."

"I believe you, Aufidius Gnaeus." Seemingly on the verge of exhaustion now, Germanicus shuffled past the general to Alope and whispered, "I will speak to your chieftains."

She closed her eyes briefly. "The Anasazi headmen refuse to enter a Roman garrison. They did so once and found themselves hostages. Will you come to the mountains of the Indee?"

Desperately, Germanicus clenched her wrists in his hands. It must have hurt, but her eyes revealed nothing but hope and expectation. "Can my visit remain a secret to all but your highest chiefs?" he asked.

"Yes."

"Then I will go." All at once, he became aware of his anxious hold on her and released his grip. "You were right. Now everything is different. I have *seen*. I wish to Hades I never had."

13

THEY HAD SPENT the morning on the prow deck of the sand-galley. A hot wind squeezed tears to the outer corners of Germanicus's eyes, but he smiled through them at dark green junipers that rolled past on undulations of red earth—a sea of desert that spread out from the dusty scar of the Nova Petra–Otacilium Trace in all directions. To the southwest, a palisade of thunderheads towered over a range of mountains shrouded in a shadow of rain. This, Alope realized with a heartache, was her homeland. But there was much to do before she could sit down at the fires of her people again.

Like all powerful men she had known, Germanicus Agricola became twisted around his dreams as soon as he was free of his burdens. A tender light had come to his face, and he spoke in a quiet voice: "Oh, there's good reason you had difficulty with Latin at the lyceum in Nova Petra, Alope. Latin has difficulty with itself. Take the provincial capital in Anatolia, my old headquarters: in strict classical, it's Antiochia Pisidiae; in Medius Latin, Nova Antiochia; and, in *nova lingua vulgata*, Novo Antioch!"

"But which name does the traveler use?"

"Any of the three—it's up to him. An urbane fellow might use all in the same conversation to show his worldliness."

"That is madness."

"The madness only begins there. Roman first names—"

"*Praenomens*."

Germanicus flashed his self-effacing smile. "That's right. There used to be just a handful of them. But people started

111

using their nomens or cognomens as first names, just to be different, so now the clan and familial meanings of an appellation are utterly confusing even to a Roman." He sighed. "So much could be done . . . but for wars."

"There is nothing else for you," she said. "You are a war chief like Skinyea."

"Isn't your uncle ruler of your people in peacetime?"

"No, he is not even a headman of one of the clans. He has no say over our lives other than in matters of war. This is only because he has great power against enemies. It is so strong all the Anasazi tribes have also accepted him as their war chief. Germanicus Agricola also has this power."

She said this in such a strangely sensuous way it sent gooseflesh down the backs of his arms. He felt proud, confused, embarrassed. "But why do you make a distinction and say I'm just a war leader?"

"Are you not different from Fabius?"

Germanicus did not answer.

"Try to understand this," she went on: "You were chosen to be war chief of the Romans."

"But I was given no mandate for conquest. The Senate never—"

"No, not the patricians, not the plebeians. You were chosen by the spirit bodies, the hidden powers that are inside your people, to lead them in an age of wars. This was done in silent knowledge."

"Are you saying Rome is doomed?"

"Only the Roman Peace." Her gaze darted to an eagle that was hanging against the sun on an updraft. "It is the Aztecae who will know what it is to be truly doomed."

Germanicus grew thoughtful. She could feel it: He was closing into himself like the flower that folds its faded purple petals before the greatest heat of the day. She stole backwards a few steps, smoothly, so the brocade of their company would not be torn all at once.

His fierce-looking bodyguard, who did not sleep nights for fear someone would make a second attempt on Caesar's life, was catnapping atop the *ballista* mount. But when she moved again, it was on a gust of wind, so the centurion would not be alerted.

Below decks, she picked her way down a passageway cluttered with the slumbering forms of the six Anatolians Germanicus had brought along. Showing no interest in the starkly beautiful wilderness lining the trace, they had retired early in the trip to the stuffy interior of the craft, where they dozed, chatted in shrill voices, or sipped tea through pieces of loaf sugar clenched between their teeth.

A hand darted out of the tangle of limbs and seized her ankle. She glared down into the eyes of their young prince.

"A word, sister . . ." Khalid whispered.

She thought to reach for the knife concealed in her legging, but decided to wait a moment longer. "What do you want?"

"It is nothing for myself. I speak on behalf of another—the Compassionate, the Merciful."

Alope sighed: one more Roman outlander hawking his religious wares. "I will listen another time, and then with the fullness of my heart."

"Yes, when your heart lies ready." But Khalid had not released her. "Wait, please."

"I wait." Her eyes narrowed with suspicion.

"I sense in you certain gifts."

"What are you saying?"

"Have you heard of a thing my people call brain-fire?"

"No," she lied, for Germanicus had mentioned a power called *massing*.

"It is to injure or kill one from afar. Do your people know of this thing?"

His grip became ever more insistent, and it was all she could do to keep her eyes outwardly calm. She believed the prince's knowledge to be fledgling, but he had obviously glimpsed inside her. Now she had to satisfy his curiosity in some way. There was no other way to get past him.

"You speak of the shooting sorcery. But it is bad for you to hear about these things. They are for those who are heavy with hatred. I should not tell you about them."

Khalid smiled. "As you wish. It is simply that I had thought so." He freed her and rolled over on his side. His long eyelashes slowly squeezed together. "I had thought so."

Alope stepped over him.

The legionary-operator was too lulled by warm, uneventful miles and the drone of the engine to take notice of her as she ducked and dodged machinery on her way aftward. Pausing at the first hatch, she knew it was locked without testing the lever. In this cabin the Nihonian was kept prisoner, still having received no word that Caesar would accept his services.

Of late, she had been wearing her long, black hair loose. Now she swept it back with her hand so she could press her ear against the iron hatch. Tora was chanting to himself—or at least the sounds he was making reminded her of some Indee invocations. Was he creating an enchantment with a spell? "Ooommm," he intoned again and again. It was quite mournful. Perhaps this was his death song.

The next cabin was Caesar's.

The lock was difficult, but nothing as intricate as the Serican variety that barred secrets in Tenochtitlan. It gave after a few probings with the tip of her knife, and she opened the hatch no more than it took to admit her slight frame. Noiselessly, she closed it again.

Laid out on the bunk was the uniform of a Tenth Legion tribune. To convince Aztecan spies that he was resting in Otacilium after his voyage, Germanicus was posing as the *tribunus aerarius* on his way to the Nova Petra garrison with the military payroll; this would account for the strength of the armored column. His spare uniform was yet fresh, and she buried her face in the cloak, then smiled mischievously. She could still catch his faint scent even after the wool had been fullered.

Then she reminded herself that it was not safe to linger here. Her movements became hurried but remained confident.

Lifting a corner of the light mattress, she removed the small hide pouch that had lain hidden there and replaced it with a similar one she had secreted inside her deerskin tunic. She reassured herself that the four sky-stones were still in place, indicating the cardinal directions. At last, she shut her eyes, softly repeated a musical phrase four times—her voice so fervent she seemed on the verge of tears—then reset the lock and sifted forward through the sand-galley again.

Germanicus did not mean to ignore Alope, but her quiet prophecy of the death of *Pax Romana* had stirred such dire worries in him he soon forgot her presence.

As feared, he had been trapped by the Novo Provinces —and swiftly, too. Now it was incumbent upon him to gain some kind of victory over Maxtla before he could return to Rome. After being humiliated at the battle of the Mare Aztecum, he must recapture some of his strength. Strength was authority, and he could never hope to restore the republic without it. Germanicus Agricola would have to remain a formidable Caesar until the instant of his abdication . . . or perish in the machinations of some noble who dreamed of soaring on imperial wings.

Yet he had not fully embraced the idea of driving on Tenochtitlan. It staggered his military sensibilities, but he decided to reserve final judgment until he could size up the Anasazi for himself. And there was always the possibility that he might convince Alope's uncle, Skinyea, to help Rome dislodge the Aztecae from Nova Baetica.

If only he might hit upon some fatal weakness in the enemy, but so far they had conducted their operations in a stalwart and courageous manner. According to Salvidienus, their attacks were often launched with pell-mell abandon, but this was to be expected of barbarian troops—and these howling advances had nevertheless bloodied the more disciplined legionaries time and again.

Eager to pursue this line of thought, Germanicus turned toward Alope. "On what do you—" He stopped short.

She was smiling at him from across the deck as if she had been contemplating his face for some time—with great pleasure.

He fought down the delight that tried to flash across his cheekbones. "On what do you base your opinion that the Aztecan Empire is doomed?"

"It is not mine, but that of Aztecae themselves."

"What?"

"To understand you must know the legend of the Fifth Sun."

Germanicus nodded gravely. "Then tell me."

"The Aztecae believe that four worlds, or suns, have come and gone before. Each was destroyed by great violence . . . " In a sad, almost plodding voice, she told him how the fifth and final sun had been stillborn and darkness stood poised to engulf the heavens forever. Only the labor and sacrifice of certain gods had finally set the golden fire of Tonatiuh into motion across the skies. Some said it was Ehecatl, the wind-god manifestation of Quetzalcoatl, who salvaged the Fifth Sun; others said it was Quetzalcoatl as his feathered serpent self; and a minority credited Nanauatzin, the syphilitic diety—these distant saviors varied according to the prejudices of each

Aztecan clan. However, the balky Fifth Sun still would not rise and set without benefit of nourishment: the preferred elixir was that of human blood and hearts, for which the sun grew increasingly ravenous as time passed. Still, the inevitable could not be postponed forever: the Fifth Sun, like the four preceding it, would fall to catastrophe. As a race, the Aztecae awaited this with a mixture of resignation and an apprehension that anything but moderate and virtuous behavior would bring the end sooner than later.

Alope finished in a hoarse whisper: "Fear makes them seem gentle. In truth, they are not so. They are murderous. And never more so than now."

"Why is that?" Germanicus persisted.

"The Fifth Sun will not die unexpectedly. The danger that it will not rise again comes every fifty-two years. That time is coming soon, and the Aztecae tremble in their hearts at its approach."

"When exactly will this be?"

"At the Ceremony of New Fire. Four days after your Saturnalia."

"Late December . . ." Germanicus realized that he had been infected by the sorrow that was suddenly oppressing her. He had no desire to go deeper into it. He traveled on his gaze to a snow-tipped cone, tiny in the far north. "The eye can really gallop away on this country."

She smiled, and he found himself wanting to hold her.

"And you have not seen the best. You have not yet seen the mountains of the Indee."

The trace began deserving its name as it wound and buckled down into a chasm, losing the resemblance to a well-engineered Roman road it had had for the first five hundred miles out of Otacilium.

The lead sand-galley overtook a lone figure, who had elected to walk through the brush rather than churn up the powdery dust of the trace with his Novo boots. He did not glance at the file of huge machines that roared past him. Stare locked on the western horizon, he continued loping through the sage at what seemed an effortless pace.

"Cornificius!" Alope shrieked, giving Germanicus a start. "Cornelius!"

Wary black eyes clicked toward the prow deck, and then a grin split the matted beard. His black hair was curly like a

Phoenician's, but the man had the animal grace of a new barbarian.

"Caesar, please, may we halt?" Alope was tugging at his arm. "He is a friend. I will not reveal who you are."

"Very well, but which is he: Cornificius or Cornelius?"

"I cannot decide yet."

Looking slightly bewildered, Germanicus gave the signal, and the craft slowed as the wild man slung his antique *pilum* over his shoulder and clambered up to hug Alope. She examined his indelibly soiled hands, then cried, "Cornificius!"

"Aye!" he growled, and they immediately began chattering in Indee.

Germanicus couldn't recall one man capable of serving up so many strong odors to his acquaintances, and he'd thought the Hibernian nobility remarkable for this kind of banquet. Through it all came a faint whiff of olive oil, the substance Cornificius had probably used to train his mustaches into long, glistening cords that he had tucked behind his ears.

"Tribune," Alope said to Germanicus, "I introduce you to brave Cornificius, who years ago sat around the fires of the Indee many times."

"A singular pleasure, I'm sure," Germanicus murmured.

Cornificius gave him a disdainful glance, then hoisted Alope off the deck with his sinewy arms to make her laugh.

Rolf had started to swing his legs over the edge of the *ballista* mount when Germanicus halted him with an outstretched hand. Germanicus sensed that this strange creature was basically shy but could be aroused to swift violence if challenged. "What tribe are you?" he asked, hoping Alope would translate if necessary.

Cornificius looked as if he'd been asked to name the last fifty kings of Parthia. His eyes had begun to water, and his lips slowly thinned. "Sicilian."

Some new barbarian bands had adopted Romanized names for themselves, and Germanicus wondered if the *Sicilians* might be one of these—although the man was far from hairless like most new barbarians. "I mean, what do your people call themselves in their own tongue?"

"*Calvii.*" The man now sounded irked. "What would they call me then but *Calvii*?"

"*You* were born on the isle of Sicilia in the Mare Nostrum?"

"Nay, nay, nay—me *pater* and *mater* be, I say."

A fly crawled out of Cornificius's beard and up a nostril. Germanicus did not breathe again until it emerged and buzzed away. "Then you, my friend, were born in Nova Baetica of Sicilian parents?"

"Almost *maximus*, by your Jove." Cornificius was now resorting to an accompaniment of hand signs. "Me *patria*"—he thumped his chest, then circled the area of his genitals—"be in Anasazi *pochs*. Me *Romulo et Remo* be Anasazi *pochs* now. And you be *bichan*?"

"I'm sorry, I don't understand . . ."

"He is telling you," Alope jumped in, "his parents were traders to the Anasazi tribes. He and his twin brother consider themselves to be Anasazi, not Sicilian. Do you see the difference?"

"Ah . . . " Germanicus's eyes brightened. "And *pochs* —from the Nahuatl *pochteca*."

"Yes."

"And what does *bichan* mean?"

Alope swallowed a giggle, but it came up again. "It is not important."

"Surely it's important if you—"

She had whispered to Cornificius, and now they both were laughing. Then the two resorted to Indee again, and Germanicus faced back into the wind. He felt taunted by her prettiness and the intimacy of language she was sharing with the unbathed Novo, but he steeled himself to appear indifferent, even bored, as Alope and Cornificius prated in soft words he imagined to be slurs.

"Tribune?" Alope said after a while, something new in her voice: an imperativeness.

Germanicus yawned. "Yes, what is it?"

Alope led the Novo by the hand to Caesar's side. "Cornificius is just now returning from a journey of three years. He saw things that will interest you."

"Where did you go?" Germanicus asked him directly.

Cornificius poked a jagged fingernail toward the north. "*Maximus* this range—"

"Hold, my friend," Germanicus interrupted. "Your Latin is too inventive for me. Alope, would you please?"

"Cornificius and his brother Cornelius followed these mountains far to the north. It was to find beaver." Her eyes smiled briefly. "He is angry you Romans will not wear furs. This keeps the prices low."

"That's something he can take up with the Germans and Britons." Germanicus was referring to the fact that northern provincials would rather shiver in silk gowns than be out of style with Tiber-side dinner parties, and the temperate Italian climate did not encourage the wearing of furs.

"The second year, after piling up many pelts, they were captured by new barbarians who sold them into slavery."

"To whom?"

"The Sericans."

Germanicus did not blink for several seconds. "Are you certain he meant the Sericans?"

"He used the Indee words for Makers of Silk. I am certain."

"Damn—where was this?"

"Their captors canoed them many weeks down a great river that became as wide as the sea. The night before they reached the salt waters, Cornificius looked westward; he thought the stars had fallen to earth and were burning whitely in the forest. But when they reached this place the next evening, he saw that these were Serican torches that did not smoke."

"Good Jupiter," Germanicus whispered to himself, "they've got *electricus motive*."

"He spent many months of hardship a prisoner in the Serican *presidium*, then escaped and made his long way home."

"How?"

"He *escaped*," Alope said with finality, as if it would be impolite to make further inquiries about the incident.

Cornificius reached inside his fur tunic to scratch his bare chest. His ribs were jacketed by an ample layer of fat. "What be new among Fabius?" he asked.

"Caesar Fabius is dead more than a year now," Alope said.

"Aye? Who be Caesar?"

Alope teased Germanicus with a brief silence. "His name is Germanicus. He's in Otalicium to make war against the Aztecae."

The Novo accepted this news with a slight nod, then tucked a strand of beard in the corner of his mouth and began chewing. Alope and he became quiet, their eyes lowered to the deck. After several moments, Germanicus sensed that there was nothing happenstance about this lapse in the conversation; only later did he learn from Alope that it was a necessary ritual in a country where death, inevitably, was reported at every reunion. The sharing of sorrow was deferred by both parties until all good tidings had been exchanged. The alternative was to have no joy at all in meeting an old friend.

"Me *Romulo et Remo* be no more," Cornificius said at last.

"How did he lose his earth body?"

"Fire-thirst disease."

"Yes, I understand. I say no more." Suddenly, Alope's eyes were spawning tears faster than she could blink them away.

Cornificius took her hands. His rough appearance accentuated the gentleness of this gesture. "You *maritus* and *filius*—among the Indee?"

"No, I speak their names no more." She leaned forward from the waist as if her back had been mounted by some massive anguish. Twisting her trunk from side to side, she wrestled to free herself of it.

"Flowery Way?" Cornificius asked gravely.

"Yes. I say no more." Then, to Germanicus's abashment, Alope started laughing through her tears. She stood upright once again, and everything about her denied the existence of that recent grief. "Will you come with us to Nova Petra?"

"Nay, Anasazi *primus*, I say . . ."

Linking her arm through Germanicus's, Alope heard Cornificius out and then translated: "He will visit friends in the Anasazi Federation before coming to the garrison. He plans to serve with the Novo militia until next spring."

"Militiamen enlist for five years," Germanicus said automatically.

"Cornificius knows that. He would not join at all, except that he needs a new *pilum* before he goes trapping again."

"But that weapon would be imperial property—" Germanicus gave up and watched with joined eyebrows as Cornificius embraced Alope in farewell. He delayed the Novo as the man was on the verge of swinging his leg over the side of the prow deck: "I would like to hear more about your experiences among the Sericans."

"Nay." Then Cornificius dropped down into the dust wreathing the tracks of the sand-galley and vanished.

14

THE ATRIUM OF the praetorian commander's villa was a cool island of Roman luxury in a sun-baked wilderness. Dangling his feet into the waters of the fountain after having enjoyed a first-rate bath, Germanicus might have imagined himself in Ostia but for the cliffs, raucous orange and red, that shone through the colonnade on the garden side of the mansion. "Then Britannicus Musa is no longer here in Nova Petra?" he asked, following a pleasant lull in conversation during which he'd nibbled succulent grapes off the stem.

"Not within the garrison itself, Caesar." The commander seemed a capable sort with a forthright manner made possible, no doubt, by his long absence from Rome. "I can take you to him, if that's what you want."

Germanicus nodded as he crushed more grapes between his teeth. "Were you able to get anything useful out of the colonel before the onset of his condition?"

"He arrived here on a litter borne by new barbarians. He was already out of his head."

"How deranged is he?"

"Hopelessly, Caesar. We tried treating him in our hospital. But he kept running away—on the advice of spirit voices, so he told us. Our patrols would find him out in the pinelands, sunburned, feet torn by rocks, nearly dead from thirst and hunger. When we attempted to transfer him to Otacilium, he worked his bonds loose and jumped from the sand-galley, breaking his wrist. I felt bad about imprisoning him with common criminals. After all, he *is* a colonel. So, in the end, I let him go where he chose."

"Which was?"

The commander rose from his couch and invited Germanicus to follow him out into the late afternoon heat.

Germanicus was squeezed between Rolf and the commander on the hard rear bench as the lorry puttered across the *castrum*. Here, years before, legionaries had slept under canvas and maintained sharp watches for marauding Indee. But now the old encampment was a quiet parade ground grazed by long shadows, its dust pelted with huge raindrops from a rogue thunderhead in an otherwise flawless desert sky.

When the smoky discharge of the engine wasn't billowing over him, Germanicus could see that Nova Petra was aptly named after the famed Nabataean "Rose City": the reddish stone faces of the palisades enclosing the garrison east and west had been skillfully carved into the appearance of a respectable forum. In bas-relief stood the majestic fronts of a curia, basilica, and Jovian temple, although the Cambrian miners had not yet tunneled out the chambers behind these facades to turn them into functional buildings. The commander promised that this was coming in due time. Even now, under the bits of clattering pneumatic tools, the florid Corinthian columns to a new praetorian headquarters were rising to the light of day out of a sheen of rock dust.

"Eventually, tribune," the commander shouted, careful to preserve Caesar's incognito, "all our facilities will be underground—like at Agri Dagi, if you recall."

"I recall," Germanicus said quietly.

At the north gate, the commander motioned for a reinforcement of two praetorians to jump upon the cowling boards. From that heavily guarded opening, a road sloped down through a desolation of red shingle to a creek shaded by sycamores. Although shadows dappled the ground only feet from where they squatted, a dozen new barbarians chose to remain in the brassy sunlight, as if to tell the legionaries manning the battlements that they, unlike Romans, were not slaves to their own comfort. They were armed with nothing more than knives, but Germanicus had no doubt these stocky, dour-looking men were warriors. As if in uniform, each wore a linen tunic, a kiltlike loincloth belted at the midriff, and soft boots that rose nearly to the knee. Bushy hair was worn shoulder-length and held in place by a thick headband.

Alope stood talking in their midst, but Germanicus would

have known even without her presence that these were the Indee.

"Say," the commander said, "isn't that the woman Alope
speaking to those warriors?"

Germanicus paused, pretending to search her out. "Why
yes, it appears it is. What business could she possibly have
with that hard-looking lot?"

"I'm going to make it *mine* to find out."

Germanicus resisted a smile.

Alope glanced up from a strident argument involving
several warriors at once. Her face was calm, and from that
Germanicus gathered that all was going according to plan. She
had told him that the Indee considered no course of action
truly settled upon unless ratified by a quarrel or two. After
this, there was no such thing as dissent.

At dawn, she had stolen out of Nova Petra to contact her
people who would escort Germanicus to the Indee heartland.
Now she and the warriors paid no attention to the passing of
Roman officialdom and went on with their discussion.

The lorry splashed across a ford. Spray shot up from the
tracks and fell across the sun like fire opals, sweet as they
broke against Germanicus's lips. The canyon began closing in
on the road; deep purple buttes loomed higher and higher
through a canopy of dusty oak leaves, the level summits
fringed with dark conifers. "This is singular country," Germanicus said. "I don't know quite what to liken it to."

"I've heard it compared to Arabia Petraea in some respects
and northern Iberia in others." The commander smiled with
something akin to affectionate pride. "But, yes, tribune,
nothing's quite like it."

"Still, you must be looking forward to a posting at the
Campus Martius."

"I've turned down rotation twice. This seems like home
now."

"I see," Germanicus said without enthusiasm: he wanted
no Roman to become too fond of Nova Petra, despite its
haunting beauties. If the quest to restore the republic brought
civil war, remote outposts such as this would have to be abandoned. Suddenly, he wanted badly to tell this loyal praetorian
that Rome must shrink to grow; some imperial provinces
might have to be ceded in order to consolidate power around
the resuscitated Senate. But such a discussion was not possible
without jeopardizing thousands of lives and perhaps the res-

toration itself. Masticated by the loneliness of this secret, his mind turned to other matters. "I have a favor to ask of you."

"Simply name your pleasure, tribune."

"How keen is your grasp on Seneca?"

"Ah . . . passable."

"Complete this for me: 'I would rather you brought about some harmony in my mind and . . .' "

" 'And...' " The commander grinned with relief. " '...and got my thoughts into tune.' "

"Yes," Germanicus sighed. "That's what I hunger to do." There were so many new things to consider. All of them so dangerous. I'd like the use of some undisturbed place—"

"Allow me the honor of vacating my villa."

"How kind of you. But I mean some place entirely out of the way. Comfort should be no consideration. It's silence I need."

The commander held his lower lip between his teeth for several moments. "Well, on a peak six miles south of the garrison we maintain a helio-flash station. It's really just an oversized hut. And the wind howls around it day and night."

"Excellent—just what I had in mind. My staff and I will retire there this evening. Please evacuate your people."

"May I ask for how long, tribune?"

"Two weeks should do."

"As you order." The commander sat back in silence, no more pleased than Marcus Gracchus had been at losing the opportunity to entertain the emperor.

Germanicus was surprised to learn that the Tenth Legion still had the helio-flash communicator in service. This device of precisely angled mirrors antedated both the Fabian *impulsus*-wire and the wireless of a decade later. At one time, the crowns of the Apenninus Range had sparkled with a string of them all the way to the Rhaetian frontier, where their glittering messages were abruptly dumped into a mounted courier station because the Alps were considered too vapor-shrouded for machines that relied on consistent sunlight. "I haven't seen a helio-flasher in ages," Germanicus chuckled. "And things were fairly primitive in eastern Anatolia."

"They're perfect for our situation." The commander clutched the brass side-rail as the lorry pitched headlong across the creek again. "Indee raiding parties, we suspect, keep cutting the wire we've strung. And our wireless is really boxed in by these endless walls of mountains. It's reliable only at night—if there's no storm. We have five helio-flash stations. The main collector here, of course, and the others sixty miles distant, one on each primary point of the *index*."

"Shut them down until I order otherwise. Restrict their surveillance to what is necessary to protect the stations."

The commander was of the old school: he immediately bottled up his surprise and said, "Aye, tribune." His nostrils were dilated, and he sniffed twice, loudly: woodsmoke was lingering in the gloom between the scruffy oaks. "Guardsmen, charge your *pili*."

There were brisk clacking noises as the praetorians and Rolf readied their weapons.

Among mounds of brush Germanicus only gradually recognized to be dwellings, he began to see hunched figures tending smudgy fires, shuffling as they moved, taking no interest in the lorry as it invaded their encampment.

Suddenly, the operator swerved: a woman was lying unconscious in the road, her arms open to the sky.

"What kind of place is this?" Germanicus demanded, displeased that no attempt had been made to check on the woman's condition.

"The legionaries call it the 'Valley of the Shades.'" Then the commander drew the attention of the guardsmen on the cowling boards to a warrior hunkering atop a boulder. The new barbarian's eyes seemed excessively moist, almost lascivious. His fingers plucked at his bowstring as if it were some kind of musical instrument. "Slay that one if he draws an arrow from his quiver."

"Aye," Rolf grumbled, swinging his *pilum* across Germanicus's face to take aim.

But the warrior cackled and flung his bow in the uppermost boughs of a juniper, and the lorry continued up the canyon unmolested.

The commander shook his head in disgust. "As soon as we vanquish a rebellious clan, the survivors drift here . . . and slowly wither in the shadow of our garrison."

"Do you mean certain plebeian elements of that clan?"

Caesar's nuance was not lost on the commander, also of patrician family: Germanicus was comparing these tribesmen to the Roman plebs on the *annona*, the imperial food subsidy, which had become so inclusive wine and lungweed were now counted among its long list of staples. "No, tribune, I mean even the nobility of a clan. With spirits readily available from the garrison shops, the distinction between good and bad is quickly eroded."

"Then we should deprive them of intoxicants. Who is the factor financing this trade?"

The commander paused. "A slave named Remmius."

Germanicus sensed the dodge that was burrowed deep in the officer's hesitancy: every Roman of good breeding retained a slave to handle his business affairs, which were considered too vulgar for a patrician's concern. In naming the slave, the commander was not revealing the noble whose money and influence were behind the commerce. "Please, I have always relied on frank subordinates."

The commander exhaled. "Marcus Gracchus."

"The proconsul?" Germanicus asked needlessly. He would say nothing more about the matter for—in his mind—there was only one way to correct the excesses of imperial government: restore the republic. He ached in silence for the day.

The lorry rattled to a stop before a round hovel that was half-buried in the earth. The operator had just bled the pneumatic brake, venting a loud reptilian hiss, when a middle-aged woman charged out of the darkened portal of the structure, whooshing a heavy club in full circle around her as she loosed oath after oath on the Romans. Rolf and the two praetorians divided her angry attention long enough to disarm her.

"What's her quarrel with us?" Germanicus asked the commander.

"She says we come to take her man. She promises to kill us first." The officer then ordered the guardsmen to bind her, explaining to Germanicus that she had gone too far, even for the diminished standards of the Valley of the Shades. She would have to be remanded to the stockade for flagellation. "Follow me, tribune, if you wish. But, believe me, you'll itch for another bath afterwards."

"Let me go in alone."

To enter the gloaming of the hovel, Germanicus had to step over a shank bone that was squirming with maggots. The stench within told him that this kind of filth pervaded the shadowy space. A figure squatted on the dirt floor a few inches behind a spill of smoky light that flowed down from an aperture in the sheaths of bark that formed the roof.

As Germanicus waited for his eyes to adjust to the dimness, he could hear Rolf pacing outside the portal, his military cadence transmitting impatience and worry through the ground.

"Well, well. Come in, Caesar," Britannicus Musa rasped as if this was just one more phantasm in an endless parade of them. He lifted a gourd to his scowling lips. His forearm was pustulated with running sores and bandaged at the wrist with gray linen. His hair was just beginning to fade in around a purplish crease on his scalp. "You've come too late, you know," he said after a noisy gulp. "We have already dined. *All* have eaten, partaken of the flesh this wilderness serves up to the innocent."

"I have come to ask you for your help, Colonel Musa."

Britannicus covered his eyes with a hand and gasped, "No, no. You've come too early. I'm not ready. I'll give Caesar this instead—" Savagely, he yanked a fistful of wispy beard off his cheek and let it flutter down onto Germanicus's bare knees.

Germanicus slapped him across the jaw.

Britannicus glowered back at him. "That was not kindly. And I loved you more dearly than myself, Gaius Julius Caesar Octavianus."

Germanicus struck him again, but less sharply this time. "You know I'm not Augustus. Who am I, Colonel Musa?"

"I have only to look upon a new coin to know that. You are Germanicus Julius Agricola."

"That's right, my friend," Germanicus grasped the man's shoulder, although the spot had just been vacated by a skittering black thing. "I have urgent need of what you know about the Aztecae."

"Ha! Damn you, ha!" Britannicus barked laughter in Germanicus's startled face. "I am so sick of this self-righteous inquiry into the savage Aztecae! Oh, and *magnified* are we, who in the name of sport cheer when limbs are hacked off living forms, when throats are cut and heads wriggle down the gullets of lions!" Then his eyes lost their violent glimmer. "We don't even have the good sense to eat what we slaughter."

Gently, Germanicus began kneading the colonel's bony shoulder. "My friend, my son, I summon you to my cause. I beg Jupiter to give you a contented mind."

Britannicus locked gazes with him, his head tremulous on the spindly stem of his neck. Then he slowly leaned his face against the back of Germanicus's hand. He wept bitterly, helplessly. "Yes, I want to . . . but I require a day or two. To restore myself, you see. To become *peninsular* again, you see. Just a day or two."

"You shall have longer than that. I'll be occupied with other matters for two weeks. During that fortnight, you are to remain inside the garrison hospital. Failure to obey the physicians will be considered insubordination toward me; escape will be treated as desertion. Do you understand your emperor?"

Sniffling, Britannicus let go of Germanicus's hand and nodded. Then, absently, he popped a small green bud from the bowl into his mouth and began chewing.

"What is that?" Germanicus demanded.

"Sweet escape from this body, Caesar."

"Spit it out."

Britannicus's jaw stopped moving. He spat onto the coals of the fire.

Outside the hovel, Germanicus stood still as the commander inspected his uniform for vermin. The praetorians were left with the unpleasant task of shouldering Britannicus to the lorry.

"Quite an improvement," the commander said under his breath. "What's the secret to your cure?"

"This isn't one. He just wanted an authority stronger than himself to punish the demons inside him. His satisfaction won't last long."

"Then shouldn't we be at Colonel Musa with our questions?"

"No," Germanicus said, "exhaustion will only make his condition more obdurate. I still have hopes for his recovery."

"I fear my physicians don't."

"Did they prescribe strong spirits?"

"All Musa wanted. What can better route the doldrums than *aqua vitae*?"

"Order the practice stopped. And let him ingest nothing but wholesome foods."

"Aye, tribune."

"I say this on the advice of Epizelus, my own physician. I'll give you one of his potions to be administered to Britannicus Musa thrice daily." Germanicus didn't add that Epizelus had invented the remedy to relieve Caesar's own periodic bouts with melancholy.

The ride back to the garrison through the gathering dusk was all the more jolting because the operator was rushing to be rid of the two new passengers. Whenever both hands were not required to steady the steering lever, he pinched his nostrils shut with his fingers.

As the lorry idled in the light of the north gate and the commander assured the centurion there with a password that he was indeed the commander, Germanicus studied Britannicus's woman. Out of the corner of his eye, he glimpsed that Rolf was doing the same. Nudging the German, he asked softly, "Who would you say she resembles?"

"The daughter Alope—it be striking."

"Yes . . . Alope."

Although he could not possibly have heard from where he slumped on the front bench, Britannicus awoke from a deep swoon at the whispering of this name and slid his frail arm around the new barbarian woman's shoulders. Her bindings prevented her from returning the embrace. The commander had explained that she was a prostitute of so rancorous a temperament she had been banished by her own people, the Yudaha, a tribe of the same ancestral blood as the Indee. But now she lovingly rubbed her nose up and down Britannicus's scraggly jawline.

If there was any tenderness between diverse peoples, it seemed to come only when all pride and advantage had been stripped away by misfortune. It blossomed only after the victorious spirit had been desolated. But Germanicus quickly rebuked himself for comparing this harlot to Alope. In fact, this woman was nothing like Alope: everything bold and handsome in her had been scoured away by years of dissipation. Still, the conundrum reared up through Germanicus's unrest: Why, when two cultures converge on the same ground, must one be shattered? Why couldn't they blend perfectly into a fresh synthesis without one predominating? Was this all too much to ask of a swaggering little mammal? These were un-Roman thoughts, he decided, as the lorry crept between clutches of legionaries out on the *castrum* to enjoy the coolness of the evening and their wineskins.

Then, unexpectedly, it came to him: He was thankful Alope had a fierce pride.

15

IT HAD ALWAYS been a singular pleasure to pack before taking to the field. There was something gratifying and completely absorbing about the small tasks; time passed lightly for Germanicus, and after a while he looked around the villa chamber for an antique water clock, the requisite adornment for tasteful guest quarters in the provinces. But there was none.

The evening star had risen. It hovered, unpulsing, at the center of the window. The glazing had been removed for the torrid summer months, and he felt he could reach right through the casement and seize Venus, who was cloaked in the robin's-egg blue seen only above pristine deserts such as this.

Dear Jupiter, he smiled to himself, *how I love taking to the field—what coltish joy arises in this old stallion!* But another thought quickly sobered him: *Have we Romans conquered half the world simply to satisfy our own restlessness?*

Some minutes before he had rediscovered among his things the olive branch he had snapped off his son's tree in Ostia. The brittle leaves were curled from their immersion in boiling water aboard the *Aeneas*. His lips tightened. Perhaps a token like this acquired value only when it was held in hopelessness. And ever since that dawn in Salvidienus's bunker, when he had witnessed Maxtla's priests ripping living hearts from the chests of Romans, Germanicus had entertained little hope of peace with the Aztecae. But he didn't crush those damaged leaves and fling them into the cold light of the star. Carefully, he put them away. His fuller had risked his life aboard the sinking trireme to save Caesar's personal possessions, although none of them mattered to Germanicus . . . except this withered link with his son.

A sandal scraped the flagstones somewhere out in the courtyard. Then the only sound was that of crickets working around the edges of the sharp silence.

Germanicus retrieved his short sword from the couch and quietly inched his way back to the window. He could sense the presence of a breathing thing on the opposite side of the casement. "Show yourself," he said over the point of his blade.

A lightly bearded face topped by a *jamadani* glided into view.

"Khalid!"

"I am sorry to present myself in such a manner, *pasa*."

The young prince had only his dagger, which was tucked in his cumberbund. But Brutus and Cassius had had only their daggers the day they cut down Gaius Julius Caesar at the foot of Pompey's statue. "Do you mean me harm this evening?" Germanicus asked quietly.

Khalid's eyes widened. "No, *pasa*! I have sworn!"

"Then swear again that you intend no treachery, but in the name of your god this time."

"Yes, I do so in the name of He who formed men from clots of blood!"

Germanicus sheathed his sword, as satisfied as he could ever be. "Then why do you seek an audience this way?"

"It is because of your bodyguard, the big Goth: he denies me a path to you."

Germanicus pulled the youth through the window by the hand. "You now have my ear."

"*Pasa*, before leaving the city of Otacilium, I received a letter from my father, the holiest of men—"

"How is he?"

"Most excellent." Khalid's brief smile faded. "But he has asked me to give an accounting of how many infidels I have slain. What can I tell him?"

"Tell the Great *Zaim* I won't waste the life of my friend's last surviving son on needless adventures."

"But when may I expect to spill blood?"

Germanicus returned to readying his kit; he cinched down a strap with the dexterity of a veteran legionary. "I was about to send word to you. Say nothing to anyone, but have your men prepared in an hour for a journey of two weeks. It's for this purpose I brought you and your best fighters to Nova Petra."

"*Inshallah!*"

"Yes . . . let us hope your god wills it."

Khalid began to climb back through the window but, on a sudden thought, turned from the perch of the casement, his eyes troubled. "*Pasa*, another matter, if I might speak frankly."

"The gods forbid. Yes, yes, go on."

"Beware of the infidel woman, Alope."

Germanicus's eyes flared at him. "What are you saying?"

"She has knowledge . . ."

"About what?" Germanicus asked when Khalid hesitated.

"Many hidden things."

"Khalid—"

"There was such a woman in the Purple Village once. She could make men do things. Even against their will." Then he leaped into the courtyard and could be heard trotting away.

The cool night wind tumbled down from higher on the peak, bearing tatters of conversation and laughter from the helio-flash station. It whistled over the sharp edges of rocks and was diced into a breathy soughing by the needles of a pinion pine, beneath which Germanicus and Rolf stood waiting.

Downslope, perhaps more than a hundred paces distant, a coyote yelped five times. "That's it," Germanicus whispered. "Something Alope told me to remember— This kind of wolf does not bark more than four times in succession."

Rolf nodded thoughtfully, then recoiled suddenly when he realized that the woman had materialized at his elbow. "By what manner of magic—?"

Briefly, she sealed the centurion's lips with her fingers as she crossed in front of him to approach Germanicus. "Silence and shadow are magic enough."

The wind had now died.

"Damn them!" Germanicus pointed downward.

On the plain far below, torch beams were bumping along the ground. Ever mindful of Caesar's safety, the commander was deploying praetorians around the base of the peak. Their lights gradually formed an arc, then stopped moving.

Alope was gazing up at Germanicus in the weak starshine.

"Will you still go?"

"I can't have all of Nova Petra alerted to my absence."

"I will see to it."

"How?"

"It is nothing. I have overcome worse. Gather the rest at this tree and await my return." Then, her feet scarcely disturbing an old talus slide, she descended the slope and quickly dropped out of sight.

Germanicus and Rolf hiked back up to the station, engulfed by a gale once again as they neared the helio-flasher on the very summit. The battens joining its mirrors were groaning like the timbers of a wooden galley despite a web of wind-strummed guys that secured the device to the ground.

A din from the station sifted through these sounds, loud enough to make Rolf remark, "A harder wind blows inside."

Germanicus strode into the hut and silenced his staff, who were in a furious debate over which one of three final candidates—the imperial fuller, signals officer, or scribe—most resembled Caesar himself and might plausibly double as the mysterious *tribunus aerarius*. "Let the emperor decide!" someone cried, and others took up the cheer until Germanicus relented and began strolling among his subordinates, flitting his head hawkishly from side to side. He got a few sniggers when he closely examined the Nihonian's features: "The nose is not Roman enough." The lantern-jawed fuller was told he had "nice bones." But, before the laughter had completely died away, Germanicus held up his hands and said, "The truth is, all three can each have a turn at it. I have the commander's reluctant word that no one will come up to this aerie for the next two weeks."

"How can we be assured that Caesar will be safe in the desert?" a voice asked earnestly.

"We cannot," Germanicus said, "for we are not the gods. But let me share with you that I have no presentiment of evil as I depart. I would not go unless I felt it vital to our interests. Hail and be well, my friends, until our next meeting."

"Hail Caesar!" his staff cried.

Marching swiftly across the hut so no one might glimpse how moved he had been by this, Germanicus greeted Tora, who, despite his polite smile, appeared to be confused by such garrulous company. "How are you faring?"

"I do well, Lord Caesar." The Nihonian's Latin showed marked improvement. "I am most indebted to Belgius for . . . for his . . ."

"Patience," the scribe whispered.

"His patience, yes."

Germanicus winked at Belgius, and the scribe gave a knowing nod before withdrawing. The emperor turned back to Tora. "Last night, I read your first report on Maxtla's defenses. I found it admirably thorough. I'm looking forward to your commentary on the Serican renovation of the Tepeyaca and Acachinanco fortresses."

"Progress slow—I apologize, Lord Caesar. We must use often Baluchi to understand, Belgius and I."

"That's fine. You have another two weeks in which to complete this task."

Tora held a deep bow. "Lord Caesar, one matter more, I beg to you—"

"You wouldn't be thinking of this, would you?"

Belgius hurried back from one of the sleeping cubicles with Tora's sword. He gave it to Germanicus, who then returned it to the Nihonian with a much abbreviated version of the *sacramentum*, the military oath of allegiance: "I commission you a tribune in the Tenth Legion, Tora."

"Tora-*san*, Caesar," Belgius said. "It is a designation of honor in his country."

"And so it shall be here as well . . . Tora-*san*."

Tora would have bowed even deeper had Germanicus not reached out and grasped his hand Roman-style. Startled, the Nihonian nevertheless beamed. "I thank Lord Caesar. I will him serve with . . ." His eyes darted to the scribe's lips.

"Loyalty will do nicely," Belgius said.

"Loyalty will do nicely," Tora echoed.

"I'm sure it will." Then Germanicus motioned for Rolf to join him in the chamber where they had stored their field kits. They changed out of their uniforms into simple brown tunics and heavy trousers of the type once favored on campaign by the Imperial Gothic Cavalry. Novo boots replaced military sandals. "Well, centurion," Germanicus said, "are you ready for this?"

"Aye, overdue. I stink of palaces."

"I, too."

Khalid and his five hand-picked tribesmen were already outside, squatting in the lee of the hut, the coals of their lungweed winking on and off. The young prince was carefully reading the stars for omens of the coming weather when he stood and grinned at Caesar's approach.

"Come," Germanicus said, "we go."

The Anatolians followed without a word.

This was the total strength of Caesar's visitation to the Anasazi Federation: six barbarians from Asia Minor, a German centurion, and himself. These tribes already understood the extent of Roman brawn, and a show of force would serve only to draw the notice of Aztecan spies. *Besides*, he admitted to himself, *the real satisfaction lies in having hoodwinked the entire praetorian guard and gone on holiday without them breathing down my neck!*

Then he reminded himself that he was not free of the praetorian octopus yet.

Alope stood beside the pine, listening to the activity below.

The torches of the guardsmen were no longer lit, but spades could be heard attacking the stony ground. True to eternal Roman regimen, they were entrenching their positions for the night.

"What's your plan?" Germanicus asked her.

"In a moment, Caesar, it will become clear."

And, while he waited for he knew not what, Germanicus felt the back of her hand tap softly against his twice. Smiling, he did not budge. A moment later, she seized his hand and held it tightly.

A trumpet blared from the far slope of the mountain. Germanicus was bewildered: the call was summoning the troops to assemble for further orders. It was absurd to gather soldiers who had already been strung out along a perimeter, but no guardsman would dare disobey the signal. Voices groused back and forth across the shadows as the praetorians abandoned their half-dug earthworks and filed in silhouette toward the sound of the trumpet.

"My people are ready now," Alope said.

"How do you suddenly know that?"

"It is not sudden. My cousin told me to wait for the trumpet."

"You mean you slipped through the praetorian perimeter?"

"Yes, Caesar, twice. But that was not the hard part." She began picking her footing down the steep mountainside, waving impatiently for the others to fall in behind her.

Germanicus was appalled that she had breezed through an elite body of imperial soldiers, sun-bronzed veterans of the Novo Provinces, without one of them sounding the alarm. "And what *was* the hard part, if I may ask?"

"Finding the praetorian with the trumpet," she whispered, "and then removing it from his person."

"But who just *played* the bloody thing?"

"My cousin, Caligula."

"*Caligula?*"

"Yes, you must remember to call him that—he likes it. Caligula was trained to be a trumpeter for the legionaries at Nova Petra. But he ran away."

"Why?" Germanicus asked.

"He was accused of taking something that was not his."

"Well, did he?"

"Yes," Alope said.

She halted the party at the base of the peak. A clear, sweet whistle split the silence and then warbled down into several chattering notes so like birdsong Germanicus found it hard to believe that the sounds had come from Alope's lips.

A sharp snort answered her from the darkness, and hooves could be heard clattering over rocks the instant before the lead horse in a riderless string of at least twenty burst out of a gully and galloped directly for Alope. One by one, the first ten were mounted by the shadowy forms of men who suddenly came astride them from having hung lengthwise along the flanks of the animals. The rest were for the imperial party. Alope swung up onto the bare back of a mare, then glanced behind her to make sure Germanicus, Rolf, and the Anatolians were ready.

"*Sumus danohwigha,*" she hissed to someone farther up the line.

"*Bil hit'ah!*" a gruff male voice cried, and the string wheeled away from the lights of the helio-flash station.

16

THE *ARCHITECTUS MAXIMUS* LEPIDUS had been longtime friends with a prostitute who lived on a pleasant sidestreet off the Via Aurelia. When the day's administrative work was done on the renovation of the quinqueremes, he invited the Abyssinian *machinator* off the ill-fated *Aeneas* to join him for dinner at the woman's house. Fiducio accepted, but with a wistful reluctance Lepidus mistook for modesty.

The Abyssinian was less than delighted because of an intricacy of reasons, none of which he could divulge to Lepidus. In the week since his arrival from the Novo Provinces, he had come to like Lepidus and admire his grasp of war galley design. If that was not complication enough, Fiducio had been caught up in the feverish spirit of his colleagues to complete the improvements by Caesar's deadline of the ides of December. After all, his life's work had been ships and making better ships. But he had also been charged with sabotaging this effort: specifically, to lure the talented *architectus maximus* away from the offices of his prefecture so he might be murdered. Now Lepidus himself was suggesting that they venture into a ward famous for its brothels, rowdy wineshops, and shadowy back streets.

It was late September, and it seemed that most of Rome's millions had poured out of their insufferably hot tenements into the only slightly cooler forums and avenues. By law, no freight lorries were permitted on the streets for another two hours, so Fiducio and Lepidus strolled down the middle of the Fabian Bridge, the gaunt iron span that had outraged

classical sensibilities when built twenty years before. A gilded
sky slashed by magenta clouds promised another breathless
day tomorrow, and Fiducio took comfort in the thought that
he'd be hidden somewhere in Etrurian highlands, enjoying the
breezes from the portico of some villa.

"Then we are agreed," Lepidus's voice welled up, "that
floatwheels add nothing but an excess of wetted surface?"

"Quite." Fiducio glanced behind: two Scythian thugs, of
the type employed by the coarser establishments of this
neighborhood, had fallen in behind them. Despite the
knowledge that the message he'd sent had loosed these
assassins, Fiducio felt his heart begin to race.

If only the flood of steam had claimed its victim aboard the
Aeneas, none of this would be necessary. In that awful moment when he had been compelled to report about the murderous device he himself had helped rig, Fiducio's hopes of
quick success sank into a bottomless well of schemes and
ruses. That which at the outset had seemed clean, even honorable—the felling of the last Julian tyrant, the kinsman of the
monster who'd crucified Fiducio's father—now thirsted for
the blood of innocent men like poor Lepidus here, who was
bleating on and on about Aztecan galleys with no inkling of
the slaughter that was stalking him.

"I was intrigued to learn from you, my dear Fiducio, how
similar their hull design is to that of our early bireme."

"Yes."

"Now *that* was a good design. Why must we Romans
always elaborate beyond the limits of efficaciousness!" But
before the Abyssinian could mumble some reply, Lepidus
caught him by the elbow and turned him up a side street.
"This is it. You can see Paulla's house from here. The golden
travertine facing there—I paid for it with all the visits I made
in my youth."

Fiducio did not attempt to chuckle.

The Scythians had finally closed with them on this deserted
lane, and one of the ruffians caught Lepidus unawares with a
hard shove that sent the *architectus maximus* sprawling to the
paving stones. He scampered back up to his height. "What is
the meaning—" Then he had time only to suck in a gasp
before the short sword entered his belly and flashed out his
back.

The second assassin spun on Fiducio and cried cheerfully,

"You who are about to die, salute us!"

The Abyssinian started walking backwards. "What madness is this?"

"We have our instructions. You *are* Fiducio, yes?"

"There must be some mistake."

"Always."

Fiducio was not certain that he could feel the penetration of the blade, except that all at once he seemed to have no legs under him. He collapsed, lay stunned with his cheek resting against the cool street, then began crawling toward a stepping-stone several yards distant. He would make use of it to rise again. Then, despite the incredible heaviness of his body, he would flee down the Via Aurelia.

Two pairs of sandals approached him as he tried to muscle up onto the elevated stone. His vision was quickly fading, but he recognized them to be military footwear: *caligae* with brass bosses bearing Germanicus's image. "Caesar?" he rasped, confused, frightening himself by how little voice he had left.

A bleared face came close to his. "Yes, that's who —Caesar."

Then Fiducio recalled: "No, no . . . can't be. Rumor from Nova Petra. Germanicus . . . gone. Out of reach."

"Why, you're privy to more than we are—and you a freed-man."

"So tell your . . . your bloody slavemaster . . . I failed."

"He already knows that."

"No . . ." Fiducio wheezed. But, however strong his out-rage, he decided not to reveal what he had discovered this past week: The work on the quinqueremes was largely done. Lepidus's capable assistants would make sure the galleys sailed before the ides of December. It was something he had intended to report in person; but now he would take it across the Styx with him. *Betrayed by all*—he would have liked that chiseled on his tomb. In the mounting dusk at the far end of the lane, he thought he could glimpse his father: the most tragic of figures, a slave with an extraordinary intelligence and energy that had mangled his sensitive mouth into a permanent scowl.

Slowly, Fiducio's head sank down onto his arms. He thought to spit at those military sandals floating in circles around his eyes. But then no time remained.

●　　●　　●

The sun raged overhead like a storm, scourging the small band with torrents of light. Germanicus's eyelashes became little prisms that disassembled the rays into dazzling flecks of red, yellow, and green. He tried to doze, but finally gave up after his own labored breathing kept him awake.

Alope had nudged him out of an exhausted sleep while the day was yet pink and vaporous in the east; this after they had spent most of the moonlit night on their mounts. But now Germanicus counted five hours since first light and the party still had not ventured out of the shallow draw in which they had camped. Alope's cousin—a giant of an Indee with a deranged grin worthy of the Emperor Caligula—had risen in the morning twilight, stretched, peered southward, and suddenly growled for everyone to rein their ponies to the ground and lie across their withers. He had not explained. It was not his habit.

As the sun rose and festered with ever-increasing brilliance, Khalid and his Anatolians had unraveled their *jamadani* and formed canopies from them to shade their heads. Rolf was so reddened after four days on the trail he appeared to be on the verge of bursting through his skin.

Agonizingly, their destination lay only ten miles across these salt flats—an island of mountains verdant with pines, rising dreamlike through the heat shimmers. The highest citadels were streaked with paler green: Alope said these were copses of aspen. And Germanicus knew aspens to be water trees, sending up their sprays of shivering leaves from cool, moist places.

The party had run out of water the evening before. Now, as the sun approached its zenith, Caligula grunted a few words in Indee to one of his warriors, and the man crept from pony to pony with knife in hand, drawing blood from the ears of the animals and collecting the liquid in a gourd. This cup was then presented to Germanicus, who declined a sip and passed it on. He sought distraction by studying the small horse reclining beneath him, its dun-colored flanks so lathered the sweat was soaking through his tunic. Even disregarding its peculiar dorsal stripe, he couldn't see where the breed was even distantly Iberian, the fountainhead of Roman strains. And since no horses had roamed the Novo Provinces prior to Isadorus Otacilius's second expedition, there remained but one explanation: These hardy ponies were of Serican origin. For once, Alope did not volunteer any information, and Germanicus surmised that the entire string had been stolen from some remote Novo settlement.

Longingly, he gazed at the mountains again, then decided to essay the reason for this torturous halt. He motioned for Alope to approach him. "Why are we roasting ourselves to death here?"

Alope drew a finger to her lips for him to be silent.

"I demand to know."

She frowned, then signaled for him to prevent her pony from rising. She crawled across the sands to Caligula, who was keeping watch at the brink of the draw. After a few moments, the warrior scuttled backwards and seized Germanicus's reins, indicating with a jut of his chin for the Roman to join Alope on the bank.

As soon as he lay down beside her, Germanicus saw why Caligula had refused to budge: Between the mountain refuge and this dry watercourse sprawled a considerable encampment. It was perhaps a mile distant, but he quickly identified the owners of the gaudily colored capes as Aztecae.

"We may talk softly now," Alope said. "Before, there was a sentry *there* . . ." She pointed at a knoll not three hundred feet distant. "But he returned to their camp for the late morning meal."

"What are they doing?"

"Those you see digging the trenches are slaves of the warriors, who are watching them work."

"Who are the idlers lounging under the awnings?"

"*Pochteca.*"

"Traders? But they look to be the lords of the place."

"They are, Caesar. *Pochteca* are Maxtla's eyes and ears in his provinces. To kill a *pochtecatl* is to bring down the full wrath of the Aztecae, for theirs is an empire built on trade and tribute. Usually they dress humbly and try to bring no notice to themselves. That they wear rich capes is a bad sign for my people."

"Your words still don't explain why they're constructing themselves a proper *castrum* out in the middle of nowhere."

At last Alope met his gaze. "This party comes to arrange a War of the Flowery Way with Skinyea, my uncle. It would have been mine to do, had I not fled from Tenochtitlan.''

"Certainly this force of fifty or so Aztecae is no match for your uncle's warriors.''

"An Aztecan army of several hundred is coming from the south. They will soon be here. These *pochteca* bear gifts for Skinyea that announce the new war: a shield, a battle club, and feathers.''

"Alope, I must ask you something . . .'' Her downcast expression revealed that she already knew what. "You told your friend Cornificius you no longer speak the names of your husband and son.''

"Yes,'' she said woodenly, "it is not proper to give voice to the names of the dead.''

"I see.'' Germanicus reached for her hand. "Then may I ask what happened to them?''

"There was a War of the Flowery Way. They were captured. They died on the Great Temple in Tenochtitlan. My son was twelve years.''

Germanicus was tempted to ask these questions another time, but then he realized that there would be no less painful occasion for Alope—ever. "The warriors of the Anasazi Federation certainly resisted, didn't they?''

"Oh, yes.'' Her eyes glistened with pride. "The Indee more bravely than all the others. It was not for want of courage that we lost our freedom.'' She became aware of Caligula, who was leering at the couple. She snapped at him in Indee, and he turned away with a sultry chuckle that convulsed his huge frame. "It is time,'' she said to Germanicus. "I will tell you how things happened.''

"Please do. I want to understand.''

"For two centuries, our warriors stole down the Mother of Mountains to raid the Aztecan *coloni*. Before that, so say the old ones, we Indee knew little of this powerful tribe. Oh, it is said they sent Yaki to try to trade with us for sky-stones. But it is also said the Yaki made up this story, and they wanted the blue stones for themselves because these are useful to make spells . . . or ward them off . . .''

Germanicus learned that, perhaps as long as five hundred years before, a reverend speaker named Moctezuma Xocoyotzin had launched a new kind of imperial expansion. Heretofore, the Aztecae had been more interested in taxing vassal states than actually governing them; but, with the valley around Tenochtitlan teeming with more and more hungry mouths, Moctezuma felt compelled to transplant large numbers of Aztecae in conquered territories that previously had been left to themselves as long as they remained current in their tribute payments. After two centuries, this string of garrisoned colonies stretched north all the way to the frontier of Anasazi Federation, and the Indee, especially, began carrying off Aztecan fowl and maize.

They plundered with near impunity until the time of Alope's grandmother, when Maxtla's brother, Cuauhtemoc III, became the *tlatoani*, or speaker, of Tenochtitlan; in effect, the emperor of the Aztecae. Then as now, a new reverend speaker was expected to put on a lavish coronation as a portent of the wealth and power of his reign. Legion victims for sacrifice were required, and the only way to win them was through a war of conquest.

Cuauhtemoc led a great army into the desert valley now shimmering before Germanicus's eyes. The Indee and their allies fought well but were overwhelmed by the seemingly numberless Aztecan host. Those too exhausted to flee into the mountains expected to be slain on the spot by eagle knights, but the reverend speaker's terms were surprisingly generous: The Indee would be allowed to live in their own country as they always had. They could keep their own leaders, customs, and language—provided they surrendered a quantity of skystones each year and submitted to a War of the Flowery Way upon demand. Not understanding what this "mock battle" truly was, nor realizing that this was how the Aztecae treated all fresh acquisitions before eventually subjecting them to a garrison state and a flood of *colonists*, the Indee rejoiced, even when a tenth of their number was marched away in tethers to die atop the Great Temple during Cuauhtemoc's triumphant coronation. They believed that they had escaped extinction.

"We Indee soon found out about the Flowery Way," Alope went on as if afraid to pause even briefly. "The next year, after rains had sprouted blossoms from the ground everywhere, the Aztecae returned. Our grandfathers were made to offer up two hundred males for a battle fought according to the Flowery Way. Some of our warriors were only twelve years, for we were afraid to give over all our most experienced fighters. Many were slain, but many more were marched south. Before departing, the Aztecan general told us to send an ambassador to Tenochtitlan to help arrange the wars and set the number of warriors for each levy . . .''

This kind of diplomacy, the politics of humiliation, was held by the tribal elders to be woman's work. By choosing a woman, they showed their disdain for Aztecan rule. Alope's grandmother had been the first ambassadress, then her mother, and finally herself—at least until Lord Tizoc hesitated before accusing her of aiding Britannicus Musa and the Roman mission, thereby giving her a few precious hours in which to steal out of Tenochtitlan. But, whatever her present status with Maxtla's court, Alope had been so skillful in negotiating levies always less than what the Aztecae demanded, she was asked by the other Anasazi tribes to do their bidding.

"Anasazi means 'ancient enemies,' '' she now said. "We came together as brothers because the Aztecae are slowly killing all of us.''

Germanicus had not yet released her hand. "But if you helped draft the levies, why couldn't you exempt your own husband and child?''

A hot breeze rose unexpectedly and scattered a thin strand of hair across her eyes. She did not push it away with her free hand. "But I would never do such a thing.''

"Not even to save your own family?''

"The Indee are my family. The levy is chosen by casting lots. Each warrior takes the same risk. I would never dishonor my husband, my son, by making others stand in their place.''

Germanicus found her answer astonishingly old Roman in spirit.

Caligula made a noise with his mouth that sounded like two pebbles being clicked together. He directed Alope's attention to a towering billow of dust at the southern threshold to the valley.

"Is it their army?'' Germanicus asked her.

"The dust of that would blot out the sun. This is no more than a hundred warriors and their porters. They come ahead to give Skinyea more reason to come down for a talk. These Aztecae will start searching for Indee camps as soon as they are rested. Now we must move."

"Won't we be seen?"

"That cannot be helped. But it is *how* we are seen that matters." Alope wrapped a scarf around her head so that little of her face showed.

The Indee let their ponies rise, then leaped astride them. Caligula swaggered up to the Anatolians. He regarded their sepia complexions, then nodded approvingly. In a bare-bones Latin, he told Khalid to have his tribesmen coil their *jamadani* into a shape more like the Indee headband.

Then, flanked by four of his stoutest comrades, the scowling titan cast his eye on the Romans. Two of the Indee were clutching rawhide thongs. "Submit," Caligula said ominously.

"What is this about?" Germanicus asked.

"Please, Caesar, we must hurry," Alope said. "My cousin is not a patient man."

"I demand an explanation—"

Caligula and his men sprang forward, but the Romans fended them off by drawing their short swords. The Anatolians could be heard charging their *pili*, gibbering in excitement at the prospect of killing infidels. "One word from you, *pasa*," Khalid cried out, "and these fools await me in paradise with a comb and a glass!"

"Hold!" Germanicus's eyes darted from Alope to her cousin and back to her again. "What kind of treachery is this?"

"None. Caesar does not understand. My cousin hates Romans as much as Aztecae. But what he does now is for the good of us all."

Germanicus lowered his blade, slightly.

"Four days now your lives have rested in our hands," she went on, "and no harm has come to you. Please—give us your weapons. They will be yours again in an hour."

Germanicus glared at her, the sweat dripping out of his eyebrows and making him blink fiercely. At last he let go of his sword and wiped his face with the dusty sleeve of his tunic. "As they say, Rolf."

"But there be—"

"You have your orders."

Rolf burrowed the tip of his blade into the sand.

"Khalid," Germanicus said firmly, "we do as these men command."

"*Inshallah, pasa*," the young prince muttered through his disappointment: another opportunity for holy violence had come and gone with no blood being spilled.

Caligula let the Anatolians keep their *pili* but instructed them to sling the pieces across their backs muzzle-downward as the Indee did to keep the mechanism free of grit. Then, with relish, he bound the wrists and ankles of the Romans, sniggering in sudden bursts of delight, cooing evil-sounding Indee oaths in their ears. Germanicus closed his eyes. Numerous hands seized him, and he was hurled over the back of his pony to dangle athwart the heaving flanks with his fingers and the toes of his boots nearly scraping the ground.

"Hail Caesar!" Caligula hissed so that none of the others could hear.

Sand dimpled by hoofprints, a tapestry of stones, and then the glistening, sun-kilned mud of the flats whisked past Germanicus's vision in a deepening blur as his mount jostled him toward the Aztecan encampment. His head was thick from the blood that was slowly pooling in his skull. No longer reassured by what he had seen in Alope's eyes, he felt fear creep up on him again. Had he come all this way only to be trussed and handed over to a band of merchant-spies? Would his dream of a new republic rot away in an Aztecan prison? He was trusting his life to a woman because once another woman, a Scandian with aquamarine eyes, had saved him at terrible cost to herself. But that had been a different woman, a different world. *So this present decision to go along with these new barbarians*, he thought as his head rocked painfully with each stride of the pony, *smacks of careless extrapolation, a flaw more Greek than Roman*.

The pony crowhopped to a halt beneath Germanicus, and beaded Indee boots padded into view. "Say nothing," Alope whispered. There was a distant murmuring of voices, and after a few minutes she explained: "My cousin is talking with the *pochtecatl maxima*. Caligula tells him we are returning from a raid on the Nova Petra–Otacilium Trace. We have two captives, lorry teamsters, and plan to sell or ransom them."

Germanicus could now make out the sharp whine of the Aztecan trader's voice. He was apparently upbraiding the Indee warrior, but in a brotherly fashion.

"The *pochtecatl* begs to know why no one has met them until now," Alope continued. "They have been camped here since noon yesterday. My cousin apologizes. He has been on a raid, as he first said. Before he left, no one had heard from the ambassadress in Tenochtitlan." Alope fell silent.

Germanicus surmised that, for whatever his reason, the Azteca had decided to keep quiet about the missing Indee woman. Perhaps he hoped that, if he pretended ignorance, the Indee would still deliver up their levy and the tribute machine would continue to grind away without interruption.

Then Germanicus sucked in a quick breath and let his body go limp. Footfalls were approaching, and Alope stepped aside. He gnashed his teeth as his forelock was grabbed and his face yanked up into the glare. Blearing his eyes, he feigned delirium. Two silhouettes confronted him, each defined by a blazing corona. After an endless moment, his head was allowed to flop down below the belly of the pony again. Caligula and the *pochtecatl* began what sounded like negotiations. They went on for centuries.

Germanicus waited, his pulse swishing in his ears. He watched through slitted eyes as his own droplets of perspiration splattered against the hardened mud and evaporated instantly. It almost sent a shudder through him—despite the heat—to imagine that the two barbarians were haggling over a fair price for his Roman carcass. But, after one final hair-wrenching examination of his face, the Azteca strode off toward Rolf's pony.

The fringes of Alope's triangular skirt floated into sight and she whispered, "The *pochtecatl* thinks Caligula asks too much for his teamsters. Especially for men who do not bear up to the sun very well. He says it is too bad they are not Roman officers. The Sericans in Tenochtitlan will pay much for a tribune or a centurion."

Germanicus sighed, thankful to be shaded by her body.

"Quiet," she snapped, for the Azteca and Caligula were farther down the string now and it was harder for her to overhear their conversation. "The *pochtecatl* sends word to Skinyea. He must ready one hundred warriors for a War of the Flowery Way. They must array themselves for battle the morning after tomorrow. Otherwise the old pact is no more.

The Aztecae will build a garrison in this valley. And then the Indee will be no more. Enough; we go." She trotted toward her own mount, and the sun spilled its fire onto Germanicus's back again.

"*Bil hit'ah!*" came Caligula's cry at long last.

Despite his misery, Germanicus smiled as his pony took its first plodding step away from the encampment of the Aztecae.

17

ENTERING THE MOUNTAINS of the Indee was an ascent into a vernal unreality. Caligula led the string of exhausted riders and ponies up a gorge shaded by sycamores and cypresses. A creek trickled from pool to pool, and in the emerald glassiness of each were the reflections of the turreted and crenellated walls of the chasm. These ramparts suggested to the martial eye every battlement imaginable, and Germanicus sensed that he was being admitted into a fortress capable of withstanding even the most persistent siege. As they paused to water their mounts for a second time, he asked Alope, "Why did the Indee of your grandmother's time fight below on the open desert when they might have harried the Aztecae from here—perhaps for years?"

"Ours was a proud and foolish war chief who wanted to prove that the Indee could fight in the manner of eagle knights."

"But, even in defeat, certainly thousands of your people could have hidden here."

"No, there has never been enough food in one place."

"But the vastness—"

"You see our lands through the eyes of a Roman farmer and wonder why they lie fallow. You think they are empty."

"Well, yes. I've asked myself why some of these fertile terraces haven't been planted with maize. And the hillsides there could be cleared for orchards."

"To eat like a Roman, one must Romanize the land."

"Is that so bad?"

"We will leave the world as it is."

An hour later, as they walked their ponies up a steep slope along a path that had grown as vague as a game trail, Alope remarked, "I have never known so many warriors to be here."

Germanicus peered around him through the dense conifers. He checked the sun-dappled earth for footprints. He saw no sign of men. "How do you know this?"

"The *dinos* bushes are stripped of their berries. Warriors eat them for strength."

Four days of hard riding had left him with little sufferance, and Germanicus found himself annoyed at this habit of hers to rush to conclusions. He decided that it was time to acquaint this self-assured new barbarian with the rudiments of Alexandrian logic. "Is it possible that a large influx of birds ate most of the berries?"

"It is," she admitted. "That happened once when I was a girl."

"Is it conceivable that the shrubs, of their own accord, set forth less fruit this year?"

There were no sounds except the thudding of hooves over a carpet of pine needles and the sigh of a thin breeze crossing the treetops. "Perhaps," she whispered at last.

When Caligula called a halt to rest the ponies after the worst of the climb, Germanicus took Alope by the hand and led her upslope into the forest. "Let's see all these warriors who have been eating the *dinos* berries."

They had not gone far through the shafted sunlight and thickets of young firs when the pair encountered a man sitting astride a log, cradling a *pilum* in his arms. A slash of yellow paint fanned out from the bridge of his nose and across both cheeks, giving his eyes a maniacal defiance. He nodded at Alope, then lapsed back into a patience so imperturbable it resembled a trance.

Within ten paces, Germanicus and Alope began encountering other tribesmen, who materialized out of ingenious hiding places and greeted the Indee woman with a respect tinged by apprehension. For some reason, her presence seemed to unnerve them. But Germanicus was irked out of reflecting about this by her triumphant tone of voice as she identified the various Anasazi tribes for him: "Ha'i'aha . . . Yudaha . . .

Tseka'kihne—do you see now? Skinyea has summoned more warriors than ever."

"You're missing my point, Alope."

Her grin was infuriatingly pretty. "What point?"

"Please try to understand: I count about fifty warriors along this streamlet. Now, if we observe the same number of warriors at the next drainage, and are diligent enough to do the same at the next, then and only then may we allow ourselves to generalize that fifty warriors are stationed along each streamlet . . ." He frowned: her gaze was fixed obstinately on the sky over his shoulder. "*And* by multiplying this figure times the number of drainages on this particular mountain, we arrive—by observation and experience, mind you—at the conclusion that—"

"There are more warriors here than ever before," she interrupted, "which I could have told you from the branches of the *dinos* bush."

"Yes, yes, but with the method I've just described to you, one can unravel any truth in the world."

"I do not wish to undo the world to gather its truths."

Germanicus sighed and preceded her down a gauntlet of warriors who showed only mild interest in the Roman stranger. From this, Germanicus believed that the Anasazi chieftains had kept their promise of safeguarding his identity.

"Tell me," he asked Alope, "why are they all here?"

"To stop the Aztecae from following us, if they had been of a mind to."

"Wouldn't that be an act of rebellion?"

She hiked one shoulder in a shrug.

Caligula welcomed the couple back to the path with gales of suggestive laughter. Using the fingers of both hands, he fashioned a sign that depicted sexual intercourse. The Anatolians looked away to avoid the evil eye, and Rolf galloped forward to shout, "Be decorous, you bloody dog!" But, for the first time on their long trek, Caligula appeared to be in a genuine good humor and had no taste for a squabble. He snorted once again as Germanicus clutched Alope by her thin waist and lifted her onto her pony. *"Bil tah'ah!"* he cackled, and the party rode on through the late afternoon shadows.

From time to time Germanicus glanced over his shoulder at her. She was passing in and out of the cool, dusty light, and when he turned forward again he was still treated by his mind's eye to these flashes of her smiling loveliness. So it was that he gradually became insensible to the drizzle of browned needles that pricked at his face after each hard gust of wind, or how the roots of the larger pines writhed along the surface of the ground like cinnamon-colored snakes; whichever way he turned he only saw Alope. She flared before and behind him, even within him, in a progression of tender miens, each more enchanting than the one preceding it—until he roused himself out of his warm languor, sensing the vulnerability he was obliged by good judgment to resist, always resist.

Caligula announced a final halt by leaping to the ground and hobbling the forelegs of his pony.

Germanicus stiffly dismounted. Woodsmoke was riffling through a colonnade of aspens, lingering in the lush pockets of the woodland. He had arrived in the heart of the Anasazi Federation. But there was no delegation to greet him. This suited him fine, for he wanted only to linger in the local baths—an impossible wish, he was sure.

"Follow," Caligula barked. "Leave kits."

The trail wound into a small meadow, and through the gap in an isthmus of firs Germanicus could see a larger grassland, its gloaming pocked by at least a hundred campfires. "Where are the dwellings of your people?" he asked Alope, for he could see robes and blankets spread across the ground but no brush huts.

"This is only a summer home. In a few weeks, my people will move down to winter camps. But sometimes a *gowa* is built for those who have married here." She blushed; he was certain of it, despite the fading light. Then she took her leave of him, explaining that a cousin had been born during her absence and she had not held a baby in a long time. She ran, and there was something plaintive about her eagerness.

Caligula clapped Germanicus and Rolf on their backs, nearly pounding their tongues out of their mouths. "Come, *Thermae.*"

"Baths . . . *here?*" Germanicus asked.

The Indee yawned in reply.

Khalid refused the offer of a bath for himself and his Anatolians, who were busy stamping out a place for themselves in a colony of ferns, isolated from any other camps, shielded by the remaining upright fronds from any wholesome sights. He did ask, once again, to borrow Rolf's legion-issue *index* so he might determine the direction of their holy city for the evening prayer.

"Follow," Caligula grunted.

Germanicus and the centurion fell in behind the towering warrior, who strode across the meadow and into a forest of ancient conifers, silent but for a faint groaning. Germanicus gazed up through a lattice of dead branches: the crowns of the trees were being rocked by a wind he could not feel down here in the mossy stillness. It was a grove that had never felt the bite of an axe, and Rolf was gaping upward with the same look of wonderment, of wistful loss, Germanicus imagined to be on his own face.

But, after quick-marching behind the Indee into the darkened timber for more than ten minutes, the Romans began to trade uneasy glances. Caligula gave no indication that he intended to stop anytime soon. "Where are these *thermae*?" Germanicus demanded.

"Follow."

Ahead, the sunset glowed in rose-colored slits between the trunks of the trees. It was wan compared to the sky-blazes of the previous evenings. They emerged from the forest and hurried along the breezy lip of a great rim that curved north and west until swallowed by haze. Across the desert basin below, the night was pooling in cobalt and azure blues. Germanicus was slowing to take in these muted glories when Caligula cried, "Do not tire!"

They scrambled down a steep cleft in the palisade, sometimes on all fours, grasping for handholds. Then, on a terrace hanging off the rim like a balcony, they finally paused, and Caligula proudly announced, "*Thermae!*"

Germanicus and Rolf could not keep the disappointment off their faces: the public baths of the Indee consisted of nothing more than a crude, hide-wrapped dome pitched beside a brook that had whitely mineralized its own banks.

"Strip!" he ordered the Romans. Then, using a forked stick, he fished several round stones out of a smoldering fire and carried them through the deerskin flaps.

"I keep my sword," Rolf said quietly.

"No, we must rely on their honor."

His preparations complete, Caligula herded Germanicus and Rolf inside and sealed the entrance so only a sliver of light leaked through. He flung water from a gourd onto the heated stones, and Germanicus recoiled from a nostril-stinging blast of steam. His pores opened like morning glories; sweat ran down his flanks in torrents. Rolf could not suppress a low groan, but the Indee sighed contentedly.

For thirty minutes, the Romans endured this torture. Then Rolf said, "Enough."

"Not enough." Caligula splashed more water on the stones.

"*Enough*," Germanicus decreed, and the Romans rushed out into a paradise of cool air, gasping as they stood with their hands braced on their knees.

Several minutes later, Caligula strode past them and waded into the brook. Germanicus and Rolf followed suit if only to cleanse themselves of their perspiration. The water was alpine-cold, but swirled into its currents were jets of warmth that invited Germanicus to slog upstream until he suddenly dunked down again, crying with delight, "Hot springs, Rolf!"

The centurion found a small pool with a temperature to his liking and slowly sank up to his shoulders. "Good as Aquae Aureliae!" Then he lowered his voice: "But that burning tent not be healthy, Germanicus."

"Agreed, my friend."

Movement in the darkness caught Rolf's eye, and Germanicus turned to see a pair of figures finish disrobing and slip inside the sweat-lodge. Caligula rose from the brook and joined these men for another half hour of steaming, marked by low murmuring punctuated every few minutes by laughter that, while not brassy or mean-spirited, made the Romans uneasy.

Finally, Caligula's huge form emerged into the night again. He lit a cedar-bark torch off the embers of the fire and illuminated the way across the bunchgrass for his two companions. One was glistening in robust middle age, but the other was so shriveled and wrinkled his naked skin only dimly reflected the torchlight.

"Caesar Germanicus," the younger Indee said, "I welcome you. I am Skinyea." It was uncanny: Alope's uncle spoke Medius Latin with a slight Macedonian accent. He had a dolorous, almost feminine set to his mouth, but his eyes were austere and thoroughly masculine. Years of squinting against desert glare had chiseled deep crow's feet at their corners. Clearly, he was a leader who had harnessed all his qualities to a single purpose; this gave him a gravity that muted his somewhat wry smile. "On my right hand is our *diyin*," Skinyea continued after a long silence which Alope had fore-warned Germanicus was part of the protocol of Indee discussions. "He calls up power against enemies. He *sees*."

Even without being told, Germanicus would have known the old man to be some kind of priest. For one thing, the *diyin* retained his skullcap, which Germanicus recognized to have been fashioned from owl feathers—he had made votive offerings of them time and again to Minerva. And then the Indee had a quality that Germanicus had seen in other aged holy men: As if to mark the final phase of his apotheosis, his spirit had begun to feed on his body, leaving him emaciated, almost transparent, as he became the invisible stuff of eternity.

"This is my centurion, Rolf," Germanicus said after his own tactful silence. "He is my best warrior."

Skinyea carefully eyed the German. "Yes, I can see that."

Caligula sank the torch stick into the soft ground, and the Indee men lowered themselves into the brook.

"Where did Skinyea learn the Roman tongue?" Germanicus asked.

"Long ago, I walked to Otacilium. I went to talk to the chief of the legionaires. But he would not talk to me unless I learned his speech. So I came home. I raided Nova Petra and took a Greek from the lyceum there. He died of the fire-thirst disease. But before he went to the other side, I learned Latin from him. Good Latin, too. But still, the chief of the legionaries would not talk to me. He was angry because he heard I had taken the Greek."

"I apologize for his bad manners."

Skinyea nodded solemnly, then turned aside to listen to the *diyin*. "He says he has read you."

"*Read* me?" Germanicus tried not to sound amused.

"Yes, from what the steam drew out of you. You have no vices that stink the air you leave behind in the *tachih*. You can be trusted to respect us, he says—as you respect yourself."

Germanicus nodded toward the old man, then said to Skinyea, "Your niece told me you are a war chieftain. She explained that this is a special honor bestowed on a man only when the need arises. Does this mean the Indee and their Anasazi allies are now ready to fight the Aztecae?"

Skinyea cupped his hands and began trickling water over his

dark shoulders. "I see already what Caesar wants. It does not please me."

Germanicus cocked an eyebrow. "What does Caesar want?"

"A levy from us to help me drive the Aztecae from Roman lands. As soon as the Flesh-Eaters are beaten back into their country, Caesar will make peace. Maxtla will live on. But even if he does not, Tizoc will. And one day, when you Romans are busy someplace else, the Aztecae will punish the Anasazi brothers—but none more so than the Indee."

"Aren't the Aztecae already punishing the Indee?"

"Yes, Caesar Gemanicus. But they choose not to kill us with a single blow. So we will have hope."

"Then I see what Skinyea wants: the destruction of Tenochtitlan."

The chieftain drank from his palm but said nothing.

"What happens if the combined armies of the Romans and the Anasazi are still not enough to destroy the Aztecae?"

"It will not be that way . . ." Skinyea paused as the *diyin* said something emphatic to him. "He tells me not to argue." The chieftain slowly smiled. A glow was rising behind the rim, heralding the full moon: he regarded this in silence for several seconds. "You will speak to all the other chiefs. They have come to this mountain to meet you. Even some who are not of the Anasazi brotherhood have walked far to sit down with Caesar Germanicus."

"How far?" Germanicus asked, eager to know the extent of dissatisfaction with Aztecan rule.

"It would be no lie to say this: Some of these chiefs can climb the mountains near their villages and see the snake head that rises above Tenochtitlan."

"Their hatred must give them sharp eyes."

"Yes," Skinyea said. "The Aztecae approach. Tomorrow, an army of many warriors will arrive in the valley below. We are now preparing to fight them. Not in a War of the Flowery Way. We will lure them into a fight of our own choosing, and rub their eagle knights off the face of our world."

"You will do this without receiving any guarantees from me?"

Again Skinyea revealed his grave smile. "One word from Caesar Germanicus will stop us. But sometimes silence speaks more surely for us than words, yes? Say nothing and we will

slay this army to the last warrior. Then together we will go
south and kill Maxtla, Tizoc, and all the rest. This is now
possible without making a promise to us."

"It is clear to me that you have already made up your minds
to engage this Aztecan force—and, for whatever your reasons,
want it to appear that I instigated the revolt. Perhaps this will
mitigate Maxtla's reprisal against your people, should you fail
on the field of battle."

"That is not so." For the first time, temper showed in
Skinyea's eyes. "Yes, we can rub out this army. But more armies will follow, one after another like the waves of the Sea of
the West, until the Indee are no more. We need Caesar Germanicus. But is for him to decide, truly. And he can do so by
saying nothing."

Suddenly, the *diyin* cried, almost deliriously. He was
pointing at the risen moon, which had an ice ring around it.

"Ah," Germanicus said evenly, mostly to calm himself
after being startled, "a sign the weather will change."

"Yes," Skinyea said. "A sign."

18

THE YOUNG WARRIOR rocked slightly against the clouds, his arms dangling behind his arched back. He did not flinch when spongy pills of snow slanted down on the west wind and began glancing off his face and bare chest. "He now feels nothing of this world," Skinyea whispered.

Germanicus took this to include the bone hooks piercing the warrior's pectoral muscles, fastening him to tethers tied to the top of the pole. He had hung there since dawn. At first, his face had been faintly tremulous, yet never fixed in a grimace or any obvious betrayal of the intense pain he must have been suffering. Between then and Germanicus's return to the encampment in the late afternoon, the warrior's features had grown placid, almost beatific—like that of some men in the last hours of crucifixion.

Skinyea continued to whisper: "He does this to ask the sun to help him fight the Aztecae. He shows he can give a blind eye to pain and death. This proves his courage, even before the battle tomorrow morning." The war chief held Germanicus's eyes.

"I doubt this fellow will be in much shape to fight *if* the Aztecae are engaged tomorrow."

"He is of a good tribe—the Horse People. He will find the strength."

At long last, Skinyea gave the signal, and the warrior was assisted down from his instrument of torture. He could not stand, but smiled with half-closed eyes from the arms of his comrades, then slowly nodded at Khalid's tribesmen, who had witnessed the entire ordeal in fascination. Not to be outdone, one of the Anatolians produced a dirk called a *dervishius*—if Germanicus recalled correctly from his Agri Dagi days—and skewered his lower lip with the triangular blade. Curiously, there was no bleeding. He spread his arms wide and danced in circles to exhibit his fortitude. The new barbarians yelped and hooted in admiration.

"Come." Skinyea led Germanicus and Rolf back toward the big meadow through a brisker snowfall than that of only moments before. Huge flakes were spinning out of the sky and melting on the shoulders of the men as they walked.

The day's inspection of the Anasazi forces had left Germanicus half-convinced that, if augmented by enough of these copper-skinned Spartans, he might be able to drive on Tenochtitlan with as little as two Roman legions—supported by Novo militia, of course. Among thousands of new barbarian warriors, he had not seen a single fat man. Most, he had been told, could trot a hundred miles in the hours between two sunsets; and, looking at their stringy leanness, Germanicus had no doubt they could *give battle* after this near quadrupling of a marathon. He wondered if, by some refractive trick of time, he was being given a glimpse of that hardy tribe of outlanders who had ensconced themselves in a hillocky basin along the Tiber when the ashes of Troy were still warm. Here was that ancient quintessence in a new and wild people: the stubbornness, the cruelty that comes naturally from a hand-to-mouth existence, the veneration of physical courage.

Yet Germanicus also had reservations about allying himself with the Anasazi Federation. He had not counted more than a hundred antiquated powder pieces all day. Wherever he had gone, the warriors, believing Germanicus to be Caesar's emissary, had taken up the chant: "*Pili! Pili! Pili!*" But did he want to arm a vast horde of un-Romanized natives who only in the past few months had suspended their raids on the farms and settlements of Nova Baetica? He might yet break the clever silence Skinyea had imposed upon him.

Then these misgivings vanished as he peered across the whitening meadow and saw Alope advancing toward him, crossing the creek on stepping-stones, holding a steaming clay bowl she had brought from her cooking pot.

"Drink," she said.

He found the liquid reminiscent of vinegar, his store of which he'd exhausted two days out of Nova Petra. "This is good. What is it?"

"*Dinos*—the berries by which I count warriors," she said with a hint of a smile.

"Are you counting me among your warriors?"

All at once, her pleasure vanished, and her face became troubled. She hurried back to her fire.

Germanicus noticed that Skinyea had been closely watching them.

"Come," the Indee commanded, "it is time for *thermae*."

Rolf turned to Caesar with pleading in his eyes, but Germanicus said quietly, "Let's step lively. They seem to put great stock in this ritual."

Over forty naked tribal chieftains were jammed into the torrid darkness of a sweat-lodge as long and wide as a sand-galley. One by one, Skinyea asked them for their "heart-thoughts" in Nahuatl, the only language known by all. After each inquiry, there followed a long, meditative pause, then a somber voice would rise up out of the silence. Skinyea translated for Germanicus in a murmur: "The chief of Yudaha says this is not a war he wants. But it is one he must fight. This is how it is for the Purple Cloaks, too. They must burn down Maxtla's great *hogan* at Tenochtitlan or he will burn down Caesar's at Otacilium. If the Purple Cloaks march down the way beside the Sea of the East, we will go along the old raiding paths through the Mother of Mountains, killing Aztecae all the way. But he says we need *pili* to do this."

"What assurance does Rome have," Germanicus asked through Skinyea, "that those weapons will not one day be used against the *coloni* of Nova Baetica?"

"The chief of the Yudaha says it would not be seemly for us to fight each other after we have become brothers of the same war party."

Germanicus was glad that no one could see the skepticism in his eyes.

One headman balked at conciliation with the Romans: "He says our enemies, the Aztecae and the Purple Cloaks, are like two bucks whose horns have become tangled. Both will starve to death in time. He says we should hasten that day and attack both."

This argument was politely considered in a calm broken
only by the sizzling of more water on the hot stones. Then it
was voted down by a volley of grunts. Skinyea whispered,
"This man will do as we agree—and bravely, too."

After an hour that had seemed like ten in the scorching con-
finement, all had had their say, even those from far to the
south—except Skinyea, who announced to Germanicus and
then the others that his *diyin* would speak for the Indee.

The holy man's voice, small but self-amused, issued from a
place near the entrance. Suddenly, it soared on a vowel up the
length of the lodge and continued from another spot in the
darkness, as if the aged man had winged over Germanicus's
head. When Skinyea began translating, he made no mention
of this feat or bit of chicanery, although his own voice was
now breathy. "Our *diyin* tells of a dream he had on this mountain when he was a boy. He had given up trying to understand
what it meant. He was sure it was supposed to stay a mystery
because he got twisted around himself whenever he thought
about it. Some dreams are like some men, and you should not
trust them. But now he thinks it was true. It shows how the Indee and their friends will win their freedom."

"Why is he making animal sounds?" Germanicus asked in a
hush.

"He is telling his dream. It goes like this: Coyote, old, with
a gray muzzle, stole Dove from the branch of the *dinos* bush.
He carried Dove back to his den in his mouth. Eagle, who is
Dove's friend, saw gray fur on the *dinos* branch and knew at
once what had happened. He flew all day but could not find
Coyote's den. He even flew at night. But Moon, who is
Coyote's ally, warned Coyote whenever Eagle was sailing
past, so Coyote could hurry back inside his den. But after a
while, Eagle overheard Moon whispering to Coyote. He
became angry and swooped down to clutch in his talons the
river that used to flow through the center of the world. Eagle
winged back up into the night sky and wrapped this river
around Moon in a ring. The waters babbled so much Coyote
could no longer hear Moon's warnings, so Eagle caught
Coyote with his nose sticking outside the hole to his den, and
killed him. Eagle then went inside but saw that Dove was
dead, too. His heart was heavy, but all the other doves were
thankful to Eagle for what he had done. This is why a dove
will never been seen pestering an eagle as other small birds will

do sometimes. They are grateful for their freedom. And this also is why when, years and years ago, some Indee warriors rubbed out many Purple Cloaks and carried home the standard of these soldiers, our *diyin* was troubled. It was the sign of the eagle."

Nothing more came from the holy man. A few chieftains could be heard scraping the sweat off their bodies.

"Now," Skinyea said in Latin and then Nahuatl, "Caesar Germanicus, chief of the Purple Cloaks, will speak."

"I have listened to all of you. I have no doubt you have suffered greatly under the Aztecae and your cause is just. But I am not ready to say yes or no."

"When will Caesar Germanicus be ready?" someone asked in Latin without waiting for translation. Germanicus suspected that it might be Caligula.

"I will make my decision known tomorrow, before the sun rises. I would like a night alone to think about the things you have told me. Sometimes it is easy to turn a small war into a great war. But it is always hard to walk away from a great war with honor. So I must think about what this could mean to my people."

Germanicus had anticipated resentment, even a few cries of anger at his postponement. But after a chorus of sighs that proved to be a signal for the deerskin flaps to be thrown open, the chieftains filed out into three inches of damp snow. They formed ranks of a sort, their brown skins steaming, then fortified themselves with war whoops and charged headlong into the creek.

Rolf shook his head at Germanicus. "If I permit this, Epizelus have my head."

Germanicus started to chuckle, but then was sobered by the still vivid image of his physician being herded across the rope bridge onto the Aztecan galley. "Well, we must not offend our hosts."

"This be barbarian madness."

"Why Rolf, don't your cousins, the Scandians, frolic away the winter in this manner?"

"Scandians be mad. And this be a practice sure to crack a heart in two!"

But Germanicus was already running toward the slate-colored waters.

"Good Jupiter!" he roared as he splashed into them, seared

by the brief uncertainty: Were they fiery or icy? The barbarians cheered him all the way in, and he lay flat across the
smooth, round stones. The scene before his distended
eyes—the grins of the chieftains, the snow sloping across the
firs, Alope smiling up from her fire, smoke tears on her
cheeks—crystallized into a notion as shocking as the chill of
the creek: He was in love with the woman. And he had no idea
how such a thing could have happened.

Rolf sank down beside him. "This be madness!"

"Yes . . . lovely madness."

And, a half hour later, when he was warmly attired and
rocking on his heels before Alope's fire, a bowl of *dinos* tea in
his hand, Germanicus was positive he had never felt better.
"I'll have more of your tea," he said, closely watching her as
she poured. "What did you think of Rome?"

"It was very big. Noisy. And crowded with too many
people."

Disappointment dimmed his eyes. "Yes, it is certainly all
those things."

"But your palace was very beautiful."

"Did you think so?"

"I have just said so."

A bonfire flared up at the center of the meadow where, in
the last few minutes, several hundred warriors had gathered in
a wide circle, segregating themselves by tribe or clan into
ragged phalanxes. A whorl of snowflakes was twisting down
around the heat of the flames as a headman led a dozen of his
men out into the firelit arena. A drum struck a tempo and the
warriors began dancing, jabbing the twilight with their spears
and plucking the strings of their bows.

"Is this the war dance?" Germanicus asked.

"Yes. Their leader sings of how he and his men will kill the
Aztecae who are on their way north. They will tempt them to
come into the mountains, then slay them one by one. After
that, they will kill all the Aztecae in the world. He says, 'Come
with me. Maxtla's warriors are very weak. They are nursed at
the breasts of their mothers. For this reason, they are soft.' "

"What of a race of men suckled at the breasts of a she-
wolf?"

Alope smiled. "They would be very powerful."

One after another, a delegation from each tribe danced out
into the flickering light and demonstrated how it would

humiliate the Flesh-Eaters according to its own particular manner of fighting. Then, while one warrior held a cowhide toward the south, his fellows engaged in a litany of chants that Alope said described the property they hoped to acquire in Tenochtitlan: feather capes, *cacao* beans to be used as money, precious gems, quills stuffed with gold dust, colorful birds, and peppers to make even rancid meat taste good.

Germanicus noticed that women had begun to drift out of the trees toward the fire. And Alope was carefully wiping the melted drops of snow off her hair.

"What happens now?" he asked.

"Come." She pulled him toward the festivities by both hands. "This is the *invite by touching* dance."

Yet Alope let go of him in the midst of the gathering throng and advanced alone toward the fire. Soon she was joined by several other women, and they began dancing among themselves, shyly, their decorum threatened all the while by giddiness.

Germanicus felt the heat of a leer on the back of his neck and glanced over his shoulder: Caligula was smirking at him. Clutching a bottle gourd, slightly unsteady on his feet, the warrior approached the Roman and offered him a drink. "From maize—it is good."

Germanicus declined.

"In the old days," the Indee went on, his boisterous good cheer unruffled, "this was part of the victory dance. But we have had no victory in a long time. So the *bizan*—"

"The what?"

"The women who have no men—they made a fuss. So it is part of the war dance now."

"Why did they protest?"

"You know nothing, but that is good." Caligula chuckled under his breath. "Because only at this dance is it proper for them to . . ." He repeated the same gesture he had made on the trail.

Germanicus was preparing to separate himself from the man when Alope shuffled up from behind. Her head was tilted to the side, and she touched Germanicus lightly on the shoulder.

He blinked at her, not knowing what to do, and she laid her hand on him once again.

Caligula nudged him forward into her arms. "Go—she asks for you. My blessings. The blessing of my people." His raven-croak of a laugh drowned out the singing for a few moments.

Germanicus studied the slow, precise movements of her feet, his face chafed by embarrassment until he found his ease in the tenderness of her eyes. She rested her forehead on his shoulder, as the other women were doing to their warriors, and they joined the circuit around the fire, their footfalls squeaking in the snow. She whispered something to him in In-dee; he would have handed over a dozen provinces to know what it was. But he didn't ask her to repeat herself in Latin, for here and there in the endless arc of new barbarian countenances was a glow deeper than that imparted by the fire: The faces of the chieftains were lit by anticipation, Skinyea's especially. The dreams of his people would soon spin off this stamping wheel of lovers. Germanicus caught Skinyea's eye to let him see that the chief of the Purple Cloaks *knew*, but was surrendering to her for reasons as much his own as theirs.

Then Germanicus was fighting doubt and suspicion. He needed to be alone; these moments might resound in the dim future, echo through the lives of untold millions. But suddenly he found himself wondering if it might be proper to enfold her in his arms. Then he realized that the other couples were embracing as they reeled and floated into the geyser of flames.

"Alope," he said, "I want to be alone with you."

He awoke, chilled, shuddering. He reached down for the furs bunched around his ankles.

Overhead was a low vault of lashed branches. Through an aperture in the dome, two stars could be seen. They were scarcely twinkling in the indigo sky. Morning. A whisper of breeze heralded the dawn.

Clutching himself in his arms, Germanicus rose to a crouch —all the higher he could in the *gowa*—and stirred the fire. The coals winked on and off, pulsed orange and black when he blew on them, but gave up no heat. Yet there was light eve-rywhere, a milky cone of it shooting down through the smoke hole and a paler triangle fanning out across the earthern floor from the portal. Germanicus ducked through the flaps and im-mediately groaned—but in awe, not pain. The full moon was

freshly risen over the aspen glade, bright on the snow. The
storm could be seen far to the east, a silvered bank of clouds.
It had left behind a deep cold.

There was the dry crack of a tree limb being broken and,
after a moment, the sound of smaller twigs being *snick-
snicked* down to size. And he was waiting for Alope to come
darting through the aspens, arms burdened, when he discovered himself—with no sense of having marked or recollected
time—peering through the flames of the wood she had somehow harvested to the mellower warmth of her bare skin. Such
tender confusion ensued that he thought the face beneath his
was Crispa's, fevered as he had never been able to see it when
she lived. But the sorrow he expected to follow such a delusion
did not come. The moistly parted lips were not Crispa's. They
were not Alope's. They belonged to all women, and he rejoiced in them until she cried out and the mouth was Alope's
again.

"Germanicus—"

"I must speak first . . . so you will understand."

"It is best for you not to speak," she said sadly.

"I love you as dearly as I loved another."

"I already know that. Please do not say these things to
me." She snaked her arms around his chest. "It is the hour
before dawn."

"I know." Germanicus lay back down. "And I thank you
for reminding me. I love you more for your honor than your
great beauty. Is that a terrible thing to say to a woman?"

She began to weep, clinging to him.

Light—the sun's, not the moon's. A drum had awakened
him. The interior of the *gowa* was chilly once again, the fire
returned to ashes. War cries drifted through the still air.

Germanicus crooked an elbow and leaned on it. "What is
it?"

"The last of the war dance," she answered without opening
her eyes. "The warriors have just sung their death song:
'There is death everywhere. You cannot go anywhere without
death. There are different kinds of death. Death comes to
everyone sometime.'" He had let go of her, and now she
refastened his hands around her waist. "But listen—the
women call out to them, 'You will not die. You will come back
all right.'"

Hearing sounds distinctly like those of pillaging, Germanicus asked, "What's going on?"

"The men are running among the camps. They will break clay pots and kill any dogs, if they find them."

"Why?"

"To show the people how they will slay the Aztecae and destroy their homes." Alope pulled him down to her and nuzzled against him. "To show the people how Caesar Germanicus and the Anasazi will sack Tenochtitlan."

Gently, he disentangled himself from her arms and reached for his boots. The leather was stiff with cold.

"Does Germanicus have second thoughts?" she asked, her voice edged with worry.

He shook his head no. The gesture was a lie. He felt he had been manipulated, but could not reasonably claim so. He had been provided with an apparently simple means of declining to ally himself with the Anasazi, but the simplicity had proved deceptive: to say no was to resist a prevailing current that combined his admiration for a vigorous people, his desperation to punish the Aztecae, and his desire to please the woman he loved. Skinyea was a master statesman.

He felt her hand grasp his shoulder, but he did not turn around.

"I love you," she said. "You must not doubt that." The hopelessness in her voice almost convinced him to meet her eyes.

Yet he trudged outside.

Rolf was keeping watch from a snow-dusted boulder. He looked away when Germanicus waved at him.

And Caesar's healer, a captive of the Aztecae, was made to lie prostrate and blindfolded before the old king, who asked, his voice trembling with anger, "Why does your lord incite our subjects to rebellion?"

The Greek answered in truth when he said he had not heard of these happenings, but that he rejoiced in news of them. "All I have seen in your realm reeks of abomination, and your warriors will be cut down as wheat is scythed, this in a harvest of wrath and darkness."

"How is it that we are abominable?" Lord Tizoc demanded. "We, my brother, who uphold the sun for all mankind?"

"The sun was set into motion long before men walked the earth, and it will shine long after the last of us has perished."

These words greatly disturbed the old king, for—in knowing nothing of the Compassionate, the Merciful—he discerned blasphemy in them. Caesar's healer was dragged from his sight.

Lord Tizoc sought to cheer his reverend speaker: "It presages well for us that not all our brother-foes are so unreasonable. There are those in their midst who would be our friends."

19

My dear Quintus,
Your father has reported to me that, in my absence, you have been remiss in some of your studies. This will not do. Great obligations may fall upon your shoulders in your lifetime, and you must prepare yourself for them now. Indeed, as you brought to my attention in your fine letter, the philosophies are less pleasurable than the histories . . .

Smiling in the privacy of his sand-galley cabin, the iron of the craft creaking around him as it cooled after the day's advance, Germanicus picked up the slip of parchment for the dozenth time and scanned the lines of oversized scrawl. Between sips of vinegar, he chuckled softly at the more imaginative distinctions between words that passed for punctuation. Then he reached for his stylus again:

Nevertheless, it is incumbent upon a Soldier of Rome to unravel these mysteries for three reasons. Firstly, he learns that, like all things of this universe, his anger is of a material substance. It has a flow that may be regulated as the occasion requires. The barbarian lacks this insight

169

*and behaves rashly for want of it, while the legionary
metes out his wrath with restraint and dispassion. Sec-
ondly, the Soldier appreciates that everything is per-
petually in the process of becoming something else; only
in such a restive state will he find the opportunities to
earn his honor. Never lament change; it is the very arena
in which we spend our lives. Finally, the Soldier takes
comfort from the knowledge that all human effort is uni-
fied in the attempt to build and then sustain order where
there was little or none before; in this, the violence we
visit upon others and suffer ourselves takes on a clearer
meaning . . .*

A distant bark of *ballista* made Germanicus lift his head.
He listened; no more followed. "Well, here it begins." He
propped his writing tablet on his knee again, but part of him
was now waiting for Gaius Nero to burst through the hatch,
reporting breathlessly that the Aztecae had been engaged at
last.

*I will now tell you of a battle I witnessed that was
fought exclusively between new barbarians:
    On the afternoon of a day that brought snow to the
mountain homeland of the Indee, the Aztecae arrived in
force on the desert plain below. Despite contrary signals
from the Anasazi tribes, Maxtla's commander still expected them to agree to a peculiar kind of battle the
Aztecae impose on their client states. A War of the
Flowery Way is not waged for annexation of territory,
but for tribute and victims whose sacrificed blood, the
Aztecae believe in their childish barbarism, will nourish
their gods and forestall the end of their world. But
unbeknown to the Aztecan commander, the Indee war
chief, Skinyea, had raised an army equal in manpower to
two of our modern legions and, being confident of
Roman aid, had decided to break the agreements his
forebears had made with their Aztecan oppressors . . .*

Germanicus's mental eye vaulted back to the ridge from
which Alope and he had overlooked the desert valley. She
calmly took stock of the Aztecan strength, her lips moving
slightly as she counted their cooking fires on that deep blue

morning after the storm. Germanicus took hold of her hand. It was like ice.

Fifty cavalrymen, led by an Indee warrior who calls himself Caligula, charged into the midst of the startled Aztecae, whose trumpeters blew furiously into their conch shells to alert the breakfasting troops. Many of these warriors were unaware of the attack until pili *began crackling above the stillness, and by then the bold Anasazi raiders were taking a fearsome toll on the defenders. But, quite abruptly, the forty or so survivors of the charge quit the fight and reeled their stout ponies back toward the foothills from which they had erupted only minutes before. They retreated at a canter, oblivious to the* pili *reports behind them, although several of the riders pitched dead to the ground.*

Aztecan officers in magnificent capes assembled bands of warriors under feather banners that streamed and fluttered despite the morning calm. Although several engine-motived lorries of sledge-track design could be spotted, these were reserved for the eagle knights, and the bulk of the cohort moved out as a mob of infantry, each man marching as he saw fit, heedless of his fellows.

The Anasazi cavalry never outdistanced their pursuers and twice wheeled to attack before withdrawing again. In this manner, Caligula drew the enemy up into a wide canyon that gradually narrowed and after several miles bifurcated into forbidding chasms. Here, the Anasazi cavalry halved itself into decuriae, each continuing up a separate ravine. As the Aztecae approached the same place, where it would have behooved their commander to sit a while in the shade of the expansive sycamore there and consider his peril, a whirlwind suddenly touched upon the ground, gathering dust, grit, and dead leaves in its revolutions before bearing down on the warriors. An Indee holy man later claimed responsibility for this phenomenon; but, whatever its origin, the stinging blast induced Maxtla's commander to keep stumbling forward, abandoning his lorries, heedless of the waiting danger as he divided his strength up the two benighted gorges . . .

• • •

Waiting atop that ridge for Skinyea to spring his trap, Germanicus found himself slowly filling with sympathy for the Aztecan soldiers. Poignancy attended the last tiny figure as the trudged into the mouth of death. He wore a humble maguey cape, signifying that he had taken no captives in his brief military career. He looked footsore.

Alope was possessed by strong emotions of her own. Her hand moved to brush something away from her face, but then she seemed to realize that the shadow lay behind her eyes. She began fighting tears as a child does, little gasps lurching up her throat. "It is hatred. I have become hatred."

Germanicus took her under his arm. "No, you are love. What are you saying?"

"You can never understand. If it were not for the Aztecae, I would be a menace to my own people. They would shun me, make me live somewhere off by myself."

"But why? They respect you."

"They fear me. They fear my *kedn*—the hatred that sent me down the path I follow." She wrapped her arms tightly around him, her face pressed against his ribs.

"These things don't matter to me, Alope."

Skinyea's skirmishers, most armed with nothing better than a short bow or a stick for hurling spears called the atlatl, lured the enemy van higher and higher up these closed draws. At great cost to themselves, they gave the Aztecae a false impression of success. Then, at the instant the victory cries of Maxtla's warriors were echoing in the chasms, Skinyea sealed the twin tombs he had prepared for his foes. Two centuries of his best warriors bottled up the outlets of the ravines, these men armed with the few pili *the Anasazi possessed. At the same time, the bulk of Skinyea's force, heretofore held in concealment, began raining arrows and stones down on the Aztecae, who halted, momentarily stunned by the ferocity of the attack, but then started withdrawing in good order. In any given moment, it appeared that only a few of Maxtla's warriors were falling. Yet remember always, my dear Quintus, that if one soldier drops at each pace an army travels, the last of ten thousand paces will find that army annihilated, for disaster is often doled out in these small pinches of death. So it was with the Aztecan force:*

*it ceased to exist down the length of those natural fun-
nels, not in a convulsion of shot and blade with bodies
heaping all around, but in a series of small parings that
were alarming only to the experienced eye.*

*Skinyea proved himself to be a resourceful tactician.
His men, of course, showed impeccable courage
throughout the long day . . .*

Germanicus put down his stylus, nudged open the
hatch, and shouted out into the passageway of the sand-
galley, "Rolf?"

After a few moments, Rolf appeared with a rag in his freck-
led hand. He smelled of brass polish. "Kaiser?"

"Find out why that *ballista* was sounded. Are the Aztecae
testing us or not?"

Shrugging, the centurion withdrew.

Germanicus collected his thoughts to write again. In his letter, young Quintus had disparaged his father, Gaius Nero, for
not being a "real legionary" like Caesar. This and other in-
timations the boy had made during their long chats in the
palace garden had convinced Germanicus that Quintus did not
hold his father in high enough regard. Germanicus suspected
that the boy's mother might be partly responsible; Claudia
was a beautiful and ambitious woman who seemed affectionate toward her husband only after he had earned some
new honor. In the hiatus between his glories, she had been
known to berate him, even in public.

*Your dear father, my legatus on this great expedition,
has accomplished the impossible. If he did not have
much time for you on his recent trip to Rome, it was only
because of the urgency of his duties. Noble Gaius Nero
apprised the Senate of the progress of the war and secured funding for the expanded campaign; expedited the
transfer of the Third Legion to Nova Baetica; and saw to
it that ten cohorts, one from each of the African and
Asian legions, were posted in the Hibernian garrisons
vacated by the Third. I relied on him to finish these tasks
before the ides of November, and he fulfilled them with
thirteen days to spare. His efforts made possible a sight
this morning that would have thrilled you to behold.*

Our army, comprised of all the Third Legion, those

units of the Tenth not entrenched with General Salvi-
dienus, and five cohorts of Novo militia, forded the
River Terminus and penetrated the arid hinterlands of
the Aztecan Empire, encountering no resistance and ad-
vancing rapidly under fair autumn skies as the auspices
foretold.

Our infantry ride in open lorries. By noon, these
legionaries were so encased in red dust that, when they
blinked or moved their hands, they appeared to be man-
sized statues sprung to life at Pygmalion's bidding!
Equally startling was to glance down from the prow deck
of a speeding sand-galley and see a score of new bar-
barians running alongside, barefooted, keeping pace
with the craft while chatting among themselves to ad-
vertise their strength of lung. These are the Raramurae, a
people who live high on the mountainous spine of this
country and are famous for their physical endurance.
Skinyea presented me with a maniple of them to convey
dispatches to the Anasazi advance, which parallels our
progress three hundred miles to the west. Recently, I sent
a message asking the Indee war chief, "Do you find war
easier with your new pili in hand?" Two mornings later,
the last Pheidippides in a relay of them raced into our
castrum with Skinyea's reply: "We find war no easier.
But Maxtla finds it much harder!"

From afar, another explosion reverberated through the hull
of the sand-galley. A corner of Germanicus's mouth hooked
downward as he quickly scribbled:

You are in my thoughts constantly, my young friend,
always with love and admiration.
                        Germanicus Julius Agricola

Crouching, Germanicus passed through the hatch into the
twilit passageway and called out, "Rolf?" There was no reply,
but if he stopped breathing Germanicus could catch whispers,
low and conspiratorial, wafting on air currents from the forward spaces. He slipped back into his cabin and donned his
short sword before venturing forward in the craft.

"Why, mates," a decidedly plebeian voice muttered,
"herein's the beggar what's been dishing us up our grief."

Germanicus's hand found the hilt to his sword.

"Due for a bleeding?" a second voice asked.

"Past due, lads, if you ask me," the first said gravely.

"Then let's do it."

Germanicus burst out of concealment, eyes flashing, jaws gnashed, and confronted three men huddled in a tight circle on the deck: two maintenance smiths and their signifer trying to repair the optical aimer, which they had reduced to its greasy components.

The signifer bolted to his feet, snatching his men by the napes of their tunics as he rose. "Hail Caesar! We beg forgiveness if we disturbed you!"

"Kindly stop shouting, signifer."

"We tried to be as quiet as we could, sir!"

"Stop shouting!" Germanicus bawled. Then he added more gently, "Please." Feeling sheepish but thankful that he hadn't drawn on them, he patted the terrified signifer on the shoulder until color returned to the man's face. "You were all quite considerate of my peace. Have you found the trouble?"

"Yes, Caesar—a defroster line requires bleeding."

"Good, good," Germanicus mumbled, starting up a ladder. "I respect what you lads can do. It's all a mystery to me. I had difficulty enough learning horses."

"Oh, it's really quite simple, Caesar—"

But Germanicus was already up on the main deck, peering southward into the first darkness for some sign of Khalid and his tribesmen, who were scouting ahead on horseback.

"You stand fast!" Gaius Nero's voice shot over the lip of the deck from the leeward side of the craft.

"Let go of me!" Alope answered.

Germanicus hurried over to the opposite railing.

Already clutching Alope by one wrist, Gaius Nero was trying to seize her free arm when he sensed Germanicus's eyes on him. Alope tracked the prefect's glare up to the main deck and Germanicus's disquieted face.

"Good evening, Caesar," Gaius Nero said at last.

Britannicus Musa spent the first day of the drive shut up in a cabin of the praetorian sand-galley following Caesar's. He squatted on the deck, arms banded around his forelegs, listening through the rumbling blackness for that first salvo, the one that would trigger a chain of events leading, inexorably, to his death on the dizzying steps of the Great Temple. He foresaw this with a paralyzing certainty, but refused to lose heart so soon, especially after the emperor had asked him to be of good cheer in the service of his peninsula. And Britannicus Musa had always been so *peninsular*.

The sand-galley slowed in jerky degrees, then stopped pitching and shuddering altogether. The engines died away with a banshee whine, a fading keen that echoed in his head for several minutes. Through the outer bulwark came no crackle of *pili*, no roar of *ballistae*. After a millennium of twenty minutes, which Britannicus spent clawing at the backs of his arms with his fingernails, a trumpet shrilled for the legionaries to fall in with their entrenching tools. The army was making its encampment for the night. "The bloody Roman army," he muttered.

Whereas his cabin had been his refuge, his snug burrow all day long, it now began to suffocate him, and he threw open the hatch to scramble forward through the mechanical clutter, banging his head without regard, grasping for handholds by which he could pull himself toward the light. Just when his skull was about to explode, he found a roundel of dark sky ringed in brass. Hyperventilating, he squirmed up into the evening.

Two praetorians stood above him on the afterdeck. "Is everything well, colonel?" one of them inquired.

Britannicus nodded yes, but his lips were puckered as if his saliva had turned to quicksilver. "Needed a bit of air. Hot below."

"You should have been with us in August, sir."

"Why?" Britannicus demanded.

"I mean the heat, sir. It was fierce."

"Oh . . . yes." Britannicus turned and descended the chain ladder into a field of flattened maize. He trudged off without purpose, first toward the dim sunset, then away from it, his shins rattling through the mummified stalks. The gourds and pumpkins ripening among the maize plants had been ruined by the treads of the Roman vehicles. The first of these Britannicus glimpsed made him reel back in horror, press his knuckles against his front teeth: he had imagined it to be a human head, smashed grotesquely, its pulp seeping into the dusty earth.

These unbridled sensations ride on your breaths, he drilled himself, as had the physicians at Nova Petra countless times. *If you find yourself panting at a rack, ease into a canter . . . and then down to a pace . . . from there to a trot . . . and finally . . . a nice slow . . . walk.* He sighed, then licked his lips before drinking from the alabaster vial his fingers had fished out of one of the slitted leather lappets dangling from his belt. The physicians had prescribed this potion to him. Reportedly, the recipe had come from Caesar himself. Britannicus eased down and sat on his heels, awaiting the arrival of its effect. Overhead, a dozen crows cawed south in a lopsided skein.

The stuff never entirely banished this mood. But it blunted his sharp sense of doom and, on rare occasions, transformed his melancholy into a lyrical sadness that, had he been a poet or a musician, might have proved quite useful. But he wasn't a poet or a musician. He was a professional soldier. And he had no use for melancholy.

This very night, he vowed, his face hardening with resolve, *I shall finally brief Caesar on Tenochtitlan's defenses: its causeway approaches, the wooden bridges, the depths of Lake Texcoco's lagoons, the great fortresses of Tepeyaca and Acachinanco, the . . .* But these things of stone and timber dissolved in his memory, and through a waxing bewilderment he could see only stack upon stack of human limbs.

As a boy in Caledonia, in the equinoctial dusk on the eve of the festival of Quinquatrus, Britannicus would steal through the heath that flowed around his father's stony fields, up over a ridge rubbed bare by the wind of everything but lichen, and then down to his uncle's distillery on the lake, where the best *aqua vitae* in the province slumbered in oak barrels. Gruffly, Gaufridus Musa would ask the boy what he had come for, pretending not to know. Before Britannicus could answer, the old man would wink and say in a low, chummy voice, "Well, a drop of the juice never harms a body when it's drunk to the glory of our good lady!" Gaufridus poured half a grown man's measure, and Britannicus gulped it down, mostly to impress his uncle and the coarse but utterly fascinating men who raked the charcoal, squinting through the smoke, smiling secretively to themselves year after year. The *aqua vitae* seared Britannicus's throat. Hot tears spilled out of his eyes and were quickly chilled by the spring westerly. But he had done what his uncle always suggested: He had thought only of Minerva as he swallowed. Then, to enjoy in private that first compassionate glow the goddess would send his way, the boy strolled down the sheltered lanes between the ricks of hardwood. But before he could savor that warmth, he realized that the lengths of ash had become human thighs, sawn free of their torsos, thousands of them piled up to the beams in that hideous factory at Tula.

From the forward perimeter of the camp, a *ballista* flashed a cupola of white light against the southern sky. The shock wave started him trembling, and he bolted off in a plodding run toward the direction he had been facing, not realizing at first that this way would soon deliver him to Caesar's sand-galley. But a glimpse of Alope stopped him short. In the lee of the craft, she was building a fire from dried maize stalks and broken crates.

Britannicus threw himself down into a furrow. So far he had been able to avoid her company, except for a happenstance encounter on the journey from Nova Petra to Otacilium, which he had broken off without a word by ducking down the closest hatch on the sand-galley deck, his face stricken as she called out his name after him. *She is Caesar's consort now*, he reminded himself. He could not dwell on this, not without sundering the cross-stitched fabric of his loyalties and desires. And it terrified him to imagine that she might be present while he briefed Caesar about Tenochtitlan. He had seen it in her eyes at that chance meeting: her revulsion at the sight of him, the mortal disrepair into which he had fallen.

Scuttling backwards like a crab, Britannicus now withdrew until he was sure she could not see him. Then he rose, dusted off his cloak, adjusted the sandal straps that laced halfway up his calves, and sauntered toward the perimeter as if he were Caesar himself on inspection.

Teams of legionaries, stripped to the waist to keep their tunics presentable, were digging a trench east and west as far as Britannicus could see in the twilight. Reclining on a pile of earth they had dredged up, he smirked at their efforts.

"Is everything all right, colonel?" a subcenturion asked.

"Tell me, optio: Why do we do this?"

"Orders, sir."

"No, no—other than that." Britannicus waited a few moments, then went on when the man made no reply: "The only reason we do this is because we have always done this and no one has the bloody courage to say let's quit doing it. But, whenever a Roman legion is on the move, you can be sure it will halt two hours before sundown and dig a ring around itself, fell trees to erect ramparts, pack dirt into battlements—only to abandon all this splendor at first light. Well, there are no Aedui or Belgae out there, optio. So what in the name of Mars are we doing?''

The legionaries within earshot were leaning on their spade handles, and the optio cut short their simpering by bellowing, ''Back to it!'' Then he stamped up to Britannicus and gave him a coolly precise salute. ''Pardons, sir, but why make their sweat sting any more than it does?''

''Because that sweat would be better invested in digging cubbies instead of trenches. Deep holes, randomly spaced, will protect the men from Aztecan *ballistae*.''

The optio puffed up his cheeks with air, then slowly released it. ''See that sand-galley yonder, sir? It conveys the Caesar and his general staff. Perhaps the colonel would care to take his suggestions there.''

Britannicus sprang up. ''Perhaps I shall.'' And he was halfway to the imposing hulk when a sense of his own foolishness came crashing down on him. His right hand darted for the thickening at the center of his chest. He tried to weep, but no tears came.

An owl whooshed overhead through the gloaming, and Britannicus dropped to his knees. ''*Minerva*. Release me from all this, good lady. Give me my peace.''

''And so you shall have it,'' a susurration of a female voice came from the darkness in front of him.

''My lady . . . ?'' He leaned toward the specter: the shape of a woman was materializing out of the maize, rustling the stalks as if she were rising out of a heap of molted snake skins.

''But no man has his final peace if he forsakes his honor.''

''I know,'' he said dismally. ''That is why I endure.''

''Of what do you speak, my friend?'' a slightly altered voice asked.

His arm flowed up from his side, and his fingers curled around the shape of the distant face. ''*Alope?*''

''Yes. How is my friend, Britannicus Musa?''

At last, his eyes flooded. ''Not so well. I cannot find my way home from Tenochtitlan.''

"Nor I." Approaching him as if he were some shy animal crouched to flee, she extended her hand. "Come. There are some things Caesar must hear from his own people. He must see Tenochtitlan through Roman eyes."

Britannicus took a half-step backwards. "How can I make him understand what I myself don't? Those things . . ." He could not finish.

"Yes, those *things*. You must be brave and live them again in his presence."

Britannicus bowed his head, breathing heavily. Then, without a word, he labored to his feet and strode toward the imperial sand-galley.

She had to trot to catch up with him. "Thank you, Britannicus Musa."

He ignored another offer of her hand. "Lake Texcoco's lagoons are quite shallow. That is significant, should Caesar decide to ford them with sand-galleys. You must remind me of this should I forget."

"I shall."

"And the distance by causeway to the Tepeyaca Fortress from the mainland—one mile perhaps?"

"I would think more like one and one-half Roman miles."

Glumly, he accepted this without argument. "How everything indispensable shrinks to confusion . . . and everything trivial swells to catastrophe."

A guardsman challenged the couple just as a *ballista* lit up the sky again.

"All is well," Alope told him when the rumbling had died away. "An officer to report to Caesar."

Britannicus kept his eyes on his sandals.

The praetorian waved them past, and Alope left Britannicus gazing into the fire while she grasped the side chains of the outboard ladder and raised her foot to the lowermost rung.

"A moment there!"

She turned: Gaius Nero was marching out of the night, flanked by two guardsmen who were unslinging their *pili*.

The prefect inclined his head toward Britannicus. "What is the colonel doing this close to Caesar?"

"He has business with the emperor."

"Then it begins with me."

"He brings useful information."

"And danger to Caesar. Just look at his eyes—he's mad.

Only the gods know what he might do on some impulse.''

"I know all kinds of spirit sickness. His will not harm others.''

"That isn't for you to decide.''

Alope started up the ladder. "I go to summon Germanicus.''

Gaius Nero caught her wrist and pulled her down. "You stand fast!''

"Let go of me!''

The prefect was reaching for her other arm when he stopped and glanced upward: Germanicus was looming over him from the main deck of the sand-galley. "Good evening, Caesar.''

"Good evening,'' Germanicus said curtly, then climbed down the ladder to stand between them. "What is the trouble here?''

"This woman insists upon abusing whatever it is the office you have afforded her. She circumvents your guard at will. And this man—'' Gaius Nero spun toward Britannicus, but the colonel was no longer standing there. "Where has he gone?''

"He fled into the darkness, prefect,'' one of the praetorians said.

"Precisely the point I was making to this woman, Caesar,'' Gaius Nero went no. "Britannicus Musa is too unbalanced to be allowed direct access to your person.''

"This is not true.'' Alope snugged her fingers into the crook of Germanicus's arm. "The colonel came to tell you what he knew of Tenochtitlan when—''

"When I quite properly executed my duties!'' Gaius Nero exploded.

Germanicus patted Alope's hand before disengaging himself from her. Then, with a nod, he drew the prefect aside. "I would consider it a great kindness, nephew, if you would inhibit the nasality that creeps into your voice whenever you refer to Alope.''

"The *nasality*, Caesar?''

"Yes, I believe that's what it's called.'' Germanicus hoisted his eyebrows. "You weren't aware of it?''

"Why, no. I'm sorry if—''

"I was sure you would be. And as to the office I have afforded her—she is the woman I love, Gaius Nero.'' For the first time, Germanicus's softly spoken words had a sting to them. "As my chief protector and *legatus* on this expedition, you should be first to know that I am giving enormous consideration to making her my wife. Of course, I rely on your discretion to keep this—"

"A *new barbarian* empress?"

"I did not say that. I declared only that I want to wed her." Germanicus smiled at his prefect's dismay, which reminded him of Juvenal's line: "What snakes are driving you mad that you think of taking a wife?" "Now, dear nephew, I hope that gives you some indication of how much I trust her with the matter of my personal well-being."

"Yes, of course, Caesar," Gaius Nero said woodenly while his pupils flitted back and forth.

"My *architectus maximus* may not be safe on the streets of Rome—"

"Yes, terrible . . . Scythian hoodlums."

"—but I feel no threat in the presence of poor Colonel Musa."

"Uncle, the man is *mad*."

"We all stand closer to the brink of that affliction than we fancy."

"How true," Gaius Nero said after a moment's deliberation. Whereas before he had been deeply distracted by hearing that Germanicus intended to marry Alope, he now seemed faintly amused, even pleased. He came briskly to attention. "The watchword for tonight, Caesar?"

Germanicus regarded her firelit face, then said, almost wistfully, "*Sporting uncropped hair*."

"From Tibullus, I believe, isn't it?"

Germanicus found the prefect's eyes disagreeably incisive. "Yes, I think so." Gaius Nero had spun on his heels to go, but Germanicus stayed him with a hand. "You should know, nephew, I've recommended to the Senate that you be awarded an ovation for your capable work this far."

"Thank you, Caesar." Then the prefect marched off to deliver the watchword to the centurions.

Alope was brewing a pot of *dinos* over her small fire. Quietly, Germanicus approached her from behind, then ran his palms down both sides of her parted hair. He could sense that she was smiling, although she was turned away from him. "I love you very much," he whispered.

One of her hands shot up to seize his and press it against her cheek.

He felt careless for having chosen a watchword so revealing of his present frame of mind. Gaius Nero, as usual, had been quite correct. It was from Tibullus:

Come exorcise the illness of this lovely girl,
come down here, Phoebus, sporting uncropped hair.
   Believe me, and hurry; you'll never regret
applying to her beauty the medicine of your hands . . .

Germanicus would soon have great need of this woman, and he did not want her attended by an Apollo with locks cropped in mourning.

Somehow, in the past few days, it had lodged in his brain that there was no hope that the republic could be restored without a civil war. Perhaps this belief had come from his increasingly strident relationship with Gaius Nero. Although he had been given no reason to doubt his nephew's loyalty, Germanicus knew that the prefect longed to be Caesar: it was shriveling the young man's face like a hunger. And if not Gaius Nero, some ambitious legion commander would leap upon the rostrum and acclaim himself emperor of the world as soon as Germanicus called for the restoration.

In this coming civil war, Alope would stand at his side, and he drew comfort from that thought. If the bloody antecedent of two thousand years before was any indication of what the future had in store, the struggle would be hammered out, year after year, on parched Greek isles or in the sun-crazed desolation of Africa. What patrician woman could be asked to shake out her bedding before retiring for fear of scorpions, or roast a lamprey over a fire of donkey chips, or have no roof over her head but a vault of stars? Clearly, the Indee woman was a gift from the gods, a sign that they would not forsake him in his odyssey to restore what justly must be restored.

Yet there was her *kedn* for the Aztecae—the heaviness of her hatred, as she herself had confessed with such sorrow. He had lied that such things didn't matter to him. Her obsession did, and he worried that it could drive them apart, as no jealousy or other kind of divisiveness could.

He stopped stroking her hair at the sound of approaching

horses. The praetorians unslung their *pili*; their *electricus* torch beams reached out across the darkness into the dusty maize fields.

Rolf's voice came out of the midst of the commotion of hooves and creaking leather: "*Sporting!*"

"*Uncropped hair!*" a praetorian shouted back from the afterdeck of the imperial sand-galley.

The centurion had returned from his errand at last. He was riding double behind Khalid, who looked weary—and furious.

"This be the reason for that *ballista* fire, Kaiser." Rolf jumped down. "These men be fired upon by Romans while they return to camp."

"Why is it, Caesar Germanicus," Khalid asked, almost shouting, "that those we come to help as brother-warriors in a holy purpose welcome us back from a long ride with explosions? Did not my father, the Great *Zaim*, the holiest of men, free you long ago when my people cried for the blood of the Roman *pasa* who had blundered into our hands?"

"Your noble father did, although I remember it as if it happened yesterday, not long ago."

"Did I not swear my heart and blood to you—not once, but twice?"

"You did."

"Then why explosions?" Khalid wailed in indignation.

"Were any of you hurt?"

"Our best horse, *pasa*—killed. A king among horses."

Mindful of countless dealings with these proud tribesmen, Germanicus turned to Rolf: "Centurion!"

Rolf snapped to. "Kaiser!"

"The officer responsible for this insult to our brave friends is to agree upon a fair price for the horse with its owner—then double it. He is to troop along with Prince Khalid and his warriors the next time they go out for us—as groom for their horses until he learns the value of a good mount."

"Hail Kaiser!" Rolf quick-marched off.

As Khalid majestically dismounted, his pride restored, Alope offered him a cup of *dinos* tea.

"I thank you, sister."

Only after they had politely discussed the temperate weather did Germanicus ask Khalid what he and his patrol had seen.

"Nothing, *pasa*, but the droppings of cowardly infidels who have withdrawn in great haste to the south. They destroyed what they could not carry, and the roads are strewn with the bodies of the very old and the very young.''

Germanicus clasped his cloak together in the front, although the night was not yet chilly. ''Did you see any of their cities?''

''One. But everything had been burned, except their temple, which we fired ourselves. Otherwise not a thing, *pasa*. Not even a kernel of grain.''

''Maxtla leaves us nothing. He realizes the importance of doing this from his own supply difficulties.''

No one around the fire spoke.

Into this silence padded the Nihonian, Tora, from the sand-galley that transported the auxiliary staff. He bowed and unfurled a chart in front of Germanicus. ''I have finished territory of Teotihuacan to Texcoco, Lord Caesar. All done in best tradition of . . .'' A corner of the parchment had dangled too near the flames and had begun to smolder. Tora yanked it back. ''. . . *Yinshaya*.''

''*Inshallah*,'' Khalid automatically intoned, then took a sip of tea.

''Yes!'' the Nihonian cried with approval, his head bobbing more vigorously than ever before. ''*Yinshaya!*''

''Good Jupiter!'' Germanicus's cup slipped out of his fingers.

''Too hot?'' Alope asked. ''But it must be drunk hot to make you strong.''

''I finally understand what this fellow has been trying to tell us!'' Germanicus grasped both Tora and Alope by the arms and pulled them toward the ladder to his sand-galley. ''Come,'' he said to her, ''we may need your Nahuatl where his Latin fails.''

20

NAHUATL PROVED TOO poetic a language with which to precisely unfold the meaning of *Yinshaya*. Listening to Alope's Latin translation, his topknot bobbing to the tempo of her words, Tora would suddenly groan, "No, that is Aztecan think! This is no magic. *Yinshaya* is the opposition of magic!"

Still, at long last, Germanicus had a glimmer of what had stirred the world forty years before—after a slumber of more than two millennia. It was not that there had been no progress in the interim between the ancient Greeks and this unfathomable awakening; but most inventions had been borne on the wings of accident, like that of niter powder following an explosion at a fertilizer factory in Egypt.

This new development in human affairs was no fortuity. Men had brought it about—extraordinary men like the Emperor Fabius and Ptolemaeus. Nor was it a gift from Mars who was reciprocating mankind for the construction of his new temple, as suggested by the *pontifex maximus*, a sniveling dotard who was high priest only because Fabius had divested himself of what he considered to be a meaningless office.

By first light, which tinged the eastern horizon blood-red, Star-Sorter's tale had been told and retold a dozen times. Germanicus thanked Tora and Alope for their patience with his endless questions for clarification. He urged them to rest. For himself, there could be no sleep until he had written everything down while it was still fresh in his mind.

Sending for his wax tablets, then climbing up to the dawn

186

coolness of the prow deck, he decided to dispatch this correspondence, like all the others, to young Quintus; but in his haste and excitement he absently addressed it to his dead son. Only when he was finished did he realize that, during this brief but cruel distraction, he had forgotten the death that still weighed heavier on him than all the rest he had suffered to survive.

My dear Cassius,
    Incredibly, adventitiously, I have just glimpsed the underpinnings of our world from a maize field in the Novo Provinces. A chance word between two men of peoples unknown to each other has resolved the mystery of what happened to Al-Hamar, mentor to Fabius and Ptolemaeus. This marvelous intellect that sprouted in the wastes of Arabia Petraea, was nurtured to fruition by the Jewish scholars of Baghdad, and then seeded the best minds of the empire at the lyceum in Alexandria—utterly vanished some years ago.
    It is now certain that, disappointed with Roman science, which he called the "imperial wattle-craft," Al-Hamar caravanned east to the Serican Empire, whose imperial family he deemed to be superior in virture to the Roman. There he established an academy and exhorted his fellowers with this creed: "Be as soldiers of a quiet army when you set forth to describe the world. Steal as close to the truth as you dare without disturbing it. When you return to tell others what you have seen, choose your words with manly care; do not allow greed, pride, or expectation to color them. Above all, remember that the cognition of even the finest mind is readily dispossessed of the truth if that mind ventures alone. And so, together, as brothers, wear down ignorance as water gradually wears down stones, satisfied that your one life is but a single drop in the continuous force of humanity. All things are possible if you adhere to this path. Truly, I believe this to be what God wills in our affairs. This, then, is the way of Inshallah.
    Yinshaya *is how a Nihonian graduate of that academy learned to pronounce this process, although it is clearly the same as that which influenced Fabius and his contemporaries.*

It is of personal interest to me that Al-Hamar's body was most likely returned to Anatolia in our own empire for burial. I am the only Roman to have visited the underground tomb at Agri Dagi, in which lie the holiest dead of the eastern provinces.

But what is critical is this: through Tora, I, Germanicus Agricola—a man who must squint into the strong and pure light of science, "a citizen more slow than swift," as an old sailor once hazarded to my face— now have the means to pick up the threads that were sundered when Fabius and Ptolemaeus were slain. For the first time, I have some meager hope that my imperium, the last of so many, will not be cast into shadow whenever the past is illuminated by Livys yet unborn!

"Caesar!" a voice lofted up from the field.

Germanicus lifted his stylus from the soft wax, then went to the rail, shaking the cramp out of his hand. Gaius Nero stood below, recovering his breath from a run. "What is it, nephew?"

"The Aztecae, I suspect. The Anatolians rode forth before first light. They've just sent back word that we face breastworks in the only pass our sand-galleys can negotiate."

Germanicus glanced southward; there were clouds, but they appeared to be as thin as fumes. "Give the word then: we advance in an hour!"

"Hail Caesar!" The young man paused, smiling. "It is heartening to see you of such good cheer."

"It is heartening to feel it again. Now go—quickly. We'll need daylight to invest their works."

"At once."

Humming softly to himself, Germanicus returned to his wax tablets. But then his heart sank as he saw his son's name, and he was filled with foreboding again. How many young Romans would cross the Styx before the sun was enfolded by another sulphurous dusk?

There was really no cause for cheer, he decided. And the feeling passed like the first glow of wine.

21

RAIN BEGAN RATTLING on the dry loam in hard drops. It bespeckled the shoulders of Germanicus's dusty uniform, shifted on the wind, then raked his back like grapeshot. "Bloody clouds," he hissed. He hobbled down the crumbly bank of a ravine, breathing through clenched teeth. He had turned his right ankle on a stone while trying to gain a higher vantage from which to study the tiers of Aztecan breastworks that had halted the Roman advance for the third time in two weeks. But there was no visibility, only a sky like wool, the dirty gray of soiled bandages. He ignored Alope's smile as he limped up to her warming fire. "Nothing. The bloody clouds are anchored to the ground."

Rolf arrived at fireside a few minutes after him. He continued to give Germanicus a wide berth as he said quietly to Alope, "Daughter, I be fond of your *dinos*."

"It will be brewed shortly, Red Wolf."

Germanicus glanced up, his face pale and humorless. "*Red Wolf?*"

"It be her name for me," Rolf said with a hint of pride.

Germanicus turned away from them and squinted up into the rain. Although Rolf had been shadowing him across the hillside above the bivouac, Germanicus felt certain the centurion had not seen what he had: a blue-black hand protruding talonlike from the ring of fresh earth surrounding a *ballista* hole. It had overpowered him with a sense of death and stagnation, of a military campaign courting doom with the

lives of young legionaries. He could overhear Alope and Rolf
whispering to each other about him. But he couldn't broach
his melancholy long enough to join them in conversation, so
he pretended not to hear.

"In dispatches from Rome last night, there be bad news
from Hibernia."

"A war?" That now-familiar trepidation was in her voice,
the panic that Germanicus might find some reason to call off
his slowing drive on Tenochtitlan. "Is there a new war on that
isle?"

"No, but there be talk of a revolt."

A breath seethed up Germanicus's throat. He had known
from his darkest dreams that this would happen: That bog-
flea, King Matholwchius, who had burrowed deep into the
green hide of Hibernia and periodically set it itching for
rebellion, was bound to take advantage of Rome's preoccupa-
tion with the Aztecae. And what malcontents in other provinces would be emboldened by this effrontery to imperial rule?
He glared at Rolf, whose mustaches were dripping with *dinos*
after a long draught. "Come, centurion, time to go back
out."

Longingly, Rolf contemplated the chunks of squash Alope
was roasting on a skewer. Alope approached Germanicus and
lightly touched his breastplate with her fingers. "It must rain
harder before it can clear."

"Alope be right. This be *in* for a spell."

Germanicus rubbed his eyes and found them very sore. "I
don't care. We're going to break out of this pestilent sink today, this afternoon. And I don't want Maxtla's entire army
standing in the way of my vanguard as they have twice this
week!"

"I be ready, Kaiser," the centurion said at last, quietly.

But just as they had turned to start trudging up the hillside
again, a lorry lumbered over the opposite ridge and skidded
sideways down into the ravine before halting. Gaius Nero
alighted from a cowling board, his uniform immaculate but
for a film of ocherous mud on his boots. "Hail Caesar!"

Germanicus gave him a bleak little nod.

"Caesar, I beg a word in private." The prefect waited for
Alope and the centurion to move out of earshot before he
whispered, "Appius Torquatus and his *comita bellica* from
the Senate arrived yesterday in Otacilium."

"For what purpose?"

"Uncle, when I was in Rome, even *I* heard talk. Any my name is linked closer to yours than any other."

"What kind of talk?"

"Well, opinion is quite divided over the Battle of the Mare Aztecum."

"How can it be divided? Our fleet would've been mauled but for the intervention of the *procella*."

"I fear . . ." Gaius Nero paused as a Serican *ballista* round trilled overhead and then exploded deep inside the Roman encampment. He tucked his hands in his armpits, but not before Germanicus saw that the man's fingertips were trembling. "I fear the Senate has a few questions about our prosecution of the war."

Germanicus said nothing for a moment, although the temptation fizzled in his eyes for him to shout: *The power of that committee emanates from me! How dare they question how I conduct this campaign?* Nevertheless, a calmer voice reminded him that this meant only that the elements of a republic were finally stretching their muscles after an atrophy of twenty centuries. It would be hypocritical for the man who hoped to restore the power of the Curia to slap down these senators like bad schoolboys and pack them off to Rome again. After taking a few deep breaths, he said, "Send this message to Otacilium: I invite the president of the Senate and his esteemed Conscript Fathers to travel, at my expense, to the *castrum* of the expeditionary army."

"I'm sure Caesar's generosity and openness will be well received by the Senate."

"Indeed."

Gaius Nero's brow became wrinkled with concern. "Is Caesar feeling well?"

Germanicus ignored the question. "Is there anything else?"

"As a matter of fact, there is. This came through the lines under a banner of truce." The prefect slipped a folded piece of paper from the sleeve of his tunic and shielded it from the rain with a wing of his cloak as Germanicus scanned the brightly painted glyphs.

"Is this writing Nahuatl?"

"Yes, Caesar—in a manner of speaking. Theirs is less a written language and more a sequence of symbols intended to prompt the speaker's memory. This juvenile caricature

here—with the flashy cape and headdress—indicates that
Maxtla himself is the author. Concerning the rest, I had the
Nihonian, Tora, look at it—"

"What does it mean?"

"Well, you might imagine the difficulty of translating—"

"The gist of it, nephew. I do not have all day. We have an
attack planned."

"It's a poem."

Germanicus's eyes narrowed. "Maxtla sends me a poem?"

"Yes. As I tried to explain, the Nihonian is working out a
more punctilious translation, but, in short, the reverend
speaker is thanking his brother, Caesar, for furnishing the
Fifth Sun with so many worthy victims for sacrifice."

"Is the bastard taunting me?"

"Tora thinks not." An ineffable smile came to Gaius
Nero's lips. "The sentiment is sincerely expressed."

"Then so is mine," Germanicus said grimly, marching off
toward the lorry, no longer favoring his right foot. "Come—I
want to speak to my legionaries. We're breaking out of here
today."

Rolf was hurrying to follow when Alope stayed him a moment by grasping his elbow. "Why is Caesar so filled with
spirit against enemies again?" she asked, bemused yet also
pleased.

"Epizelus be among Maxtla's captives. Germanicus fight
hardest from love, not anger. It be his way." Then the centurion shrugged as if to ask if she understood.

"Yes, Red Wolf." But her face became somber as she
watched the Romans depart. Finally, she stopped staring after
them and turned the pieces of squash on their skewer.

The downpour began riding on crosswinds, lashing the
legionaries both front and back at the same time. The men
were already chilled, weary, but Germanicus would ask them
to fight through the night and perhaps well into tomorrow
morning—at least those who would survive this first bloody
slitting of the Aztecan breastworks. Maxtla's troops fought as
a ferocious mob, a great clot of howling men that inevitably
formed around the Roman van, each warrior clamoring for
victims, heedless of the depth of his comrades piling up
underfoot. The Aztecan disdain for tactical formation was
unnerving to the legionaries, who were familiar with foes who

inevitably arrayed themselves for battle in some variation of the Greek phalanx, especially when massed fire at close range was called for. But these barbarians attacked in the manner of a pack of wild dogs. Their losses would have been unacceptable to any other people in the world, but not to the children of the Fifth Sun, who believed that their blood nourished the same golden star that turned their corpses black after a few days under its heat.

Germanicus strode down the ranks of his men, showing them that he too had skin roughed by goosebumps, a nose running from the wet cold, an an exhaustion that was making him feel as old as the Pantheon. But if he could vault above all this, so could they. He stepped up onto a boulder and nodded at them, the silent faces numbering in the thousands. Hail had begun clicking off their helmets, dancing on their shoulders. "Lads! Are you tired of this mudhole?"

"Aye!" they roared.

"Well, so am I. What do you say we punch out of here today?"

"Aye!"

"These feathered bastards have had a few lucky guesses as to where we tried to push through. But they can't keep guessing right all the time. Nor can they keep losing a dozen warriors each time they rub noses with a Roman legionary!"

"Aye!"

"Beyond here, it's open plains all the way to the mountains that harbor Maxtla's palace. Perfect country for our sandgalleys." His eyelids flinching from the swift drops, Germanicus grimaced up into the rain. "Let's get out of here before our cloaks rot off our backs!"

"Hail Caesar!"

A trumpet called for the army to unravel itself into a column of eight files. This formation wound down into the mist-shrouded gulley from which these legionaries would charge toward the Aztecan lines in the next half hour.

Then the reports of at least a score of *pili* crackled through the dense air, and Germanicus turned to Gaius Nero. "Have the Aztecae beaten us to the first blow? Find out what this is about."

"Aye, Caesar."

Awaiting the prefect's return, Germanicus clasped his hands behind him, then before him, and finally crossed his arms over his cuirass before abruptly motioning for Rolf to follow him across the muddy camp to a cohort of Novo militiamen, who were waiting in reserve as part of the second line. They were slouching in ranks of questionable trim, and Caesar's inspection did little to neaten them up. Swaddled in fur togas, which gave off a vivid stink now that they were soaked, the colonials leaned on their *pili* as they greeted Germanicus with nods and shrugs instead of salutes. He turned a blind eye on this breach of Campus Martius etiquette and stayed their Tenth Legion tribune, who seemed on the verge of decimating them for their casual bearing in the presence of the most regal man on earth: "That's all right, tribune." Germanicus then inquired of a signifer who wore his hair shoulder-length in the fashion of an Indee warrior: "What is your assignment today?"

"Not be *maximus*, by your Jove." The man bared his big, square teeth. "But we steal the meat of the nut these squirrels silver and red crack for us *cum* their heads!"

The other Novos whooped and cheered.

Looking ill, the Italian-born tribune croaked, "He means, Caesar, that our role this afternoon is secondary. We will exploit the gap in the Aztecan defense created by the legionary vanguardists."

"Ah . . ." Germanicus said at last, then strolled down the line. He could not understand how a group of men gathered under the same standard could so thoroughly subvert the principle of uniformity. While all were bearded and dressed in dripping furs, each was so appointed in his own distinctive way: one irregular sported mustaches that hung down to his chest; the next in line had none but, to compensate for the lack, had trained his beard into a quilt of ringlets reminiscent of Assyrian statuary; the third, having half new barbarian blood, had no beard at all, except one that had been tattooed onto his pockmarked cheeks and chin! Some togas draped down into the mud; others revealed scarred forelegs; and a few were no longer than tunics, with the wearer preserving modesty only by adding a breechcloth.

One of the Novos he passed was staring at him sullenly.

Germanicus backed up a step. "Is something troubling you?" Then he recognized the man: Alope's friend of Sicilian extraction whom she had invited aboard Germanicus's sandgalley on the Nova Petra–Otacilium Trace. "I remember you."

"Cornificius, *tribune*." He seemed remarkably unruffled to discover the *tribunus aerarius* of that occasion to be the emperor. "Why Alope tell me not?" he asked almost resentfully.

"There were important reasons. Why do you join our army on its drive south?" Germanicus smiled at him. "I see you've already received your new *pilum*."

"To see 'Titlan. Most *maximus* handsome city, I hear."

"You should see Rome before you say that."

Cornificius apparently mistook this for an order. "No. I see 'Titlan first, then maybe Rome—if Romans be ready to buy furs."

"Caesar!" Gaius Nero came bounding from island to island across the sea of gumbo that was gradually inundating the camp. He splashed to a halt and saluted, his brief silence an exquisite pantomime of shame. "The *pili* you heard—my praetorians were attempting to halt the flight of two Aztecan prisoners from the stockade."

"How did they escape?"

"That last *ballista* round—it struck the wall, opening a breach in the timbers. My guardsmen killed one of the warriors. But—"

"The other made his way through the lines."

Gaius Nero looked down. "Yes."

"We must call off the attack. The bastard will have seen where we plan to push through. Quickly—"

But then trumpets declared the moment of attack. Germanicus's back stiffened as his legionaries, screened by a bank of mist, cried, "Hail Caesar!" A smattering of *pili* reports swelled into a roar. He spun on Gaius Nero, his eyes accusatory. "All captives are to be transported north to Otacilium at once! No Aztecae are to be held this close to our front!"

"Of course, Caesar." The prefect came smartly to attention, then strolled off with his head held high, as if refusing to accept the chastisement.

Germanicus listened to the ever-increasing tumult of battle, wincing when a shriek was borne to him on some caprice of the wind. Still gazing southward, he said to Rolf, "I want you to find out what's going on inside that stockade." After several seconds in which he had heard no retreating footfalls, he turned to glare at the centurion, who was standing with his arms akimbo. "Did you hear me?"

"Aye." Rolf started to say something, but then thought better of it.

Germanicus sighed. "Out with it."

"I thought we be of an agreement."

"What about?"

"I guard you close by—as long as I be no bother."

"Yes, that's true."

With undisguised suspicion, Rolf regarded the praetorians standing off by themselves in the distance. "Well, you keep sending me away . . ."

"And?"

"And I be sent away no more. From now on, I stay at your side."

"In chains then?"

Rolf gave a fierce nod. "If need be—aye."

"You insolent Goth!"

The centurion's shrug said that he would not back down this time. "Aye."

"You—!" Germanicus had formed a fist; but, in suddenly realizing the loyalty at the heart of the man's doggedness, his anger went slack. "You," he said far less vehemently, "are the only person I can trust out of my sight."

Rolf considered this in silence—as if struck by the curious loneliness in these words, but then fell in step with Germanicus when he saw that the emperor was striding for the front. "I be cursed with another trust: to keep Kaiser alive! What if you be slain while running errands?"

"Then we are both relieved of our great burdens."

The centurion stared askance at him for a long moment. Then a strange sound akin to a hiccup or even a belch racked his throat and burst out his nose. A moment afterwards, Germanicus realized that it had been a snort of laughter; his remark had tickled the German affinity for imperturbability in the face of total disaster.

"So, my friend," Germanicus said earnestly, "please do as I ask. I would not beg if it weren't absolutely necessary."

"You be willing to go back to your sand-galley?"

Germanicus hesitated, but Rolf's eyes shone with insistence. "Very well, centurion."

A lorry came wallowing down two galena-colored slashes

that were ruts in the ooze. The Third Legion colonel on the rear bench gawked at Germanicus, riffling through some mental congealment for the right words.

"Report," Germanicus said at last.

"The men are turning back. May we . . . ?"

"Yes"—Germanicus's voice seemed thin and faraway even to his own ears—"you may dignify this rout with the order to retreat."

"Do you think it is I who sends word to Tizoc?" she asked out of the languid stillness that weighed upon them. It had nearly dampened their lovemaking.

Germanicus made no reply other than to hold her more tightly in his arms.

"Do not believe so, Germanicus." Her breath gusted warmly inside the cup of his ear. "Do not do this to the time we have left."

Suddenly, he turned her face with his palms so she could meet his gaze. "You will not leave me, Alope. I won't allow that. I will fight it—make no mistake."

"I will never leave you."

Confusion tapered his eyes. "Then what . . . ?"

She pressed her fingertips against his lips. And when he did not try to speak again, her touch trickled down his throat and across his chest.

A soughing of rain-scented air drew his attention to the small porthole in his sand-galley cabin. Beyond was a chaos of dim blue clouds. In another few minutes they would be lost in darkness. Germanicus exhaled. "I don't trust the way I once did —completely or not at all. Nor do I love as I did."

"It is so for those who have lost much."

"Yes . . . yes."

"Then we must speak plainly to each other, as friends who have lost much before they ever met."

Germanicus rested his chin on the crown of her head. "Very well."

"Why are you losing your stomach for this war?"

And finally it gushed out of him, the great secret at the core of his life he had never revealed to anyone. "Do you know what I mean by the republic?" He waited, his heart thundering as he considered the enormousness of what he was risking.

"Of course I know. It was very bad. By making war on
Pompey's clan, the warriors of Caesar's clan saved Rome
from this republic."

"Good Jupiter—is *that* what they teach in a provincial
lyceum?"

"Do I recall it wrong?"

"No, my love. I'm sure it's the instruction that's faulty.
Even Gaius Julius, if alive, would take issue with such over-
simplification. In some ways, he loved Pompey."

"Then you think it better that this republic had won?"

"In the long view, yes, despite the excesses of the senatorial
class at that time."

"But of which clan are you—Pompey's or Caesar's?"

"Both, perhaps. It depends on how the lineage is reckoned.
But these men were tied to the same clan: Pompey was at one
time Caesar's son-in-law."

"Did not Caesar have the chief of the Egyptians slay Pompey?"

"Yes, Alope."

"Such wickedness—a relative of this own clan! The Indee
would put such a person to death!"

"Well, we Romans, too, as things worked out for poor
Gaius Julius." Through the porthole, Germanicus watched a
flare fester down through the clouds, dripping cold sparks. He
snugged the blanket around her bare shoulders. "That's the
unavoidable evil of a civil war. A clan is pitted against itself."
His chuckle was morose: "I once imagined that I could just
stop being emperor. I would simply walk off the Palatine Hill,
and that would be that. But such a dream can never be. The
hour I abdicate is the one in which Roman will start murdering
Roman. Fighting and destruction will erupt wherever in this
world the coinage bears my countenance."

"If you say this republic is best, then so do I. And so will
Skinyea. The Indee will add their arms to yours."

"Oh, Alope . . ."

"But what has this to do with the punishment Maxtla
deserves for making war on your Romans?"

"I must look beyond this campaign. Most of the legions, I
believe, will remain loyal to me, even if the men are undecided
about the republic. I can't afford to squander legionaries I will
so desperately need to quell the forces of reaction, especially in

an interminable struggle with a daft barbarian like Maxtla. I must leave off being Caesar with all my *personal* authority intact, for I'll no longer be able to lay claim to imperial authority. Don't you see what a war like this could do to the esteem in which my people hold me?"

Alope remained silent. Germanicus ached for her to say something, anything. He rested the side of his face against hers. Her pulse was swishing through her temple, swiftly, irregularly. "My love—"

"The heartland of the Aztecae would make a rich province," she said with smarting in her voice.

"We Romans are bloated on provinces. We already hold more than we can safely manage. If only you could understand how short I am of capable governors. Do you remember learning at the lyceum about Periclean Athens? How its downfall was hastened by military adventurism in Sicilia?"

She had sat up and slid across the bunk to lean against the bulkhead opposite him. The profile of her face was downcast as she spoke: "I have hoped many times that you might love me."

"I do, woman. And I don't care to imagine a future without you."

"You are a good man, Germanicus. That is nothing unusual of itself. But your goodness does not come from weakness, as it does with some men who act this way so others will not harm them. Your goodness springs from power. It is only this way with the greatest chiefs." She lowered her voice until he could barely hear it. "Often I have hungered for the one whose name is no longer spoken. This is natural, yes?"

"Of course."

"But I have wanted you with a different kind of yearning. Never have I imagined you to be that one."

Germanicus's eyes closed on a twinge of guilt.

"If there were a way," she went on, "would you make peace with Maxtla?"

"Perhaps."

"What of the Indee and our Anasazi brothers who already race for Tenochtitlan?"

"It would be a condition of the peace that your people go unmolested, free of this Flowery Way business."

"And what of me?"

"I don't understand . . ."

"Would it be a condition of the peace that you still love me?"

Germanicus groaned. "I have no wish to live without you. I want you to be my wife."

"Will I live in your palace?" she demanded, fighting back tears.

"For a time—but only a short one. Then we must encamp on whatever shore the war tosses us."

"If I became your wife, you could say go and I would go. If I became your wife, I would find your arms palace enough for me. But it matters only that you love me."

"Good Jupiter, woman . . ." He reached across the space to seize her. "You are everything."

"Then it is finished," she whispered. "And I am content."

Yet Germanicus could sense no joy in her body. The sensations he took from her frantic embrace suggested loss and sadness, and this was confirmed when, after they had made love again, she whispered, "I can never be your wife. But if it were mine to say yes or no . . ." Her voice trailed off. She slept—or pretended to.

22

GERMANICUS HAD HOPED that by the time he had doused his face with cold water and donned a fresh uniform the shock would have dissipated, even mellowed into the serenity of self-denial. But, by breakfast, the heaviness at the center of his chest had not eased, and even the oil-and-honey bread, his favorite, was ashes in his mouth. One by one, aides approached his couch, which was protected from the drizzle by an awning hung off the leeward bulwark of the imperial sand-galley. Each of these officers took one glance at the emperor's stunned, almost owlish expression, then promptly about-faced and hurried off toward some bureaucratic necessity without disturbing him.

At first light, Germanicus had awakened to find his arms empty, sprawled whitely across the blankets like those of a dead man.

She has gone back to her people, he kept having to remind himself. *She has run off to tell Skinyea the bitter news*. The Anasazi chieftains would feel betrayed, but Germanicus now admonished them with a glower as if these new barbarians were arrayed in a semicircle around his couch: *I never swore I'd go all the way to Tenochtitlan. All of you simply assumed I would* . . . Regardless of the Anasazi cravings for vengeance, now was the time for Germanicus to reopen negotiations with Maxtla: a Roman army was threatening Tenochtitlan and an Aztecan one was investing the approaches to Otacilium.

As for the practices of the Aztecae, the barbarian world was rife with these kinds of abomination, and Rome would never have legionaries enough to root them all out. Still, there remained Epizelus. Germanicus could not recall his beloved physician without pain shooting through his heart. Yet there was hope even in this matter: with infuriating courtesy, the Aztecan commander had delivered to General Salvidienus a list of all Roman prisoners sacrificed to date so that the families of the deceased "might rejoice in the knowledge that their sons and daughters have helped feed the majesty of the Fifth Sun." Epizelus's name had been absent from this bloody manifest. In fact, it seemed that Maxtla was sparing the lives of all high-ranking Romans. Again, Germanicus gleaned a small kernel of hope from what otherwise seemed a blighted field.

He was on the verge of summoning Belgius to draft a missive to Maxtla proposing a truce when Alope's face flashed through the light and shadow of his mind as it had with arresting beauty that afternoon on the holy mountain of the Indee.

He had been wrong before—and now prayed that his deepest, most incisive instincts were deceiving him. He could not stand the thought of such appalling desperation in someone who had lain so tenderly in his arms.

All at once, the resolve that had made him sit upright to do business was gone, and he slumped back before drawing a servant near with a weary flick of his fingers. "A cup of wine."

"*Wine*, Caesar?" the man asked in astonishment. It was the first time he had ever heard such a request from the emperor.

"To dip my bread in," Germanicus muttered. "It's stale."

"But we baked fresh this morning—"

Germanicus cut him short with a glare. But when the cup was nestled in his palms, the vintage rocking in a purple tide from lip to lip, he suddenly growled and flung the wine out. "Bring me vinegar!"

Before this new request could be filled, he bolted up off his couch and climbed the ladder to the main deck of the sandgalley, where he stood for several seconds, face pinched against the sting of the rain, and gazed all around in search of a glimpse of buckskin. Then he ducked down a hatch to his cabin and began tearing through his possessions, dumping the contents of his kit onto his bunk, rummaging through leather satchels and soiled tunics. He had just overturned the thin mattress when a roar rattled through the iron plates of the sand-galley. It continued unabated for five minutes, a seam-less explosion hammering the earth. When it abruptly ceased, his ears were ringing so fiercely he found it difficult to understand a flustered Gaius Nero, who was shouting from the passageway.

"What?" Germanicus growled.

"The Aztecae hurl themselves at our lines, Caesar!"

Germanicus appeared to be unaffected by the report. "What do you make of this?" He was pointing at a small hide pouch and four blue gemstones neatly arrayed on the iron pallet that supported his mattress. There was also a sprinkling of leaves that had been crushed into fine flakes. Germanicus knew by the gray-green color that this is all that remained of the sprig of olive he had intended to give Maxtla in the name of peace.

"Good Mars, Caesar," the prefect said at last, "these are the trappings of sorcery!"

Germanicus nodded absently as he opened the pouch and examined its powdery contents.

"Wasn't Alope carrying one of those aboard the *Aeneas*?"

Germanicus ignored the question and tasted the golden substance with the tip of his tongue.

"Uncle, please—that might well be noxious."

"Do you really think so?" Germanicus's eyes seemed unusually large and moist.

Gaius Nero laid his hand on Germanicus's forearm. "I know that she's left you."

"Did anyone see her depart?"

"No. She must've gone under the cover of darkness."

"Yes . . . she can move like a ghost."

"Truly, uncle, I'm sorry for you. But permit me to say that I never trusted the woman."

"Not once did she speak poorly of you."

"I'm surprised—but not flattered." The prefect reached for the pouch. "I want to preserve these banes for examination."

"No, nephew."

"Surely you'd want to know if they're poisonous!"

"I do not." Germanicus opened the porthole and inverted the hide so that the powder was borne away in a dusty billow.

Gaius Nero could be heard sniggering, and Germanicus turned back toward him, eyes flashing.

"Forgive me, uncle, but something keeps occurring to me."
"*What?*"

His nephew's smile slowly faded. "There isn't a man in the world who wouldn't trade places with you. Yet you always seem so grave. So unhappy. Never once have I seen you enjoy your *imperium*."

"And you would delight in being emperor?"

"Yes," the prefect said quietly, "I would delight if it fell upon me. That is the Roman way: to find pleasure in adversity, to accept what the gods give us."

"If we are fortunate, the gods grant us power only after we've lost our taste for it." Germanicus saw that Rolf was lingering in the passageway.

Gaius Nero winked as he tilted his head toward the centurion. "I understand, uncle, that your man has been visiting my praetorians assigned to the stockade."

"I must give Rolf leave now and again. His is a solitary posting. He has no comrades with whom he can share the annoyance I must cause him."

"Well," Gaius Nero said, "I know how that can be remedied: have him transferred to the praetorian guard. I welcome a man of his experience."

Germanicus looked to Rolf. "What do you say about becoming a praetorian, as you once were?"

"I be satisfied with my status."

"Which is?" Gaius Nero asked with a complacent grin.

"On detached service from my legion in Anatolia, prefect."

Germanicus shrugged. "There you have it, nephew, from the man himself. He's content."

"A blessing, I'm sure. But the offer remains open, centurion."

"I thank the prefect."

Gaius Nero listened to the distant cacophany of *pili* reports, then saluted. "Very well, Caesar, I shall check on the progress of the battle. Hail and be well."

Germanicus waited until he was well down the passageway, then motioned for Rolf to step inside the cabin and seal the hatch behind him. "What did you learn at the stockade?"

"These praetorians be tight-lipped."

"No Germans among them to gossip with you?"

"Nay, and the new guardsmen be gladiators."

Germanicus's face darkened: it had never boded well for the

emperor when his praetorian prefect had started enlisting his troops from the arena. The foremost loyalty of such men was to gold. "Are you certain?"

"I recognize one who once be called the Aquitanian—a *retiarius*. Many did die inside his net."

"Are they still holding Aztecan prisoners there?"

"For a bit. Then they be transported north as ordered."

"I want you to keep an eye on praetorian activities for the next several days." Germanicus noticed that Rolf was grasping a slip of parchment in his hand. "What's that?"

"It be in my kit when I come back from the stockade just now. From Alope for you."

Germanicus seized it from him. The uncial Alope had mastered at the lyceum was elegant and feminine; it reminded him of Crispa's.

> *My Great Friend,*
> *Nothing is possible where there is distrust.*
> *Only one man inside your camp knows the face of the traitor. He is the guilty one himself. But Tizoc and his lords will know who this one is. One tongue can keep a secret. But many tongues cannot.*
> *Soon I will be with you always,*
>
> *Alope of the Indee*

Germanicus drifted past Rolf, his face stunned.

In the next three days, as he ambled around the rust-brown hull of his sand-galley or stood gazing southward from its highest deck, he refused to relinquish the piece of parchment. It became as soft as kidskin from the oil of his fingers. He referred to it time and again with a bewildered expression as if it were some ambiguous Delphic poem he was helpless to decipher.

Finally, on the third evening, he glanced up from an aromatic fire of juniper wood to see a Raramuran messenger hesitating outside the praetorian perimeter. Germanicus ordered the captain of the guard to let the runner approach.

The new barbarian handed Germanicus a sweat-discolored wad of rawhide, then trotted back into the darkness. It resisted unfolding after being clutched over so many miles, but when Germanicus had pried its corners flat he could see a single word painted in uncial upon its wrinkled surface—a praenomen. Quickly, as if afraid of being discovered with the missive in his grasp, he flung it down into the hottest cove of flames and appeared to breathe again only after it had shrunk and twisted into a black cinder. "The sorrow comes from being only half-surprised," he whispered to himself.

"Lord Caesar!"

Germanicus started, his hand flashing to the hilt of his short sword before he fully realized who had hailed him. "Yes, Tora-san, what is it?"

"The Aztecan message that came through lines this day—"

"Yes?"

The Nihonian paused, then lowered his face to show his discomfiture. "I have translated: it is another list."

Germanicus found it painful to form the words: "Who now has been sacrificed?"

"No one, Lord Caesar."

"No one?"

"They are being saved for Ceremony of New Fire. Their blood will be used to renew sun." Tora still had not lifted his eyes from the muddy ground, and Germanicus at last learned why: "Your physician, the woman Alope—they will die."

Germanicus's head was jarred as if he had been struck: it had been a shudder he'd been able to control until it reached his neck. "*When?*"

"Twenty-five days, Lord Caesar."

"Dear Jupiter, however can I do it?" Germanicus's eyes, frenzied, almost hysterical, lit upon the Nihonian's wretched expression. "However can I take Tenochtitlan in that time?" He spun on his heels toward the sand-galley. "Rolf!"

The centurion's face shot over the railing. "Kaiser?"

"Assemble my officers!"

"Aye."

Germanicus lowered his voice: "And then see me in private." It was more than an afterthought.

Rolf hobbled his pony on the dark side of the ridge, then hurried through the bright starshine to the crest and concealed himself in the cleft of a great boulder that had split in two. He swept his optics up to his eyes and brought the distant stockade into focus. He waited.

From afar came a soft and deep rustling sound the centurion recognized at once: Roman legionaries on the move.

Within the hour, he had been listening to Germanicus exhorting his officers to finally break through the Aztecan resistance: "Five cohorts of the Third Legion and one of Novo
militia shall advance and outflank the enemy from here . . ."
Germanicus had hammered the map with his fist at a fording
on the seasonal river ten miles west of the camp. "The men
must quick-march noiselessly and with no more light than that
of the stars. Can they do this, my *legatus*?"

"They can, Caesar," Gaius Nero answered, not taking his
eyes off the place Germanicus had thumped on the serpentine
streak of blue that indicated the river.

"Are there any prisoners in the stockade?"

"One—he was captured at dusk."

"We cannot afford an escape on the eve of our attack."

"Of course, Caesar."

"Very well, Gaius Nero. I want you to command the
cohorts at the fording. That way, I can rest assured that all
will go smoothly there."

"An honor, Caesar—and I will personally attend to the
removal of the prisoner before I march."

Germanicus had nodded, smiling warmly at his nephew.
Then he'd fervently clasped his hands together. "Forward to
the shores of Lake Texcoco, my sons!"

Now, glimpsing sudden movement in the darkness below,
Rolf strained to distinguish silhouette from shadow. Soon, a
squad of a dozen praetorians marched out of the night and
into the fan of dim torchlight that issued from the portal of
the stockade. It was Gaius Nero and his retinue of former
gladiators, who promenaded rather than tramped forthrightly
like soldiers. Bringing up the rear was a figure in a fur toga, a
Novo militiaman, who entered the compound with the
cautious steps of a feline and stood by restlessly until an
Azteca, wrists bound behind him, was herded up the steps
from an underground bunker. The captive was addressed by
the prefect, and the Novo appeared to translate, but Rolf
could hear nothing of what was being said. Visibly, in the
gradual sloping of his shoulders and the unraveling of his fists,
the Azteca began to relax, and by the time his bindings were
cut away by a praetorian the warrior was grinning.

"These be merry foes," Rolf muttered.

Then the Azteca was invited to share the rear bench of a
lorry with a pair of guardsmen, which he did without hesita-

tion. Two more praetorians leaped aboard, and one of them steered the vehicle out of the stockade. The cones of light from its prow lanterns swept across the dingy tents of the *castrum* and eventually aligned with the ruts of the northbound trace. The guardsmen passed through a sentry post without being challenged.

Scrambling down the slope, Rolf swung up onto the pony's back and urged it with sharp kicks to the top of the ridge, which paralleled the road. Laboriously, the lorry was churning over its ribbon of ooze no faster than Rolf's mount was negotiating the game trail that meandered along the lip of the bluff. He felt no thrill of pursuit; there was a vague taint of dishonor on this detail he had accepted. In his brief moment alone with Germanicus, the centurion had argued, "If Kaiser be aware of the guilty one, arrest him. Otherwise, this be a test of the daughter Alope!" Wearily, Germanicus had rubbed his eyes with his fingers before speaking: "Yes, it's a test. Most men can completely trust those whom they love. Emperors are not so fortunate."

Rolf now halted and raised up from his saddle.

Ahead, in a shadowy vale, loomed a sand-galley, so like a ship riding at anchor on the black waters of a lagoon it seemed to bob slightly. This was no ordinary armored craft: sitting astride its main deck was a huge figure of Charon, pulling on brass oars and scowling over his shoulder for a glimpse of the benighted shore of the Styx. A chimney jutted up out of his head and from it spewed a panicle of orange sparks, a continuous swarm of fireflies that skittered far up into the darkness before winking out.

A half dozen priests had ringed a brazier with their couches, their white togas appearing saffron-colored in the amber lamplight. At any given moment, one of them was either giggling or hoisting his cup for it to be filled by a dwarf.

Rolf spat on the ground.

Prior to the Emperor Fabius's reign, there had been no special caste of Jovian priests. All Romans had been charged with nurturing the mutual trust between the gods and men. But Fabius, in order to spare himself the endless ritual that went along with being *pontifex maximus*, had struck a bargain with the Senate: The imperial treasury would support an order of holy men so that the House of Jupiter would not be neglected while Caesar concerned himself with other matters.

This priesthood soon became a patrician dumping ground for dull or dissipated sons. Rolf had never had any time for Jovian priests. On campaigns, they usually stayed aboard "Libitina's Barge," as their funerary galley was called, and wiled away the days in debauchery.

The glow from their lantern spilled across the ground and illuminated row upon row of lifeless legionaries. The cloaks of the soldiers had been unhitched and draped over their faces. Working among these silent ranks were three slaves, two bearing a litter and the third lighting their way with a torch.

"This citizen has been surrendered to death!" the torchbearer cried as soon as his comrades had picked up another corpse. "For those who find it convenient it is now time to attend the funeral!" The little procession shuffled to a halt beneath the afterdeck. All three stared upward, waiting.

After several moments, a priest grumbled up off his couch and pitched three handfuls of Italian earth down onto the deceased, pelting the slaves at the same time. Then, without even a brief prayer, he plodded back to the warmth of the brazier.

"That be no way to honor a legionary," Rolf whispered. Then he realized that the praetorian lorry was lumbering toward the sand-galley, but with its prow lanterns extinguished. He rode farther along the ridge until he was within earshot of the priests' conversation, which concerned a Roman courtesan with shameful talents.

The slaves laid the body at the foot of a flickering seam in the hull of the galley, then swung open two iron doors to reveal a conflagration that twisted and crackled up through a heap of bones and skulls. They had just ripped a pendant from the dead legionary's neck and were prying open the man's mouth to fish out the coin placed there by his bereaved comrades to pay the Styx ferryman for the crossing when two praetorians strolled up from their lorry, which they had left some distance back in the darkness.

The torchbearer hid the plunder behind his back. "Hail Caesar!"

"Hail. We're searching for a friend of ours. He's been missing since yesterday, and we fear the worst."

"We've fed no guardsmen to the flames," the torchbearer said.

There was movement somewhere out in the dusky field, and

Rolf saw that the two other praetorians—their indentity betrayed by the cut of the Attic crests on their helmets—were dragging a corpse back to the lorry. The Azteca could still be seen on the rear bench, unguarded, patiently awaiting the return of his Roman captors. The guardsmen loaded the body onto the vehicle, then hurried back through the low brush to snatch another fare from Charon.

But, from the afterdeck, the priests took no notice of this theft. One of them bawled drunkenly at the slaves, "Do not permit these praetorians to depart until they have been thrice sprinkled with holy water and thus purified!"

"You'll not put spots on my brass!"

The priest unsteadily approached the railing and glowered down at the offending guardsman. "Shame—time was when praetorians were held up to the citizenry as examples of devotion."

"Time was when the same was said of priests—before they went on the dole." Laughing, the guardsmen turned on their heels and marched back to their lorry, where their comrades were already seated, flanking the Azteca once again.

With lanterns blazing, the lorry continued north, faster now that the ground was higher and less muddy, forcing Rolf to goad his pony into a gallop. He was compelled to keep his attention on the dim luminescence of the game trail, especially where it threaded across slopes of scree, and so it did not surprise him when he glanced up after a particularly hazardous stretch and failed to see the lorry. He expected the glow of its lanterns to show any instant around some bend in the narrowing chasm below. But, after several minutes, the centurion became alarmed. He dismounted and stood away from the labored breathing of his pony so he could listen to any sounds carried his way by the slight breeze.

Finally, just when he was growing frantic that the praetorians had slipped away from him, Rolf caught snatches of their conversation from below. Hobbling his pony once again, he unslung his *pilum* and began zigzagging down a hogback toward the voices. The sandy spur dipped steeply, then rose again to a rocky knob, whose summit Rolf achieved after several minutes of careful climbing. From this vantage he could clearly see the lorry, which was idling on a brightness of chalky ground.

Two of the guardsmen were chuckling softly as they ex-

changed uniforms with the dead legionaries. The other pair
was busy gesticulating to the Azteca, who stood motionless
before them, arms splayed out slightly from his sides as if he
were bemused, until, at last, one of the guardsmen thrust a
scroll-shaped object in his hands and shouted, "Go!" The
warrior bowed and began trotting southwest—the direction by
which it would be easiest to circumvent the Roman lines; his
path took him up a ravine that passed directly beneath the
knob on which Rolf crouched. The centurion watched this
through the aimer of his *pilum*, but did not fire. "You live,"
he whispered, "thanks to Germanicus Julius Agricola."

Meanwhile, the praetorians had propped the corpses up on
the rear bench of the lorry and snugged crested helmets onto
the sagging heads. They stood back to admire their handiwork
before discharging their *pili* into the bodies and the vehicle.
The individual reports were curdled by echoes into a clattering
din that had not completely died away when one of the
guardsmen splashed petrol over the lorry and set it ablaze.

Then, briskly, like gladiators entering the arena to cheers,
they set off back toward the camp, the fire casting their co-
lossal shadows ahead of them. But the praetorians had not
gone far when the two in Third Legion uniforms took their
leave and found concealment in a thicket of willows.

"Tomorrow, lads . . . Stay in the same place, now," their
comrades farewelled them, continuing on their way toward
that breathless moment in which, surrounded by Caesar's
staff, they would recount how the cunning Aztecae had am-
bushed their lorry, killing two fine praetorians and freeing the
captive.

Rolf surmised that these praetorians would not wander back
into the camp until dawn, after another Roman attack would
have been launched and repelled. He would have gladly slain
them, but he had curious orders to allow all the treachery to
unfold without hindrance.

Of the six cohorts slated to proceed to the fording, only
one—the Novo militia—had departed into the night. Before
the next cohort in the column could troop forward to join
them, an order delayed the march. Hearsay filtered down to
the legionaries that just before the First Cohort had fallen in
behind the militiamen, the clatter of hooves had broken the
stillness out in front of them. It was believed that Aztecan

cavalry had infiltrated the Roman column, although no one could remember having ever heard of Aztecan cavalry. Now it was hoped that the enemy had stumbled into this small gap without realizing it, and—if all the lads kept quiet—Maxtla's horsemen might return to their own lines none the wiser.

Here and there, legionaries began shedding their cloaks to use them as blankets. The salts in their thirties and forties, the *principles* and the *triarii* who would comprise the second and third lines in the heavy infantry attack, took their helmets off their chests, where they had been slung for the march, and made pillows of them. They sensed that this would be one more long wait.

Outside his sand-galley, Germanicus stood beside a brazier sipping vinegar, studying each of his aides one by one as if he'd never seen any of them before in his life.

Three hours before first light, a messenger from Gaius Nero came staggering through the praetorian cordon, red-rimmed eyes flitting from face to face in search of the emperor's.

"Here, tribune," Germanicus said quietly.

The messenger pivoted toward him frantically. "Hail Caesar! The prefect sends his compliments, but begs to know where the imperial cohorts are. He has nothing but Novo auxiliaries to command at the fording!"

"Did you observe Aztecan cavalry on your run here?"

"Aztecan cavalry?" The man was too exhausted to mask his incredulity.

"Yes, that's the cause of this delay. As soon as we feel confident that the enemy has passed out of the area in front of our column, the five cohorts will resume their march."

"Pardons, Caesar, but the prefect is quite concerned that he cannot mount the attack with the insufficient force he presently has."

"Is he really?"

"*Profoundly*, Caesar."

Germanicus smiled humorlessly. "My nephew shouldn't deprecate our provincial cousins. At any rate, the situation will clarify itself shortly. Rest here a while—I may have further orders in regard to Gaius Nero's *profound* concern. Have you the wind to cross this plain of Marathon twice in the same night?"

The praetorian nodded yes, but grimly. His heart had not yet stopped visibly pounding under his woolen tunic.

• • •

The false dawn seemed so luminous Gaius Nero could no longer contain himself. He abandoned his cover behind the berm atop the riverbank and began pacing down the long line of prostrate Novo militiamen. Their Etrurian-born colonel gave chase, rising no higher than a crouch, and respectfully asked the praetorian prefect not to show himself. He was ignored.

After half an hour, the vague sky-glow had failed to burgeon into day and night blackened the east again. "Aurora taunts me as well!" Gaius Nero hissed, savagely kicking the foot of a Novo, who started awake, gasping and punching at the air.

When sunrise came in earnest, its first rays found the prefect's face so wan it appeared to have been chiseled out of rose marble. He peered eastward toward the *castrum*. Instead of seeing five imperial cohorts—three thousand legionaries —on the march, he glimpsed nothing but light and shadow bandying for possession of the low hills. Birdlike, his face snapped southward: he imagined dust being raised by thousands of pairs of Aztecan sandals, clinging to the rolling highlands there and betraying the presence of a vast host. Reeling once again, he confronted the gaze of the colonel, who had sidled up to him noiselessly. "Dammit, don't sneak upon my person—what is it?"

"Your orders, prefect?"

Gaius Nero clenched his teeth to keep his chin from trembling. "Orders?"

"It is now dawn. We were to proceed south at dawn."

"With *one* cohort of half-barbarian rabble?"

"Your voice, prefect—please."

"How dare you tell—" But he suddenly closed his mouth and turned his ear to the east: hobnailed *caligae* were approaching over the stony ground. A moment later, the messenger he had dispatched to Germanicus last night came plodding over a rise and stumbled into the arms of two militiamen, who assisted him the last paces to the prefect.

"Where in the name of Mars are my five cohorts?" Gaius Nero demanded.

"Not . . . coming." The tribune sank to his knees as soon as the Novos let go of him.

"Then how am I to advance this morning?"

"You, sir, are not."

"Why?"

When the messenger paused to wheeze for breath, Gaius Nero cuffed the man across the face. "*Why?*" The tribune was too spent to respond to the humiliation of being struck by another Roman, but the officers encircling the two men looked away.

"Caesar says . . . you are in excellent position . . . to defend . . . right flank of the attack he's launching."

"From where, you fool?"

"Directly from the *castrum*."

"What happened to my cohorts?"

"Delayed too long . . . Aztecan cavalry infiltrated the column."

After several moments of no sound other than the morning breeze fluting through body armor, the officers began glancing back at the prefect. He was wearing a shocked grin, his teeth bared in a last rampart against self-annihilating fear. Now, with peculiar warmth—given the derision he had just heaped on the man—Gaius Nero rested his pale hand on the colonel's shoulder and asked, "I want you and my praetorians to remain around my person."

"Of course, prefect, we legionaries will be honored to do so. But your special squad of praetorians didn't march with us."

Gaius Nero's eyes flickered up and down the line. The light was now strong enough for him to see what he should have realized even in the darkness and confusion of last night: His guard was no longer on the fringe of his presence. "Why was this done?"

"Caesar's order, sir. Moments before we set out, your praetorians were transferred to the Third Cohort, which is badly undermanned. I thought you knew."

Gaius Nero continued to smile, although his left shoulder was being racked by spasms. "Yes, of course. I'd forgotten," he lied. He began walking backwards, keeping the officers in sight as he moved down the line of sprawling Novos, who were smirking at their disconcerted Roman overlords. The prefect began looking over his shoulder, searching among the hairy faces with mounting desperation. Finally he cried, "Come forth, you bastard!"

A lank figure slowly rose to his slouching height. Above his corded mustaches, which he had tucked behind his ears, his eyes were wide and troubled.

Gaius Nero strode up to him and whispered, "Get across the way and tell Tizoc it's off."

"*Off?*" Cornificius asked, dazed.

"The Roman attack will be launched directly out of the *castrum*."

"If I go, I must stay—*maximus* time."

"Yes, yes, of course—I'll arrange for your release when the campaign's concluded."

"And me *Romulo et Remo*?"

"Yes, your brother as well. Hurry, man!"

Cornificius had taken only a few strides to the south when the colonel asked in a hard voice, "Prefect, where is that militiaman going?"

"To reconnoiter—on Caesar's orders."

"Fire on that fleeing traitor!" the colonel commanded the line.

The Novos hesitated, and the Roman officers seized *pili* from the militiamen closest to them.

Cornificius was sprinting headlong across the shallow river, raising a spray with his boots, when the volley caught him, twisted his trunk so that his shoulder splashed first into the silty waters. He came up choking, clutching a bloody shin with his hands, and hobbled up the far bank into the brush. A second burst of fire pitched him down again. This time he did not rise.

"Are you mad?" Gaius Nero screamed at the colonel. "That man is acting on Caesar's personal orders!"

"No, prefect." The veteran seized Gaius Nero's right hand and, before the man could protest, stripped the signet ring off his middle finger. "I'm the only one present acting on Caesar's orders." He turned to his officers: "Arrest Gaius Nero Agricola."

Cornificius reminded himself that he had suffered greater pain before. While trapping in the basin of steamy geysers far to the north, as far north as one could go without beginning to encounter the Flatheaded People, he had been mauled by a humpbacked bear. Now *those* had been searing wounds, unlike these from *pili*, which would remain numb for several minutes before the burning ache would commence in his right foreleg and along his ribs. Of course, this time he would have no brother to nurse him through the fever and delirium. And it almost panicked him to realize that the pink strand dangling off the nearest saltbush was a piece of his own lung tissue. He refused to test the damage with a deep breath, but his mouth was already coppery with the taste of blood.

He had lied to Alope: his twin brother had not perished on the long trek. He was being held captive at Lord Tizoc's mansion in Tenochtitlan.

It was true that the detestable Flatheaded People had sold Cornelius and him into slavery at the Serican settlement along the Sea of the West. But Cornelius had not died of fire-thirst disease, and Cornificius had not escaped and walked south to make his way to the Nova Petra–Otacilium Trace, where Germanicus and Alope had encountered him. A month after their capture, the twins had been put aboard a Serican merchant galley, which eventually called on the Aztecan port of Aztlan, where Lord Tizoc took possession of them. The Sericans had believed that their new allies might find greater use for a pair of scruffy Novos than they.

His brother held on pain of death, Cornificius had been sent north to join the Novo militia and report on Roman activities at Nova Petra. Had he known at the time that the gruff-looking paymaster aboard the sand-galley was Caesar, he would have attempted to seize and carry him away—all to win Cornelius's freedom. Then, united once again, the brothers would have vanished forever into the country of meadows and quick waters. He cared little for emperors, even less for their garrisons and cities.

But that opportunity had been missed and, a few days later, when he had learned and reported that Germanicus was largely unguarded in the land of the Indee, Cornificius had been instructed by Tizoc's minion in Nova Petra to take no action. Caesar was to be permitted to complete his visitation unmolested, and Cornificius was to await contact by friends of the Aztecae in the Roman camp. This had not occurred for several months, but then, secretly, he was brought before the praetorian prefect, Caesar Germanicus's own nephew, who further intimidated the Novo with warnings about what would happen to his brother in Tenochtitlan should he betray the conspiracy. He had expected Gaius Nero to enlist him in an attempt against the emperor's life, but it soon became evident that the plotters had some ploy other than outright assassination in mind. Cornificius did not care—he only desired Cornelius's safe return.

Now that would never be. Cornelius would be handed over to the Aztecan priests for a Flowery Death, the thought of which filled Cornificius with rage. There was a second cause for his anger, a more immediate one: Freedom had made life precious to him, and soon he would have no eyes with which to light up distant snowfields or the thunderheads painted on a summer sky. Wind would no longer cool his face, fire crackle in his ears on deep, black nights. Unless . . . the Indee had been right all along about death.

Unknotting his tunic sash, he tied it around his thigh to stem the gush of blood. "By your Jove—damn Rome!" he hissed through the first sunburst of pain. "Damn 'Titlan!"

Horses were approaching. He could feel the vibrations pass through the dewy sands beneath his face. They were coming from the south—could that laughable rumor of Aztecan cavalry have been true after all? But he kept his mind on surviving—not his earth body, but that fragile essence of him that, if able to overcome these moments of fear and hatred, would pass through pines like the wind and stone like a hard frost. It was the spirit body of which the Indee spoke.

Then dozens of hooves were thudding the soft ground around him. He rolled on his back and discharged his *pilum* into the glare of the risen sun, to catch a rider full in the chest. But by the time he had craned his head and wheeled his weapon in another direction—seemingly impossible for limbs that had become leaden and sight that was fading—a dagger was pressed against his jugular.

"By your Jove," Cornificius said, his voice phlegmatic from the blood welling up in his throat, "give me the Flowery Way."

"*Inshallah*," the strange barbarian said. "A cross is waiting."

But the Novo's eyes had turned to opals: he no longer had an earth body worth crucifying.

The afternoon sunlight came yellowly through the canvas of the tent. Gaius Nero's face had the pallor of raw suet. He glared at Germanicus's intrusion, then turned his ear south toward the distant sounds of the Roman breakthrough—the only acknowledgment of his star-crossed machinations until he said with a mirthless smile, "A while ago, uncle, I over-heard the readministering of the *sacramentum* to your praetorian guard. I found it quite moving, really."

"There were those who refused to take it." Germanicus's voice was a croak. He had personally commanded the successful attack; his features and hands had been grayed by smoke. "Many of your followers closed their rebellious days with honor."

"Whatever I have or have not done in defense of the empire will be judged by the Senate, not by my own sword. That is my final word, uncle."

As he spoke, Gaius Nero canted his chin upwards—an arrogant gesture Quintus had inherited. The sight of it now pierced Germanicus's heart, made him want to beg—against his soundest judgment—for the young man to avow his loyalty as if for the first time. "Then you must know that the Senate which tries you will have a new *princeps senatus*."

Gaius Nero's eyes suddenly clicked toward Germanicus's face, but he held his tongue.

"Appius Torquatus was detained while on his way here from Otacilium. He was implicated by others in your plot. Confronted with this charge, he opened his veins—but not before confessing *all* that you and he had done to supplant my *imperium*. The failed assassination aboard the *Aeneas*. The murder of my *architectus maximus*, made all the more perfidious by the betrayal of your fellow conspirator, Fiducio. And finally this latest course—to thwart my prosecution of this campaign in the hope that the Senate and praetorian guard might declare you my regent. Then, I suppose, I would have died in my sleep one night, and been quickly cremated."

"Are you trying to persuade me to take my life?" Gaius Nero was grinning incredulously. "Who are you but an insipid republican who has bungled this war at every turn?"

"I am a friend who loves your family enough to acquaint you with the legal quandary in which you find yourself. Had you served as a magistrate you'd realize what your conviction would mean to them: the loss of all social advantage, all property, all—"

"Leave this tent!" Gaius Nero cried. "Your insincerity is stinking up the air!"

Germanicus's eyes were enraged, but he stayed Rolf, who

had bolted through the flaps with his sword drawn. "Perhaps I am being insincere, nephew," Germanicus said, his hands fisted as he wavered on the brink of either tears or shouting. "In truth, if you were to take your life, I don't know what I could say to Quintus."

"If you feel moved to execute me, uncle, tell him I died trying to save the empire."

"Yes, but for whom, Gaius Nero? Quintus may one day have the wisdom to ask."

And this reversal so distressed the old king he recalled his lord general from the northern lands where Tizoc was fighting the forces of the Compassionate, the Merciful.

"These enemies race like two arms of fire toward the heartland of our world!" Maxtla wailed. "Surely they are aided by the gods, perhaps even by Quetzalcoatl himself, who announces his return in this manner. And is this not further proof that the Fifth Sun will not be renewed? Is it not clear now that these waning years of two and fifty will not be tied to a fresh bundle of two and fifty?"

"No, reverend one—do not lose heart." Lord Tizoc had anticipated the old man's despair and brought with him to the palace a diviner, who had read the future in a scattering of maize kernels. "This priest assures us that an impossible thing must happen before our world, our gleaming city can be overthrown."

"Yes, reverend speaker, it is described in an ancient hymn of the Mexicae," the diviner said humbly from the floor. "Chaos shall not visit us until the waters of Lake Texcoco crawl up into the sky of stone."

But the old king was not mollified by these words. He felt the darkness closing on his soul.

23

"GIVE ME A quick way to win ground." Germanicus's lips felt sluggish from the cold. He paused to glide his palms back and forth across the coals throbbing in the brazier, staring all the while at the most trusted members of his immediate staff: Khalid, with the snowfall collecting in the folds of his *jamadani*; Tora, with head bowed pensively; and Britannicus Musa standing off a short distance, shivering either from the chill mountain air or his relentless affliction. "Five days," Germanicus went on, straining not to sound too desperate. "That is all the time our hostages have remaining before this Ceremony of New Fire."

"It has been revealed to me how we will win our way into the high valley of the infidel Maxtla," Khalid said matter-of-factly. "This will come to pass without the loss of another Roman life."

Weeks before, Germanicus might have cast a dubious glance in the prince's direction for making such a boast. But in these past days of hard-fought but swift advancing, the Great *Zaim*'s son had lived up to his promises time and again. Given command of a maniple of Novo militiamen, the young Anatolian had appropriated more Serican ponies—only the gods knew where—and whipped the irregulars into a capable light cavalry. His horsemen had become increasingly useful as the terrain buckled up into snowy ranges too precipitous for the facile deployment of sand-galleys. Twice Khalid's force had ferreted out Lord Tizoc's ambushes before they could be

221

sprung and, on the latter occasion, put a host of warriors to flight, the Aztecae leaving a trail of feathers that shouted red, orange, and blue from the drifted whiteness.

"Go on, Khalid," Germanicus said at last.

"Tora-san has often said the Aztecae foresee the death of their world in many signs."

"That is true, prince." The Nihonian lifted his face, smiling. Finally, he seemed comfortable with Latin. "They contemplate their end in the way Romans do their beginnings."

"And it is written of non-believers such as Maxtla: 'When evil befalls him he is despondent; but blessed with good fortune he grows niggardly.' My father, the holiest of men, told me before I ever rode for Rome: 'A vision will be yours after both deceivers and waters are crossed by Caesar's men in the same hour.' That did happen nineteen days past, yes? Last night, returning to Caesar's camp, I slept in my saddle. And the answer was revealed to me . . . *Inshallah*."

"*Yinshaya*," Tora echoed.

"Before the battle of Badr, three warriors of the Prophet challenged three Meccans to combat. It was fought in the sight of both armies. The believers slew the infidels, and the Meccans lost courage. They ran from the might of God."

Khalid's eyes became both dreamy and troubled, as if it were all a personal memory, a day of mixed emotions, of death and triumph. "I saw this struggle perfectly. No—" he corrected himself with a frown. "I took the place of one of these holy warriors. And a brace of my men from this time stood at my side. The Meccans were the Aztecae, and we slew them. I wore a long plume of feathers into battle." Khalid shook off the reverie. "I awoke as Jalaludin and Ismail galloped up to me. They were amazed: both had fallen asleep and been visited by the same dream. My men were even more astonished when, before they could tell it, I described their dream to them. 'It is everything you say, Prince Khalid,' Ismail cried, 'except the best part—Jalaludin and I lying nestled in the scented bosoms of *houris*!' " The Anatolian's eyes became dolorous. "They did not understand what this foretold of their fate. You see, in my vision, I was not comforted by the maidens of paradise."

Germanicus turned to Tora: "What do you think? Should I grant Khalid the chance to do single combat?"

"It would be reasonable, like *Yinshaya*, to use the Aztecae's own fears against them. Lord Tizoc's warriors might lose heart if the prince wins."

"What if Caesar's troops lose heart?"

Tora begged for apology with a grin, but spoke frankly nevertheless: "Yes, Romans are as superstitious as Aztecae. But Lord Caesar's legionaries will see no bad omen in the death of Anatolians."

In short, Germanicus would be risking the loss of a capable young commander of irregular cavalry. Tizoc would have to play for higher stakes than that, if he chose to gamble at all. "What if their lord general refuses our invitation?"

"He won't." Britannicus Musa's voice crackled dryly from infrequent use. His eyes shone despite their dark, swollen lids. Upon learning that Alope faced death on the Great Temple, he had put aside his qualms about joining any concerted effort, although his poise was repeatedly attacked by spasms in his lips and fingers, and often his voice grated to silence mid-thought. "His religion will not permit him to decline a battle. The Fifth Sun grows ever more voracious for human hearts. Long ago, a few hundred sacrifices each new growing season were thought sufficient to keep Tonatiuh satisfied—and the maize green. Now tens of thousands are given a Flowery Death. If Tenochtitlan is not destroyed, a hundred . . . two hundred thousand victims will be believed necessary. Tizoc is as much trapped by an ancient obsession as we are. And then there are the practical ramifications . . ." He shuddered involuntarily. "Once, they partook of small pieces of flesh simply to serve some ritual. But now I'm sure the Aztecan masses subsist on it. And if we triumph, Caesar, you should pray to the gods that Africa and Syria have bounteous enough harvests to share with your new clients."

Snuffling quietly, he at last crept up to the brazier and opened his pale, trembling hands to the heat. His pained expression slowly turned quizzical. "But I was unaware, prince, that the men of Agri Dagi adorn themselves with feathers."

"It is not our custom," Khalid admitted.

Britannicus's eyes lit on the Nihonian. "You would know: Of all their gods, which one haunts the Aztecan imagination?"

"Quetzalcoatl." Then Tora caught the drift of Britannicus's thought. "Yes, Quetzalcoatl, most certainly!"

"What's this about?" Germanicus asked impatiently.

"Quetzalcoatl," Britannicus explained, "was a noble but fallible deity. He committed some unmentionable sin and exiled himself by floating away to the east on a raft of snakes."

"So?"

"Before departing, Caesar, he promised to return one day—"

"In the year of One Reed," Tora said with rising enthusiasm.

"Yes—and this is that year in the Aztecan calendar. Everywhere I went," Britannicus went on, "bargemen, temple attendants, even eagle knights—begged me to tell if I'd seen Quetzalcoatl."

"Why you, colonel?" Germanicus asked.

"Well, I was a stranger who'd come out of the east."

"What did you tell them?"

"That I hadn't met Quetzalcoatl." Britannicus studied Khalid's regal figure for a moment. "But, then again, I'd never ventured far enough east . . . to Agri Dagi, let us say, where lonely and pious gods serve out their banishment."

Lord Tizoc promptly replied to Caesar's missive by sending his own courier back with the Roman envoy under the same banner of truce. This aquiline-nosed Azteca was a repeater: instead of bearing a sealed document in Nahuatl—which had only confused communication on previous occasions—he regurgitated every last syllable his general had fed him. Tora translated: Tizoc considered it a brotherly honor that the Emperor Germanicus had invited the Sons of the Mexicae to participate in a War of the Flowery Way. The three eagle knights he had chosen would enter into this combat with no spirit of enmity, nor was it their wish to infer which gods —Roman or Aztecan—would eventually predominate in the world. There would be enough richly nourishing blood to sate all the deities, and the blood of Rome's finest warriors would be like honey and their flesh like soft, warm breads to the heavenly beings.

At this, Germanicus hiked an eyebrow. "*What* Roman warriors?"

After Tora repeated the question in Nahuatl, the courier lapsed into a confused silence. The Nihonian suppressed a smile. "He does not understand, Lord Caesar."

"Tell him that those who will fight on my behalf are not my countrymen. They are visitors to my empire from a place called Tula."

Even without benefit of a translation, the Azteca recoiled at mention of this ancient city, which Germanicus had learned from Tora was the legendary abode of Quetzalcoatl. The courier returned to his lines a distracted man, his arms limp at his sides.

The appointed place for the contest was a snowy vale between two ridges that formed the most recent battleground, one slope held by the Romans and the one facing it by the Aztecae.

Germanicus's praetorians stamped out a place for him in a waist-high drift, then established him on a curule chair. Across the gulf, which had been swept clear of mists by a wind that burned with cold, Tizoc could be espied being similarly attended by his retinue. The distance was too great for Germanicus to catch his rival's expression, but there was a decided air of expectation surrounding the tiny figure: the Azteca's gestures were hammer blows, and at one point he batted away a golden cup that had been offered to him as he argued vociferously with a priest.

"It weighs upon you," Germanicus whispered. "And on them as well . . ." His gaze swept over the centuries of Aztecan warriors loosely arrayed across the face of the hillside like flocks of brightly colored birds, stunning to behold in their feather capes and animal-skin tunics. They were silent and kept watch as if their own fates hinged on the clash that was only minutes away from unfolding.

The legionaries, on the other hand, awaited the combat as if it would be some gladiatorial sport in the Circus Fabius. Germanicus had encouraged this spirit by ordering the dispensing of a modest wine ration (although the two cohorts he had held in reserve received only vinegar as they stood ready at the rear in full panoply); and not only were the optios winking at any wagering in the ranks, some of the subcenturions had even doffed their helmets to hold the bets until the fight was concluded.

Once again, Britannicus had removed himself from the press of any close company and was standing alone, rocking from foot to foot, ready to bolt at the first hint of disturbance. He nearly caved in to this urge seconds later when conch

trumpets bleated from the Aztecan ranks. His face twisted
into a mask of anguish, but he held his ground. Germanicus
tried to hearten him with a smile. Britannicus nodded grate-
fully. When this campaign was finished, the colonel would be
given a long rest.

Germanicus watched in fascination as three Aztecae promenaded out into the small valley, black eyes shining from the
gaping beaks of their eagle-head helmets. Tizoc's forces
greeted the appearance of these champions by slapping their
palms against their mouths, and the elite warriors responded
to this cry of encouragement by whooshing their bladed clubs
through the air in intricate loops and arcs that revealed endless
hours spent in such drill.

Germanicus hid a frown behind his fist: the Anatolians were
certainly fearless combatants, but they were short on discipline. For the first time, it occurred to him that Khalid and his
men might actually fall, toughening Aztecan resolve to stand
fast against the invaders . . . and Alope would be prostrated
on the sacrificial stone before Germanicus could ever hope to
reach Tenochtitlan. This did not mean that he imagined the
eagle knights to be invincible. Germanicus had learned from
Tora that, five hundred years before, one thousand of these
soldiers of the sun god had been reduced to a fifth of that by
their Tarascan enemies. But, ironically, this only enhanced
their reputation in Germanicus's eyes: to be genuinely professional, an army had need of a scroll or two of defeats in its
catalogue of triumphs.

Rolf was squinting through optics at the eagle knights, who
were beginning to fidget at being kept waiting. "They be not
fully traditional."

"In what way?"

"Their clubs be edged with steel, Kaiser, not that black
stone."

"In fairness, we must grant them that much. Our swords
shatter their obsidian." The agreement with Tizoc had been
that only traditional weapons would be used.

"I be of a mind to grant nothing to barbarians what murder
their prisoners," Rolf grumbled. Then he blanched when he
saw the effect of his hasty words on Germanicus, who turned
back to the scene below, his eyes flickering beneath a film of
sudden moisture.

All this time, Khalid and his two men had been shielded

from view in a small tent pitched halfway up the Roman-occupied hillside. Now, to a flourish of trumpets, a century of spit-and-polish praetorians formed double ranks, and its centurion threw back the flaps before—quite un-Romanly—prostrating himself toward the triangular opening.

Germanicus rose from his curule chair.

The Lord Quetzalcoatl created by Britannicus and Tora was resplendent as he swept down the corridor of bowing guardsmen. His elaborate headdress undulated back from fanged jaws in a serpentlike plume of dazzling white feathers. One of Germanicus's imperial vestments of woven gold had been used to fashion a knotted breechclout that now, in an errant burst of late afternoon sunlight, scintillated brisk demands for attention. At Khalid's heels were Ismail and Jalaludin, both attired in rather plain quilted cotton body armor that only served to accentuate Quetzalcoatl's gorgeousness. Their bare forelegs were rent by what appeared to be bloody lacerations but were actually only smears of sheep's blood: adherents to this god drew blood from the calves of their legs as a form of penance.

Germanicus took this in only briefly, for his greater interest lay in how the Aztecae would react to the appearance of a deity absent from their country for centuries. The faces of two of the three eagle knights showed a kind of stunned incredulity which caused them to share uncertain glances—the warriors were hoping to draw confidence from each other. The third knight was without expression; he, like many of the Aztecae on the slope behind him, had suffered petrifaction—as would any Roman should the Capitoline marble of Jupiter suddenly shudder to life in a flurry of stone dust. Tizoc had come to his feet and was consulting with his chief priest again, this time with far less animation.

As Khalid and his tribesmen bore down on the eagle knights, a silence impressed itself upon the valley, and the only sounds to escape it were the footfalls of the Anatolians crunching across the snowfield. Motionless, the Aztecan warriors watched this approach as if they were resisting the urge to sneak a tentative step backwards. Then one of them did something that made Germanicus hold his breath in anticipation.

The knight who had been most visibly affected by Quetzalcoatl's appearance reeled slightly as if swooning and gently lowered himself to his knees in supplication. His comrade beside him barked a command, but the warrior refused to obey it.

"He was told to rise—or die," Britannicus whispered, then gasped when he found it impossible to turn his face away from what swiftly followed: A steel-edged club flashed through the air and became embedded in the nape of the kneeler's neck, nearly decapitating him. Reflexively, the Azteca stiffened and thereby freed himself off the bladelike flakes before flopping down face-first in the snow. His comrade who had slain him now ignored the cries welling up behind him ("Sacrilege! Remove yourself! You will be crusty bread for the gods!" Britannicus translated in a rasp) and mounted his attack on the Anatolians, catching Jalaludin off guard with a raking blow to the head that instantly killed him. And before this motion was completely spent, the knight redirected it against Ismail's abdomen. The man's bowels spilled out of him; he toppled over, his eyes turning inward, presenting nothing but whites to the hillside gallery of Romans.

His sword had never left its scabbard.

This threw the legionaries into a confusion equal to that of the Aztecae, and their consternation was doubled an instant later when, instead of pressing their advantage against Khalid, who stood alone now, the two eagle knights began squabbling between themselves.

"What is being said?" Germanicus asked.

"Quetzalcoatl. Every other word they speak is Quetzalcoatl." Suddenly, Britannicus pointed sharply below. "Another Azteca quits the field!"

The knight who had slain Ismail and Jalaludin was left snarling as his surviving comrade strode toward the rear, presenting his back to an attack that never occurred because the fanatical Azteca now had his hands full with Khalid, who closed on him with an array of thrusts and parries that drove the knight into a retreat of a dozen staccato steps. Then, incredibly, he caught Khalid's next overhand strike on the flat head of his club, and the tips of the two weapons were embedded together, leaving both men to grunt as they strained to wrench them apart. The knight bashed Khalid backwards with his wicker shield, which might have proved fatal to the young Anatolian had not Khalid's sword come free at the insistence of this savage buffet. Khalid kept himself from going down into the snow by propping an arm behind him, and readied his blade for the Azteca's next strike, which came swooping out of the dim pearl of a winter sun and echoed throughout the valley.

"The eagle knight is more practiced. More masterful." Germanicus slowly shook his head as he watched the combatants begin circling in a plodding dance of death.

"Aye"—Rolf took an urgent gulp of wine—"but our barbarian be a brave one."

Germanicus became aware that the priest who had been attending Tizoc had sifted down the warrior-crowded hillside and now stood on the fringe of the contest. At closer range, the filth of his body, which Aztecan holy men upheld as an abstinence from the pleasure of bathing, was appalling: his face and bare arms were black with soot; his braided hair hung like a horse's tail down to his knees. He held up a quavering hand as if pleading for a halt to the strife until it could be determined if this bearded presence was truly Quetzalcoatl.

Britannicus hurriedly explained, "Even they're not too sure how human this god was."

"Do they think he can be slain?"

Grimly, the colonel lifted his chin at the priest, who was now wringing his hands together. "See for yourself, Caesar —the Aztecae themselves do not know. But it appears we shall all soon find out."

Khalid was being worn down. The outcome seemed inexorable: his movements were less precise after each exchange of steel. The eagle knight wore a patronizing, almost affectionate smile; he had sniffed the end, and it reeked of blood other than his own.

Then one of his hammering blows glanced along the length of Khalid's blade and sank in the Anatolian's upper arm. The prince struggled not to lose consciousness. This effort he won, but a moment later he gawked in helplessness as the hilt of his sword slipped out of his cricked and useless fingers. "*Inshallah!*" he cried defiantly, awaiting the club swing that would drive the light from his head. He refused to stem the flow of blood that was issuing from his wound. Instead, with eyes blazing, he riddled every quarter of the sky with prayers.

The priest began yowling in outrage at the eagle knight, who grunted a reply over his shoulder.

His mouth almost too dry to form words, Britannicus said, "The holy man insists that Khalid be spared. He thinks that the Fifth Sun might hang in the balance."

"What does the knight say?"

"He wants to kill Khalid here and now, to put to rest this Roman nonsense."

The knight was tightening his grip on the club's handle when a dartlike arrow whisked past his shoulder into the snow beyond. It had flown from the Aztecan—not Roman—side of the valley, and he turned to fix his enraged eyes on the priest, at whose side hung the gilded *atlatl* that had been seized from a warrior to launch the bolt.

In this Khalid glimpsed a fleeting chance to save his own life. He picked up his sword with his left hand and, as the knight instinctively recoiled, slashed the Azteca along the thigh before the warrior could deliver the counterblow he was already winding up. The knight pitched over on his side and scuttled backwards, hoping to gain distance so he might stand up again, ignoring how richly his own blood was dyeing the snow. But, with his last strength, Khalid was hounding him, cutting him wherever he was not protected by his quilted body armor—ineffectually, until one strike found the Azteca's club, knocking it down, and the next his throat, stilling him.

Finally, an ashen-faced Khalid collapsed athwart the knight's corpse.

"You have won, Caesar," Britannicus said with an utter lack of satisfaction. "Look."

The Aztecan ranks, which had stood frozen during the last moments of the contest, were beginning to sway and fracture under the force of quarrels. Then, without being commanded to do so, one man, then another, and suddenly a clot of twenty began trudging up the slope. Within seconds, their entire army was in retreat, despite Tizoc's most vehement efforts. Those warriors topping the crest of the hill broke into a trot, which infected those behind them to pick up their pace or be left behind to encounter the wrath of a wounded and grossly offended god.

Germanicus raised his fist, and a red flare was lofted into the overcast. This signal launched the two cohorts held in reserve to pursue the Aztecae. They poured down off the ridge and flowed around him. He himself was starting forward when Rolf took hold of his arm. "You remain," the centurion said firmly. "I look after Khalid."

Germanicus nodded, then slowly sank back into his chair.

At last, Tizoc apparently realized that he alone could not halt the refluxing tide of warriors. He stopped spinning this way and that, beseeching all who passed near him to halt and fight. Then, burying his face in his hands, he joined the flight —and, from that moment on, Germanicus knew that the fifth world of the Aztecae was truly doomed.

The Aztecan general slipped out of sight several hundred paces above a line of sprinting legionaries.

24

GERMANICUS AND SKINYEA strode down through an effulgence of mist and dawn sunlight. Moss venerated the branches of the ancient firs, gathered the moisture, then shed it on the breeze, providing the only sound—a soft pelting like rain.

During the night, the Roman and Anasazi armies had converged upon each another. Germanicus had immediately met with Skinyea. Unable to contain himself during the customary silence that followed the greeting of an Indee, he had blurted, "Alope has been taken captive."

"This I know." Skinyea gave him a smile so overripe with satisfaction Germanicus wanted to slap it off the chieftain's face.

"I intend to rescue her."

"We shall see."

"See what?" Germanicus demanded, knowing full well that the heartsickness in his face seemed unmanly to the Indee headman.

"What this day shall bring." After enforcing the continuation of the moment of silence with a stern expression, Skinyea had gone on to explain that, in the murk of two evenings past, his scouts had seen Tizoc's army running pell-mell down these wooded slopes into the Valley of the Mexicae. This had made no sense to the chieftain until he had learned from a Raramuran runner of Khalid's single combat and its demoralizing effect on the Aztecae. "He must have been protected by great power against enemies to go unscathed," Skinyea said. "Eagle knights are seldom defeated."

"My young friend did not go unscathed, Skinyea."

"Ah, yes—but what is an arm wound? I have had several."

"He suffered the loss of his sword arm."

"Ah." For the first time, Skinyea's expression was sympathetic.

"Prince Khalid rests in my sand-galley, attended by my centurion. He refuses to be consoled. I've tried everything to rouse him from this mood. But because he will be useless in battle, he sees no further reason to live."

"Your warrior is wise for his years. It would be best if he died soon. He has shrouded himself in honor. It is a good time to die."

Now, as they slipped down through the forest, Germanicus suddenly halted Skinyea with a touch on the shoulder: a song was sifting through the tilted trunks of the patriarchs.

"My warriors sing their death song. They say they will welcome death if only they might be allowed to die bravely inside the walls of Tenochtitlan."

A short distance later, shards of dim light slanted down through the tossing boughs and played among a dozen or so warriors, who were squatting on their haunches. For those who still had them, linen tunics were in tatters. Hair, without exception, was greasy and flecked with burrs. Faces that had been round and full-fleshed prior to the campaign were now wolfish-lean. Yet Germanicus sensed no loss of determination in the Indee.

Caligula glanced up long enough to bare his lascivious grin at Germanicus. Then his expression became as somber as the song he was singing, and he seemed aware of nothing but the gruff sound of his own voice.

"Come . . ." Skinyea led him toward a precipice Germanicus sensed more than saw through the mist that dampened his face as it scudded past. Climbing hand and foot, they filed up a narrow cleft in the porphyry face and eventually emerged into a sky that seared Germanicus's eyes with a molten blue. The chilly breeze that was sifting through his cloak had scythed the broad valley to the southwest clear of clouds, and only a ring of them clung funguslike to the eastern rim on which he stood.

Otherwise, Tenochtitlan shone beneath a peerless morning.

"Dear Jupiter, Lord of Light . . ." he murmured, but did

not finish the thought. His silence growled back at him with twice the awe he had expressed.

Never could have Alope, Tora, nor even his fellow Roman, Britannicus, prepared him for this. It was a vista no man could adequately imagine; and, upon viewing it for the first time with his own eyes, he was half-persuaded to disbelieve them. Perhaps he would never fully trust them again; a glimpse of the Aztecan capital was that unsettling. Germanicus had gazed upon Alexandria, Antioch, Londinium, and Rome, of course, the queen of cities; but all of these combined on one commanding piece of ground could not surpass the grandeur of Tenochtitlan. "Why are we fighting men who can build such things?" he exclaimed before he remembered himself.

Skinyea grunted, but said nothing.

Forests of gigantic cypresses swept down in shaggy billows to an elipse of white Germanicus had first mistaken for vast numbers of snow geese flocking the shores of Lake Texcoco. After a few moments, his appreciation of distances was honed by comparison of objects to the serpent-shaped chimney rising from the imperial city—which Britannicus had informed him was three hundred feet tall, and he realized that these white glints ringing Texcoco were the buildings of the lesser Aztecan cities. The crowning jewel of this alabaster necklace was the island of Tenochtitlan, its profile jagged with gleaming temples made all the more brilliant and colorful by the thin atmosphere. Germanicus espied watercraft plying the network of canals, stitching between the graceful buttresses of the aqueducts at a brisk pace that belied mechanization. Some of the more expansive structures—palaces, undoubtedly—were topped with gardens. From one of these Arcadian rooftops, Alope was perhaps gazing toward the northern mountains at this very moment, ever-composed, unstinting in the silence she threw up to her captors . . .

Germanicus cut short these thoughts and turned his reckoning eye on the capital, as a redoubt and not a splendor. Although the Aztecan army had bolted out of the mountains in twilight, Skinyea believed that Tizoc had withdrawn all his forces onto the island and not the heights beyond. The populations of the cities bordering the lake had been evacuated to the provinces south of the Valley of the Mexicae. This, Germanicus surmised, was so that Tizoc's men could loose their Serican *ballistae* on the Roman seige without killing their own kinsmen. He further supposed that the Aztecae would await relief in the form of their expeditionary force presently in Nova Baetica, which Germanicus was surprised had not been pulled off the beaches facing Gnaeus Salvidienus's Tenth Legion and relanded to be driven into the flank of the advancing Roman army like a spike.

Britannicus's appraisal of Tenochtitlan's defenses had been accurate. There would be no bloodless way to approach those fortified walls: the north and south causeways were each straddled by a cylindrical fortress—the Tepeyaca and the Acachinanco, structures every bit as massive as the Great Pyramid of Cheops. Even if they could be captured, the legionaries would then be prevented from reaching the city if the Aztecae destroyed the wooden spans they had built into each of the long and exposed causeways, and the aqueduct bridges were too slender to be considered useful for an infantry assault.

A stone dike, stoutly built, cleaved the lake and, according to Britannicus Musa, prevented storm-tossed waves that were brewed in the eastern portion of Texcoco from battering the foundations of Tenochtitlan. For this reason, the lagoon surrounding the capital like a moat was deeper than the remainder of the lake. Breaching the dike would lower the water level, but Britannicus did not know if it would be enough for sand-galleys to ford the shallows without being swamped through their exhaust tubes and leaky hatches.

"Oh, Mars, what I'd give for a few months," Germanicus whispered. He had no doubt that a traditional Roman seige predicated on Herculean engineering projects would succeed in this instance. He would simply select a suitable small city on the shores of the lake, preferably the one nearest Tenochtitlan —Tlacopan—and reduce its buildings to rubble. This material he would use to construct a broad ramp right up to the walls of the city. Then, under a thunderstorm of *ballistae*, he would hurl his armored craft and most experienced legionaries against Maxtla's crumbling defenses.

And, if he considered everything quite sensibly, there was no tactical reason to invade Tenochtitlan at all: Tizoc, by withdrawing onto the island rather than escaping with his army into the southern provinces, had sealed himself in his own funerary urn. The maize and amaranth preserved in the airtight chambers of the Tepeyaca and Acachinanco fortresses could not last forever. The aqueducts would be pinched off, and petroleum dumped into the potable waters of the western lagoon. Disease, abetted by the press of humanity that was now packed into the ten square miles of the capital, would fell more Aztecae than dust and stone splinters.

But, to work, a seige required time—often months or even years. And Germanicus had less than three days remaining. Even at this moment, a thread of white smoke could be seen twisting up from the landing between the blue and red monuments atop the Great Temple. He knew from Britannicus and Tora what this signaled: the morning firing of the braziers used to roast human hearts. His eyes began smarting. He was tempted to stop fighting the warm clutch of self-pity and quietly admit that his *gravitas*, his dignity as a man of self-restraint, was about to be hauled down by the soft hands of his desire.

Rome conquered patiently. She ruled patiently. Patience was as much expected of a patrician as courage. Yet Germanicus stood wavering on the verge of acting as passionately as a Greek—as Menelaus of old, who risked the lives of thousands, although uncertain in his heart of hearts whether Helen was Paris's captive or lover. His desperation became the world's.

Without turning, Germanicus knew that Skinyea was staring at him. "Let's go down into the valley," he said.

And their combined army had no sooner trooped down out of the mountains, across the fields of maize stubble, through the scrupulously tidy but deserted Aztecan cities and onto Texcoco's shore, than Germanicus's resolve *to remain a Roman* was immediately tested.

The wooden bridge on the Tlacopan causeway, which had been obscured from view by the Great Temple, was still in place. Feverishly, Skinyea began assembling the other Anasazi headmen around him in a war council.

Britannicus drifted up to Germanicus. The colonel was shivering, although he was awash in warm sunlight. "Be wary, Caesar—Tizoc's no dullard."

"But the bridge *is* intact." Germanicus called for vinegar. He met no one's eyes as he took careful sips from the cup. "Imagine the time that can be saved if we secure this causeway and penetrate Tenochtitlan's defenses before they are soundly organized."

"Lord Caesar!" Tora cried above the growing tumult. "The Aztecae begin most battles by luring enemies in this way!"

Skinyea scowled at the Nihonian: "Maxtla has decided not to fight. And if he does, we will finish him. All the Flesh-Eaters are finished."

Tora refused to back off, although his voice was now brittle with anger. "How you know this?"

"Our *diyin* has had a vision—"

"Such things are not in accordance with *Yinshaya*!"

Germanicus realized that, while the argument raged, the chieftains had been dispatching messengers, apparently to mass their warriors for an assault down the Tlacopan cause-way. Then, before their Roman allies might stay them, the headmen began trickling away to join their men, leaving Skinyea behind to divide Caesar's attention long enough for them to organize their hasty plan.

Germanicus fully understood this ruse, and did nothing but slowly drain his cup of vinegar.

"Caesar," Britannicus was shouting, his sunken cheeks blotched with red, "these barbarians are susceptible to the fancy that victory will be easy! In the name of *sanity*, I beg you to—" With that word, Britannicus exhausted his last argument. He simply stood gawking at the emperor, his hands clasped before him, flinching as if *ballista* rounds were thumping the earth around him, although none had been fired from Tenochtitlan.

Germanicus peered across the turbid waters at the cause-way. He said nothing more. Not even in his most painful long-ing to save Alope would he consider ordering his Anasazi allies down that narrow corridor of death. Yet, immobilized by dis-appointment in himself, finally plumbing the depths of a lone-liness he had never imagined to be bottomless, he admitted in numb silence that he would not stop the warriors. He wanted them to try. Perhaps it had come to this: there was no risk he would decline if he might clutch her in his arms again. From the midst of a half dozen bellowing Roman officers, Skinyea was quietly smirking at him.

Yes, my clever friend, Germanicus glowered back at him wordlessly, *you shall now have the satisfaction of watching me confirm my desires in blood.*

• • •

Britannicus grinned up at the stars: "Why, you're all as sharp as toothaches tonight."

The colonel quelled a spate of giddiness by taking deep, rhythmic breaths, as he had been taught by the physicians at Nova Petra, and then started as a chorus of laughter exploded from a large dugout. He shuffled toward the friendly glow of lanterns. Within the shelter reclined nine officers, the perfect number for a dinner party, comfortably sprawled on their couches, enjoying a rich red vintage despite the Aztecan rounds that were warbling down into the Roman encampment every few minutes. The young patricians were making jokes about the virtue of a certain woman. Britannicus really had no idea who they were talking about, but the impulse seized him to stagger over the earthen embankment that ringed their bunker and bawl down at them: "Just *who* the bloody Mars are you defaming?"

A wet-lipped tribune would raise himself up off his couch rugs and sneer, "I beg the colonel's pardon?"

"You're making light of the woman I love"—Britannicus's face became exquisitely thoughtful—"as the Aztecae shall soon make *light* of the woman I love . . ."

But that would not do—interrupting healthy company with his affliction. He thanked the gods that he could still rein in such impulses when he had to. Soon he might not have that ability. Soon he would cartwheel before the wind like a dead leaf. "So be it," he declared with great conviction, whipping a flask of *aqua vitae* out of his cloak. He drank and damned the emperor for not listening to him.

There had been days—or perhaps only minutes of an extraordinary capaciousness—in which he had believed it was with Alope he had shared a hogan in the Valley of the Shades outside Nova Petra. He had been told—and had no reason to doubt the word of those who had told him—that he had been living desolately, vilely, with a Yudaha prostitute even the least cautious legionaries refused to touch. Yet that did not seem possible. Those days had been demarcated from illusion by a sad fragility: being sequestered in a wilderness of purple light with a woman who wore all the masks of love and ultimately promised to unmask the thing itself, so he might gaze nakedly into the blaze and be blinded from that moment on to all things but love, the radiance of human love. But then he had been awakened, if that was the right term, on the threshold of joy by Caesar himself.

That in itself was worth a giggle: his affliction could influence reality!

"To Alope . . . my Minerva." Britannicus lowered the flask from his lips and pitched forward through the encampment, crossing those areas occupied by the Anasazi tribesmen, now silent and ashamed for the mauling they had suffered on the Tlacopan causeway that evening. The scene returned to Britannicus in a mangled glut of images.

Against a golden sun dissolving into the horizon, the stream of warriors had boiled down the causeway in silhouette, relentless in forward momentum and unmolested by the Aztecae until, unexpectedly, a squad of eagle knights promenaded through the armored gateway in Tenochtitlan's western wall and stood in their path, unflinching. The Anasazi vanguard halted halfway down the bridge, not in alarm but in curiosity as to what kind of battle the eagle knights were proposing. The horde behind these foremost warriors continued to press onward, pushing them ahead another fifty paces against their wishes. Within seconds, a mass of confused, jostling Anasazi was clogging the span. At this instant, Britannicus and the other Romans who were awaiting the outcome three miles distant on the promontory at Tepeyaca gasped—the wooden structure vanished in a pall of smoke. Flaming timbers began tumbling out of the sky, slapping the waters around the freshly formed gap, and a shock wave could be seen crazing Lake Texcoco in an ever-widening ring.

The detonation was still reverberating across the valley when Tenochtitlan's Serican *ballistae* began raking the length of the causeway. The wounded were trampled underfoot or abandoned by their comrades to flounder in the lake. Britannicus could not witness this slaughter of fleeing warriors with the professional detachment of his fellow officers, who murmured between puffs on lungweed what they would have done differently had it been their gambit. Nor could he even watch with a stricken expression like that on the emperor's face. Britannicus simply could not touch his eyes to the scene without being whiplashed by pain. So he withdrew from the company of others and kept faith with his sense of horror by weeping.

Yet Britannicus was not cheered in the least when, beginning an hour later, nothing but good news arrived in the camp.

General Salvidienus reported that during the preceding night the Aztecan invasion army had been pulled off the trench-combed beaches of Nova Baetica. The enemy fleet that was bearing it homeward had been engaged by the newest Roman quinqueremes, which had held their own against the Serican-designed war galleys and then sunk seven of their transportation craft, sending much of Maxtla's most tested infantry to the bottom of the Mare Aztecum. And then came news from Rome's new Tarascan allies that the Serican deputation, which numbered in the hundreds, had fled Tenochtitlan before the arrival of Caesar's cohorts and was now scurrying toward the port of Aztlan for the ships that would ferry these soldiers and *machinators* back across the Sea of the West (reluctant to give the Serican emperor a cause for war, Germanicus had ordered their safe conduct). Finally, a rumor had been noted in the dispatches from Hibernia that King Matholwchius, Rome's old nemesis in that unruly province, had been assassinated by his own ragtag nobles.

Yet, despite a growing frenzy of glee, Britannicus had shrunk into himself when a Third Legion colonel recognized him from their Hibernian service together and jostled him by the shoulders. "Isn't it all too marvelous, Britannicus Musa? You must feel so vindicated!"

"What did you say?" Britannicus snapped back at him.

"I merely suggested—"

"Did you accuse me of being *peninsular*?"

"Pen . . . insular?" the man repeated hollowly.

Britannicus continued to leer at him until the colonel withdrew, whispering something to his fellows Britannicus believed to be menacing. "Look to Caesar before you dance to the Saturnalia, you fools!" he had bawled at them before stumbling up a twilit hill thick with cacti, the spines snatching at the hem of his grimy cloak.

Britannicus felt certain that he alone of the entire Roman host knew why Germanicus had refused dinner and continued to slump on a curule chair, ignoring all petitioners, rousing slightly only when a conch trumpet keened across the lake from Tenochtitlan, announcing the loss of another hour. The expressions on the faces of his legionaries were the source of Caesar's gloom: the campaign was nearly won, and no soldier was eager to court death in the final days of a contest that had already been decided. The imperative to rescue Alope and the other Roman-Anasazi captives was melting away under a bright, festive mood that might have degenerated into a full-fledged Bacchanalia but for the presence of an emperor who did nothing but stare off toward the Great Temple, darkened now like all of the city for the silent hiatus the Aztecae were maintaining prior to the Ceremony of New Fire—broken only when they felt compelled to lob an occasional shell into the Roman encampments.

No soldier in his right mind could justify spending five thousand lives to save five hundred—no one except Germanicus Agricola and Britannicus Musa, whose fingers now crept up the backside of his head like a spider and began twirling a lock of his fine reddish hair between them.

Alope and Caesar: Britannicus's feelings toward these unlikely lovers were couched in an outward indifference. Secretly, he wavered constantly between murderous jealousy and affection toward both of them; this was an oscillation so frenetic, like that of the tension skein on an antique catapult being strummed, it suggested to the naked eye a bleared inertia, and to the ear, a single note as plaintive as a child's moan. But never once did it manifest itself as mutiny against Germanicus. To the contrary, Britannicus began hungering for vengeance against Caesar's enemies, real and imagined, whom he despised as if they had personally wronged him as well. Perhaps they had. He was not certain. And he often wondered if these troubled emotions were being deflected off his *patria* and his love for the personage of the emperor (the Ultimate Peninsular One, after all).

Whatever its meaning, the colonel had found himself intricately plotting the assassination of Gaius Nero and gave up the notion only upon learning that the accused traitor was being held on a bireme anchored several miles off the eastern coast.

"I must give all this some noble expression," he muttered to himself, then realized that a circle of Indee warriors around a small fire had broken off their conversation at his intrusion.

Britannicus smiled at them.

These barbarians had a different attitude toward him than that of his fellow Romans. Caught unawares by his presence, legionaries exuded a revulsion that all but the most callous quickly tried to disguise beneath a cloying pity; Britannicus wanted to cut out their eyes for that. Primitives such as the Indee, on the other hand, were of the opinion that a man in the colonel's condition was like a cracked door left open to the spirit world. In the Valley of the Shades, they had valued his company and sought his counsel whenever they sensed that their spirit bodies were threatened by some hidden force.

Now one of the tribesmen invited Britannicus to join them. "Sit, brother." Politely, he fell silent for several moments, then asked, "Do you know our tongue?"

"I know all tongues." Britannicus smirked at his own boast.

"You speak Indee well. Will you have some *pulque*?"

"Yes, if you will share my *aqua vitae* with me."

They exchanged vessels and drank with loud slurping noises. Then Britannicus locked gazes across the flames with a bony-chested warrior of forty or so years.

"He *sees*," this man suddenly declared to the others. "What will happen, brother?"

Britannicus peered at the Great Temple. His eyes seemed to fill with quicksilver, although he continued to grin.

"Tell us nothing, brother. Your words will not make us braver. We are already much too twisted around ourselves." This giant of an Indee seemed capable of searing insolence, especially toward Romans; but he spoke to Britannicus with a cautious civility. "We already know that most of us will die tonight," the warrior went on. "But still we will have strong power against enemies. And what does it matter if we are killed? For each of us who falls a baby boy will be born. We made sure of that before we left our mountain, yes? At least I did. There will be another Caligula if I fall." His philosophical smile turned cruel. "We will have shame on our heads when we get back home."

"This is true," another Indee murmured.

"And it will be easier to talk about this shame if we also have spoils to share with everybody . . ."

"It was not our fault the Flesh-Eaters tricked us onto the stone path across the waters."

"It is always our fault when we are tricked." Caligula stared down the warrior who had interrupted him. "We should have swum across the place of no bridge. We should have fought the eagle knights. Some of us should have come back with wounds on the *front* of us."

"A man must let go of his *pilum* to swim. That would have left us only our knives. They would have killed us!"

Caligula spat into the fire. "We have faced worse and come out all right."

"Tonight you will know worse," the colonel whispered.

Caligula smiled at Britannicus. "And we will come out all right."

"You plan to go into Tenochtitlan, don't you?"

There were a few admiring grunts of surprise from the warriors, then Caligula slapped him on the back. "Yes, to raid Maxtla's house of treasure—and bring back our kin who are captive. Do you want to go?"

"No . . ."

"Ah. The choice is yours, brother."

"I don't want to go, but I *must*."

Caligula and the others took heart from Britannicus's decision. "Why must you go?"

"Your plan is perfect."

Caligula chortled. "You know nothing about it!"

But Britannicus had turned toward Tenochtitlan again. Already he was gliding across the night in a canoe, the seven stars of the Pleiades glittering above and then below as well on the liquid blackness of Texcoco. Ordinarily, only six of these impossibly distant suns were visible, but there would be nothing ordinary about this final adventure. "Your plan is perfect because it serves two purposes—my love for a woman of your tribe and my esteem for Germanicus Julius Agricola—with one simple act. Anything else would pit these affections against each other, and I would die less nobly. Like most men, I have waited dismally all my life for a simple act such as this." But then the colonel was not certain he had said this aloud.

Caligula rose and barked for the others to pick up their weapons.

25

GERMANICUS STOOD BEFORE Lake Texcoco, which was wind-ruffled, glinting silver and green beneath the mid-morning sun. "How deep does it become between here and Tenochtitlan?"

"I saw charts when I served the Sericans," Tora said. "It is fifteen feet at deepest off Tepeyaca Promontory."

Germanicus slowly shook his head. "Too much for our sand-galleys. Water would cover the hatches—and they're not watertight. It might even spill down the exhaust tubes." He began breathing through his mouth, resisting a spate of nausea brought on by another sleepless night.

"It is shallower off Tlacopan's shore."

"How much?"

Tora hesitated a moment. "Perhaps five feet, Lord Caesar."

Germanicus sighed.

"But there is the Great Dike—"

Caesar's eyes widened. "Yes?"

"It raises the level of this lagoon . . ." Tora went on to confirm what Britannicus Musa had said about the six-mile-long barrier of cemented stone: It had been built centuries before to keep the foundations of Tenochtitlan's structures from being weakened by storm-tossed waves; at one time, currents had been exchanged through a gap in the dike, but eventually even this narrow wooden gate had been closed in order to keep the more alkaline waters of the eastern arm from contaminating the fresher stuff of the western, which was drunk by the city's population in times of crisis.

Enviously, Germanicus watched a white gull waft over the shimmering expanse toward the city. "Tora-san, if we breach this dike, how much will the lake drop around Tenochtitlan?"

"A foot, Lord Caesar. I cannot be certain. But if we shut intakes to the aqueducts from Chapultepec and Coyohuacan, perhaps it will be enough. I cannot say. It will take time to calculate the volume of this lagoon. I no longer have charts—"

"It will be enough. It *must* be enough."

Pacing up and down the spongy mud along the shore, Germanicus waited until the morning breeze shifted and began blowing out of the north. Then he signaled for the oil pots to be lit. Ugly black roils issued out of these cast-iron *amphorae* and bumped along the surface of the lake before curling around Tenochtitlan's durable stone monuments, which had been only slightly pocked by Roman *ballistae*.

Germanicus had already dispatched squads to close the two aqueducts that fed the capital. This task would require considerable adroitness: the blasting of the conduit bridges would not solve the problem, as the spring-fed streams would continue to gush into Texcoco, perhaps even raising the level of the lagoon once the flow was no longer regulated and pent up in the huge masonry cisterns on the island.

The waters would have to be stemmed underground, perhaps deep within the headlands from which they issued. That called for nerve, strong backs, and an intimate knowledge of tunneling; Germanicus located these qualities in the Cambrian legionaries of a sapper century—stocky, blunt-faced men who, prior to service, had spent more time below ground than above it. He saw to it that they received their daily wine ration early, and they had raised their cups in his honor, assuring him that this would be no great matter "for lads what got slurry instead of blood" in their veins. Whatever the difficulties they encountered, the Cambrians would shut down the aqueducts.

Germanicus wished he felt as confident that the detail charged with breaching the Great Dike would succeed. His doubt had nothing to do with the leadership of these hand-picked praetorians—they would be commanded by Rolf, who at this moment was readying the niter explosives. It had to do

with the half mile of exposure to Aztecan fire they would have
to risk in order to reach the cedar floodgate, the only vulner-
able place in a barrier twenty feet thick and of impeccable
craftsmanship.

"There isn't enough smoke!" Germanicus barked.

A dozen staff tribunes tripped over each other to see that
more oil was poured on the guttering flames.

The breeze shifted once again and began billowing the choking screen over the Roman positions. Out of this unnatural
twilight, Rolf materialized and took his place at Germanicus's
elbow. "There be enough smoke," he said, squinting.

Germanicus gazed through burning eyes at his centurion.
Rolf looked much as he had years before at their first meeting
in Anatolia: a scrapper, for sure, securely ensconced in his
own calm dignity. He was loaded down with enough niter to
raze the Forum Romanum.

"There never be enough smoke for cowards," Rolf went on
quietly. He was on the verge of saying something more when
he clenched his teeth and looked away.

Germanicus tried to fill the silence. "My friend, I thank
you—"

"I go now." The centurion waved for the squad of praetorians to fall in behind him. He and his volunteers were
quickly enfolded by the tendrils of smoke, leaving Germanicus
behind to feel foolish and bewildered.

Several minutes later, a brisk crumping noise echoed across
the lake from Chapultepec Hill, then a second from slightly
north of the city of Coyohuacan. Germanicus trusted that the
springs at those locations no longer flowed down their aqueducts into Tenochtitlan.

Germanicus sank into his curule chair. He called for vinegar, which he then forgot to drink. He waited, tapping out the
seconds with his right foot.

Thirty minutes later, in the clear space between two mountainous waves of smoke, Rolf's detail could be seen trotting at
intervals down the Great Dike, every other man encumbered
by a bulky pack. They stitched through garlands of haze,
emerging now and again into brassy sunlight at an ever-
quickening run, and Germanicus began to believe that the
smoke was dense enough to mask them from Aztecan spotters
and that the Romans might go unchallenged all the way to the
floodgate.

"Boats!" a colonel at Germanicus's side shouted. "The Aztecae have launched boats!"

They had cast off from quays tucked beneath the north wall of Tenochtitlan and were slitting the lake toward the Great Dike, leaving long white scars of wake. Now Germanicus knew that nothing escaped Tizoc's attention: the Aztecan general had simply decided to answer the new threat with watercraft rather than wasting precious *ballistae* fire on scarcely visible targets. Rounds from the Roman batteries on the Tepeyaca promontory began punching white fountains in Texcoco's surface, disintegrating a boat here and there. But most of the craft buzzed on toward their clash with Rolf's men, who were now sprinting for the floodgate, the unburdened men pulling on the shoulder straps of those who were loaded down with niter.

"Britannicus Musa warned me about mechanized barges." Suddenly, Germanicus turned to Tora, who had been standing off by himself, lost in contemplation: "Where is poor Britannicus? I haven't seen him since yesterday afternoon."

"No one does know, Lord Caesar."

"Has anyone looked for him?"

"I did this dawn to discuss matters with him. But his trail grows cold in the camp of Anasazi."

For the past several moments, the breeze had been slackening. Now it died away entirely. The pall flattened out into a limpid storm that dimmed the sun to a bead paler than the moon. Germanicus could hear nothing but the plaints of gulls that were trying to circle above the noisome cloud.

"Damn!" Germanicus cried through a rumbling cough. "How will I know if it has worked?!"

"Come down to shore, Lord Caesar," Tora said. "Please follow."

They groped their way through tules that bristled javelinlike in the gloaming.

"Wait here, yes?" Tora waded out into Texcoco until the waters were lapping around his knees. Then he drew his curved sword and planted the blade upright in the muck of the bottom. He slogged back to Germanicus's side. Both men said nothing as they listened to an exchange of *pili* fire raucous enough to be heard over the gulls.

The shallows here were coated with a film of cattail pollen, a golden mantle that rocked with the gentle action of the waves. Alope, Germanicus was sure, would have been delighted by such an abundance of the stuff that was holy to her. He could see her dipping her skirts into the waters to harvest it, the weak sunshine the same amber tone as the spangles in her hair. She craned her slender neck so he might glimpse her smile—beguiling, ineffable, a burst of radiance that lanced him with joy. Only the thunder of an explosion from the direction of the Great Dike freed him from this bittersweet reverie.

Tora's eyes were fixed on his sword. Nothing had changed: the waters were at the same level on the steel.

"Shouldn't it be . . . already . . . ?" Germanicus could not finish.

"I think not, Lord Caesar. The gate is narrow. It may require our patience . . ." Then the Nihonian braced his hands on his knees and leaned forward once again. By remaining as motionless as sculpture, he seemed to suspend time, freeze it like a bas-relief, and Germanicus was taken by surprise when Tora finally clapped his hands together and cried, "It descends!"

Germanicus was starved for the slightest bit of hope, but it was some moments before he could truly see where the receding waters had left a thin stripe of pollen on the sword. Over the next half hour, this dusty-looking band grew and grew until it was nearly a foot in length, then stopped: the western and eastern arms of Lake Texcoco had equalized at the same level. The moat around Tenochtitlan was now that much less deep.

"Quickly—to Tlacopan!" Germanicus had already begun hiking up the slope. "More smoke . . . more!" he bawled at any legionary who dared stop feeding the pots to gape at him.

Nearly dragging the shorter-legged Nihonian along, Germanicus commandeered a lorry loaded with olive oil and promised the startled operator a hogshead of wine if he could dash them around to the western side of the lagoon. There, Tora had suggested, sand-galleys might have enough draft to make the crossing—if the floodgate was destroyed.

One of the ponderous craft had been alerted to standby for Caesar's arrival, and its eager-looking centurion now saluted over the main deck railing. "What is Caesar's pleasure?"

"Can you swim?" Germanicus shouted back at him.

"Aye . . ." The officer no longer sounded so accommodating.

"What about the rest of your lads?"

"We can all get by in the water, sir."

Tora asked Germanicus, "Will Lord Caesar carry infantry on sand-galleys when he attacks Tenochtitlan?"

"Of course; it'd be pointless otherwise."

"Then this craft should weigh what it will on the day of attack. If not, we learn nothing about the softness of Texcoco's bottom."

Germanicus exhaled, then ran his hand through his hair. He was gazing lakeward when a break in the smoke revealed the Tepeyaca Fortress. Much closer to the Roman batteries than Tenochtitlan, the huge redoubt had been sheared of the serpentine ramp that coiled up around the outer wall to its domed summit of battlements and barracks, which had also been ravaged by *ballistae*. Its surviving warriors were no longer capable of interdicting Roman sallies against the capital's defenses, although the main cylindrical structure, the granary, looked as sound as ever. It had astounded Germanicus to learn that the Aztecan builders had not used iron cramps to hold the stones together—the mortarless fits were that precise.

He looked back up at the centurion. "Have a century of heavy infantry board your craft."

"In light panoply, Caesar?"

"No, full, but see to it that they set their gear on the decks and strip down to their tunics."

"That's a load of men for a galley, sir."

"We shall require 'a load of men' if we are to overrun Tenochtitlan's walls."

Nevertheless, Germanicus had the praetorians scour the reeds for canoes Aztecan fishermen had abandoned when forced to flee south. Then, ignoring the protests of his guardsmen, he slid into one of the slim craft between the paddlers and impatiently waved for Tora to join him. "We and our flotilla will follow in the event—" He decided not to finish.

The century of infantry, looking like a shipment of slaves in their buff-colored tunics, sang out a "Hail Caesar!" and the sand-galley inched forward into the smoke-shrouded lake.

"Caesar!" its centurion shouted from the crowded afterdeck. "How far will we go?"

"Watch for my signal!"

For the longest time, the level of the water rose no higher than midway up the tracks, which shot twin roostertails of

spray over the canoes that were following. Germanicus did not
pause to wipe his dripping face. He was at the point of believing that this shelf might stretch all the way to Tenochtitlan
when, suddenly, the prow of the sand-galley dipped nose-first
into the surface. The legionaries scrambled for handholds,
and the centurion glared back at Germanicus with pleading in
his eyes.

But, after several moments in which the cleats churned and
boiled the waters for another purchase on the oozy bottom,
the craft righted itself and continued to wallow forward. The
waterline was now within a foot of overlapping the main deck;
the centurion elbowed his way through the tightly packed
troops to check all the portholes and hatches.

The Emperor Fabius had designed the sand-galley as an armored seige vehicle. Its most notable successes as a weapon
had been against rebel strongholds in desert country. Never, as
best Germanicus could recall, had his cousin boasted of its
amphibian qualities. Even had it been buoyant, which it was
not, there existed no mechanical means to propel the craft
over water should the tracks float clear of the lake bottom.
The operator's cubicle beneath the prowdeck was relatively
airtight, but this was simply a precaution against Greek fire-
attack. No one, until now, had tested the integrity of the entire
craft against flooding.

Water was beginning to sheet over the main deck. Those
men who had not already done so now shed their *caligae*.

Germanicus turned back toward Tora, who was squeezing
the moisture out of his topknot with his fist. "How far have
we come?"

"Halfway—perhaps, Lord Caesar."

"Does it get deeper beyond here?"

"I think not."

Then the prow of the sand-galley lurched downward again.
A few of the younger legionaries hollered in alarm as water
began slopping around their shins.

"Caesar!" the centurion cried. "My main deck hatch is
leaking! And we're getting a trickle now and again down the
exhaust tube!"

"Continue."

"We're out too far. If the smoke clears, the Aztecae will
have us with their *ballistae*!"

Germanicus snugged his cloak around his throat with one

hand and gestured for the officer to press on with the other.

The sand-galley engine was racked by a sequence of phleg-matic coughs, the chugging reminiscent of the sounds made by its steam antecedent. The exhaust was now tainted blue from unspent fuel; its flue drum, built low to the afterdeck to avoid entanglement in tree limbs and clotheslines strung across city lanes, was now accepting the top inch of each wave that cleared the bulwarks. And, if this was not the cause of the sickly behavior of the galley, the blame could be rested on the air intake louvers, which lay flush to the main deck beneath a grate and were relied upon to seal out flashes of Greek fire—not liquids.

Suddenly, the *ballista* mount hatch clanged open, and through it scuttled the crew as if they consisted of one body—a centipede wriggling out of a burning log. "There's a bloody cloudburst down there!" the operator clamored to his cen-turion. Just then, the deck beneath him yawed slightly, and there followed a shrill hiss like the bright redness of a hot poker being snuffed out in cold water. "The exhaust tube! Swim for it, lads!"

Legionaries began tumbling headlong into the lake, thrash-ing for the canoes.

"But for a foot less of water . . ." Germanicus closed his eyes: it was the loss of the *Aeneas* all over again. He reopened them on an adolescent legionary fanning his arms for help. Germanicus seized him by the front of his tunic and hauled the boy aboard.

"Many thanks, Caesar!" he gasped. "I shall never forget this!"

"Nor I," Germanicus said dismally. Sunlight began basting the back of his neck with warmth. Vaguely, it occurred to him through his thickening melancholy that this would herald something perilous, but he could not think what until the distinctive warble of Serican *ballistae* was reverberating in his ears and billows of crazed water were sprouting on all sides of the flotilla. Yet Germanicus seemingly paid no mind to the Aztecan barrage; grasping the gunwales, he turned completely around and faced Tora: "Can water be pumped out of this lake?"

"Of course, Lord Caesar, but how? This valley is a very deep bowl. Texcoco has not one outlet."

Germanicus's eyes flickered back and forth in search of

another answer. "Do you know what I mean by a *siphon?*"

"I do. There are many of these water-lifters on the Sericans' Bridle on the Dragons Canal . . ."

Germanicus's eyes brightened. "And so?"

"The last completed by the Sericans required three years . . . two hundred thousand laborers."

Even after a lengthy pause, Germanicus could not rid his voice of its desperate inflection. "Is there any other way to lower Lake Texcoco?"

Tora dropped his gaze. "I am not certain, my lord. I will apply every principle of *Yinshaya* to the question—"

Then they were drenched by the spray of a near miss.

As, one by one, the troop-laden craft of the flotilla bumped against the shore, the Aztecan *ballistae* fire died away, leaving a somber peace cross-stitched with fading wisps of smoke. The praetorian centurion who assisted Germanicus out of the canoe said, "We could watch their salvos walk out only so far, Caesar. They must be running out of niter. These rounds are loaded light. They have no range."

Having only half-listened, Germanicus took several moments to respond: "Yes . . . then they're saving everything for our final assault . . ." He became aware of a familiar presence not by sight or sound, but as if by some reassuring texture that was suddenly in the air around him.

Rolf was standing among the guardsmen, his face burned crimson. His eyebrows had been singed off as well, but he ignored his discomfort as, with a slight lifting of his shoulders, he seemed to ask if the blasting of the floodgate on the Great Dike had proved enough.

Germanicus nodded no, but then tried to thank the centurion with a dispirited smile.

Rolf stared away, looking no less vexed than he had at their last meeting.

"Caesar!" a praetorian sentry cried from the uppermost tier of a small temple above them. "The Aztecae approach under a flag of truce!"

Germanicus spun wildly around: a barge was puttering out of the haze toward him, flying a gold mesh banner.

Yet, instead of immediately beaching his craft, the Aztecan courier instructed his steersman to lay offshore within hailing distance of the Romans. Then he cried out in Nahuatl and waited patiently for someone to respond.

Tora hurried to Germanicus's side. "Maxtla's messenger begs permission to land. He bears a gift for Lord Caesar."

"Is it possible Maxtla is prepared to capitulate?"

The Nihonian dropped his eyes.

"Well," Germanicus sighed, "let him approach."

"*After* I see the gift of this beggar," Rolf said. Flanked by two German praetorians, he waded out to the barge and motioned with his short sword for the Aztecae to open a long and slender chest of hammered gold leaf. Almost eagerly, they cracked the lid so the centurion could peer inside.

Rolf froze for a long moment, then seized the lid with his free hand to admit more light into the chest. "Ach!" he roared and raised his sword to cut down the astonished courier.

"Hold!" Germanicus cried. "Is it something to injure my person?"

Rolf strained against the moment to let the blade fall.

"Centurion—answer me!"

"It be something to . . . to injure your spirit!"

"Have them bring it here."

The Aztecae trotted through the shallows but, despite their haste, made certain the chest was not jarred. Reverently, they laid it at Germanicus's feet, then fell upon their knees. His eyes glistening, the courier began beseeching the emperor as if trying to win his affection.

Germanicus's face was like stone until his eyes shifted toward Tora for a translation.

"He says he bears the love of Maxtla for Caesar Germanicus as one brother to another . . ."

Rolf spat into Texcoco's limpid waters.

"Once again, Maxtla thanks Lord Caesar for providing Tonatiuh with delicious breads, softened by courage, by piety. And if Romans are gods themselves, he understands all the better how they can serve up such good morsels to satisfy the Fifth Sun. For was it not the sacrifice of Quetzalcoatl that gave birth to this world?"

Suddenly, Rolf had pushed aside the courier and planted his sandal atop the gilded chest. "These be the morsels this demon speaks of!" Then he threw back the lid with his foot. Germanicus's face went ashen, except where a blue vein forked down the center of his brow. Behind him, a tribune howled, "Good Juno—that one there is Britannicus Musa!"

Germanicus took a vicious stride toward the Aztecae, then forced himself to halt. The steersman lost his nerve and bolted back to the barge.

Baffled by the horror experienced by the Romans, the courier implored Caesar's favor by offering him one of the hideous objects. Germanicus recoiled: Caligula's leer was as unsettling in death as it had been in life. Growing even more disconcerted, the Azteca exchanged the head for another, yammering all the while.

"Does Lord Caesar wish me to translate?" When Germanicus continued to look too sickened to answer, Tora whispered to him, "He says these brother-heroes you see before you came to Tenochtitlan during the night. They fought their way to the square of the temples, giving many eagle knights the joy of a Flowery Death. This one—the one with hair like fire—climbed halfway up the Great Temple before earning the delight of his own death."

"What terrible process . . . ?" Germanicus's croak faded to silence.

"I have seen this before, Lord Caesar," Tora went on. "The head is flayed. Then the skin is wrapped on a skull of crystal stone. The Aztecae think this to be a great honor."

Briefly, for he could bear no more than a glimpse, Germanicus peered through the copper-colored eyelashes into a glittering void. Then he batted the thing out of the Azteca's grasp and began shouting, obsessively wiping his hand on his tunic all the while, "If any of our hostages is harmed, Anasazi or Roman, I shall make deadly certain that before the sun sets on my wrath . . . !" Seething, waiting for Tora to catch up with his torrent of words, he reached down to scoop up a pebble: ". . . nothing larger shall remain of your Great Temple than this!" Then he flung the stone against the courier's chest.

Convulsed by tears, the Azteca began tripping backwards toward the barge, his pathetic smile seeping through the jagged rent Germanicus had put in his dignity. "Brother . . . brother," he kept moaning with perhaps the only Latin word he knew.

Then, surprising everyone with a suddenly different tone of voice, Germanicus cried out to the courier in dire pleading: "Why does your lord refuse to surrender? I will let him live. I will let him continue to serve his people as my client king. Why does he insist on destroying his own country?"

The Azteca's moist eyes darted toward Tora's lips, and his expression grew increasingly anguished as he listened. Then, tenderly, almost lovingly, he spoke directly to Caesar before clambering aboard the barge and ordering the steersman to come about for Tenochtitlan.

Only after they were gone did Tora whisper, "He said, Lord Caesar, 'No mortal can decline to take part in the death of his world. Not even you, Caesar Germanicus, when your hour is at hand. We are raised up and struck down by the gods. We must show courage to them. Even when they forsake us.'"

26

A CANOE HAD been snagged by the reeds along the shore. An evening breeze out of the north tried to free the craft, let it glide toward Tenochtitlan, but the tules held it fast.

Germanicus had unhitched his cloak and was sitting on it. His gaze alternated between the canoe and a sun-dazzled cloud that was rearing up over one of the two volcanoes in the southeast, blanching the forested slopes with snow.

"Father of Romulus, I will not be denied," he prayed, his lips thinned by the selfishness he was feeling, although there was nothing unseemly about addressing Mars in this manner. As a child, he had been told time and again that the most efficacious prayers were those which struck a balance between the desires of the gods and men; and this was the bargain he was proposing: If Alope were spared tomorrow, Germanicus would not only revive a republic governed by pious farmer-soldiers instead of a dissipated oligarchy, he would restore the preeminence of Mars in the Roman pantheon.

The shame he now felt had little to do with this betrayal of Jupiter: he would have bartered away each and every self-absorbed deity on Olympus just to glimpse Alope through the fading light. It arose from the confession he made to himself that he ached to save her less for Rome's good than his own. Yes, certainly, he did not believe he could endure a long civil war without her at his side. And, of necessity, such a struggle would preface the new order. But, when he imagined wading out to that canoe gently rocking in the cradle of the tules, truly he was thinking only of the tender set of her eyes, the honey of her skin, the laughter that flowed from her mouth all too rarely.

Suddenly he began dickering with Mars on the most violent of terms: "If she is taken, I will take myself!"

He paused, struck silent by his own desperation, then chuckled helplessly. "Even in this awful extremity, I'm not sure I *believe*." And with these words, distant Olympus, hooded by god-wrath only seconds before, became no more or no less than a volcanic cone on the rim of the Valley of the Mexicae, rapidly dissolving under a winter storm. "But, believe in the gods or not, I won't be left alone again."

The canoe.

He then realized with the blazing certainty of divine revelation that the canoe offered any solution he might desire. If it amused these restless gods, he might be permitted to penetrate Tenochtitlan's defenses and free her. And if he failed—well, Death, even when stripped of her mostly charming promises, could still seduce a man with a naked offer of peace.

It would be dark soon: the canoe waited as impatiently as he did, straining against the reeds.

Yet, as he sat there testing the edge of his short sword with his thumb until it was crisscrossed with thin lines of red, the sense of duty that underscored his melancholy began creeping back up on him, quibbling with him from its hiding place in the shadows behind his eyes: *If you die tonight there shall never arise another republic, Germanicus Julius. And what would be the effect of Caesar's death on those here who trust you with their lives?*

"Yes, yes," he muttered. Even at this moment, *pili* fire could be heard crackling across the lake: his legionaries and praetorians were dealing with the last Aztecan resistance in the Tepeyaca Fortress. "But I cannot abandon Alope any more than I can set fire to Curia."

Nor could he hope for a spate of Dog Star weather, warm nights and blistering days that might evaporate enough water off Texcoco to allow his sand-galleys to ford. Even now there was a musty hint of rain in the air; the Pleiades and not Sirius dominated the darkening skies.

Germanicus rose, clasped his cloak around his shoulders, assured himself that his short sword was snug in its scabbard, then strode into the shallows. He had just set one foot inside the canoe when a voice halted him. Dropping his sandal back into the water, he averted his eyes from the figure standing on the bank.

"Lord Caesar?" Tora repeated himself.

"Yes . . . what is it?"

"Will you come with me? *Yinshaya* reveals a solution to us."

Germanicus chased Tora's heels to the bunker the Nihonian had appropriated to keep his charts and instruments out of the weather. Germanicus could recognize nothing in the idiosyncratic clutter that might bring Tora's astounding promise to life, although he could not help but admire a relief map of Lake Texcoco for its accuracy: there loomed Tenochtitlan at the intersection of its web of causeways, safeguarded on the north and south by the Tepeyaca and the Acachinanco fortresses. Tora's forefinger tapped the crowns of the cylindrical twins. "Herein lies the secret, Lord Caesar."

Germanicus hiked an eyebrow. "To what?"

"To lowering the lake. It was foolish of me not to think of this sooner. One of Star-Sorter's first lessons at the Serican academy was 'The Might of the Void.' " Tora grinned triumphantly, as if with one word he had explained everything.

"What constitutes this *void*?"

"Nothing. It is a complete absence."

Germanicus was in no humor to bandy with him over *machinalis scientia*. "There is no such state," he said crossly. "Even the upper heavens are constantly filled with a medium. We call this the *aether*. How else could light issue from place to place if not conveyed by a rarified material like this?"

Tora fought down an amused smile. "Void can exist, Lord Caesar. And once formed, it is so powerful teams of horses cannot tear it apart."

Germanicus slowly shook his head. His thoughts were gravitating back toward the canoe.

"Does Lord Caesar doubt this?"

"I'm sorry, Tora-san, but I'm weary. Much remains to be done tonight. There's the securing of the Tepeyaca Fortress—"

"Yes!" the man cried urgently. "Permit me to show you what the void has to do with Maxtla's fortresses!"

Germanicus nodded sullenly.

"When I served the Aztecae with the Sericans, I visited the

Tepeyaca many times. Its walls are made of huge stones, three paces thick and fitted so tightly even dust cannot sift between. But still, to keep moisture out of the grain, the Aztecae lined inside walls with sheets of bronze. These they did lath and plaster over with many inches of lime. It is quite difficult to open the portal at lowermost level—several men must strain to do so.''

"I don't see—"

"They can be made airtight—I can form voids within these structures. But they must be captured first, Lord Caesar."

Germanicus sighed. "The Tepeyaca is nearly ours. But this is only so we can use it to launch an infantry assault down the last stretch of its causeway in the morning.''

"No, unnecessary. I will show!" Tora scurried around the model to a tripod table, returning with a tray clasped in his scrawny hands.

Germanicus's heart sank even more: he had no idea what miracles could be worked with this jumble of mundane items: a pitcher of water, an earthenware dish, a chalice of inferior Alexandrian glass, a dollop of jelly that appeared to be Greek fire, some tinder vials, and a cork bung.

"Please, Lord Caesar. Imagine this to be the waters of Lake Texcoco." Tora poured enough liquid into the dish to cover its bottom to a depth the thickness of his thumbnail. "The problem has been to lower them around Tenochtitlan, yes?"

Germanicus gazed at the dish, his eyes disinterested.

"We did breach the Great Dike, but it was not enough. We can build siphons, perhaps, but there is no time." Tora coated one surface of the cork with Greek fire, then set this bung afloat on his artificial lake. It bobbed in time with his excited breath. "This will be Greek fire—much of it—placed in upper chambers of the fortresses." Then he reached for a tinder vial. The legionary's best friend in wet country like Hibernia, it was really no more than a twist of waxed paper tipped with phosphorous and sealed in a tube of glass so sheer it could be cracked with a light touch of the fingers. The phosphorous ignited as soon as it was exposed to oxygen.

The Nihonian now crushed one of these and touched the sallow flame to the cork. Quickly then, he covered this miniature conflagration by setting the upturned chalice on the dish. "This, let us say, is the Tepeyaca with Greek fire raging inside." After a few seconds, the flare-up guttered and succumbed to wisps of smoke that befogged the inside of the glass.

Germanicus had been staring at the chalice several seconds before it dawned on him that—mysteriously, magically—three fingers of water had been sucked up into the vessel, leaving the dish as dry as a desert lake. "Good Jupiter—can this really work on the scale we require?"

"*Yinshaya* assures me so, Lord Caesar."

"But will enough volume be drawn up into the Tepeyaca Fortress so we can cross with our sand-galleys?"

Tora's smile faded slightly. "With just one fortress . . . it is in doubt."

"Then we absolutely require the Acachinanco as well?"

Tora dipped his head once, then evaded Germanicus's eyes. Neither man had to say that this redoubt was not yet in Roman hands.

Germanicus rushed up the steps.

He did not have far to go to find Rolf.

The centurion was sitting on his heels in the dithering light thrown by a praetorian warming fire, his cloak gathered around his legs. Anticipating Germanicus's wishes before any word had been spoken, he rose a bit stiffly, grimacing. Even the whites of his eyes had been scorched by the blast on the Great Dike that afternoon. "Hail Kaiser," he said quietly.

With his right hand, Germanicus pressed down on the man's shoulder until they were both cross-legged on the ground—a display of equality that discomfited the nearby German guardsmen. Rolf smoothed his mustaches with his fingers. Tiny waves lapped the nearby shore, barking over a gravel of pumice. When Germanicus finally spoke, it was in a whisper. "The sister fortress to the Tepeyaca—"

"The Acachinanco?"

"Yes, it must be taken."

"At first light then." Rolf started to rise.

"No, tonight, my friend—*now*."

Expressionless, the centurion sat again.

"Both fortresses must be readied as soon as possible for something Tora has in mind. Something extraordinary. For this assault on the Acachinanco, I require capable men, veterans—"

"Germans." Rolf nodded at the guardsmen: "I be sure of these praetorians. Good lads."

Germanicus's lips tussled down a sudden smile. "Yes, of course . . . Germans. Requisition whatever you need—make it known that this is at my bequest. And Rolf . . ." He started to reach for the man's forearm, but found the gesture awkward and slowly withdrew his hand. "Preserve yourself. At all costs, preserve yourself. Only desperation makes me risk you like this. It shames me to make such extravagant use of your loyalty to me—"

"Nay." The centurion had straightened his back, and his eyes were brassy with challenge. "This assault, today's thing on the Great Dike—these not be for you, Germanicus Julius Agricola."

Not knowing what to say, Germanicus ventured a baffled grin. "For *Caesar*, then."

These words spurred the centurion to an even hotter obstinacy, one that Germanicus knew could not be effaced by their affection for each other. "Nay, tomorrow's attack be madness. A month no bread, no water—this city be ready to give up. So it not be for Rome either."

The German praetorians who had been sharing the fire with Rolf started trickling away into the darkness. None wanted to be on hand when the order flew from Caesar to behead the insolent centurion.

The silence between Germanicus and his bodyguard turned cold and a little sinister. They avoided each other's eyes.

"I be of few words," Rolf went on at last, "and none serve me well enough now." He stirred the coals with the heel of his boot, sending up a galaxy of sparks that quickly died in the dark chill.

"Is it that I seem of two minds?" Germanicus asked quietly.

Rolf chuckled humorlessly.

And Caesar knew then that that was it.

In his long experience with German legionaries, Germanicus had found that they would do anything demanded of them —unless they caught the slightest whiff of ambivalence lingering around their commander's tent. Then, like children catching their parents in a mealy-mouthed lie, they became surly, even intractable. There was something in the soul of a Goth that hungered for singularity of purpose, and something in the sophistication of a Roman that denied the very existence of such a thing.

"You do not wish to attack the Acachinanco fortress."

Rolf looked as if he had been cuffed. "I be of no mutinous mind. I do as I be commanded. You say. I go. Always!"

"Very well." Hesitating, Germanicus knew that at last he had to unleash the unreasoning truth. "Then you don't want to take the fortress for Alope's sake."

"I be fond of your consort. But a Roman hostage expects no rescue, and she now be a Roman hostage—aye?"

Germanicus slowly nodded. Then he sensed what might restore the balance between them. It was Rolf's uncertainty that was rebelling; he needed a grasp on his leader's motives, even if they were imprudent. "You believe it wrong for me to risk an entire army to save a single woman."

Rolf hitched his cloak around the lower half of his face so only his blazing eyes showed. He did not answer.

"I too believe it to be wrong, centurion. The worst thing I have ever done in arms."

The German raised an eyebrow.

"What I intend is madness. But I am powerless against it. I cannot lose this woman—and live. She is more than desire. She—like you, my old friend—is necessity."

Rolf remained enfolded in his cloak for a long moment, then lowered it from his face as he carefully studied Germanicus's eyes. "You *know* this to be high foolishness?"

"Yes. That is the reason for my low spirits."

"You be mindful of your own madness?"

"Without lapse."

Rolf gave a soft grunt of satisfaction, then rose. "I go now to rouse the lads for the Acachinanco fortress." But he had taken only a few strides toward the praetorian bunkers when he spun around and said sternly, "Kaiser must show a new face to his legions, what if he be planning to take Tenochtitlan tomorrow. If this be madness—let it be a merry one!"

27

THE SWEET ODOR of ripe grain flowed out of the lowermost chamber of the Tepeyaca Fortress. Germanicus found it slightly sickening as he paced back and forth on one of the titanic bronze doors his legionaries had blasted down during their seizure of the bastion that afternoon. The lake chuckled around the foundations of the causeway he had just crossed without incident from the mainland. He now felt somewhat foolish that his guardsmen had persuaded him to trot all the way, his armor jingling with each hurried step.

This squad of praetorians had tramped on ahead to secure his way up the labyrinth staircases of the structure. They had been gone ten minutes, and Germanicus was growing increasingly impatient with their over-cautiousness in his behalf. The Nihonian and he needed to get inside—without further delay—to assess the *ballista* damage the walls might have sustained.

From the direction of the Acachinanco Fortress came a cacophany of *pili* reports, so furious the multitudinous sounds melded into a consonance, a new and violent voice bellowing across the lake. Reflexively, he muttered a prayer to Mars in Rolf's behalf, then turned to Tora, who was so deep in thought it was several seconds before he responded to Germanicus's clearing of his throat.

"Lord Caesar?"

"Where do you intend to punch this large hole in the fortress wall?"

"Come, please . . ." Tora said. The catwalk wound along the base of the redoubt a foot above its waterline. "Here. I will have your Cambrians tunnel through this wall below the waters."

The surface of the lake was lustrous with oil rainbows from the leaking fuel of the swamped sand-galley. Germanicus fought the urge to ask once again, "Are you positive this will work?" Instead he murmured, "How long should it take the sappers to blast their way through?"

"I have been told no more than seven packs of niter—two hours."

Germanicus nodded morosely, then strode back to the portal, resting his sandal on the enormous door. "What will you do about this?"

"Your maintenance smiths are making new—two for this fortress and two for Acachinanco."

"I see."

Approaching footfalls echoed out of the chamber to their ears. Then a cedar-bark torch—most of the *electricus* variety were now useless for want of power cells which were probably corroding on a distant beach at the far end of the long supply line—began pushing back the darkness in an ever-widening circle. The praetorian centurion could be seen at its center, his shadow yawning out to greet Germanicus before he himself arrived to salute: "All's well within, Caesar."

Germanicus led Tora through the portal. A cool mustiness enfolded them. It was tomblike.

The stone floor was golden with grain dust, although it quickly became evident by the absence of a single whole kernel of maize that, during the past months of hardship, Maxtla had exhausted all of the food reserves he had stored here. They must have been considerable, for this chamber was half as wide as the spina of the Circus Maximus was long; and, although the walls tapered in toward a domed roof, the chambers were so expansive the Aztecan *architectus* had been constrained to support their ceilings with groves of stone columns.

At Tora's beckoning, they made a circuit of the exterior wall. The Nihonian meticulously inspected the plaster, then ran his fingers along the smooth, endlessly curving surface. His verdict came with an apologetic smile: "Built according to *Yinshaya*, yes? It withstood all your *ballistae* could give." He motioned for Germanicus to follow him up a broad flight of stairs.

A trough, its granite abraded to a slick glistening, ran up the center of the incline. "What was this for?" Germanicus asked.

"Packs of grain. They were hauled up this channel by men with tumplines on foreheads."

"How was that considered practical? It would've required millions of man-trips to put up even a modest harvest."

"Thousands of slaves did make it practical, Lord Caesar."

Germanicus's eyes seemed to be watching teams of gaunt men trudging up the ramp, sweaty heads bent forward, grunting like beasts against the drag of their burdens. "Entire tribes enslaved for want of a block and tackle?"

Tora smiled approvingly. "Yes—a question worthy of Star-Sorter himself."

The landing delivered them into another chamber only slightly less echoic than the one beneath it. "How many of these levels are there?"

"Five, Lord Caesar. We must place the *amphorae* of Greek fire up on the fourth. That way, it will be fed air from both below and above."

"Then you anticipate that the two lowest chambers will be flooded?"

"That is not possible, my lord."

Germanicus cast a suspicious eye at the man. "Just how *high* will the waters rise?"

"Even in a most perfect void, water will rise but thirty-four feet."

"Damn your *Yinshaya*!" he exploded, his pessimism surging out of its fumarole with even more force than he himself had expected. "That's not even to the ceiling of the first level!"

"Yes, and this will not be a perfect void." The Nihonian remained calm, almost icy as he returned Germanicus's stare, although his Latin suffered from the strain: "That is reason I have ask for other things to be accomplished as well."

Mindlessly, Germanicus started down the stairs, then halted and pounded up them again. "She goes to the sacrificial stone in less than twenty-four hours!"

Tora said nothing.

Blinking to rid himself of this paralyzing image that might come to pass atop the Great Temple, Germanicus stood still except for the unconscious flexing of his jaw muscles. He took inventory of the efforts that were underway at this very moment: The floodgate in the Great Dike was being repaired so that, once the waters began flowing up into the fortresses, spillage from Texcoco's eastern arm would not refill the western lagoon; sand-galleys with blades on their prows were building an earthen levee to close off Lake Chalco's shallow inlet and reduce the volume of Tenochtitlan's moat by that much more; and, taking advantage of the moonless dark, legionaries were dumping canoe-loads of stones into the sumps known to lie in the lakebed path of tomorrow's assault. Everything, he reminded himself, that could be done was being done. And he could not change his mind now—not without making Rolf's undertaking at the Acachinanco Fortress utterly meaningless. "You must forgive me, Tora-san," he said at last with a ghastly smile. "Time beats on me with a hammer tonight."

The Nihonian accepted these words with a slight bow. "If Lord Caesar will excuse me, I must look to transportation of Greek fire."

"Of course."

Tora flew down the stairs three at a time. When Germanicus turned and began tramping upward, the centurion dutifully stepped between the roof and him. "Caesar, please—it's not safe above."

Germanicus gently patted the praetorian's arm, then circumvented him.

The Serican-style barrack with its cursive eaves and the other battlements that had clung like mud daubers' nests to the dome were now gone, scorched off by Roman *ballistae*, leaving a black and pitted desert on the far side of the horizontal doors that had been propped open to the starlight. Germanicus clambered up into this desolation at the instant two praetorians were doing something his eye did not immediately comprehend.

Facing each other while standing at the parapeted brink of the precipice, the guardsmen were swinging a bundle endwise out toward the abyss. After grunting out a count of three, they released their burden. Then, only when the object was forever gone, did Germanicus realize that it had been the corpse of an

Aztecan defender, for the praetorians had turned with mechanical indifference and were plodding toward a neat pile of more of these neophyte warriors cocooned in their maguey capes. Ordinarily, he would have given his guardsmen the lash of his tongue: it was un-Roman not to afford a fallen warrior some measure of dignity. But he could not find it within himself to speak. They seized the next Azteca and, after winding up with the same ritual to a count of three, pitched it into the night. Even after an inordinately long wait, there came no splashing sound from below. Unchallenged, the moment had blended seamlessly into memory, and Germanicus felt diminished by his own silence. Never before had he felt unworthy of censuring his troops. But tonight was ungodly different. Tomorrow these praetorians might die, not for the cause of *Pax Romana* but in the attempt to rescue Alope.

He withdrew to the opposite side of Tepeyaca's pocked dome before the praetorians became aware of his presence.

This vantage afforded him a panorama of Tenochtitlan. But he did not want to torture himself with the exquisite mixture of admiration and abhorrence that glazed his eyes whenever he viewed those ramparts and monuments, even when they loomed faintly in silhouette.

He began walking again, pausing only when he could overlook the Roman-held causeway that joined the fortress to the Tepeyaca Promontory. His eyes were tracing its length when he noticed an orb of curiously emerald waters where the lake butted against the submerged foundations of the redoubt, and it was only after several minutes of peering below that Germanicus realized that Tora had promptly mustered the Cambrians to begin boring through both sides of Tepeyaca's formidable wall. The underwater glow was from their thermitic torches, and here and there dim apparitions could be seen drifting through this aqua-dreamscape—miners in diving panoply, drawing their oxygen from umbilicals that looked as thin as threads from this height.

There was movement on the causeway, and Germanicus saw that the first lorries loaded with *amphorae* of Greek fire were inching toward the fortress. Their operators were not using their prow lanterns for fear of attracting Aztecan attention. But then a dazzling *electricus* beam shot down from the summit of the Great Temple and raked the lorries nearest the mainland with its claws of splayed light. An Aztecan barrage, the first in six hours, began tussling the lake waters on both sides of the causeway. Yet Lord Tizoc's accuracy was waning: where a dozen lorries should have been destroyed, only one was struck. An orange and white cloud rumbled up from the vehicle, and Greek fire began rippling across the lake.

A Roman battery swiftly blinded this eye festering from the very pinnacle of Tenochtitlan. Once it was extinguished, the Aztecan *ballistae* fell silent. Unbelievably, Tizoc had not pre-plotted targets should the capital ever be threatened. Perhaps he had truly believed invasion impossible: the Valley of the Mexicae could be violated only by the gods. Or perhaps the lord general imagined that, if the fortunes of his people ever deteriorated to the point of Tenochtitlan being beseiged, there was nothing any mortal could do to save the Aztecan Empire. Whatever the case, these salvos were the death rattles of the Aztecae. If only that death could be hastened . . .

The Greek fire rapidly consumed itself. Legionaries wended their way between the stalled vehicles, then formed a gang to jettison the blackened iron bones of the lorry over the side of the causeway.

The column lumbered on toward the fortress again.

Germanicus glanced skyward: the constellation Pleiades had risen to its zenith, and he found it remarkable that all seven sisters were visible, whereas a night on the Capitoline Hill was commemorated if three of Atlas's daughters could be espied through Rome's vault of smoke and river mist. From what Tora and Britannicus had told him, he knew that the hopes and trepidations of the Aztecae were now fixed on these same stars. Tomorrow night, when the Pleiades again glimmered highest in the heavens, the priests would prostrate their most noble captive on the sacrificial stone, rip his heart from his chest, and attempt to kindle a flame in the gaping wound. If the Ceremony of New Fire was successful, the Fifth Sun would be born again in that pale flickering, and the Aztecae could be expected to shake off the spiritual lethargy that attended the five days preceding this crucial midnight. They might even counterattack.

His pulse suddenly racing, Germanicus wondered how the world would strike him in twenty-four hours. Would life be too painful to be endured? Or would Alope be sleeping in his arms, both he and she too drained by the sweet exhaustion of relief to make love?

Over the next three hours, in which he lorried to Tlacopan to oversee his sand-galleys form battle lines in a wooded estate behind the shoreline, he was never unmindful of the constellation's inexorable slide down the backside of its arc, until finally, two hours before sunrise, the sisters entered the nimbus rimming the horizon. Merope, the dimmest, who hid in shame for having loved a mortal, for having made love itself her god, was first to wink out. And in the time it took Germanicus to board the craft that would convey him to Tenochtitlan's walls, the others followed, one by one: Electra, Maia, Taygete, Alcyone, Celoeno, and Sterope; then he was alone on a main deck crowded with legionaries.

His head began sinking forward, and he resisted drowsiness with spasmodic jerks. But finally he gave up. His chin rested against the chilled metal of his breastplate. His pupils flickered back and forth beneath their lids, then his eyes snapped open. *I musn't sleep*, he admonished himself. *However profound my exhaustion, it's nothing compared to Rolf's.*

Concussively asleep, the centurion was sprawled across the afterdeck, one foot dangling over the iron ledge so that his hobnailed *caliga* nearly touched Germanicus on top of the head. Few of his fellow Germans had survived the assault all the way to the smoking dome of the Acachinanco Fortress.

Climbing the ladder to the afterdeck, Germanicus lingered over the unmoving man. His eyes grew moist. Removing his brilliantly red *paludamentum*, which was of the finest Caledonian wool and lined with silk, he laid it atop Rolf's legion-issue *sagum*. At first look the centurion's face seemed pinched by the mountain cold, but perhaps the contorted expression came from some remembrance he was helpless to fend off during the sad vulnerabilities of his sleep. *"I be of few words . . . and none serve me well enough . . ."*

Through the cypresses, Germanicus could see Lake Texcoco. Its waters were slack, as if the stars glistening there in reflection had tacked them flat and glassy. Somewhere midlagoon floated a raft manned by legionaries who had been tasked with firing a green flare should the surface suddenly recede a measured distance on the pole they had pounded into the muck of the bottom. Hopefully, this would occur one half hour before sunrise. That way, the crossing would be screened by twilight, but the surmounting of Tenochtitlan's walls could be attempted in the first rays, whose light the legionaries would need if they were to direct *ballistae* fire against pockets of resistance.

"It be time?" Rolf had opened a heavy eyelid.

"Soon, my friend. Word came a while ago that the last airtight door on the Acachinanco has been soldered into place."

Rolf sat up stiffly. Mystified, he passed the soft wool and silk of Germanicus's cloak between his fingers until at last he understood. In silence, he handed it back to Caesar.

"You were right," Germanicus said.

"Kaiser?"

"My legionaries require some cheer from me." Then, without waiting to glimpse the centurion's expression, Germanicus lowered himself down a hatch into the bowels of the sand-galley. Slumbering praetorians crowded the passageway. Delicately, he picked his way over them to the space occupied by the operator, who jolted to his feet. "Hail—!"

"Sssh, lad—you'll wake the lot of them."

"Sorry, Caesar." The legionary was a typical Campagnian with wrists as thick as ox shanks and a broad nose. "Are we off to 'Titlan now?"

"Not yet. But as soon as we're underway, I want you to see to it that this is done—"

"Anything, Caesar."

"Wireless the other galleys in the first line. Tell them that, as we near the wall, they should fall back, allowing this craft to reach Tenochtitlan first."

"Very well, sir." Then the young man's face became exceedingly grave as he tried not to stumble over the most important words of his life: "I just want to say, Caesar, that this . . . this is the greatest honor I shall ever know."

Germanicus's attempt to smile became a grimace, and as the seconds burned away in silence he could find no words of his own to share with the legionary. Before he himself realized what he'd done, he had wriggled off a signet ring that had belonged to his grandfather and pressed it upon the astonished youth.

He was spinning around to flee when he became aware of another presence in the cubicle.

Skinyea was sitting cross-legged in the warm niche of a U-shaped bend in the exhaust tube, sipping from a gourd cup of what smelled like *dinos*. "Not long," he said simply, but with a look of intense satisfaction.

Germanicus had invited the foremost Anasazi chieftains to make the fording in his sand-galley. Skinyea had been the last to appear, explaining that he had been delayed by a "cry dance," which Germanicus took to be some kind of funeral for Caligula and other Indee raiders. He now said to the headman, "I was saddened to hear of the deaths of your tribesmen in Tenochtitlan."

Skinyea did not reply. To discuss the dead, Alope had said, was to invite some spiritual malady she called "ghost sickness." But it seemed to Germanicus, who had passed the ornate monuments of the Via Appia a thousand times, the departed clamored to be remembered, even by strangers of the road.

"Will you take some air with me?" he asked.

Skinyea nodded yes.

There was an efflorescence in the east, a wisp of light resting on the horizon like a hoarfrost. But no flare had been sent aloft from the raft. Then it stunned Germanicus to imagine that the conflagrations Tora had rigged inside the fortresses had accomplished nothing. The opportunity to save Alope had come and gone. He began prattling to Skinyea, mostly to ward off a rising panic. "The secret is in keeping the structures as airtight as possible," he heard himself saying. "The bronze doors on both roofs and causeways have been sealed with a liquid alloy that quickly hardens."

"Who will stay inside to light the fires—and die?"

"This will be done by igniter devices timed to go off after all our men have been removed from the fortresses."

Skinyea's starlit face looked amused. "It does not matter what the one with pulled-up eyes does."

"What do you mean?"

"*You* are the one with the great power against enemies. He takes everything from you."

"Power . . . ?"

"I see the final changes." The Indee was now grinning. "I heard them awakening when you spoke to the teamster of this land-ship. You are not afraid. You do not try to avoid that which is dangerous. Nothing can stand in your path from this moment on. I will say no more, but that is how things are."

"No, I would like to *understand* before we cross this morning."

Skinyea waited, his eyes more austere than ever.

"What did Alope mean when she said to me that, but for the Aztecae, she would be a menace to her own people?"

The chieftain's lips remained compressed.

"And she would be an outcast in her own country—why?"

"Hatred is a dangerous thing," Skinyea said quietly.

"But isn't hers for the Aztecae?"

"*Kedn* is like fire. It burns everybody the same."

"But I felt nothing but love in her presence."

"Yes," Skinyea said with a tiny smile. "Still, these are not things to talk about. This is no insult. Even among ourselves we do not discuss these things. I will say no more." Germanicus was not prepared to give up, but all at once he heard a deep soughing from the Tepeyaca or the Acachinanco or perhaps both at once. He half-expected the fortresses to rip themselves open like enraged volcanoes, disgorging rivers of fire through their cracked walls. But the redoubts remained intact, and the sound died away—if it had existed at all outside his frayed expectations.

A thermitic torch pulsated in flashes on Lake Texcoco's silty floor. Globs of spirulina glided past it like green clouds. The ponderous current that drove the algae was like the wind, and the night above the surface was like the void that was wrapped around the world. With enough imagination, even the simplest of things became models for the most complex and mysterious.

Clutching a handful of long and elegant quetzal feathers, Tora turned from where he had been leaning over the catwalk railing and admired the rotund wall of the Tepeyaca Fortress looming over his head, curving away into the stars. The igniters up there—and in the Acachinanco as well—would touch off the Greek fire at any second. Then his heart would know.

But his mind already trusted: a bit of flame, a cork, a chalice, a dish, and *Yinshaya* had revealed the reality to him. Now he was simply waiting for it to be replicated on a grander scale.

The preparations had taken longer than he had expected. He had been close to completion when it occurred to him that the grain dust littering the flagstones of the chambers might cause an explosion—he'd seen the aftermath of such an accident in the Serican capital. So, overriding the protests of the legionaries, he ordered the floors swept as cleanly as possible. This had taken more than an hour.

He peered down over the railing once again. Directly below was the elongated portal to the tunnel the Cambrian sappers had blasted through the immense stones into the lowermost chamber.

Then he gaped upward.

A rumble was coming from deep within the fortress. He less heard than felt it—through the soles of his feet, like one of the nearly imperceptible earthquakes of his homeland whose very existence one doubted until, from the garden, came a tinkling of wind chimes in a breezeless moment.

Immediately, he let one of the feathers tumble down onto the waters. It rode a vague current but refused to budge toward the submerged tunnel.

Tora closed his eyes.

The rumbling sensation was now so pronounced he could feel it through his hands as they clutched the railing. And suddenly these tremblers were amplified by sound, that of the foamy swash of a wave sighing toward shore. It became a roar. Only after several anxious moments could he force himself to look downward again.

The feather was gone. Vanished. Something—more like many things in one assemblage—whisked through the glare of the torch. He imagined it to have been a school of small fish until it dawned on him that a broken mass of spirulina had been sucked into the tunnel. Again, he let a feather skitter down. It remained stationary, bowed from quill to tip across the surface, until all at once it joined the growing momentum of a whorl. Then, without warning, it ducked into the opening as if it had been yanked into the black mouth on a string.

"Great Void, drink more deeply of these waters . . ."

Tora released every last feather and—as if he had cast a spell with this impulse—the surface suddenly depressed, deeply, almost to the bottom of the lake. Then a surge rushed in to fill this bowl, and the waters erupted into a white fountain that gurgled and hissed twenty feet over his head, knocking him flat with the sheer weight of its frenzy. Holding his palms open to this brief, leaden rain, Tora gasped and howled. Finally, he began to weep—not for his personal triumph, although failure would have called for the sincerest form of apology to Caesar Germanicus. There was little regard for himself in his tears: they were for the beauty, the grace, the inevitability of *Yinshaya*.

Rolf strode back from the shore and through the cypresses to Germanicus's sand-galley. "The lads on the raft be shouting something—"

"How do they sound?"

"Sound, Kaiser?"

"Are their voices excited?"

"Aye, a bit," Rolf said. "But these lads be Gauls. They always—"

"Damn," Germanicus groused to Skinyea, who was looking on with amusement, "if only we had a wireless that isn't as big as a pony."

"Caesar, there—!"

The Third Legion colonel who had cried out did not have to finish, for the faces all around Germanicus took on a bright emerald sheen.

"Go! Go now!" he chanted, striking the exhaust tube with the flat of his sword to alert the operator. "For the love of Mars, go!"

Rolf swung his legs over the bulwark onto the main deck just as the craft began lumbering forward between the trees. "Move below, Kaiser!" he shouted. "Surely, the Aztecae be ready with their *ballistae*!"

"Not for the world, my friend." Germanicus had begun to grin, his suddenly buoyant spirits surprising no one more than himself.

"Ach . . ." Dejectedly, the centurion turned to watch the cleated tracks boil through the shallows, shredding tules to pulp.

Germanicus felt a hand squeeze his upper arm.

"Savor this feeling you have," Skinyea whispered. "It is your courage. Your courage is pushing away the night. Everything will turn out all right for you."

"But what of Alope?" Germanicus asked helplessly, almost losing his voice. "What will happen to her?"

The Indee's grip became even tighter. "There are different kinds of death. Everything will turn out all right. Even she would think so."

The legionaries on the raft cheered the first line of sand-galleys that left them bobbing in their wake. But the men aboard the craft remained silent, their eyes clasped to Tenoch-titlan's walls, whose jagged crenellations were yet softened by mist and shadow.

In the east was an umbrage of low clouds, its belly growing more and more fiery by the second. Germanicus was reminded of Lucretius's "flaming ramparts of the world," that cosmic wall the Aztecae apparently also believed in—and feared would one day come tumbling down on their heads. "*Today it falls,*" he muttered as a fan of orange wraiths broke over the mountains. Then he looked sidelong at Rolf, who stared back at him from the crowded main deck. Carefully, the German examined the light of Caesar's eyes, plumbed the hazel depths with vague suspicion.

"Why don't they commence their *fire*?" a young praetorian asked, contemptuous of the Aztecae's inactivity.

"Would you bother, lad?" a colonel said jauntily, indicating with a sweep of his arm the three long lines of sand-galleys closing on the Aztecan capital, streaking the twilit lake with cream-colored wakes. "I honestly expect no serious resistance," he went on, loud enough so Caesar would overhear. "So keep a keen watch for a gold mesh banner of truce."

"A hull goes under!" someone shouted from the prow deck.

"Where?" Germanicus demanded.

"First line, southwest of us!"

Germanicus crossed the deck in time to glimpse a galley, tiny in the shrouded distance, sink bow-first into the waters, leaving its legionaries to thrash above the spot it had been last seen. The craft on both its flanks had slowed and halted, the operators obviously fearful to advance any farther.

"Colonel!" Germanicus cried. "Go below—wireless those galleys to keep advancing! Tell them we must expect some uncharted sumps here and there!"

"Yes, Caesar." The officer's high spirits had deserted him, leaving him slightly embarrassed.

Germanicus turned away from the sight of legionaries floundering toward the nearest craft. In the space of seconds, their number had been halved: only the strongest swimmers had found the time in which to shuck off their panoply.

"It will turn out all right," Skinyea intoned, encouraging the Romans around him who kept checking the water level as it crept up the hull of their own sand-galley.

A thin skein of water—turned magenta by the dawn light—rippled over the main deck, and a cluster of praetorians reared back from the wash as if it were blood. Rolf gave no sign that he had felt it lap around his ankles.

The first line was now midway between the mainland and Tenochtitlan. Clearly, there was ample light for Aztecan spotters to discern the shapes of approaching sand-galleys, and Germanicus could think of no reason why their *ballistae* remained silent. No torches glowed from the lanes of the city; no braziers burned atop the temples. Was he advancing on another Masada, a necropolis of zealots who had chosen suicide over subjugation? And if this were true, what did it bode for the captives of the Aztecae?

As the moments began to weigh upon him like ballast stones, he awaited the first salvo as a source of relief; the expectation was much worse to bear than the reality of explosives mushrooming in deadly spouts among the sand-galleys.

The fortresses loomed over the morning, pregnant with their vast stores of lake water, which Tora had assured him would only be released when the sand-galleys were safely inside the city.

The colonel was standing again at Germanicus's side, saluting with the self-consciousness of a cadet. "Caesar, all craft have acknowledged your order to continue advancing. But do you now have . . . fresh orders?"

"What do you mean?"

The officer pointed downward: water was splashing around the shins of the troops on the main deck, darkening the hems of their cloaks.

"No," Germanicus said quietly. "My orders stand."

"Of course, Caesar. I was merely relating the concern of some officers—"

Another alarming cry came from the prow deck: "A second galley goes under!"

"Caesar, please," the colonel said, his fingers already gravitating toward his cuirass straps. "I spoke too hastily before. Perhaps the Aztecae are not overwhelmed by our presence. Perhaps they realize the futility of our fording so deep a body of water."

"That's possible."

The colonel sighed through a faint smile. "Shall I give the order, Caesar?"

"Order?" Germanicus repeated hollowly.

"To halt and withdraw in formation?"

"No . . . continue." Then Germanicus descended the ladder to the main deck, intertwining his fingers behind him as he waded into the overflow, using his severest glare to douse the panic that enflamed any eyes that met his. "Sky's ruddy this morning," he mentioned to a legionary, who for the first time stopped gaping at the water covering his boots.

"Yes, Caesar."

"Red sky at morn—storm must be coming."

The youth appeared to glean the seed of irony from this: a smile twitched across his lips. "Yes, Caesar—a big one today."

Germanicus winced, but quickly masked it behind his hand; why did so many of these legionaries have to resemble his dead son? "Well, you can let down your cloak now, lad."

"Caesar?"

Germanicus drew the legionary's attention to the main deck again: it was free of water. "We seem to have survived the worst Texcoco has to offer."

Then, ignoring the cheer that rose all along the first line as the noses of the sand-galleys began sloping upward, Germanicus ambled through his men to the prow deck and faced squarely into the city, a rain-scented breeze curling around him in gusts of velvet, trailing his conspicuous *paludamentum* behind him. *I should be afraid*, he mused, *but I'm not. It has never been like this before—the mindless certainty. I know perfectly what I must do. And everything will turn out all right.* He would now manifest his great power against enemies. Alope's voice told him in a whisper of a thought, a brief scintillation that shot along the worn paths of his nerves, that he had been born for this moment, and he was smiling through frosted eyes when he realized that the gray embankment less than a hundred paces ahead was the outer defensive wall of Tenochtitlan. No warriors, no knights in feathery costume could be seen manning its network of battlements.

Following Germanicus's orders, the operator had gained distance on the rest of the sand-galleys in the foremost line. Germanicus felt emboldened by the thousands of gazes that

were converging on his back. He glanced over his shoulder as
Rolf, who had been charging his *pili*, stopped short, suddenly
grasping what Germanicus intended to do.

"No!" the centurion bawled, trying to flail his way through
the phalanx of legionaries and praetorians that was forming
on the main deck. "Kaiser!" He was pounding up the prow
deck ladder when the snout of the craft bumped against the
wall and Germanicus leaped outward, caught the lip of a balustrade, and clambered over.

First to reach Tenochtitlan, the emperor came to his height,
his blood-red cloak whipping around his legs in the wind. He
had thought to exhort his army with remembrance of the ashes
of their forefathers. Of the gods. Of Mother Rome. But all he
cried, as his arms opened to embrace the advancing sand-
galleys, was "*Please!*"

Then Germanicus's pleading figure was backdropped by a
detonation that burgeoned out from its blazing core in roils of
smoke and upended him. He was gone in the same instant the
concussion spalled the waters and raked the iron hulls with
stone chips.

On the night before the infidel capital was penetrated by the forces of the Compassionate, the Merciful, Lord General Tizoc of the Aztecae was summoned to the chambers of the old king.

"In these, the hours before the Ceremony of New Fire," said Maxtla, full of trembling, "it has always been our way to remain obsequious and silent. Do we not extinguish the flames of our hearths and smash our crockery so as not to offend the gods? And might not these invaders be messengers of Lord Quetzalcoatl, who will report our resistance as sacrilege?"

"Reverend one," answered Tizoc, "Caesar Germanicus and his men are cunning enchanters. But was not the Quetzalcoatl they proffered us a false one? We should fight these brother-foes—and heartily, too."

Maxtla did not speak. In his heart, he knew Tenochtitlan to be a spider's cobweb, the frailest of all dwellings, and that the wardens of the sky had come to destroy it. As it is written: "Men cannot forestall their doom, nor can they retard it."

"Besides," Lord Tizoc continued, "no harm may befall us until the waters of Lake Texcoco are coaxed up into a sky of stone. Have not the priests assured us so? I have seen tonight's sky, and it is—"

"Black like obsidian!"

As dawn approached and the righteous host in its legion chariots could be seen crossing the waters toward Tenochtitlan, Maxtla decreed: "We must do nothing. Surely, the Romans will founder and die."

"But if they do not?" Lord Tizoc asked.

"Then we shall make one last appeal to the gods, and present them with those noble brothers and sisters who await a Flowery Death. But do not molest the approach of our enemies. This is an issue for our guardians of old to decide."

"I shall commence the sacrifices, reverend one." Then Lord Tizoc whispered so the old king could not hear: "And mangle a great heart without the use of a knife."

When Caesar Germanicus bestowed upon himself the praise of later generations and stood under a shower of fire to rouse the faithful to humble the proud city, Lord Tizoc commanded that the first Aztecan retortion be directed on the imperial person. But when Caesar was felled, the forces of the Compassionate, the Merciful, were not enfeebled. Nay, these soldiers surged over the walls on the wings of vengeance.

"Fool!" Maxtla cried when the lord general told him what had been done. "By this the nation passes away!"

"No, my most reverend one, with this we cast off our fecklessness."

Then the lord general embraced the old king with great love, as son to father, and strangled him with his hands.

28

GERMANICUS'S GAZE SKIMMED back and forth across a sea of light, trying to fathom it. Wondering if he still possessed a body, he waved his right hand in front of his murky vision. His palm, so bloodless it appeared to be translucent, sprouted ashen lips that wheezed: "The emperor's in there, lads—quiet!" Then it snapped with centurion authority: "The surgeon wants these body parts hauled outside. It's unwholesome to have them laying about. That's it—stack those thighs on the cloak and . . ."

Germanicus could not remain conscious. He resisted losing the light. But . . .

"Caesar?" a voice, sad and gentle, sighed in his ear, inviting him to cross the lowest threshold of wakefulness. "Can you hear me?"

"Alope . . . ?"

"Can you hear me, sir?"

"Alope . . ."

"Do you think that's a response?" another voice whispered.

"No, he's been saying that to any sound we make."

"When'd he start?"

"As soon as the praetorians dug him out of the rubble." Wearily, the voice pleaded, "Germanicus Julius Agricola, please answer me. Say anything."

"Where is Alope?" he cried. But it was like shouting from the bottom of a well. The voices did not respond from far above. His legs began transmitting fierce, sharp aches to his brain, and nausea brewed in his stomach. He chose sleep, the numbing blackness.

Once he asked quite lucidly, "What is the progress of the fighting? Have they reached the Great Temple yet?" Through a portal he could see that it was raining heavily outside. Either smoke or steam was drifting through the streaking droplets. "What hour is it?"

The faces enclosing him showed such astonishment he repeated the question. But then time lapsed into disarray and he couldn't recall what his surgeons had answered—if they had done so at all.

"Caesar?"

"Yes . . . ?"

"Praise the gods! Can you hear me?"

"Of course."

"Can you see us?"

Germanicus cracked his lids to narrow slits, but found the chamber painfully bright from cedarbark torches, pulsing wildly and filling the air with pungent smoke. He closed his eyes, then flinched at the report of a sinister rumble. "Was that *ballistae*?"

"Yes, Caesar. Our forces are now clearing the summit of the Great Temple. Tizoc and his eagle knights have ensconced themselves in one of the shrines there, awaiting the end."

Germanicus's head began buzzing: he desperately feared to venture the question. The expectation of agony was so great he was tempted to swallow the words before his tongue and teeth could give them shape. Perhaps he could coexist with the misery of not knowing—forever. But then he realized that he could not. "The hostages? What of—?"

"Caesar," someone said brightly, "there's someone here you'll be delighted to see."

"Indeed," another voice added before chuckling arose from the throats of the staff officers.

"*Where?*"

"Being attended to in the next chamber, Caesar."

"Hurt?"

"Nothing more injurious than exhaustion."

"Bring . . . bring . . ." Germanicus's voice deteriorated into hoarseness.

"Directly, Caesar."

Swallowing a groan, Germanicus shifted his weight so he could peer down the passageway that led to the adjoining chamber. He waited without breathing. The happy looks of anticipation on the faces of his officers cheered him beyond reckoning. After an interminable wait, a slender human form materialized at the far end of the corridor and drifted toward him. Arms flowed up as if to implore him to laugh or cry out with relief. The graceful approach continued to the accompaniment of the soft padding of deerskin slippers. He had recognized the triangular kilts, the tunic tassels, the lie of her hair . . . when this glorious phantasm transformed itself into Epizelus, whose skin was now slashed with red and white stripes of paint. Otherwise, his physician was caparisoned only with a breechclout, its excess cloth dangling from groin to shins, and tufts of white down that had been glued to his head.

"You must forgive my appearance, Caesar," the Greek rasped. "But this is how they adorn their victims for sacrifice—"

Germanicus loosed a bellow as if he had been pierced by a javelin.

It was late night—although Germanicus had superimposed darkness on everything—when Rolf stole into his chamber and knelt beside the pallet. The centurion did not violate the silence, and hours passed before Germanicus croaked, "Is this one of those places where men and women are . . . dismembered?"

"Aye, it be the one with the chimney like a serpent."

Germanicus lay perfectly still again, his eyes opaque. Suddenly he seized the centurion's wrist. "I must speak to Epizelus. I was much relieved to see him alive—he must not think otherwise."

"He be aware."

"But I must say it to him, before he believes otherwise."

Rolf nodded, then pried himself free of Germanicus's clutch. "I find him."

"Thank you . . . thank you."

Struggling to compose himself, Germanicus lay still again and tried to slow his heartbeats, although not convinced this could be done. He had achieved some measure of decorum when Epizelus shuffled into his presence. Then, helplessly, his eyes overflowed and he spread his arms, motioning for the physician to fill them.

Epizelus dropped to his knees and embraced the emperor. Then, awkwardly, the men disengaged themselves from each other's grasp.

"You have your work cut out for you," Germanicus said when he could speak again. "They advise me my legs are in rather poor shape."

"Yes." Epizelus's skin hung off his skull like dough. He talked as if he had no feeling in his lips. "The neck of the right femur snapped—only Galen knows how. And your left tibia is in at least three pieces. This much the surgeons could feel with their fingers. If only we had a way to examine bone without making incisions."

Germanicus buried his chin in his chest to prevent his lower jaw from trembling, but his eyes clouded. "The Indee woman Alope—how . . . ?"

Epizelus studied him for a long moment, as if gauging his strength.

"Please, my friend, I must know."

A consoling smile slowly melted off the Greek's lips. "She crossed the sacrificial stone when the sun was straight up. She was first. I suspect Tizoc knew what she meant to you. And he was consumed with spite. He wanted to punish you. And I"—he hesitated, shamefaced—"I was to be last. The grandest honor in their reckoning—the living hearth in which the New Fire would be kindled. I wasn't to die until midnight, when the Pleiades would be at its zenith. But as our forces encircled the Great Temple, the Aztecae began slaughtering in a frenzy. There were just three ahead of me"—a shudder racked his body, and he steadied himself by wrapping himself in his thin arms—"when the guardsmen swept up to us and freed me. I shall never again mock the praetorian guard."

"I wonder if she knew . . ." Germanicus squeezed his eyes shut.

"Knew what, Germanicus Julius?"

". . . how I loved her."

A spark of censure flashed in Epizelus's yellowed eyes. "Do you understand what this woman's love for you cost her?"

"No, my dear Greek, it was all done for her people. I can understand that. It would have been enough for her to share my life."

"She discussed this very thing with me."

Germanicus gaped at him. "You met with her?"

"Yes, male captives were segregated from female. But there was a banquet some weeks ago—a great honor on our behalf, the Aztecae thought. We were allowed to mingle, but only briefly. I had learned from legionaries recently captured of your relationship with Alope. So I sought her out."

Germanicus tried to prop himself up on his elbows, but proved too weak for the effort. "What did she say?" he moaned from his pillow. "Dear Jupiter, what things did she—?"

"Remarkable things." Epizelus looked down, ever the physician as he paused, unsure what to tell and not to tell. "She admitted to me that it'd been her purpose to create desperation in your heart where there had been none before."

"Oh no, please—"

"Hold a moment. Then she whispered that she'd been snared by the trap she herself had set. She'd never intended to love you, for she'd suspected from the beginning she would have to die. And loving you, she said, would turn her death into a feast of bitter herbs. For herself, she wanted only to go with you. Help you fight those who have wronged your clan—whatever that meant. Yet, for the sake of her people, she was compelled to lure you to Tenochtitlan." Epizelus thought to ease the mood with a smile, but failed. His face was desolate no matter what his expression. "I've never seen a more lonely-looking human being. She tried to ask me things about you—harmless, personal things, I suppose. But an eagle knight pushed her along. I did not see her again until . . ." Epizelus chose not to finish.

Germanicus lay silent for more than an hour, not moving a muscle until a praetorian colonel strode into the chamber. His eyes lost some of their glassiness as they focused on the officer's grimy face.

"Yes, what is it?" Epizelus demanded.

"It is my pleasure to report to Caesar that Maxtla, reverend speaker of the Aztecae, and Tizoc, his lord general, are confirmed dead. The Aztecan Empire is no more. Hail Caesar!"

Germanicus slanted his forearm across his eyes.

29

BEFORE DAWN, GERMANICUS had a detail of four praetorians bear him on a litter to the foredeck of the *Romulus*. The last hour of the night was fair, and the Mare Nostrum smooth. He reveled in the breeze, which was springlike and lacking the bite of blue-water gales.

The officer on the *pontis* deck announced his presence. This, like all the calcified practices of the fleet, was required by the codex: "Germanicus Julius Agricola Aztecus is now topside! Hail Caesar!" The Senate had already granted him the *cognomen ex virtute* of Aztecus, and this afternoon he would be paraded through the streets of Rome to be acclaimed with a triumph.

Yet, when informed of these senatorial tributes while still recovering from his wounds in Tenochtitlan, Germanicus had stared at the envoy from the Curia as if he were mad: "What are you saying?"

"Why, Caesar, your colonels tell me even the southernmost Aztecan provinces, which were expected to remain rebellious, have sued for Roman peace and rule."

"Yes . . ."

"Then how can this be anything but a conquest of enormous proportions?"

Germanicus paused, then carefully measured his words: "We've conquered much. Resolved nothing. Empires seem to grow outward—or not at all."

"Why, of course," the Senator cheerfully assented.

Germanicus had said nothing more about the matter for fear of confirming his republican intentions. Rumors were already being whispered among his staff and—more dangerously—among the praetorian guard that Caesar was not enamored of being Caesar.

Now on the foredeck, he started as Rolf wrapped a blanket around his shoulders. "I'm not cold."

"Then why you be shivering?"

Germanicus stared at the centurion for a long moment, then sadly smiled. "I'm going over recent days . . ."

"That be wise?"

"Yes, I must . . . especially this morning, as we near home . . . and my poor Quintus. It's as if I never experienced some of those things, or I lived them in a trance, shut up within myself."

"Aye, it be that way for you in Nova Britannia."

"But now it all comes to life within me as if for the first time . . ." Germanicus's thin voice trailed off into silence. Remembrance burnished his eyes.

In the fortnight following the fall of Tenochtitlan, he had closeted himself in Tizoc's palatial home, which had been spared destruction while Roman attention was focused on eagle knights holding out in Maxtla's palace. He granted no audiences and admitted only Rolf or Epizelus, the latter to treat the emperor's melancholy with that curious potion that lifted a man's spirits regardless of the blackness of his thoughts—and Germanicus's were so dark he could scarcely speak.

One afternoon during that time, Khalid had created a row by attempting to force entry into the emperor's chamber. It was fortunate that Germanicus called out to intervene, for—deprived of his right arm—the Anatolian prince was no match for the praetorians.

"I wish no visitors, Khalid," Germanicus muttered and then turned his back on the young man.

"As I did not, *pasa*, in the days after the loss of my arm. But you came to me nevertheless. And you reminded me of my duty to God. So I chose to live."

Germanicus glared at him, but remained silent.

"My father, the holiest of men, trusted me with this before I set forth." He held a vellum packet under the stump of his

right arm, from which he produced a sheet of parchment. A
praetorian prevented him from approaching the emperor, but
then the guardsman grudgingly delivered the letter for the
Anatolian.

The missive was in Greek, which the Great *Zaim* said he had
learned in order to read Aristotle. This, Germanicus realized
with a gaunt smile, was part of the man's obdurate attitude
toward things Roman, for there existed a dozen excellent
Latin translations of the philosopher's works. He slanted the
parchment toward the glow of the oil lamp; Tenochtitlan's
rather primitive *electricus motive* system had not yet been
restored.

> *Germanicus Julius,*
>   *Long ago, by the will of the Compassionate, the Mer-
> ciful, you were my prisoner. My people cried for the
> blood of the Roman pasa, but I did not grant their desire
> for revenge. For the holiest of holy, my blessed shaykh,
> had a vision of the conquest I trust you have now made.
> That night of rage, when you suddenly donned one of
> our soof robes, he whispered to me alone: "So it is writ-
> ten: 'The son of the she-wolf will garb himself like the
> lamb of God. This man will secure a new land of fallow
> souls for the Compassionate, the Merciful.' " This is all
> I will tell . . .*

Germanicus realized that Khalid's eyes were hard on him.

> *. . . except that I rely on you to value my son's services
> as you would mine. I now share the saddest secret of my
> heart: Khalid shall never return to me. He shall perish in
> your new province. So, as your brother, I beg that none
> of his light, so pure and honest, be wasted . . . Inshallah.*

That was all: it was not even signed.

Germanicus regarded the young Anatolian with care.
"Have you read this?"

"No—I was commanded not to."

"So be it," Germanicus said. He touched the parchment to
the wick of the oil lamp and let it spin in flames down to the
stone floor.

"*Pasa*, there remains something else, if you please."

"Of course," Germanicus said gently.

"Your colonels—they deny me the opportunity to convert infidels."

"Khalid," Germanicus sighed, "there's a Roman tradition of liberality in these matters. Forced conversions—"

"Oh, no, *pasa*, I do not suggest that kind of persuasion. None is needed. If you will permit me, I have proof—a merchant of their race. He wisely absented himself far to the south during the *jhad*, and has just returned to Tenochtitlan."

Frowning, Germanicus watched the ashes of the letter being tumbled apart by a draft. "Very well."

Khalid snapped his fingers and a *pochtecatl* scampered in through the portal and prostrated himself before Germanicus's bed. The Azteca fixed his eyes on the flagstones.

"Speak," Khalid commanded.

"Caesar Germanicus, reverend lord of we the Mexicae—"

"Please rise," Germanicus said.

The Azteca hesitated.

Khalid snapped his fingers again. "Caesar bids you to rise."

The *pochtecatl* came to his feet as if afraid the Roman could immolate him with a single glance. His lower jaw flapped noiselessly a few times before he could speak again, but he finally found the courage to meet Germanicus's inquiring gaze. "Caesar Germanicus—"

"How do you speak Latin, my friend?"

"At one time, I traded in the country of your Novos." The Azteca was not quick enough to hide his own look of distaste at mention of these grubby colonials. "I made certain Lord General Salvidienus got the finest *cacahuhel*. I was very fond of the lord general—"

"Yes . . ."

"And now I wish to declare for *Inshallah* . . ." Then he added rather hopefully: ". . . if I can no longer have the gods of my fathers?"

"You cannot. You'll understand in time that the sun requires no feast of blood and flesh. It rises and sets regardless of what we humans do." Germanicus ignored the man's dubious expression. "It seems to me that you pledge yourself to a new religion rather hastily. Have you heard of the Cult of Isis? Of Reformed Mithraism? Not to mention the House of Jupiter?"

The *pochtecatl* shrugged. "I have, lord."

"Well, what did you think of Jupiter, Juno, the other deities?"

"They bicker too much among themselves. They are more like in-laws than gods."

"I see. And what qualities do you see in the religion of my friend, Prince Khalid?"

"It has a good discipline. It forbids drinking of spirits, which is the wellspring of all evil. Without these restraints, there will be chaos among my people."

"Do you not see, *pasa*?" Khalid beamed.

Germanicus lay back down. The brief audience had exhausted him. "Please go now. I'll make my pleasure known tomorrow."

He did not sleep that night, for—in addition to his oppressive melancholy—it distressed him to think that the import of these decisions might outlive him for centuries. But by morning, when his staff, the Anasazi chieftains, and the surviving Aztecan hierarchy had convened at his order, Germanicus appreciated that he could no longer defer judgment on a host of concerns; his silence was bewildering half the world.

"Now that the war is done," he said in a tired but firm voice from his curule chair, "it is time to rebuild and reshape—"

Suddenly, in the space that separated Germanicus from the assembly, a jaguar padded across the floor. This greatly alarmed the Anasazi headmen for, as Germanicus later learned, they were convinced the animal was Tizoc's ghost. It halted, glared at Germanicus, who steeled himself to betray no fright, and then continued on its way out of the lord general's feasting chamber.

"One of our first orders of business," Germanicus broke the unpleasant calm, "will be to repair the walls of the royal menagerie."

There was tentative, then boisterous, laughter.

But Germanicus did not join in. "Soon I will sail for Rome. I have been absent from the capital too long, but it pleases me how well the Senate has functioned while I was occupied here —especially in the matter of preserving order and peace in Hibernia." He paused. "This morning, I announce whom and what manner of administration I leave here to govern in my stead." He unfurled a scroll that, by its ancient style, indicated an incalculable imperial gravity. "This I dispatched to the commander of the garrison at Nova Petra: 'Hail and be well! I order the immediate dismantling of your command and the transfer of all Tenth Legion troops in that region called the Anasazi Federation to Otacilium. Henceforth, the federation shall be deemed a district of extraterritoriality and entered by Romans only by invitation of its inhabitants. This *pactum—*' ''

A whoop flew up from the gaggle of Anasazi headmen; Skinyea was swiftly translating the edict for them.

'' 'This *pactum* shall be considered abrogated should any tribe or faction within the federation raid or make violence upon *coloni* of Rome or her client states, and the weapons Caesar has dispensed to the Anasazi for their services rendered to us during the Aztecan campaign shall be confiscated.' '' At this moment, Germanicus met Skinyea's keen eyes. He knew exactly what the Indee was thinking: *What then of raids we conduct against the burgeoning Serican colonies along the Sea of the West?* Germanicus had no intention of forbidding these activities. In fact, with the gift of tens of thousands of *pili*, he was encouraging them. But to openly say so was to declare war on the Sericans. That was coming, he was certain, but hopefully not in his lifetime. If the likes of the Indee could not be broken of raiding, then Germanicus intended to put their bad habits to good use: the creation of a buffer between the Novo Provinces and the Serican enclaves.

"But Caesar—" A colonel took advantage of Germanicus's momentary pensiveness. "Does this mean we may expect no tribute from the Anasazi?"

"It does."

"But who shall bear the burden of their defense?"

"They shall . . . as we bear our own." Germanicus motioned for Skinyea to approach him. Then, without hesitation, he said, "Alope . . ."

The chieftain startled.

"She lives in your liberty, and can die only in the event of your enslavement. So I believe we can speak her name without offending the funereal spirits." Germanicus's eyes clouded. "And rest assured: I shall always recall her name, the loveliness of her person, with a solemn affection."

Skinyea nodded and stepped back again, the usually dolorous cant of his lips now smug. Alope had won everything for him and his people, but he revealed no tenderness at her mention. Perhaps an Indee warrior did not have such feelings —Germanicus didn't honestly know, even after having campaigned with them. Yet on one issue Skinyea's and his eyes could lock in complete agreement: The Indee could never be Romanized without being annihilated in the process. This understanding would be the foundation for future relations between their peoples.

"And now to the matter of my government here—"

Khalid, who had been lost in some musing, lifted his face at the emperor's words.

"I will suggest to the Senate that Mexicae be considered a department of Nova Baetica in the same kind of dependency that Greater Judea enjoys with Syria. Proconsul Marcus Gracchus shall have ultimate provincial authority in this instance, but directing the immediate affairs of the Department of Mexicae shall be a procurator . . ."

The chamber fell quiet with expectation. Each man waited breathlessly for his own name to sing out over the throng.

"Prince Khalid—approach me." Germanicus seemed oblivious to the dismay that plowed through the ranks of his staff like a shock wave. These patricians had assumed that the first governor would be chosen from their pool of Latin lineage. Even the selection of a Gaul or an Iberian would have been going too far. But an Anatolian? And one who legally wasn't even a citizen?

Taking another scroll from the sleeve fold of his toga, Germanicus unfurled it and flashed the bold word CIVITAS! so all might see, then said to Khalid, "Your name is the first to be duly enrolled in Tenochtitlan, henceforth to be known as Nova Britannia in honor of a brave soldier of Rome who sacrificed more than his life to the cause of peace. Citizenship makes possible your appointment as procurator of Mexicae. You shall have first authority in all matters profane and religious, and I call upon you to uphold the Twelve Tables and its Forty-eight Codicils. What I have seen of your character in these past months gives me confidence that you will govern prudently and humanely."

"I thank you, Caesar Germanicus," Khalid said, accepting the scroll with his left hand. He appeared to be moved, but not terribly surprised.

There was a stirring from the crowd as it recovered from its bewilderment, and a voice boldly asked, in obvious hope of snatching some sinecure: "What will be the noble procurator's first act?"

The Anatolian was now grinning. "I will write a history of the glories we have so recently lived, before they are blurred by time and too much Roman wine."

"An apposite enterprise," Germanicus said. "We should pause and soberly reflect—"

"Caesar!"

Annoyed, Germanicus spun around and met the buoyant grin of a signal's centurion. "What is so important that it must interrupt these inaugural proceedings?"

The officer was too ecstatic to be deterred. "I hold a message just received from our fleet in the Mare Aztecum: 'Manlius Julius Agricola Ahenobarbianus, a traitor to the empire more commonly known as Gaius Nero, upon hearing of the extent of Caesar's victories, has taken his own life aboard the bireme that was conveying him to the Curia and justice!'" The officer waited for Germanicus to show some sign of pleasure. When none followed, the man's expression became confused.

A colorless Germanicus struggled to ask: "How . . . in what manner . . . ?"

"He hanged himself with his toga, Caesar."

There was a smattering of grim applause, which Germanicus viciously waved off. Then he rose out of his chair but appeared so unsteady Rolf rushed forward to bolster him by the arm. Germanicus stared at the centurion as if the man were a complete stranger. At last, his glower melted under some desperate warmth of recognition: "*Rolf* . . . I never wanted this. Didn't I order that Gaius Nero be kept from such news?" His mouth twisting into a scowl, he shouted at the stunned assembly: "Didn't I order thus?" Then he clutched Rolf's cloak and whispered, "Take me from this place, quickly. Dear Jupiter, what will I tell young Quintus of his father? What can I say to a child?"

Even now on the prow of the *Romulus*, with Rome and all her incumbencies only a few hours away, Germanicus had not yet decided what he would say to the boy. Rolf had suggested the truth, but the truth had too many jagged edges to be

touched by such tender hands. He prayed that, when this
awful moment finally arrived, he would be rescued by some
inspiration.

"Light . . . the Appeninus!" Rolf said, his voice sharpened
by excitement.

"My crook—bring it!" Germanicus snapped, and a servant
brought him a staff that had been fashioned from an aspen
sapling. Then Germanicus hobbled to the railing with Rolf
dancing nervously at his elbow in case he should stumble.
Caesar's eyes narrowed as he studied the eastern horizon. "Go
below and awaken Tora, centurion. Tell him I want to treat
him to his first glimpse of Italia."

"Aye, Kaiser."

In truth, Germanicus had wanted a few moments in which
to be alone. He had elected to voyage home on the *Romulus*,
although the admirals had singled out a magnificent new quinquereme for that honor. But it was on this deck, under a light
rain, that he had sailed into Otacilium. Alope had been standing at his side. Her hands might easily have been wrapped
around this piece of brass rail he was grasping. *Eternally, I'm
a prisoner of little significances like these. And how foolish
of me to seek moments of joy in this captivity,* he sighed. *But
I can never again journey to the country of the Indee. That
would be too much, even for a nature steeled to melancholy
like mine. Everything would resound with her touch, her
voice, the shining of her eyes.*

The last Roman legionary perhaps to ever venture into the
Anasazi Federation had been Rolf. The centurion had taken it
upon himself to preserve Alope's remains for cremation, and
for this Germanicus told him: "You've restored my love to
me, my dearest friend. Now, even in death, she is restored to
me."

Weeks later, when Rolf joined Germanicus for embarkation
in Otacilium, sunburned and markedly thinner, there was an
air of peace about the man more substantial than the weariness that mellows a soldier after a long campaign. It seemed as
if, at long last, he'd been able to cast off a demon he had
borne ever since he had taken Crispa's life in Anatolia.

Germanicus never had to ask Rolf where he had sprinkled
Alope's ashes. He knew from the German's averted eyes that
it had been in the vale of the *gowa*—where, whenever he
pleased to remember, she smiled up at him from her blankets

of fur, blinding him with love that failed to dim, even when the Novo Provinces vanished in the wake of the *Romulus*.

Only in the past few days had he realized her extraordinary bequest to him: The conquest of the Aztecan Empire had given him more personal *authoritas* than any man alive, something he had not had upon embarking from Ostia six months before. Now there was no doubt in his heart that only he, Germanicus Julius Agricola Aztecus, of all Romans living, could restore the republic. Hardship and great loneliness would attend all his remaining days. But he would survive. And he would prevail. For he was an instrument of his people, as she had been of hers. There was sustenance in this thought, and it enabled him to endure the jarring light between sleeps.

All at once, he found himself flanked by Rolf and Tora. "Is that cloud or mountain, Lord Caesar?" the Nihonian asked, pointing landward.

"A range of mountains—the Appeninus, the backbone of my country."

"It is sadly amusing to think . . ." Tora paused.

"What is, my friend?"

"In me, Star-Sorter returns to Rome. In you, Lord Caesar, Rome will perhaps prove worthy of his teachings."

Germanicus smiled: there was more courage in that *perhaps* than all the legions of the empire. It was good to be surrounded by brave men once again.

"Italia," Rolf said, "she be riding on the breeze."

This prompted Germanicus to inhale: it was a fragrance so familiar it could only be relished after long absence. He drank deeply of these first sweet, vegetative inklings of home. "There's Ostia off the port bow. And starboard—those are the lights of my villa. My household has set out torches for me."

And Caesar was consoled.

Acknowledgements of classical and anthropological sources: from *The Oedipus Cycle* (New York: Harcourt Brace, 1949), on p. 31 of this work; *Meditations* by Marcus Aurelius (Baltimore: Penguin Classics, 1964), p. 101; *Seneca: Letters from a Stoic* (Baltimore: Penguin Classics, 1969), p. 124; *Latin Poetry in Verse Translation*, edited by Levi R. Lind (Boston: Houghton Mifflin Riverside Editions, 1957), p. 183; *The Koran* (Baltimore: Penguin Classics, 1968), pp. 222 and 279; and *Western Apache Raiding and Warfare* by Grenville Goodwin, edited by Keith H. Basso (Tucson: University of Arizona Press, 1971), p. 166. The author would also like to thank hydrological engineer Andrew Boyd, Jr., C. E., and the staff of the White Mountain Apache Culture Center at Fort Apache, Arizona.